Greek Mavericks: Giving Her Heart to the Greek

DANI COLLINS

JENNIFER FAYE

JENNIFER TAYLOR

MILLS & BOON

First Published in Great Britain 2019
By Mills & Boon, an imprint of HarperCollins *Publishers*
1 London Bridge Street, London, SE1 9GF

ISBN: **978-0-263-27564-3**

0719

MIX
Paper from responsible sources
FSC™ C007454

This book is produced from independently certified FSC™ paper to ensure responsible forest management.

For more information visit: www.harpercollins.co.uk/green

Printed and bound in Spain
by CPI, Barcelona

THE SECRET BENEATH THE VEIL

DANI COLLINS

To you, Dear Reader, for loving romance novels as much as I do. I hope you enjoy this one.

CHAPTER ONE

THE AFTERNOON SUN came straight through the windows, blinding Viveka Brice as she walked down the makeshift aisle of the wedding she was preventing—not that anyone knew that yet.

The interior of the yacht club, situated on this remote yet exclusive island in the Aegean, was all marble and brass, adding more bounces of white light. Coupled with the layers of her veil, she could hardly see and had to reluctantly cling to the arm of her reviled stepfather.

He probably couldn't see any better than she could. Otherwise he would have called her out for ruining his plan. He certainly hadn't noticed she wasn't Trina.

She was getting away with hiding the fact her sister had left the building. It made her stomach both churn with nerves and flutter with excitement.

She squinted, trying to focus past the standing guests and the wedding party arranged before the robed minister. She deliberately avoided looking at the tall, imposing form of the unsuspecting groom, staring instead through the windows and the forest of masts bobbing on the water. Her sister was safe from this forced marriage to a stranger, she reminded herself, trying to calm her racing heart.

Forty minutes ago, Trina had let her father into the room where she was dressing. She'd still been wearing this gown, but hadn't yet put on the veil. She had promised Grigor she would be ready on time while Viveka had kept well out of sight. Grigor didn't even know Viveka was back on the island.

The moment he'd left the room, Viveka had helped Trina out of the gown and Trina had helped her into it. They had hugged hard, then Trina had disappeared down a service elevator and onto the seaplane her true love had chartered. They were making for one of the bigger islands to the north where arrangements were in place to marry them the moment they touched land. Viveka was buying them time by allaying suspicion, letting the ceremony continue as long as possible before she revealed herself and made her own escape.

She searched the horizon again, looking for the flag of the boat she'd hired. It was impossible to spot and that made her even more anxious than the idea of getting onto the perfectly serviceable craft. She hated boats, but she wasn't in the class that could afford private helicopters to take her to and fro. She'd given a sizable chunk of her savings to Stephanos, to help him spirit Trina away in that small plane. Spending the rest on crossing the Aegean in a speedboat was pretty close to her worst nightmare, but the ferry made only one trip per day and had left her here this morning.

She knew which slip the boat was using, though. She'd paid the captain to wait and Stephanos had assured her she could safely leave her bags on board. Once she was exposed, she wouldn't even change. She would seek out that wretched boat, grit her teeth and sail into the sunset, content that she had finally prevailed over Grigor.

Her heart took a list and roll as they reached the top of the aisle, and Grigor handed her icy fingers to Trina's groom, the very daunting Mikolas Petrides.

His touch caused a *zing* of something to go through her. She told herself it was alarm. Nervous tension.

His grip faltered almost imperceptibly. Had he felt that static shock? His fingers shifted to enfold hers, pressing warmth through her whole body. Not comfort. She didn't fool herself into believing he would bother with that. He was even more intimidating in person than in his photos, exactly as Trina had said.

Viveka was taken aback by the quiet force he emanated, all chest and broad shoulders. He was definitely too much masculine energy for Viveka's little sister. He was too much for *her*.

She peeked into his face and found his gaze trying to penetrate the layers of her veil, brows lowered into sharp angles, almost as if he suspected the wrong woman stood before him.

Lord, he was handsome with those long clean-shaven plains below his carved cheekbones and the small cleft in his chin. His eyes were a smoky gray, outlined in black spiky lashes that didn't waver as he looked down his blade of a nose.

We could have blue-eyed children, she had thought when she'd first clicked on his photo. It was one of those silly facts of genetics that had caught her imagination when she had been young enough to believe in perfect matches. To this day it was an attribute she thought made a man more attractive.

She had been tempted to linger over his image and speculate about a future with him, but she'd been on a mission from the moment Trina had tearfully told her she was being sold off in a business merger like sixteenth-century chattel. All Viveka had had to see were the headlines that tagged Trina's groom as the son of a murdered Greek gangster. No *way* would she let her sister marry this man.

Trina had begged Grigor to let her wait until March, when she turned eighteen, and to keep the wedding small and in Greece. That had been as much concession as he'd granted. Trina, legally allowed to marry whomever she wanted as of this morning, had *not* chosen Mikolas Petrides, wealth, power and looks notwithstanding.

Viveka swallowed. The eye contact seemed to be holding despite the ivory organza between them, creating a sense of connection that sent a fresh thrum of nervous energy through her system.

She and Trina both took after their mother in build, but Trina was definitely the darker of the two, with a rounder face and warm, brown eyes, whereas Viveka had these icy blue orbs and natural blond streaks she'd covered with the veil.

Did he know she wasn't Trina? She shielded her eyes with a drop of her lashes.

The shuffle of people sitting and the music halting sent a wash of perspiration over her skin. Could he hear her pulse slamming? Feel her trembles?

It's just a play, she reminded herself. Nothing about this was real or valid. It would be over soon and she could move on with her life.

At one time she had imagined acting for a living. All her early career ambitions had leaned toward starving artist of one kind or another, but she'd had to grow up fast and become more practical once her mother died. She had worked here at this yacht club, lying about her age so they'd hire her, washing dishes and scrubbing floors.

She had wanted to be independent of Grigor as soon as possible, away from his disparaging remarks that had begun turning into outright abuse. He had helped her along by kicking her out of the house before she'd turned fifteen. He'd kicked her off this island, really. Out of Greece and away from her sister because once he realized she had been working, that she had the means to support herself and wouldn't buckle to his will when he threatened to expel her from his home, he had ensured she was fired and couldn't get work anywhere within his reach.

Trina, just nine, had been the one to whisper, *Go. I'll be okay. You should go.*

Viveka had reached out to her mother's elderly aunt in London. She had known Hildy only from Christmas cards, but the woman had taken her in. It hadn't been ideal. Viveka got through it by dreaming of bringing her sister to live with her there. As recently as a few months ago, she had pictured them as two carefree young women, twenty-three and eighteen, figuring out their futures in the big city—

"I, Mikolas Petrides..."

He had an arresting voice. As he repeated his name and spoke his vows, the velvet-and-steel cadence of his tone held her. He smelled good, like fine clothes and spicy aftershave and something unique and masculine that she knew would imprint on her forever.

She didn't want to remember this for the rest of her life. It was a ceremony that wasn't even supposed to be happening. She was just a placeholder.

Silence made her realize it was her turn.

She cleared her throat and searched for a suitably meek tone. Trina had never been a target for Grigor. Not just because she was his biological daughter, but also because she was on the timid side—probably because her father was such a mean, loudmouthed, sexist bastard in the first place.

Viveka had learned the hard way to be terrified of Grigor. Even in London his cloud of intolerance had hung like a poison cloud, making her careful about when she contacted Trina, never setting Trina against him by confiding her suspicions, always aware he could hurt Viveka through her sister.

She had sworn she wouldn't return to Greece, certainly not with plans that would make Grigor hate her more than he already did, but she was confident he wouldn't do more than yell in front of all these wedding guests. There were media moguls in the assemblage and paparazzi circling the air and water. The risk in coming here was a tall round of embarrassed confusion, nothing more.

She sincerely hoped.

The moment of truth approached. Her voice thinned and cracked, making her vows a credible imitation of Trina's as she spoke fraudulently in her sister's place, nullifying the marriage—and merger—that Grigor wanted so badly. It wasn't anything that could truly balance the loss of her mother, but it was a small retribution. Viveka wore a grim inner smile as she did it.

Her bouquet shook as she handed it off and her fingers felt clumsy and nerveless as she exchanged rings with Mikolas, keeping up the ruse right to the last minute. She wouldn't sign any papers, of course, and she would have to return these rings. Darn, she hadn't thought about that.

Even his hands were compelling, so well shaped and strong, so sure. One of his nails looked… She wasn't sure. Like he'd injured it once. If this were a real wedding, she would know that intimate detail about him.

Silly tears struck behind her eyes. She had the same girlish dreams for a fairy-tale wedding as any woman. She wished this were the beginning of her life with the man she loved. But it wasn't. Nothing about this was legal or real.

Everyone was about to realize that.

"You may kiss the bride."

* * *

Mikolas Petrides had agreed to this marriage for one reason only: his grandfather. He wasn't a sentimental man or one who allowed himself to be manipulated. He sure as hell wasn't marrying for love. That word was an immature excuse for sex and didn't exist in the real world.

No, he felt nothing toward his bride. He felt nothing toward anyone, quite by conscious decision.

Even his loyalty to his grandfather was provisional. Pappoús had saved his life. He'd *given* Mikolas this life once their blood connection had been verified. He had recognized Mikolas as his grandson, pulling him from the powerless side of a brutal world to the powerful one.

Mikolas repaid him with duty and legitimacy. His grandfather had been born into a good family during hard times. Erebus Petrides hadn't stayed on the right side of the law as he'd done what he'd seen as necessary to survive. Living a corrupt life had cost the old man his son and Mikolas had been Erebus's second chance at an heir. He had given his grandson full rein with his ill-gotten empire on the condition Mikolas turn it into a legal—yet still lucrative—enterprise.

No small task, but this marriage merger was the final step. To the outside observer, Grigor's world-renowned conglomerate was absorbing a second-tier corporation with a questionable pedigree. In reality, Grigor was being paid well for a company logo. Mikolas would eventually run the entire operation.

Was it irony that his mother had been a laundress? Or appropriate?

Either way, this marriage had been Grigor's condition. He wanted his own blood to inherit his wealth. Mikolas had accepted to make good on his debt to his grandfather. Marriage would work for him in other ways and it was only another type of contract. This ceremony was more elaborate than most business meetings, but it was still just a date to fix signatures upon dotted lines followed by the requisite photo op.

Mikolas had met his bride—a girl, really—twice. She was young and extremely shy. Pretty enough, but no sparks of attraction had flared in him. He'd resigned himself to affairs while she grew up and they got to know one another. *Therein might be another advantage to marriage*, he had been thinking distantly, while he waited for her to walk down the aisle. Other women wouldn't wheedle for marriage if he already wore a ring.

Then her approach had transfixed him. Something happened. *Lust.*

He was never comfortable when things happened outside his control. This was hardly the time or place for a spike of naked hunger for a woman. But it happened.

She arrived before him veiled in a waterfall mist that he should have dismissed as an irritating affectation. For some reason he found the mystery deeply erotic. He recognized her perfume as the same scent she'd worn those other times, but rather than sweet and innocent, it now struck him as womanly and heady.

Her lissome figure wasn't as childish as he'd first judged, either. She moved as though she owned her body, and how had he not noticed before that her eyes were such a startling shade of blue, the kind that sat as a pool of water against a glacier? He could barely see her face, but the intensity of blue couldn't be dimmed by a few scraps of lace.

His heart began to thud with an old, painful beat. *Want.* The real kind. The kind that was more like basic necessity.

A flicker of panic threatened, but he clamped down on the memories of deprivation. Of denial. Terror. Searing pain.

He got what he wanted these days. Always. He was getting *her*.

Satisfaction rolled through him, filling him with anticipation for this pomp and circumstance to end.

The ceremony progressed at a glacial pace. Juvenile eagerness struck him when he was finally able to lift her veil. He didn't celebrate Christmas, yet felt it had arrived early, just for him.

He told himself it was gratification at accomplishing the goal his grandfather had assigned him. With this kiss, the balance sheets would come out of the rinse cycle, clean and pressed like new. Too bad the old man hadn't been well enough to travel here and enjoy this moment himself.

Mikolas revealed his bride's face and froze.

She was beautiful. Her mouth was eye-catching with a lush upper lip and a bashful bottom one tucked beneath it. Her chin was strong and came up a notch in a hint of challenge while her blue, blue irises blinked at him.

This was no girl on the brink of legal age. She was a woman, one who was mature enough to look him straight in the eye without flinching.

She was *not* Trina Stamos.

"Who the hell are you?"

Gasps went through the crowd.

The woman lifted a hand to brush her veil free of his dumbfounded fingers.

Behind her, Grigor shot to his feet with an ugly curse. "What are you doing here? Where's Trina?"

Yes. Where was his bride? Without the right woman here to speak her vows and sign her name, this marriage—*the merger*—was at a standstill. *No.*

As though she had anticipated Grigor's reaction, the bride zipped behind Mikolas, using him like a shield as the older man bore down on them.

"You little bitch!" Grigor hissed. Trina's father was not as shocked by the switch as he was incensed. He clearly knew this woman. A vein pulsed on his forehead beneath his flushed skin. "Where is she?"

Mikolas put up a hand, warding off the old man from grabbing the woman behind him. He would have his explanation from her before Grigor unleashed his temper.

Or maybe he wouldn't.

Another round of surprised gasps went through the crowd, punctuated by the clack of the fire door and a loud, repetitive ring of its alarm.

His bride had bolted out the emergency exit.

What the *hell*?

CHAPTER TWO

VIVEKA RAN EVERY DAY. She was fit and adrenaline pulsed through her arteries, giving her the ability to move fast and light as she fled Grigor and his fury.

The dress and the heels and the spaces between planks and the floating wharf were another story. *Bloody hell.*

She made it down the swaying ramp in one piece, thanks to the rails on either side, but then she was racing down the unsteady platform between the slips, scanning for the flag of her vessel—

The train of her dress caught. She didn't even see on what. She was yanked back and that was all it took for her to lose her footing completely. *Stupid heels.*

She turned her ankle, stumbled, tried to catch herself, hooked her toe in a pile of coiled rope and threw out an arm to snatch at the rail of the yacht in the slip beside her.

She missed, only crashing into the side of the boat with her shoulder. The impact made her "oof!" Her grasp was too little, too late. She slid sideways and would have screamed, but had the sense to suck in a big breath before she fell.

Cold, murky salt water closed over her.

Don't panic, she told herself, splaying out her limbs and only getting tangled in her dress and veil.

Mom. This was what it must have been like for her on

that night far from shore, suddenly finding herself under cold, swirling water, tangled in an evening dress.

Don't panic.

Viveka's eyes stung as she tried to shift the veil enough to see which way the bubbles were going. Her dress hadn't stayed caught. It had come all the way in with her and floated all around her, obscuring her vision, growing heavier. The chill of the water penetrated to her skin. The weight of the dress dragged her down.

She kicked, but the layers of the gown were in the way. Her spiked heels caught in the fabric. This was futile. She was going to drown within swimming distance to shore. Grigor would stand above her and applaud.

The back of her hand scraped barnacles and her foot touched something. The seabed? Her hand burned where she'd scuffed it, but that told her there was a pillar somewhere here. She tried to scrabble her grip against it, desperately thinking she had never held her breath this long and couldn't hold it any longer.

Don't panic.

She clawed at her veil with her other hand, tried to pull it off her hair. She would never get all these buttons open and the dress off in time to kick herself to the surface—

Don't panic.

The compulsion to gasp for air was growing unstoppable.

A hand grabbed her forearm and tugged her.

Yes, please. Oh, God, please!

Viveka blew out what little air she still had, fighting not to inhale, fighting to kick and help bring herself to the blur of light above her, fighting to reach it…

As she broke through, she gasped in a lungful of life-giving oxygen, panting with exertion, thrusting back her veil to stare at her rescuer.

Mikolas.

He looked murderous.

Her heart lurched.

With a yank, he dragged her toward a diving ramp off the back of a yacht and physically set her hand upon it. She slapped her other bleeding hand onto it, clinging for dear life. Oh, her hand stung. So did her lungs. Her stomach was knotted with shock over what had just happened. She clung to the platform with a death grip as she tried to catch her breath and think clear thoughts.

People were gathering along the slip, trying to see between the boats, calling to others in Greek and English. "There she is!" "He's got her." "They're safe."

Viveka's dress felt like it was made of lead. It continued trying to pull her under, tugged by the wake that set all the boats around them rocking and sucking. She shakily managed to scrape the veil off her hair, ignoring the yank on her scalp as she raked it from her head. She let it float away, not daring to look for Grigor. She'd caught a glimpse of his stocky legs and that was enough. Her heart pounded in reaction.

"What the *hell* is going on?" Mikolas said in that darkly commanding voice. "Where is Trina? Who are you?"

"I'm her sis—" Viveka took a mouthful of water as a swell bashed the boat they clung to. "*Pah.* She didn't want to marry you."

"Then she shouldn't have agreed to." He hauled himself up to sit on the platform.

Oh, yes, it was just that easy.

He was too hard to face with that lethal expression. How did he manage to look so action-star handsome with his white shirt plastered to his muscled shoulders, his coat and tie gone, his hair flattened to his head? It was like staring into the sun.

Viveka looked out to where motorboats had circled to see where the woman in the wedding gown had fallen into the water.

Was that her boat? She wanted to wave, but kept a firm grip on the yacht as she used her free hand to pick at the buttons on her back. She eyed the distance to the red-and-gold boat. She couldn't swim that far in this wretched dress, but if she managed to shed it…?

Mikolas stood and, without asking, bent down to grasp her by the upper arms, pulling her up and out of the water, grunting loud enough that it was insulting. He swore after landing her on her feet beside him. His chest heaved while he glared at her limp, stained gown.

Viveka swayed on her feet, trying to keep her balance as the yacht rocked beneath them. She was still wearing the ridiculously high heels, was still in shock, but for a few seconds she could only stare at Mikolas.

He had saved her life.

No one had gone out of their way to help her like that since her mother was alive. She'd been a pariah to Grigor and a burden on her aunt, mostly fending for herself since her mother's death.

She swallowed, trying to assimilate a deep and disturbing gratitude. She had grown a thick shell that protected her from disregard, but she didn't know how to deal with kindness. She was moved.

Grigor's voice above her snapped her back to her situation. She had to get away. She yanked at her bodice, tearing open the delicate buttons on her spine and trying to push the clinging fabric down her hips.

She wore only a white lace bra and underpants beneath, but that was basically a bikini. Good enough to swim out to her getaway craft.

To her surprise, Mikolas helped her, rending the gown

as if he cursed its existence, leaving it puddled around her feet and sliding into the water. He didn't give her a chance to dive past him, however. He set wide hands on her waist and hefted her upward where bruising hands took hold of her arms—

Grigor.

"Nooo!" she screamed.

That ridiculous woman nearly kicked him in the face as he hefted her off the diving platform to the main deck of the yacht. Grigor was above, taking hold of her to bring her up. What did she think? That he was throwing her back into the sea?

"Noooo!" she cried and struggled, but Grigor pulled her all the way onto the deck where he stood.

She must be crazy, behaving like this.

Mikolas came up the ladder with the impetus of a man taking charge. He hated surprises. *He* controlled what happened to himself. No one else.

At least Grigor hadn't set this up. He'd been tricked as well, or he wouldn't be so furious.

Mikolas was putting that together as he came up to see Grigor shaking the nearly naked woman like a terrier with a rat. Then he slapped her across the face hard enough to send her to her knees.

No stranger to violence, Mikolas still took it like a punch to the throat. It appalled him on a level so deep he reacted on blind instinct, grabbing Grigor's arm and shoving him backward even as the woman threw up her arm as though to block a kick.

Stupid reaction, he thought distantly. It was a one-way ticket to a broken forearm.

But now was not the moment for a tutorial on street fighting.

Grigor found his balance and trained his homicidal gaze on Mikolas.

Mikolas centered his balance with readiness, but in his periphery saw the woman stagger toward the rail. Oh, hell, no. She was not going to ruin his day, then slip away like a siren into the deep.

He turned from Grigor's bitter "You should have let her drown" and provoked a cry of "Put me down!" from the woman as he caught her up against his chest.

She was considerably lighter without the gown, but still a handful of squirming damp skin and slippery muscle as he carried her off the small yacht.

On the pier, people parted and swiveled like gaggles of geese, some dressed in wedding regalia, others obviously tourists and sailors, all babbling in different languages as they took in the commotion.

It was a hundred meters to his own boat and he felt every step, thanks to the pedal of the woman's sharp, silver heels.

"Calm yourself. I've had it with this sideshow. You're going to tell me where my bride has gone and why."

CHAPTER THREE

VIVEKA WAS SHAKING right down to her bones. Grigor had hit her, right there in front of the whole world. Well, the way the yacht had been positioned, only Mikolas had probably seen him, but in the back of her mind she was thinking that this was the time to call the police. With all these witnesses, they couldn't ignore her complaint. Not this time.

Actually, they probably could. Her report of assault and her request for a proper investigation into her mother's death had never been heeded. The officers on this island paid rent to Grigor and didn't like to impact their personal lives by carrying out their sworn duties. She had learned that bitter lesson years ago.

And this brute wouldn't let her go to do anything!

He was really strong. He carried her in arms that were so hard with steely muscle it almost hurt to be held by them. She could tell it wasn't worth wasting her energy trying to escape. And he wore a mask of such controlled fury he intimidated her.

She instinctively drew in on herself, stomach churning with reaction while her brain screamed at her to swim out to her hired boat.

"Let me go," she insisted in a more level tone.

Mikolas only bit out orders for ice and bandages to a

uniformed man as he carried her up a narrow gangplank, boarding a huge yacht of aerodynamic layers and spaceship-like rigging. The walls were white, the decks teak, the sheer size and luxury of the vessel making it more like a cruise liner than a personal craft.

Greek mafia, she thought, and wriggled harder, signaling that she sincerely wanted him to put her down. *Now.*

Mikolas strode into what had to be the master cabin. She caught only a glimpse of its grand decor before he carried her all the way into a luxurious en suite and started the shower.

"Warm up," he ordered and pointed to the black satin robe on the back of the door. "Then we'll bandage your hand and ice your face while you explain yourself."

He left.

She snorted. *Not likely.*

Folding her arms against icy shivers, she eyed the small porthole that looked into the expanse of open water beyond the marina. She might fit through it, but even as the thought formed, a crewman walked by on the deck outside. She would be discovered before she got through it and in any case, she wasn't up for another swim. Not yet. She was trembling.

Reaction was setting in. She had nearly drowned. Grigor had hit her. He'd do worse if he got his hands on her again. Had he come aboard behind them?

She wanted to cry out of sheer, overwhelmed reaction.

But she wouldn't.

Trina was safe, she reminded herself. Never again did she have to worry about her little sister. Not in the same way, anyway.

The steaming shower looked incredibly inviting. Its gentle hiss beckoned her.

Don't cry, she warned herself, because showers were

her go-to place for letting emotion overcome her, but she couldn't afford to let down her guard. She may yet have to face Grigor again.

Her insides congealed at the thought.

She would need to pull herself together for that, she resolved, and closed the curtain across the porthole before picking herself free of the buckles on her shoes. She stepped into the shower still wearing her bra and undies, then took them off to rinse them and— Oh. She let out a huff of faint laughter as she saw her credit card stuck to her breast.

The chuckle was immediately followed by a stab of concern. Her bags, passport, phone and purse were on the hired boat. Was the captain waiting a short trot down the wharf? Or bobbing out in the harbor, wondering if she'd drowned? Grabbing this credit card and shoving it into her bra had been a last-minute insurance against being stuck without resources if things went horribly wrong, but she hadn't imagined things would go *this* far wrong.

The captain was waiting for her, she assured herself. She would keep her explanations short and sweet to Mikolas and be off. He seemed like a reasonable man.

She choked on another snort of laughter, this one edging toward hysteria.

Then another wave of that odd defenselessness swirled through her. Why had Mikolas saved her? It made her feel like— She didn't know what this feeling was. She never relied on anyone. She'd never been *able* to. Her mother had loved her, but she'd died. Trina had loved her, but she'd been too young and timorous to stand up to Grigor. Aunt Hildy had helped her to some extent, but on a quid-pro-quo basis.

Mikolas was a stranger who had risked his life to preserve hers. She didn't understand it.

It infused her with a sense that she was beholden to him. She hated that feeling. She had had a perfect plan to get Hildy settled, bring Trina to London once she was eighteen and finally start living life on her own terms. Then Grigor had ruined it by promising Trina to this… *criminal.*

A criminal who wasn't averse to fishing a woman out of the sea—something her stepfather hadn't bothered doing with her mother, leaving that task to search and rescue.

She was still trembling, still trying to make sense of it as she dried off with a thick black towel monogrammed with a silver *M.* She stole a peek in his medicine chest, bandaged her hand, used some kind of man-brand moisturizer that didn't have a scent, rinsed with his mouthwash, then untangled her hair with a comb that smelled like his shampoo. She used his hair dryer to dry her underwear and put both back on under his robe.

The robe felt really good, light and cool and slippery against her humid skin.

She felt like his lover wearing something this intimate.

The thought made her blush and a strange wistfulness hit her as she worked off his rings—both the diamond that Trina had given her and the platinum band he'd placed on her finger himself—and set them on the hook meant for facecloths. He was *not* the sort of man she would ever want to marry. He was far too daunting and she needed her independence, but she did secretly long for someone to share her life with. Someone kind and tender who would make her laugh and maybe bring her flowers sometimes.

Someone who wanted her in his life.

She would *not* grow maudlin about her sister running off with Stephanos, seemingly choosing him over Viveka, leaving her nursing yet another sting of rejection. Her sister was entitled to fall in love.

With a final deep breath, she emerged into the stateroom.

Mikolas was there, wearing a pair of black athletic shorts and towel-dried hair, nothing else. His silhouette was a bleak, masculine statue against the closed black curtains.

The rest of the room was surprisingly spacious for a boat, she noted with a sweeping glance. There was a sitting area with a comfortable-looking sectional facing a big-screen TV. A glass-enclosed office allowed a tinted view of a private deck in the bow. She averted her gaze from the huge bed covered with a black satin spread and came back to the man who watched her with an indecipherable expression.

He held a drink, something clear and neat. Ouzo, she assumed. His gaze snagged briefly on the red mark on her cheek before traversing to her bare feet and coming back to slam into hers.

His expression still simmered with anger, but there was something else that took her breath. A kind of male assessment that signaled he was weighing her as a potential sex partner.

Involuntarily, she did the same thing. How could she not? He was really good-looking. His build was amazing, from those broad, bare shoulders to that muscled chest to those washboard abs and soccer-star legs.

She was not a woman who gawked at men. She considered herself a feminist and figured if it was tasteless for men to gaze at pinup calendars, then women shouldn't objectify men, either, but seriously. *Wow.* He was muscly without being overdeveloped. His skin was toasted a warm brown and that light pattern of hair on his chest looked like it had been sculpted by the loving hand of Mother Nature, not any sort of waxing specialist.

An urge to touch him struck her. Sexual desire wasn't

something that normally hit her out of the blue like this, but she found herself growing warm with more than embarrassment. She wondered what it would be like to roam her mouth over his torso, to tongue his nipples and lick his skin. She felt an urge to splay her hands over his muscled waist and explore lower, push aside his waistband and *possess*.

Coils of sexual need tightened in her belly.

Where was the lead-up? The part where she spent ages kissing and nuzzling before she decided maybe she'd like to take things a little further? She never flashed to shoving down a man's pants and stroking him!

But that fantasy hit her along with a deep yearning and a throbbing pinch between her legs.

Was he getting *hard*? The front of his shorts lifted.

She realized where her gaze had fixated and jerked her eyes back to his, shocked with herself and at his blatant reaction.

His expression was arrested, yet filled with consideration and—she caught her breath—yes, that was an invitation. An arrogant *Help yourself.* Along with something predatory. Something that was barely contained. Decision. Carnal hunger.

The air grew so sexually charged, she couldn't find oxygen in it. The rhythm of her breaths changed, becoming subtle pants. Her nipples were stimulated by the shift of the robe against the lace of her bra. She became both wary and meltingly receptive.

This was crazy. She shook her head, as if she could erase all this sexual tension like an app that erased content on her phone if she joggled it back and forth hard enough.

With monumental effort, she jerked her gaze from his and stared blindly at the streak of light between the curtains. She folded her arms in self-protection and kept him in her periphery.

This was really stupid, letting him bring her into his bedroom like this. A single woman who lived in the city knew to be more careful.

"Use the ice," he said with what sounded like a hint of dry laughter in his tone. He nodded toward a side table where an ice pack sat on a small bar towel.

"It's not that bad," she dismissed. She'd had worse. Her lip might be puffed a little at the corner, but it was nothing like the time she'd walked around with a huge black eye, barely able to see out of it, openly telling people that Grigor had struck her. *You shouldn't talk back to him*, her teacher had said, mouth tight, gaze avoiding hers.

Grigor shouldn't have called her a whore and burned all her photos of her mother, she had retorted, but no one had wanted to hear *that*.

Mikolas didn't say anything, only came toward her, making her snap her head around and warn him off with a look.

Putting his glass down, he lifted his phone and clicked, taking a photo of her, surprising her so much she scowled.

"What are you doing?"

"Documenting. I assume Grigor will claim you were hurt falling into the water," he advised with cool detachment.

"You don't want me to try to discredit your business partner? Is that what you're saying? Are you going to take a photo after you leave your own mark on the other side of my face?" It was a dicey move, daring him like that, but she was so *sick* of people protecting *Grigor*. And she needed to know Mikolas's intentions, face them head-on.

Mikolas's stony eyes narrowed. "I don't hit women." His mouth pulled into a smile that was more an expression of lethal power than anything else. "And Grigor has discredited himself." He tilted the phone to indicate the photo. "Which may prove useful."

Viveka's insides tightened as she absorbed how cold-blooded that was.

"I didn't know Grigor had another daughter." Mikolas moved to take up his drink again. "Do you want one?" he asked, glancing toward the small wet bar next to the television. Both were inset against the shiny wood-grain cabinetry.

She shook her head. Better to keep her wits.

"Grigor isn't my father." She always took great satisfaction in that statement. "My mother married him when I was four. She died when I was nine. He doesn't talk about her, either."

Or the boating accident. Her heart clenched like a fist, trying to hang on to her memories of her mother, knotting in fury at the lack of a satisfactory explanation, wanting to beat the truth from Grigor if she had to.

"Do you have a name?" he asked.

"Viveka." The corner of her mouth pulled as she realized they'd come this far without it. She was practically naked, wearing a robe that had brushed his own skin and surrounded her in the scent of his aftershave. "Brice," she added, not clarifying that most people called her Vivi.

"Viveka," he repeated, like he was trying out the sound. They were speaking English and his thick accent gave an exotic twist to her name as he shaped out the *Vive* and added a short, hard *ka* to the end.

She licked her lips, disturbed by how much she liked the way he said it.

"Why the melodrama, Viveka? I asked your sister if she was agreeable to this marriage. She said yes."

"Do you think she would risk saying no to something Grigor wanted?" She pointed at the ache on her face.

Mikolas's expression grew circumspect as he dropped his gaze into his drink, thumb moving on the glass. It was the only indication his thoughts were restless beneath that rock-face exterior.

"If she wants more time," he began.

"She's marrying someone else," she cut in. "Right this minute, if all has gone to plan." She glanced for a clock, but didn't see one. "She knew Stephanos at school and he worked on Grigor's estate as a landscaper."

Trina had loved the young man from afar for years, never wanting to tip her hand to Grigor by so much as exchanging more than a shy hello with Stephanos, but she had waxed poetic to Viveka on dozens of occasions. Viveka hadn't believed Stephanos returned the crush until Trina's engagement to Mikolas had been announced.

"When Stephanos heard she was marrying someone else, he asked Trina to elope. He has a job outside of Athens." One that Grigor couldn't drop the ax upon.

"Weeding flower beds?" Mikolas swirled his drink. "She could have kept him on the side after we married, if that's what she wanted."

"Really," Viveka choked.

He shrugged a negligent shoulder. "This marriage is a business transaction, open to negotiation. I would have given her children if she wanted them, or a divorce eventually, if that was her preference. She should have spoken to me."

"Because you're such a reasonable man—who just happens to trade women like stocks and bonds."

"I'm a man who gets what he wants," he said in a soft voice, but it was positively deadly. "I want this merger."

He sounded so merciless her heart skipped in alarm. *Gangster.* She found a falsely pleasant smile.

"I wish you great success in making your dreams come true. Do you mind if I wear this robe to my boat? I can bring it back after I dress or maybe one of your staff could come with me?" She pushed her hand into the pocket and gripped her credit card, feeling the edge dig into her palm. Where was Grigor? she wondered. She had no desire to pass him on the dock and get knocked into the water again—this time unconscious.

Mikolas's expression didn't change. He said nothing, but she had the impression he was laughing at her again.

Something made her look toward the office and the view beyond the bow. The marina was tucked against a very small indent on the island's coastline. The view from shore was mostly an expanse of the Aegean. But the boats weren't passing in front of this craft. They were coming and going on both sides. The slant of sunlight on the water had shifted.

The yacht was moving.

"Are you kidding me?" she screeched.

CHAPTER FOUR

MIKOLAS THREW BACK the last of his ouzo, clenched his teeth against the burn and set aside his glass with a decisive *thunk*. He searched for the void that he usually occupied, but he couldn't find it. He was swirling in a miasma of lascivious need, achingly hard after the way Viveka had stared at his crotch and swallowed like her mouth was watering.

He absently ran a hand across his chest where his nipples were so sharp they pained him and adjusted himself so he wouldn't pop out of his shorts, resisting the urge to soothe the ache with a squeeze of his fist.

His reaction to her was unprecedented. He was an experienced man, had a healthy appetite for sex, but had never reacted so immediately and irrepressibly to any woman.

This lack of command over himself disturbed him. Infuriated him. He was insulted at being thrown over for a gardener and unclear on his next move. Retreat was never an option for him, but he'd left the island to regroup. That smacked of cowardice and he pinned the blame for all of it on this woman.

While she stood there with her hand closed over the lapels of his robe, holding it tight beneath her throat. Acting virginal when she was obviously as wily and experienced as any calculating opportunist he'd ever met.

"Let's negotiate our terms, Viveka." From the moment she had admitted to being Trina's sister he had seen the logical way to rescue this deal. Hell, by turning up in Trina's gown she'd practically announced to him how this would play out.

Of course it was a catch-22. He wasn't sure he wanted such a tempting woman so close to him, but he refused to believe she was anything he couldn't handle.

Viveka only flashed him a disparaging look and spun toward the door.

He didn't bother stopping her. He followed at a laconic pace as she scurried her way out to the stern of the mid-deck. Grasping the rail in one hand, she shaded her eyes with the other, scanning the empty horizon. She quickly threw herself to the port side. Gazing back to the island, which had been left well behind them, she made a distressed noise and glared at him again, expression white.

"Is Grigor on board?"

"Why would he be?"

"I don't know!" Her shoulders relaxed a notch, but she continued to look anxious. "Why did you leave the island?"

"Why would I stay?"

"Why would you take me?" she cried.

"I want to know why you've taken your sister's place."

"You didn't have to leave shore for that!"

"You wanted Grigor present? He seemed to be inflaming things." Grigor hadn't expected his departure, either. Mikolas's phone had already buzzed several times with calls from his would-be business partner.

That had been another reason for Mikolas's departure. If he'd stayed, he might have assaulted Grigor. The white-hot urge had been surprisingly potent and yes, that too had been provoked by this exasperating woman.

It wasn't a desire to protect *her*, Mikolas kept telling himself. His nature demanded he dominate, particularly over bullies and brutes. His personal code of ethics wouldn't allow him to stand by and watch any man batter a woman.

But Grigor's attack on this one had triggered something dark and primal in him, something he didn't care to examine too closely. Since cold-blooded murder was hardly a walk down the straight and narrow that was his grandfather's expectation of him, he'd taken himself out of temptation's reach.

"I had a boat hired! All my things are on it." Viveka pointed at the island. "Take me back!"

Such a bold little thing. Time to let her know who was boss.

"Grigor promised this merger if I married his daughter." He gave her a quick once-over. "His stepdaughter will do."

She threw back her head. "Ba-ha-ha," she near shouted and shrugged out of his robe, dropping it to the deck. "No. 'Bye." Something flashed in her hand as she started to climb over the rail.

She was fine-boned and supple and so easy to take in hand. Perhaps he took more enjoyment than he should in having another reason to touch her. Her skin was smooth and warm, her wrists delicate in his light grip as he calmly forced them behind her back, trapping her between the rail and his body.

She strained to look over her shoulder, muttering, "Oh, you—!" as something fell into the water with a glint of reflected light. "That was my credit card. Thanks a *lot*."

"Viveka." He was stimulated by the feel of her naked abdomen against his groin, erection not having subsided much and returning with vigor. Her spiked heels were gone, which was a pity. They'd been sexy as hell, but when it came to rubbing up against a woman, the less clothes the better.

She smelled of his shampoo, he noted, but there was an intriguing underlying scent that was purely hers: green tea and English rain. And that heady scent went directly into his brain, numbing him to everything but thoughts of being inside her.

Women were more subtle than men with their responses, but he read hers as clearly as a billboard. Not just the obvious signs like the way her nipples spiked against the pattern of her see-through bra cups, erotically abrading his chest and provoking thoughts of licking and sucking at them until she squirmed and moaned. A blush stained her cheeks and she licked her lips. There was a bonelessness to her. He could practically feel the way her blood moved through her veins like warm honey. He knew instinctively that opening his mouth against her neck would make her shiver and surrender to him. Her arousal would feed into his and they'd take each other to a new dimension.

Where did that ridiculous notion come from? He was no sappy poet. He tried to shake the idea out of his head, but couldn't rid himself of the certainty that sex with her would be the best he'd ever known. They were practically catching fire from this light friction. His heart was ramping with strength in his chest, his body magnetized to hers.

He was incensed with her, he reminded himself, but he was also intrigued by this unique attunement they had. Logic told him it was dangerous, but the primitive male inside him didn't give a damn. He *wanted* her.

"This is kidnapping. And assault," she said, giving a little struggle against his grip. "I thought you didn't hurt women."

"I don't let them hurt themselves, either. You'll kill yourself jumping into the water out here."

Something flickered in her expression. Her skin was very white compared with her sister's. How had he not noticed that from the very first, veil notwithstanding?

"Stop behaving like a spoiled child," he chided.

She swung an affronted look to him like it was the worst possible insult he could level at her. "How about you stop acting like you own the world?"

"This *is* my world. You walked into it. Don't complain how I run it."

"I'm trying to leave it."

"And I'll let you." Something twisted in his gut, as if that was a lie. A big one. "After you fix the damage you've done."

"How do you suggest I do that?"

"Marry me in your sister's place."

She made a choking noise and gave another wriggle of protest, heel hooking on the lower rung of the rail as if she thought she could lift herself backward over the rail.

All she managed to do was pin herself higher against him. She stilled. Hectic color deepened in her cheekbones.

He smiled, liking what she'd done. Her movement had opened her legs and brought her cleft up to nestle against his shaft. She'd caught the same zing of sexual excitement that her movement had sent through him. He nudged lightly, more of a tease than a threat, and watched a delicate shiver go through her.

It was utterly enthralling. He could only stare at her parted, quivering mouth. He wanted to cover and claim it. He wanted to drag his tongue over every inch of her. Wanted to push at his elastic waistband, press aside that virginal white lace and thrust into the heat that was branding him through the thin layers between them.

He had expected to spend this week frustrated. Now he began to forgive her for this switch of hers. They would do very nicely together. Very. Nicely.

"Let's take this back to my stateroom." His voice emanated from somewhere deep in his chest, thick with the desire that gripped him.

Her eyes flashed with fear before she said tautly, "To consummate a marriage that won't happen? Did you see how Grigor reacted to me? He'll never let me sub in for Trina. If anything would make him refuse your merger, marrying me would do it."

Mikolas slowly relaxed his grip and stepped back, trailing light fingers over the seams at her hips.

Goose bumps rose all over her, but she ignored it, hoping her knickers weren't showing the dampness that had released at the feel of him pressed against her.

What was *wrong* with her? She didn't even *do* sex. Kissing and petting were about it.

She dipped to pick up the robe and knotted it with annoyance. How could she be this hot when the wind had cooled to unpleasant and the sky was thickening with clouds?

She sent an anxious look at the ever-shrinking island amid the growing whitecaps. It was way too far to swim. Mikolas might have done her a favor taking her out of Grigor's reach, but being at sea thinned her composure like it was being spun out from a spool.

"You're saying if I want Grigor to go through with the merger, I should turn you over to him?" he asked.

"What? *No!*" Such terror slammed into her, her knees nearly buckled. "Why would you even think of doing something like that?"

"The merger is important to me."

"My *life* is important to me." Tears stung her eyes and she had to blink hard to be able to see him. She had a feeling her lips were trembling. Where was the man who had saved her? Right now, Mikolas looked as conscienceless as Grigor.

Crushed to see that indifference, she hid her distress by averting her gaze and swallowed back the lump in her throat.

"This is nothing," she said with as much calm as she could, pointing at her face, trying to reach through to the man who had said he didn't hurt women. "Barely a starting point for him. I'd rather take my chances with the sharks."

"You already have." The flatness of his voice sent a fresh quake of uncertainty through her center.

What did it say about how dire her situation was that she was searching for ways to reach him? To persuade *this* shark to refrain from offering her giftwrapped to the other one?

"If—if—" She wasn't really going to say this, was she? She briefly hung her head, but what choice did she have? She didn't have to go all the way, just make it good for him, right? She had a little experience with that. A very tiny little bit. He was hard, which meant he was up for it, right? "If you want sex…"

He made a scoffing noise. "*You* want sex. I'll decide if and when I give it to you. There's no leverage in offering it to me."

Sex was a basket of hang-ups for her. Offering herself had been really hard. Now she felt cheap and useless.

She pushed her gaze into the horizon, trying to hide how his denigration carved into her hard-won confidence.

"Go below," he commanded. "I want to make some calls."

She went because she needed to be away from him, needed to lick her wounds and reassess.

A purser showed her into a spacious cabin with a sitting room, a full en suite and a queen bed with plenty of tasseled pillows in green and gold. The cabinetry was polished to showcase the artistic grains in the amber-colored wood and the room was well-appointed with cosmetics, fresh fruit, champagne and flowers.

Her stomach churned too much to even think of eating, but she briefly considered drinking herself into oblivion. Once she noticed the laptop dock, however, she began looking for a device to contact…whom? Aunt Hildy wasn't an option. Her workmates might pick up a coffee or cover for her if she had to run home, but that was the extent of favors she could ask of them.

It didn't matter anyway. There was nothing here. The telephone connected to the galley or the bridge. The television was part of an onboard network that could be controlled by a tablet, but there was no tablet to be found.

At least she came across clothes. Women's, she noted with a cynical snort. Mikolas must have been planning to keep his own paramour on the side after his marriage.

Everything was in Viveka's size, however, and it struck her that this was Trina's trousseau. This was her sister's suite.

Mikolas hadn't expected her sister to share his room? Did that make him more hard-hearted than she judged him? Or less?

Men never dominated her thoughts this way. She never let them make her feel self-conscious and second-guess every word that passed between them. This obsession with Mikolas was a horribly susceptible feeling, like he was important to her when he wasn't.

Except for the fact he held her life in his iron fist.

Thank God she had saved Trina from marrying him. She'd done the right thing taking her sister's place and didn't hesitate to make herself at home among her things, weirdly comforted by a sense of closeness to her as she did.

Pulling on a floral wrap skirt and a peasant blouse—both deliberately light and easily removed if she happened to find herself treading water—Viveka had to admit she was relieved Mikolas had stopped her from jumping. She *would* rather take her chances with sharks than with Grigor, but she didn't have a death wish. She was trying not to think of her near drowning earlier, but it had scared the hell out of her.

So did the idea of being sent back to Grigor.

Somehow she had to keep a rational head, but after leaving Grigor's oppression and withstanding Aunt Hildy's virulence, Viveka couldn't take being subjugated anymore. That's why she'd come back to help Trina make her own choices. The idea of her sister living in sufferance as part of a ridiculous business deal had made her furious!

Opening the curtains that hid two short, wide portholes stacked upon each other, she searched the horizon for a plan. At least this wasn't like that bouncy little craft she'd dreaded. This monstrosity moved more smoothly and quietly than the ferry. It might even take her to Athens.

That would work, she decided. She would ask Mikolas to drop her on the mainland. She would meet up with Trina, Stephanos could arrange for her things to be delivered, and she would find her way home.

This pair of windows was some sort of extension, she realized, noting the cleverly disguised seam between the upper and lower windows. The top would lift into an awning while the bottom pushed out to become the railing on a short balcony. Before she thought it through, her finger was on the button next to the diagram.

The wall began to crack apart while an alarm went off with a horrible honking blare, scaring her into leaping back and swearing aloud.

Atop that shock came the interior door slamming open.

Mikolas had dressed in suit pants and a crisp white shirt and wore a *terrible* expression.

"I just wanted to see what it did!" Viveka cried, holding up a staying hand.

What a liability she was turning into.

Mikolas moved to stop and reverse the extension of the balcony while he sensed the engines being cut and the yacht slowing. As the wall restored itself, he picked up the phone and instructed his crew to stay the course.

Hanging up, he folded his arms and told himself this rush of pure, sexual excitement each time he looked at Viveka was transitory. It was the product of a busy few weeks when he hadn't made time for women combined with his frustration over today's events. Of course he wanted to let off steam in a very base way.

She delivered a punch simply by standing before him, however. He had to work at keeping his thoughts from conjuring a fantasy of removing that village girl outfit of hers. The wide, drawstring collar where her bra strap peeked was an invitation, the bare calves beneath the hem of her pretty skirt a promise of more silken skin higher up.

Those unpainted toes seemed ridiculously unguarded. So did the rest of her, with her hair tied up like a teenager and her face clean.

Some women used makeup as war paint, others as an invitation. Viveka hadn't used any. She hadn't tried to cover the bruise, and lifted that discolored, belligerent chin of hers in a brave stare that was utterly foolish. She had no idea whom she was dealing with.

Yet something twisted in his chest. He found her nerve entirely too compelling. He wanted to feed that spark of energy and watch it detonate in his hands. He bet she scratched in bed and was dismayingly eager to find out.

Women were *never* a weakness for him. No one was. Nothing. Weakness was abhorrent to him. Helplessness was a place he refused to revisit.

"We'll eat." He swept a hand to where the door was still open and one of the porters hovered.

He sent the man to notify the chef and steered her to the upper aft deck. The curved bench seat allowed them to slide in from either side, shifting cushions until they met in the middle, where they looked out over the water. Here the wind was gentled by the bulk of the vessel. It was early spring so the sun was already setting behind the clouds on the horizon.

She cast a vexed look toward the view. He took it as annoyance that the island was long gone behind them and privately smirked, then realized she was doing it again: pulling all his focus and provoking a reaction in him.

He forced his attention to the porter as he arrived with place settings and water.

"You'll eat seafood?" he said to Viveka as the porter left.

"If you tell me to, of course I will."

A rush of anticipation for the fight went through him. "Save your breath," he told her. "I don't shame."

"How does someone influence you, then? Money?" She affected a lofty tone, but quit fiddling with her silverware and tucked her hands in her lap, turning her head to read him. "Because I would like to go to Athens—as opposed to wherever you think you're taking me."

"I have money," he informed, skipping over what he intended to do next because he was still deciding.

He stretched out his arms so his left hand, no longer wearing the ring she'd put on it, settled behind her shoulder. He'd put the ring in his pocket along with the ones she had worn. Her returning them surprised him. She must have known what they were worth. Why wasn't she trying to use them as leverage? Not that it would work, but he expected a woman in her position to at least try.

He dismissed that puzzle and returned to her question. "If someone wants to influence me, they offer something I want."

"And since I don't have anything you want…?" Little flags of color rose on her cheekbones and she stared out to sea.

He almost smiled, but the tightness of her expression caused him to sober. Had he hurt her with his rejection earlier? He'd been brutal because he wasn't a novice. You didn't enter into any transaction wearing your desires on your sleeve the way she did.

But how could she not be aware that she *was* something he wanted? Did she not feel the same pull he was experiencing?

How did she keep undermining his thoughts this way?

As an opponent she was barely worth noticing. A brief online search had revealed she had no fortune, no influence. Her job was a pedestrian position as data entry clerk for an auto parts chain. Her network of social media contacts was small, which suggested an even smaller circle of real friends.

Mikolas's instinct when attacked was to crush. If Grigor had switched his bride on purpose, he would already be ruined. Mikolas didn't lose to anyone, especially weak adversaries who weren't even big enough to appear on his radar.

Yet Viveka had slipped in like a ninja, taking him unawares. On the face of it, that made her his enemy. He had to treat her with exactly as much detachment as he would any other foe.

But this twist of hunger in his gut demanded an answering response from her. It wasn't just ego. It was craving. A weight on a scale that demanded an equal weight on the other side to balance it out.

The porter returned, poured their wine, and they both sipped. When they were alone again, Mikolas said, "You were right. Grigor wants you."

Viveka paled beneath her already stiff expression. "And you want the merger."

"My grandfather does. I have promised to complete it for him."

She bit her bottom lip so mercilessly it disappeared. "Why?" she demanded. "I mean, why is this merger so important to him?"

"Why does it matter?" he countered.

"Well, what is it you're really trying to accomplish? Surely there are other companies that could give you what you want. Why does it have to be Grigor's?"

She might be impulsive and a complete pain in the backside, but she was perceptive. It *didn't* have to be Grigor's company. He was fully aware of that. However.

"Finding another suitable company would take time we don't have."

"A man with your riches can't buy as much as he needs?" she asked with an ingenuous blink.

She was a like a baby who insisted on trying to catch the tiger's tail and stuff it in her mouth. Not stupid, but cheerfully ignorant of the true danger she was in. He couldn't afford to be lenient.

"My grandfather is ill. I had to call him to tell him the merger has been delayed. That was disappointment he didn't need."

She almost threw an askance look at him, but seemed to read his expression and sobered, getting the message that beneath his civilized exterior lurked a heartless mercenary.

Not that he enjoyed scaring her. He usually treated women like delicate flowers. After sleeping in cold alleys that stank of urine, after being tortured at the hands of degenerate, pitiless men, he'd developed an insatiable appetite for luxury and warmth and the sweet side of life. He especially enjoyed soft kittens who liked to be stroked until they purred next to him in bed.

But if a woman dared to cross him, as with any man, he ensured she understood her mistake and would never dream of doing so again.

"I owe my grandfather a great deal." He waved at their surroundings. "This."

"I presumed it was stolen," she said with a haughty toss of her head.

"No." He was as blunt as a mallet. "The money was made from smuggling profits, but the boat was purchased legally."

She snapped her head around.

He shrugged, not apologizing for what he came from. "For decades, if something crossed the border or the seas for a thousand miles, legal or illegal, my grandfather—and my father when he was alive—received a cut."

He had her attention. She wasn't saucy now. She was wary. Wondering why he was telling her this.

"Desperate men do desperate things. I know this because I was quite desperate when I began trading on my father's name to survive the streets of Athens."

Their chilled soup arrived. He was hungry, but neither of them moved to pick up their spoons.

"Why were you on the streets?"

"My mother died. Heart failure, or so I was told. I was sent to an orphanage. I hated it." It had been a palace, in retrospect, but he didn't think about that. "I ran away. My mother had told me my father's name. I knew what he was reputed to be. The way my mother had talked, as if his enemies would hunt me down and use me against him if they found me...I thought she was trying to scare me into staying out of trouble. I didn't," he confided drily. "Boys of twelve are not known for their good judgment."

He smoothed his eyebrow where a scar was barely visible, but he could still feel where the tip of a blade had dragged very deliberately across it, opening the skin while a threat of worse—losing his eye—was voiced.

"I watched and learned from other street gangs and mostly stuck to robbing criminals because they don't go to the police. As long as I was faster and smarter, I survived. Threatening my father's wrath worked well in the beginning, but without a television or computer, I missed the news that he had been stabbed. I was caught in my lie."

Her eyes widened. "What happened?"

"As my mother had warned me, my father's enemies showed great interest. They asked me for information I didn't have."

"What do you mean?" she whispered, gaze fixed to his so tightly all he could see was blue. "Like...?"

"Torture. Yes. My father was known to have stockpiled everything from electronics to drugs to cash. But if I had known where any of it was kept, I would have helped myself, wouldn't I? Rather than trying to steal from them? They took their time believing that." He pretended the recollection didn't coat him in cold sweat.

"Oh, my God." She sat back, fingertips covering her faint words, gaze flickering over her shoulder to where his left hand was still behind her.

Ah. She'd noticed his fingernail.

He brought his hand between them, flexed its stiffness into a fist, then splayed it.

"These two fingernails." He pointed, affecting their removal as casual news. "Several bones broken, but it works well enough after several surgeries. I'm naturally left-handed so that was a nuisance, but I'm quite capable with both now, so…"

"Silver lining?" she huffed, voice strained with disbelief. "How did you get away?"

"They weren't getting anywhere with questioning me and hit upon the idea of asking my grandfather to pay a ransom. He had no knowledge of a grandson, though. He was slow to act. He was grieving. Not pleased to have some pile of dung attempting to benefit off his son's name. I had no proof of my claim. My mother was one of many for my father. That was why she left him."

He shrugged. Female companionship had never been a problem for any of the Petrides men. They were good-looking and powerful and money was seductive. Women found *them*.

"Pappoús could have done many things, not least of which was let them finish killing me. He asked for blood tests before he paid the ransom. When I proved to be his son's bastard, he made me his heir. I suddenly had a clean, dry bed, ample food." He nodded at the beautiful concoction before them: a shallow chowder of corn and buttermilk topped with fat, pink prawns and chopped herbs.

"I had anything I wanted. A motorcycle in summer, ski trips in winter. Clothes that were tailored to fit my body in any style or color I asked. Gadgets. A yacht. Anything."

He'd also received a disparate education, tutored by his grandfather's accountant in finance. His real estate and investment licenses were more purchased than earned, but he had eventually mastered the skills to benefit from such transactions. Along the way he had developed a talent for managing people, learning by observing his grandfather's methods. Nowadays they had fully qualified, authentically trained staff to handle every matter. Arm-twisting, even the emotional kind he was utilizing right now, was a retired tactic.

But it was useful in this instance. Viveka needed to understand the bigger picture.

Like his grandfather, he needed a test.

"In return for his generosity, I have dedicated myself to ensuring my grandfather's empire operates on the right side of the law. We're mostly there. This merger is a final step. I have committed to making it happen before his health fails him. You can see why I feel I owe him this."

"Why are you being so frank with me?" Her brow crinkled. "Aren't you afraid I'll repeat any of this?"

"No." Much of it was online, if only as legend and conjecture. While Mikolas had pulled many dodgy stunts like mergers that resembled money laundering, he'd never committed actual crimes.

That wasn't why he was so confident, however.

He held her gaze and waited, watching comprehension solidify as she read his expression. She would not betray him, he telegraphed. Ever.

Her lashes quivered and he watched her swallow.

Fear was beginning to take hold in her. He told himself

that was good and ignored the churn of self-contempt in his belly. He wasn't like the men who had tormented him.

But he wasn't that different. Not when he casually picked up his wineglass and mentioned, "I should tell you. Grigor is looking for your sister. You could save yourself by telling him where to find her."

"No!" The word was torn out of her, the look on her face deeply anxious, but not conflicted. "Maybe he never hit her before, but it doesn't mean he wouldn't start now. And this?" She waved at the table and yacht. "She had these trappings all her life and would have given up all of it for a kind word. At least I had memories of our mother. She didn't even have me, thanks to him. So no. *I* would rather go back to Grigor than sell her out to him."

She spoke with brave vehemence, but her eyes grew wet. It wasn't bravado. It was loyalty that would cost her, but she was willing to pay the price.

"I believe you," he pressed with quiet lack of mercy. "That Grigor would resort to violence. The way he spoke when I returned his call—" Mikolas considered himself immune to rabid foaming at the mouth. He knew first-hand how depraved a man could act, but the bloodlust in Grigor's voice had been disturbing. Familiar in a grim, dark way.

And educational. Grigor wasn't upset that his daughter was missing. He was upset the merger had been delayed. He was taking Viveka's involvement very personally and despite all his posturing and hard-nosed negotiating in the lead-up, he was revealing impatience for the merger to complete.

That told Mikolas his very thorough research prior to starting down this road with Grigor may have missed something. It wasn't a complete surprise that Grigor had kept something up his sleeve. Mikolas had chosen Grigor because he hadn't been fastidious about partnering with the Petrides name. Perhaps Grigor had thought the sacrifice to his reputation meant he could withhold certain debts or other liabilities.

It could turn out that Viveka had done Mikolas a favor, giving him this opportunity to review everything one final time before closing. He could, in fact, gain more than he'd lost.

Either way, Grigor's determination to reach new terms and sign quickly put all the power back in Mikolas's court, exactly where he was most comfortable having it.

Now he would establish that same position with Viveka and his world would be set right.

"Even if he finds her, what can he do to her?" she was murmuring, linking her hands together, nail beds white. "She's married to Stephanos. His boss works for a man who owns news outlets. Big ones. Running her to ground would accomplish nothing. No, she's safe." She seemed to be reassuring herself.

"What about you?" He was surprised she wasn't thinking of herself. "He sounded like he would hunt you down no matter where you tried to hide." It was the dead-honest truth.

Dead.

Honest.

"So you might as well turn me over and save him the trouble? And close your precious deal with the devil?" So much fire and resentment sparked off her it was fascinating.

"This deal *is* important to me. Grigor knows Pappoús is unwell, that I'm reluctant to look for another option. He wants me to hand you over, close the deal and walk away with what I want—which is to give my grandfather what he wants."

"And what I want doesn't matter." She was afraid, he could see it, but she refused to let it overtake her. He had to admire that.

"You got what you wanted," he pointed out. "Your sister is safe from my evil clutches."

"Good," she insisted, but her mouth quivered before she clamped it into a line. One tiny tear leaked out of the corner of her eye.

Poor, steadfast little kitten.

But that depth of loyalty pleased him. She was passing her test.

He reached out to stroke her hair even though it only made her flinch and flash a look of hatred at him.

"Are you enjoying terrorizing me?"

"Please," he scoffed, taking up his glass of wine to swirl and sip, cooling a mouth that was burning with anticipation as he finalized his decision. "I'm treating you like a Fabergé egg."

He ignored the release of tension inside him as what he really wanted moved closer to his grasp.

"Grigor makes an ugly enemy. You understand why I don't want to make him into one of mine," he said.

"Is it starting to grate on your conscience?" she charged. "That he'll beat me to a pulp and throw me into the nearest body of water? I thought you didn't shame."

"I don't. But I need you to see very clearly that the action I'm taking comes at a cost. Which you will repay. I will not be leaving you in Athens, Viveka. You are staying with me."

CHAPTER FIVE

VIVEKA'S VISION GREW grainy and colorless for a moment. She thought she might pass out, which was not like her at all. She was tough as nails, not given to fainting spells like a Victorian maiden.

She had been subtly hyperventilating this whole time Mikolas had been tying his noose around her neck. Now she'd stopped breathing altogether.

Had she heard him right?

He looked like a god, his neat wedding haircut finger-combed to the side, his mouth symmetrical and unwavering after smiting her with his words. His gray eyes were impassive. Just the facts.

"But—" she started to argue, wanting to bring up Aunt Hildy.

He shook his head. "We're not bargaining. Actions have consequences. These are yours."

"You," she choked, trying to grasp what he was saying. "*You* are my consequence?"

"It's me or Grigor. I've already told you that I won't allow you to hurt yourself, so yes. I have chosen your consequence. We should eat. Before it gets warm," he said with a whimsical levity that struck her as bizarre in the middle of this intense, life-altering conversation.

He picked up his spoon, but she only stared at him.

Her fingers were icicles, stiff and frozen. All of her muscles had atrophied while her heart was racing. Her mind stumbled around in the last glimmers of the bleeding sun.

"I have a life in London," she managed. "Things to do."

"I'm sure Grigor knows that and has men waiting."

Her panicked mind sprang to Aunt Hildy, but she was out of harm's reach for the moment. Still, "Mikolas—"

"Think, Viveka. Think hard."

She was trying to. She had been searching for alternatives this whole time.

"So you're abandoning the merger?" She hated the way her voice became puny and confused.

"Not at all. But the terms have changed." He was making short work of his soup and waved his spoon. "With your sister as my wife, Grigor would have had considerable influence over me and our combined organization. I was prepared to let him control his side for up to five years and pay him handsomely for his trouble. Now the takeover becomes hostile and I will push him out, take control of everything and leave him very little. I expect he'll be even more angry with you."

"Then don't be so ruthless! Why aggravate him further?"

His answer was a gentle nudge of his bent knuckle under her chin, thumb brushing the tender place at the corner of her mouth.

"He left a mark on my mistress. He needs to be punished."

Her heart stopped. She jerked back. "Mistress!"

"You thought I was keeping you out of the goodness of my heart?"

Her vision did that wobble again, fading in and out. "You said you didn't want sex." Her voice sounded like it was coming from far away.

"I said I would decide if and when I gave it to you. I have decided. Are you not going to eat those?" He had switched to his fork to eat his prawns and now stabbed one from her bowl, hungrily snapping it between his teeth, but his gaze was watchful when it swung up to hers.

"I'm not having sex with you!"

"You've changed your mind?"

"*You* did," she pointed out tartly, wishing she was one of those women who could be casual about sex. She'd been anxious from the get-go, which was probably why it had turned into this massive issue for her. "I'm not something you can buy like a luxury boat with your ill-gotten gains," she pointed out.

"I haven't purchased you." He gave her a frown of insult. "I've earned your loyalty the same way my grandfather earned mine, by saving your life. You will show your gratitude by being whatever I need you to be, wherever I need you to be."

"I'm not going to be *that*! If I understand you correctly, you want to live within the law. Well, pro tip, forcing women to have sex is against the law."

"Sex will be a fringe benefit for both of us." He was flinty in the face of her sarcasm. "I won't force you and I won't have to."

"Keep. *Dreaming*," she declared.

His fork clattered into his empty bowl and he shifted to face her, one arm behind her, one on the table, bracketing her into a space that enveloped her in masculine energy.

She could have skittered out the far side of the bench, but she held her ground, trying to stare him down.

His gaze fell to her mouth, causing her abdominals to tighten and tremble.

"You're not thinking about it? Wondering? *Dreaming*," he mocked in a voice that jarred because he did *not* sound angry. He sounded amused and knowing. "Let's see, shall we?"

His hand shifted to cup her neck. The caress of his thumb into the hollow at the base of her throat unnerved her. If he'd been forceful, she would have reacted with a slap, but this felt almost tender. She trusted this hand. It had dragged her up to the surface of the water, giving her life.

So she didn't knock that hand away. She didn't hit him in the face as he neared, or pull away to say a hard *No*.

Somehow she got it into her head she would prove he didn't affect her. Maybe she even thought she could return to him that rejection he'd delivered earlier.

Maybe she really did want to know how it would be with him.

Whatever the perverse impulse that possessed her, she sat there and let him draw closer, keeping her mouth set and her gaze as contemptuous as she could make it.

Until his lips touched hers.

If she had expected brutality, she was disappointed. But he wasn't gentle, either.

His hold firmed on her neck as he plundered without hesitation, opening his mouth over hers in a hot, wet branding that caused a burn to explode within her. His tongue stabbed and her lips parted. Delicious swirls of pleasure invaded her belly and lower. Her eyes fluttered closed so she could fully absorb the sensations.

She *had* wondered. Intrigue had held her still for this kiss and she moaned as she basked in it, bones dissolving, muscles weakening.

He kissed her harder, dismantling her attempt to remain detached in a few short, racing heartbeats. He dragged his lips across hers in an erotic crush, the rough-soft texture of his lips like silken velvet.

All her senses came alive to the heat of his chest, the woodsy spice scent on his skin, the salt flavor on his tongue. Her skin grew so sensitized it was painful. She felt vulnerable with longing.

She splayed her free hand against his chest and released a sob of capitulation, no longer just accepting. Participating. Exploring the texture of his tongue, trying to compete with his aggression and consume him with equal fervor.

He pulled back abruptly, the loss of his kiss a cruelty that left her dangling in midair, naked and exposed. His chest moved with harsh breaths that seemed triumphant. The glitter in his eye was superior, asserting that *he* would decide *if* and *when.*

"No force necessary," he said with satisfaction deepening the corners of his mouth.

This was how it had been for her mother, Viveka realized with a crash back to reality. Twenty years ago, Grigor had been handsome and virile, provoking infatuation in a lonely widow. Viveka's earliest memories of being in his house had been ones of walking in on intimate clinches, quickly told to make herself scarce.

As Viveka had matured, she had recognized a similar yearning in herself for a man's loving attention. She understood how desire had been the first means that Grigor had used to control his wife, before encumbering her with a second child, then ultimately showing his ugliest colors to keep her in line.

Sex was a dangerous force that could push a woman down a slippery slope. That was what Viveka had come to believe.

It was doubly perilous when the man in question was so clearly not impacted by their kiss the way she was. Mikolas's indifference hurt, inflicting a loneliness on her that matched those moments in her life that had nearly broken her: losing her mother, being banished from her sister to an aunt who should have loved her, but hadn't.

She had to look away to hide her anguish.

The porter arrived to bring out the next course.

Mikolas didn't even look up from his plate as he said, "What is the name of the man who has your things? I would like to retrieve your passport before Grigor realizes it's under his nose."

Viveka needed to tell him about Aunt Hildy, but didn't trust her voice.

Mikolas said little else through the rest of their meal, only admonishing her to eat, stating at the end of it, "I want to finish the takeover arrangements. You have free run of the yacht unless you show me you need to be confined to your room."

"You seriously think I'll let you keep me like some kind of pirate's doxy?"

"Since I'm about to stage a raid and appoint myself admiral of Grigor's corporate fleet, I can't deny that label, can I? You call yourself whatever you want."

She glared at his back as he walked away.

He left her to her own devices and there must have been something wrong with her because, despite hating Mikolas for his overabundance of confidence, she was viciously glad he was running Grigor through.

At no point should she consider Mikolas her hero, she cautioned herself. She should have known there'd be a cost to his saving her life. She flashed back to Grigor calling her useless baggage. To Hildy telling her to earn her keep.

She wasn't even finished repaying Hildy! That hardly put her in a position to show "gratitude" to Mikolas, did it?

Oh, she hated when people thought of her as some sort of nuisance. This was why she had been looking forward to settling Hildy and striking out on her own. She could finally prove to herself and the world that she carried her own weight. She was not a lodestone. She wasn't.

A rabbit hole of self-pity beckoned. She avoided it by getting her bearings aboard the aptly named *Inferno.* The top deck was chilly and dark, the early night sky spitting rain into her face as the wind came up. The hot tub looked appealing, steaming and glowing with colored underwater lights. When the porter appeared with towels and a robe, inviting her to use the nearby change room, she was tempted, but explained she was just looking around.

He proceeded to give her a guided tour through the rest of the ship. She didn't know what the official definition for "ship" was, but this behemoth had to qualify. The upper deck held the bridge along with an outdoor bar and lounge at the stern. A spiral staircase in the middle took them down to the interior of the main deck. Along with Mikolas's stateroom and her own, there was a formal dining room for twelve, an elegant lounge with a big-screen television and a baby grand piano. Outside, there was a small lifeboat in the bow, in front of Mikolas's private sundeck, and a huge sunbathing area alongside a pool in the stern.

The extravagance should have filled her with contempt, but instead she was calmed by it, able to pretend this wasn't a boat. It was a seaside hotel. One that happened to be priced well beyond her reach, but *whatever.*

It wasn't as easy to pretend on the lower deck, which was mostly galley, engine room, less extravagant guest and crew quarters. And, oh, yes, another boat, this one a sexy speedboat parked in an internal compartment of the stern.

Her long journey to get to Trina caught up to her at that point. She'd left London the night before and hadn't slept much while traveling. She went back to her suite and changed into a comfortable pair of pajamas—ridiculously pretty ones in peacock-blue silk. Champagne-colored lace edged the bodice and tickled the tops of her bare feet, adding to the feeling of luxuriating in pure femininity.

She hadn't won a prize holiday, she reminded herself, trying not to be affected by all this lavish comfort. A gilded cage was still a prison and she would *not* succumb to Mikolas's blithe expectation that he could "keep" her. He certainly would not *seduce* her with his riches and pampering.

I won't force you and I won't have to.

She flushed anew, recalling their kiss as she curled up on the end of the love seat rather than crawl into bed. She wanted to be awake if he arrived expecting sex. When it came to making love, she was more about fantasy than reality, going only so far with the few men she'd dated. That kiss with Mikolas had shaken her as much as everything else that had happened today.

Better to think about that than her near-drowning, though.

Her thoughts turned for the millionth time to her mother's last moments. Somehow she began imagining her mother was on this boat and they were being tossed about in a storm, but she couldn't find her mother to warn her. It was a dream, she knew it was a dream. She hadn't been on the other boat when her mother was lost, but she could feel the way the waves were battering this one—

Sitting up with a gasp, she sensed they'd hit rough waters. Waves splashed against the glass of her porthole and the boat rocked enough she was rolling on her bed.

How had she wound up in bed?

With a little sob, she threw off the covers and pushed to her feet.

Fear, Aunt Hildy would have said, was no excuse for panic. Viveka did not consider herself a brave person at all, but she had learned to look out for herself because no one else ever had. If this boat was about to capsize, she needed to be on deck wearing a life jacket to have a fighting chance at survival.

Holding the bulkhead as she went into the passageway, she stumbled to the main lounge. The lifeboat was on this deck, she recalled, but in the bow, on the far side of Mikolas's suite. The porter had explained all the safety precautions, which had reassured her at the time. Now all she could think was that it was a stupid place to store life jackets.

Mikolas always slept lightly, but tonight he was on guard for more than old nightmares. He was expecting exactly what happened. The balcony in Viveka's stateroom wasn't the only thing alarmed. When she left her suite, the much more discreet internal security system caused his phone to vibrate.

He acknowledged the signal, then pushed to his feet and adjusted his shorts. That was another reason he'd been restless. He was hard. And he never wore clothes to bed. They were uncomfortable even when they weren't twisted around his erection, but he'd anticipated rising at some point to deal with his guest so he had supposed he should wear something to bed.

He'd expected to find release *with* his guest, but when he'd gone to her room, she'd been fast asleep, curled up on the love seat like a child resisting bedtime, one hand pillowing her cheek. She hadn't stirred when he'd carried her to the bed and tucked her in, leaving him sorely disappointed.

That obvious exhaustion, along with her pale skin and the slight frown between her brows, had plucked a bizarre reaction from him. Something like concern. That bothered him. He was impervious to emotional manipulations, but Viveka was under his skin—and she hadn't even been awake and doing it deliberately.

He sighed with annoyance, moving into his office.

If a woman was going to wake him in the night, it ought to be for better reasons than this.

He had no doubt this private deck in the bow was her destination. He'd watched her talk to his porter extensively about the lifeboat and winch system while he'd sat here working earlier. He wasn't surprised she was attempting to escape. He wasn't even angry. He was disappointed. He hated repeating himself.

But there was an obdurate part of him that enjoyed how she challenged him. Hardly anyone stood up to him anymore.

Plus he was sexually frustrated enough to be pleased she was setting up a midnight confrontation. When he'd kissed her earlier, desire had clawed at his control with such savagery, he'd nearly abandoned one for the other and made love to her right there at the table.

His need to be in command of himself and everyone else had won out in the end. He'd pulled back from the brink, but it had taken more effort than he liked to admit.

"Come on," he muttered, searching for her in the dim glow thrown by the running lights.

This was an addict's reaction, he thought with self-contempt. His brain knew she was lethal, but the way she infused him with a sense of omnipotence was a greater lure. He didn't care that he risked self-destruction. He still wanted her. He was counting the pulse beats until he could feel the rush of her hitting his system.

Where *was* she?

Not overboard again, surely.

The thought sent a disturbing punch into the middle

of his chest. He didn't know what had made him throw off his jacket and shoes and dive in after her today. It had been pure instinct. He'd shot out the emergency exit behind her, determined to hear why she had upended his plans, but he hadn't been close enough to stop her tumble into the water.

His heart had jammed when he'd seen her knock into the side of the yacht, worried she was unconscious as she went under.

Pulling her and that whale of a gown to the surface had nearly been more than he could manage. He didn't know what he would have done if the strength of survival hadn't imbued him. Letting go of her hadn't been an option. It wasn't basic human decency that had made him dive into that water, but something far more powerful that refused, absolutely refused, to go back to the surface without her.

Damn it, now he couldn't get that image of her disappearing into the water out of his head. He pushed from his office onto his private deck, where the rain and splashing waves peppered his skin. She wasn't coming down the stairs toward him.

He climbed them, walking along the outer rail of the mid-deck, seeing no sign of her.

Actually, he walked right past her. He spied her when he paused at the door into the bridge, thinking to enter and look for her on the security cameras. Something made him glance back the way he'd come and he spotted the ball of dark clothing and white skin under the life preserver ring.

What the hell?

"Viveka." He retraced his few steps, planting his bare feet carefully on the wet deck. "What are you doing out here?"

She lifted her face. Her hair was plastered in tendrils

around her neck and shoulders. Her chin rattled as she stammered, “I n-n-need a l-l-life v-v-vest.”

“You’re freezing.” *He* was cold. He bent to draw her to her feet, but she stubbornly stayed in a knot of trembling muscle, fingers wrapped firmly around the mount for the ring.

What a confounding woman. With a little more force, he started to peel her fingers open.

The boat listed, testing his balance.

Before he could fully right himself, Viveka cried out and nearly knocked him over, rising to throw her arms around his neck, slapping her soaked pajamas into his front.

He swore at the impact, working to stay on his feet.

“Are we going over?”

“No.”

He could hardly breathe, she was clinging so tightly to his neck, and shaking so badly he could practically hear her bones rattling. He swore under his breath, putting together all those anxious looks out to the water. This was why she hadn’t shown the sense to be terrified of *him* today. She was afraid of boats.

“Come inside.” He drew her toward the stairs down to his deck.

She balked. “I don’t want to be trapped if we capsize.”

“We won’t capsize.”

She resisted so he picked her up and carried her all the way through his dark office into his stateroom, where he’d left a lamp burning, kicking doors shut along the way.

He sat on the edge of his bed, settling her icy, trembling weight on his lap. “This is only a bit of wind and freighter traffic. We’re hitting their wakes. It’s not a storm.”

There was no heat beneath these soaked pajamas. Even in the dim light, he could see her lips were blue. He ran his hands over her, trying to slick the water out of her pajamas while he rubbed warmth into her skin.

"There doesn't have to be a storm." She was pressing into him, her lips icy against his collarbone, arms still around his neck, relaxing and convulsing in turns. "My mother drowned when it was calm."

"From a boat?" he guessed.

"Grigor took her out." Her voice fractured. "Maybe on purpose to drown her. I don't know, but I think she wanted to leave him. He took her out sailing and said he didn't know till morning that she fell, but he never acted like he cared. He told me to stop crying and take care of Trina."

If this was a trick, it was seriously good acting. The emotion in her voice sent him tumbling into equally disturbing memories buried deep in his subconscious. *Your mother died while you were at school.* The landlord had made the statement without hesitation or regret, casually destroying Mikolas's world with a few simple words. *A woman from child services is coming to get you.*

So much horror had followed, Mikolas barely registered anymore how bad that day had been. He'd shuffled it all into the past once his grandfather had taken him in. The page had been turned and he never leafed back to it.

But suddenly he was stricken with that old grief. He couldn't ignore the way her heart pounded so hard he felt it against his arm across her back. Her skin was clammy, her spine curled tight against life's blows.

His hand unconsciously followed that hard curve, no longer just warming her, but trying to soothe while stealing a long-overdue shred of comfort for himself from someone who understood what he'd suffered.

He recovered just as quickly, shaking off the moment of empathy and rearranging her so she was forced to look up at him.

"I've been honest with you, haven't I?" Perhaps he sounded harsh, but she had cracked something in him. He didn't like the cold wind blowing through him as a result. "I would tell you if we were in danger. We're not."

Viveka believed him. That was the ridiculous part of it. She had no reason to trust him, but why would he be so blunt about everything else and hide the fact they were likely to capsize? If he said they were safe, they were safe.

"I'm still scared," she admitted in a whisper, hating that she was so gutless.

"Think of something else," he chided. The edge of his thumb gave her jaw a little flick, then he dipped his head and kissed her.

She brought up a hand to the side of his face, thinking she shouldn't let this happen again, but his stubble was a fascinating texture against her palm and his lips were blessedly hot, sending runnels of heat through her sluggish blood. Everything in her calmed and warmed.

Then he rocked his mouth to part her lips with the same avid, possessive enjoyment as earlier and cupped her breast and she shuddered under a fresh onslaught of sensations. The rush hurt, it was so powerful, but it was also like that moment when he'd dragged her to the surface. He was dragging her out of her phobia into wonder.

She instinctively angled herself closer, the silk of her pajamas a wet, annoying layer between them as she tried to press herself through his skin.

He grunted and grew harder under her bottom. His arms gathered her in with a confident, sexual possessiveness while his knees splayed wider so she sat deeper against the firm shape of his sex.

Heat rushed into her loins, sharp and powerful. All of

her skin burned as blood returned to every inch of her. She didn't mean to let her tongue sweep against his, but his was right there, licking past her lips, and the contact made lightning flash in her belly.

His aggression should have felt threatening, but it felt sexy and flagrant. As the kiss went on, the waves of pleasure became more focused. The way he toyed with her nipple sent thrums of excitement rocking through her.

She gasped for air when he drew back, but she didn't want to stop. Not yet. She lifted her mouth so he returned and kissed her harder. Deeper.

Her breast ached where he massaged it and the pulse between her legs became a hungry throb as he shifted wet silk against the tight point of her nipple.

His hand slid away, pulling the soggy material up from her quivery belly. He flattened his palm there, branding her cold, bare skin. His fingers searched along the edge of her waistband and he lifted his head, ready to slide his hand between her closed thighs.

"Open," he commanded.

Viveka gasped and shot off his lap, stumbling when her knees didn't want to support her. "What—no!"

She covered her throat where her pulse was racing, shocked at herself. He kept turning her into this...*animal*. That's all this was: hormones. Some kind of primal response to the caveman who happened to yank her out of the lion's jaws. The primitive part of her recognized an alpha male who could keep her offspring alive so her body wanted to make some with him.

Mikolas dropped one hand, then the other behind him, leaning on his straight arms, knees wide. His nostrils flared as he eyed her. It was the only sign that her recoil bothered him.

Contractions of desire continued to swirl in her abdomen. That part of her that was supposed to be able to take his shape felt so achy with carnal need she was nearly overwhelmed.

"You said you wouldn't make me," she managed in a shaky little voice.

It was a weak defense and they both knew it.

He cocked one brow in a mocking, *I don't have to*. The way his gaze traveled down her made her afraid for what she looked like, silk clinging to distended nipples and who knew what other telltale reactions.

She pulled the fabric away from her skin and looked to the door.

"You're bothered by your reaction to me. Why? I think it's exciting." The rasp of his arousal-husky voice made her inner muscles pinch with involuntary eagerness. "Come here. I'll hold you all night. You'll feel very safe," he promised, but his mouth quirked with wicked amusement.

She hugged herself. "I don't sleep around. I don't even know you!"

"I prefer it that way," he provided.

"Well, I don't!"

He sighed, rising and making her heart soar with alarmed excitement. It fell as he turned and walked away to the corner of the room.

She had rejected *him*, she reminded herself. This sense of rebuff was completely misplaced.

But he was so appealing with his tall, powerful frame, spine bracketed by supple muscle in the way of a martial artist rather than a gym junkie. The low light turned his skin a dark, burnished bronze and he had a really nice butt in those wet, clinging boxers.

She ought to leave, but she watched him search out three different points before he drew the wall inward like an oversize door. The cabinetry from her stateroom came with it, folding back to become part of his sitting room, creating an archway into her suite.

"I haven't used this yet. It's clever, isn't it?" he remarked.

If she didn't loathe boats so much, she might have agreed. As it was, she could only hug herself, dumbfounded to see they were now sharing a room.

"You'll feel safer like this, yes?"

Not likely!

He didn't seem to expect an answer, just turned to open a drawer. He pawed through, coming up with a pink long-sleeved top in waffle weave and a pair of pink and mint green flannel pajama pants. "Dry off and put these on. Warm up."

She waved at the archway. "Why did you do that?"

"You don't find it comforting?"

Oh, she was not sticking around to be laughed at. She snatched the pajamas from his hand, not daring to look into his face, certain she would see mockery, and made for the bathroom in her own suite. *Infuriating* man.

She would close the wall herself, she decided as she clumsily changed, even though she preferred the idea of him being in the same room with her. He was not a man to be relied on, she reminded herself. If she had learned nothing else in life, it was that she was on her own.

Then she walked out and found a life vest on the foot of her bed. When she glanced toward his room, his lamp was off.

She clutched the cool bulk of the vest to her chest, insides crumpling.

"Thank you, Mikolas," she said toward his darkened room.

A pause, then a weary "Try not to need it."

CHAPTER SIX

VIVEKA WAS SO emotionally spent, she slept late, waking with the life vest still in her crooked arm.

Sitting up with an abrupt return of memory, she noted the sun was streaming in through the uncovered windows of Mikolas's stateroom. The yacht was sailing smoothly and she could swear that was the fresh scent of a light breeze she detected. She swung her feet to the floor and moved into his suite with a blink at the brightness.

He didn't notice her, but she caught her breath at the sight of him. He was lounging on the wing-like extension from his sitting area. It was fronted by what looked like the bulkhead of his suite and fenced on either side by glass panels anchored into thin, stainless steel uprights. The wind blew over him, ruffling his dark hair.

She might have been alarmed by the way the ledge dangled over the water, but he was so relaxed, slouched on a cushioned chair, feet on an ottoman, she could only experience again the pinch of deep attraction.

He had his tablet in one hand, a half-eaten apple in the other and he was mostly naked. Again. All he wore were shorts, these ones a casual pair in checked gray and black even though the morning breeze was quite cool.

Her heart actually panged that she had to keep fighting

him. He looked so casually beau
her, though, but Aunt Hildy.

He lifted his head and turned to look at h
he'd been aware of her the whole time. "Are yo
to come out here?"

She was terrified, but it had nothing to do with the water and everything to do with how he affected her.

"Why are you allowed to have your balcony open and I got in trouble for it?" she asked, choosing a tone of belligerence over revealing her intimidation, forcing her legs to carry her as far as the opening.

"I had a visitor." He nodded at the deck beside his ottoman.

Her bag.

Stunned, she quickly knelt and rifled through it, coming up with her purse, phone, passport… Everything exactly as it should be. Even her favorite hair clip. She gathered and rolled the mess of her hair in a well-practiced move, weirdly comforted by that tiny shred of normalcy.

When she looked up at him, Mikolas was watching her. He finished his apple with a couple of healthy bites and flipped the core into the water.

"Help yourself." He nodded toward where a sideboard was set up next to the door to his office.

"I'm in time-out? Not allowed out for breakfast?"

No response, but she quickly saw there was more than coffee and a basket of fruit here. The dishes contained traditional favorites she hadn't eaten since leaving Greece nine years ago.

Somehow she'd convinced herself she hated everything about this country, but the moment she saw the *tiganites*, nostalgia closed her throat. A sharp memory of asking her mother if she could cut up her sister's pancakes and pour

sted quite like grape
er mouth watered and
ger.

d, hoping he didn't hear
anced out to see he didn't

helping of the smoked pork om-
ele s and topped up his coffee, earning a co k as she served him.

Yes, she w ng to soften him up. A woman had to create advantages where she could with a man like him.

"Efcharistó," he said when she joined him.

"Parakaló." She was trying to act casual, but she had chosen to start with yogurt and thyme honey. The first bite tasted so perfect, was such a burst of early childhood happiness, when her mother had been alive and her sister a living doll she could dress and feed, she had to close her eyes, pressing back tears of homecoming.

Mikolas watched her, reluctantly fascinated by the emotion that drew her cheeks in while she savored her breakfast. Pained joy crinkled her brow. It was sensual and sexy and poignant. It was *yogurt*.

He forced his gaze to his own plate.

Viveka was occupying entirely too much real estate in his brain. It had to stop.

But even as he told himself that, his mind went back to last night. How could it not, with her sitting across from him braless beneath her long-sleeved nightshirt? The soft weight of her breast was still imprinted on his palm, firm and shapely, topped with a sensitive nipple he'd longed to suck.

Instantly he was primed for sex. And damn it, she'd

been as fully involved as he had been. He wasn't so arrogant he made assumptions about women's states of interest. He took pains to ensure they were with him every step of the way when he made love to them. She'd been pressing herself into him, returning his kiss, moaning with enjoyment.

Fine, he could accept that she thought they were moving too fast. Obviously she was a bit of a romantic, flying across the continent to help her sister marry her first love. But sex would happen between them. It was inevitable.

When he had opened the passageway between their rooms, however, it hadn't been for sex. He had wanted to ease her anxiety. She had been nothing less than a nuclear bomb from the moment he'd seen her face, but he'd found himself searching out the catch in the wall, giving her access to *his* space, which had never been his habit with any woman.

He didn't understand his actions around her. This morning, he'd actually begun second-guessing his decision to keep her, which wasn't like him at all. Indecision did not make for control in any situation. He certainly couldn't back down because he was *scared.* Of being around a particular *woman.*

Then the news had come through that Grigor was, indeed, hiding debts in two of his subsidiaries. There was no room for equivocating after that. Mikolas had issued a few terse final orders, then notified Grigor of his intention to take over with or without cooperation.

Grigor had been livid.

Given the man's vile remarks, Mikolas was now as suspicious as Viveka that her stepfather had killed her mother. Viveka would stay with him whether he was comfortable in her presence or not.

Whether she liked it or not. At least until he could be sure Grigor wouldn't harm her.

She opened her dreamy blue eyes and looked like she was coming back from orgasm. Sexual awareness shimmered like waves of desert heat between them.

Yes. Sex was inevitable.

Her gaze began to tangle with his, but she seemed to take herself in hand. She sat taller and cleared her throat, looking out to the water and lifting a determined chin, cheekbones glowing with pink heat.

He mentally sighed, too experienced a fighter not to recognize she was preparing to start one.

"Mikolas." He mentally applauded her take-charge tone. "I *have* to go back to London. My aunt is very old. Quite ill. She needs me."

He absorbed that with a blink. This was a fresh approach at least.

She must have read his skepticism. Her mouth tightened. "I wish I was making it up. I'm not."

If he expected her trust—and he did—he would have to trust her in return, he supposed. "Tell me about her," he invited.

She looked to the clear sky, seeming to struggle a moment.

"There's not much to tell. She's the sister of my grandmother and took me in when Grigor kicked me out, even though she was a spinster who never wanted anything to do with children. She had a career before women really did. Worked in Parliament, but not as an elected official. As a secretary to a string of them. She had some kind of lofty clearance, served coffee to all sorts of royals and diplomats. I think she was in love with a married man," she confided with a wrinkle of her nose.

Definitely a sentimentalist.

She shrugged, murmuring, "I don't have proof. Just a few things she said over the years." She picked up her coffee and cupped her hands around it. "She was always telling me how to behave so men wouldn't think things." She made a face. "I'm sure the sexism in her day was appalling. She was adamant that I be independent, pay my share of rent and groceries, know how to look after myself."

"She didn't take her own advice? Make arrangements for herself?"

"She tried." Her shoulder hitched in a helpless shrug. "Like a lot of people, she lost her retirement savings with the economic crash. For a while she had an income bringing in boarders, but we had to stop that a few years ago and remortgage. She has dementia." Her sigh held the weight of the world. "Strangers in the house upset her. She doesn't recognize me anymore, thinks I'm my mother, or her sister, or an intruder who stole her groceries." She looked into her cooling coffee. "I've begun making arrangements to put her into a nursing home, but the plans aren't finalized."

Viveka knew he was listening intently, thought about leaving it there, where she had stopped with the doctors and the intake staff and with Trina during their video chats. But the mass on her conscience was too great. She'd already told Mikolas about Grigor's abuse. He might actually understand the rest and she really needed it off her chest.

"I *feel* like I'm stealing from her. She worked really hard for her home and deserves to live in it, but she can't take care of herself. I have to run home from work every few hours to make sure she hasn't started a fire or caught a bus to who knows where. I can't afford to stay home with her all day and even if I could..."

She swallowed, reminding herself not to feel resentful, but it still hurt. Not just physically, either. She had tried from Day One to have a familial relationship with her aunt and it had all been for naught.

"She started hitting me. I know she doesn't mean it to be cruel. She's scared. She doesn't understand what's happening to her. But I can't take it."

She couldn't look at him. She already felt like the lowest form of life and he wasn't saying anything. Maybe he was letting her pour out her heart and having a laugh at her for getting smacked by an old lady.

"Living with her was never great. She's always been a difficult, demanding person. I was planning to move out the minute I finished school, but she started to go downhill. I stayed to keep house and make meals and it's come to this."

The little food she'd eaten felt like glue in her stomach. She finished up with the best argument she could muster.

"You said you're loyal to your grandfather for what he gave you. That's how I feel toward her. The only way I can live with removing her from her home is by making sure she goes to a good place. So I have to go back to London and oversee that."

Setting aside her coffee, she hugged herself, staring sightlessly at the horizon, not sure if it was guilt churning her stomach or angst at revealing herself this way.

"Now who is beating you up?" Mikolas challenged.

She swung her head to look at him. "You don't think I owe her? Someone needs to advocate for her."

"Where is she now?"

"I was coming away so I made arrangements with her doctor for her to go into an extended-care facility. It's just for assessment and referral, though. The formal arrangements have to be completed. She can't stay where she is and she can't go home if I'm not there. Her doctor is expecting me for a consult this week."

Mikolas reached for his tablet and tapped to place a call. A moment later, the tablet chimed. Someone answered in German. They had a lengthy conversation that she didn't understand. Mikolas ended with, *"Dankeschön."*

"Who was that?" she asked as he set aside the tablet.

"My grandfather's doctor. He's Swiss. He has excellent connections with private clinics all over Europe. He'll ensure Hildy is taken into a good one."

She snorted. "Neither of us has the kind of funds that will underwrite a private clinic arranged by a posh specialist from Switzerland. I can barely afford the extra fees for the one I'm hoping will take her."

"I'll do this for you, to put your mind at ease."

Her mind blanked for a full ten seconds.

"Mikolas," she finally sputtered. "I *want* to do it. I definitely don't want to be in your debt over it!" She ignored the fact that he had already decided she owed him.

Men expect things when they do you a favor, she heard Hildy saying.

A lurching sensation yanked at her heart, like a curtain being pulled aside on its rungs, exposing her at her deepest level. "What kind of sex do you think you're going to get out of me that would possibly compensate you for something like that? Because I can assure you, I'm not that good! You'll be disappointed."

So disappointed.

Had she just said "you'll"? Like she was a sure thing?

She tightened her arms across herself, refusing to look at him as this confrontation took the direction she had hoped it wouldn't: right into the red-light district of Sexville.

* * *

"If that sounds like I just agreed to have sex with you, that's not what I meant," Viveka bit out, voice less strident, but still filled with ire.

Mikolas couldn't think of another woman he'd encountered with such an easily tortured conscience or with such a valiant determination to protect people she cared about while completely disregarding the cost to herself.

She barely seemed real. He was in danger of being *moved* by her depth of loyalty toward her aunt. A jaded part of him had to question whether she was doing exactly what she claimed she wasn't: trying to manipulate him into underwriting the old woman's care, but unlike most women in his sphere, she wasn't offering sex as compensation for making her problems go away.

While he was finding the idea of her coming to his bed motivated by anything other than the same passion that gripped him more intolerable by the second.

"Let us be clear," he said with abrupt decision. "The debt you owe me is the loss of a wife."

She didn't move, but her blue eyes lifted to fix on him, watchful and limitless as the sky.

"My intention was to marry, honeymoon this week, then throw a reception for my new bride, introducing her to a social circle that has been less than welcoming to someone with my pedigree when I only ever had a mistress du jour on my arm."

Being an outsider didn't bother him. He had conditioned himself not to need approval or acceptance from anyone. He preferred his own company and had his grandfather to talk to if he grew bored with himself.

But ostracism didn't sit well with a nature that demanded to overcome any circumstance. The more he worked at growing the corporation, the more he recognized the importance of networking with the mainstream. Socializing was an annoying way to spend his valuable time, but necessary.

"Curiosity, if nothing else, would have brought people to the party," he continued. "The permanence of my marriage would have set the stage for developing other relationships. You understand? Wives don't form friendships with women they never see again. Husbands don't encourage their wives to invite other men's temporary liaisons for drinks or dinner."

"Because they're afraid their wives will hear about their own liaisons?" she hazarded with an ingenuous blink.

Really, no sense of self-preservation.

"It's a question of investment. No one wants to put time or money into something that lacks a stable future. I was gaining more than Grigor's company by marrying. It was a necessary shift in my image."

Viveka shook her head. "Trina would have been hopeless at what you're talking about. She's sweet and funny, loves to cook and pick flowers for arrangements. You couldn't ask for a kinder ear if you need to vent, but playing the society wife? Making small talk about haute couture and trips to the Maldives? You, with your sledgehammer personality, would have crushed her before she was dressed, let alone an evening trying to find her place in the pecking order of upper-crust hens."

"Sledgehammer," he repeated, then accused facetiously, "Flirt."

She blushed. It was pretty and self-conscious and fueled by this ivory-tusked, sexual awareness they were both pretending to ignore. Her gaze flashed to his, naked and filled with last night's trance-like kiss. Her nipples pricked to life beneath the pink of her shirt. So did the flesh between his legs. The moment became so sexually infused, he almost lost the plot.

That's how he wanted it to be between them: pure reaction. Not installment payments.

He reined himself in with excruciating effort, throat tight and body readied with tension as he continued.

"Circulating with the woman who broke up my wedding is not ideal, but will look better than escorting a rebound after being thrown over. Since you'll be with me until I've neutralized Grigor, we will be able to build that same message of constancy."

"What do you mean about neutralizing Grigor?"

"I spoke to him this morning. He's not pleased with my takeover or the fact you're staying with me. You need some serious protections in place. Did you have your mother's death investigated?"

That seemed to throw her. Her face spasmed with emotion.

"I was only nine when it happened so it was years before I really put it all together and thought he could have done it. I was fourteen when I asked the police to look into it, but they didn't take me seriously. The police on the island are in his pocket. The whole island is and I don't really blame them. I've learned myself that you play by his rules or lose everything. Probably the only reason he didn't kill me for making a statement was because it would have been awfully suspicious if something happened to me right after my complaint. But stirring up questions was one of the reasons he kicked me out. Why?"

"I will hire a private investigator to see what we can find. If something can be proved and he's put in prison, you'll be out of his reach."

"That could take years!"

"And will make him that much more incensed with

you in the short term," he said drily. "But as you say, if he's under suspicion, it wouldn't look good if anything happened to you. I think it will afford you protection in the long term."

"You're going to start an investigation, take care of my aunt and protect me from Grigor and all I have to do is pretend to be your girlfriend." Her voice rang with disbelief. "For how *long*?"

"At least until the merger completes and the investigation shows some results. Play your part well and you might even earn my forgiveness for disrupting my life so thoroughly."

Her laugh was ragged and humorless. "And sex?"

She tossed her head, affecting insouciance, but the small frown between her brows told him she was anxious. That aggravated him. He could think of nothing else but discovering exactly how incendiary they would be together. If she wasn't equally obsessed, he was at a disadvantage.

Not something he ever endured.

With a casual flick of his hand, he proclaimed, "Like today's fine weather, we'll enjoy it because it's there."

Did a little shadow of disappointment pass behind her eyes? What did she expect? Lies about falling in love? They really were at an impasse if she expected that ruse.

Her mouth pursed to disguise what might have been a brief tremble. She pushed to stand. "Yes, well, the almanac is predicting heavy frost. Dress warm." She reached for her bag. "I'm going to my room."

"Leave your passport with me."

She turned back to regard him with what he was starting to think of as her princess look, very haughty and down the nose. "Why?"

"To arrange travel visas."

"To where?"

"Wherever I need you to be."

"Give me a 'for instance.'"

"Asia, eventually, but you wanted to go to Athens, didn't you? There's a party tonight. Do as you're told and I'll let you off the boat to come with me."

Her spine went very straight at that patronizing remark. Her unfettered breasts were not particularly heavy, but magnificent in their shape and firmness and chill-sharpened points. He was going to go out of his mind if he didn't touch her again soon.

As if she read his thoughts, her brows tugged together with conflict. She was no doubt thinking that the return of her purse and arrival in Athens equaled an excellent opportunity to set him in the rearview mirror.

He tensed, waiting out the minutes of her indecision. Oddly, it was not unlike the anticipation of pain. His breath stilled in his lungs, throat tight, as he willed her to do as he said.

Do not make me ask again.

Helplessness flashed in her expression before she ducked her head and drew her passport out of her bag, hand trembling as she held it out to him.

A debilitating rush of relief made his own arm feel like it didn't even belong to him. He reached to take it.

She held on while she held his gaze, incredibly beautiful with that hard-won determination lighting her proud expression. "You *will* make sure Aunt Hildy is properly cared for?"

"You and Pappoús will get along well. He holds me to my promises, too."

She released the passport into his possession, averting her gaze as though she didn't want to acknowledge the significance. Clearing her throat, she took out her phone. “I want to check in with Trina. May I have the WiFi code?”

“The security key is a mix of English and Greek characters.” He held out his other hand. “I’ll do it for you.”

She released a noise of impatient defeat, slapped her phone into his palm and walked away.

CHAPTER SEVEN

MIKOLAS HAD SET himself up in her contacts with a selfie taken on her phone, of him sitting there like a sultan on his yacht, taking ownership of her entire life.

She couldn't stop looking at it. Those smoky eyes of his were practically making love to her, the curve of his wide mouth quirked at the corners in not quite a smile. It was more like, *I know you're naked in the shower right now.* He was so brutally handsome with his chiseled cheekbones and devil-doesn't-give-a-damn nonchalance he made her chest hurt.

Yet he had also forwarded a request from the Swiss doctor for her aunt's details along with a recommendation for one of those beyond-top-notch dementia villages that were completely unattainable for mere mortals. A quick scan of its website told her it was very patient-centric and prided itself on compassion and being ahead of the curve with quality treatment. All that was needed was the name of her aunt's physician to begin Hildy's transfer into the facility's care.

Along with Trina's well-being, a good plan for Aunt Hildy was the one thing Viveka would sell her soul for. It was a sad commentary on her life that it was the only thing pulling her back to London. She had no community there, rarely had time for dating or going out with friends.

Her neighbor was nice, but mostly her life had revolved around school, then work and caring for Aunt Hildy. There was no one worrying about her now, when she had been stolen like a concubine by this throwback Spartan warrior.

She sighed, not even able to argue that her job was a career she needed to get back to. One quick email and her position had been snapped up by one of the part-timers who need the hours. She'd be on the bottom rung when she went back. If she went back. She'd accepted that job for its convenience to home, and in the back of her mind, she'd already been planning to make a change once she had Hildy settled.

But Aunt Hildy had faced nothing but challenges all her life and, in her way, she'd been Viveka's lifeline. The old woman shouldn't have to suffer and wouldn't. Not if Viveka could help it.

And now that Mikolas had spelled out that sex wasn't mandatory…

Oh, she didn't want to think about sex with that man! He already made her feel so unlike herself she could hardly stand it. But she couldn't help wondering what it would be like to lie with him. Something about him got to her, making her blood run like cavalry into sensual battle. Sadly, Viveka had reservations that made the idea of being intimate with him seem not just ill-advised but completely impossible.

So she tried not to think of it and video-called Trina. Her sister was both deliriously joyful and terribly worried when she picked up.

"Where *are* you? Papa is furious." Her eyes were wide. "I'm scared for you, Vivi."

"I'm okay," she prevaricated. "What about you? You've obviously talked to him. Is he likely to come after you?"

"He doesn't believe this was my decision. He blames

you for all of it and it sounds—I'm not sure what's going on at his office, but things are off the rails and he thinks it's your fault. I'm so sorry, Vivi."

"That doesn't surprise me," Viveka snorted, hiding how scared the news made her. "Are you and Stephanos happy? Was all of this worth it?"

"So happy! I knew he was my soul mate, but oh, Vivi!" Her sister blushed, growing even more radiant, saying in a self-conscious near-whisper, "Being married is even better than I imagined it would be."

Lovemaking. That's what her little sister was really talking about.

Envy, acute and painful, seared through Viveka. She had always felt left out when women traded stories about men and intimacy. Dating for her had mostly been disastrous. Now even her younger sister was ahead of her on that curve. It made Viveka even more insecure in her sexuality than she already was.

They talked a few more minutes and Viveka was wistful when she ended the call. She was glad Trina was living happily-ever-after. At one time, she'd believed in that fairy tale for herself, but had become more pragmatic over the years, first by watching the nightmare that her mother's romance turned into, then challenged by Aunt Hildy for wanting a man to "complete" her.

She hadn't thought of it that way, exactly. Finding a soul mate was a stretch, true, but why shouldn't she want a companion in life? What was the alternative? Live alone and lonely, like Aunt Hildy? Engage in casual hookups like Mikolas had said he preferred?

She was not built for fair-weather frolics.

Her introspection was interrupted by a call from Hildy's doctor. He was impressed that she was able to get her aunt into that particular clinic and wanted to make arrangements to move her the next morning. He assured Viveka she was doing the right thing.

The die was cast. Not long after, the ship docked and Viveka and Mikolas were whisked into a helicopter. It deposited them on top of *his* building, which was an office tower, but he had a penthouse that took up most of an upper floor.

"I have meetings this afternoon," he told her. "A stylist will be here shortly to help you get ready."

Viveka was typically ready to go out within thirty minutes. That included shampooing and drying her hair. She had never in her life started four hours before an appointment, not even when she had fake-married the man who calmly left her passport on a side table like bait and walked out.

Not that this world was so different from living with Grigor, Viveka thought, lifting her baleful gaze from the temptation of her passport to gaze around Mikolas's private domain. Grigor had been a bully, but he'd lived very well. His island mansion had had all the same accoutrements she found in Mikolas's penthouse: a guest room with a full bath, a well-stocked wine fridge and pantry, a pool on a deck overlooking a stunning view.

None of it put her at ease. She was still nervous. Expectation hung over her. Or rather, the question of what Mikolas expected.

And whether she could deliver.

Not sex, she reminded herself, trying to keep her mind off that. She turned to tormenting herself with anxiety over how well she would perform in the social arena. She wasn't shy, but she wasn't particularly outgoing. She wasn't particularly pretty, either, and she had a feeling every other woman at this party would be gorgeous if

Mikolas thought she needed four hours of beautification to bring her up to par.

The stylist's preparation wasn't all shoring up of her looks, however. It was pampering with massage and a mani-pedi, encouragement to doze by the pool while last-minute adjustments were made to her dress, and a final polish on her hair and makeup that gave her more confidence than she expected.

As she eyed herself in the gold cocktail dress, she was floored at how chic she looked. The cowled halter bodice hung low across her modest chest and the snug fabric hugged her hips in a way that flattered her figure without being obvious. The color brought out the lighter strands in her hair and made her skin look like fresh cream.

The stylist had trimmed her mop, then let its natural wave take over, only parting it to the side and adding two little pins so her face was prettily framed while the rest fell away in a shiny waterfall around her shoulders. She applied false eyelashes, but they were just long enough to make her feel extra feminine, not ridiculous.

"I've never known how to make my bottom lip look as wide as the top," Viveka complained as her lips were painted. The bruise Grigor had left there had faded overnight to unnoticeable.

"Why would you want to?" the woman chided her. "You have a very classic look. Like old Hollywood."

Viveka snorted, but she'd take it.

She had to acknowledge she was delighted with the end result, but became shy when she moved into the lounge to find Mikolas waiting for her.

He took her breath, standing at the window with a drink in his hand. He'd paired his suit with a gray shirt and charcoal tie, ever the dark horse. It was all cut to perfection against his frame. His profile was silhouetted against the glow of the Acropolis in the distance. *Zeus*, she thought, and her knees weakened.

He turned his head and even though he was already quite motionless, she sensed time stopping. Maybe they both held their breath. She certainly did, anxious for kind judgment.

Behind her, the stylist left, leaving more tension as the quiet of the apartment settled with the departure of the lift.

Viveka's eyes dampened. She swallowed to ease the dryness in the back of her throat. "I have no idea how to act in this situation," she confessed.

"A date?" he drawled, drawing in a breath as though coming back to life.

"Is that all it is?" Why did it feel so monumental? "I keep thinking that I'm supposed to act like we're involved, but I don't know much about you."

"Don't you?" His cheek ticked and she had the impression he didn't like how much she did know.

"I guess I know you're the kind of man who saves a stranger's life."

That seemed to surprise him.

She searched his enigmatic gaze, asking softly, "Why did you?" Her voice held all of the turbulent emotions he had provoked with the act.

"It was nothing," he dismissed, looking away to set down his glass.

"Please don't say that." But was it realistic to think her life had meant something to him after one glimpse? No. Her heart squeezed. "It wasn't nothing to me."

"I don't know," he admitted tightly. His eyes moved over her like he was looking for clues. "But I wasn't thinking ahead to this. Saving a person's life shouldn't be contingent on repayment. I just reacted."

Unlike his grandfather, who had wanted to know he

was actually getting his grandson before stepping in. *Oh, Mikolas.*

For a moment, the walls between them were gone and the bright, magnetic thing between them tugged. She wanted to move forward and offer comfort. Be whatever he needed her to be.

For one second, he seemed to hover on a tipping point. Then a layer of aloofness fell over him like a cloak.

"I don't think anyone will have trouble believing we're involved when you look at me like that." He smiled, but it was a tad cruel. "If I wasn't finally catching up to someone I've been chasing for a while, I would accept your invitation. But I have other priorities."

She flinched, stunned by the snub.

Fortunately he didn't see it, having turned away to press the call button to bring back the elevator.

She moved on stiff legs to join him, fighting tears of wounded self-worth. Her throat ached. Compassion wasn't a character flaw, she reminded herself. Just because Grigor and Hildy and this *jackass* weren't capable of appreciating what she offered didn't mean she was worthless.

She couldn't help her reaction to him. Maybe if she wasn't such an incurable *virgin*, she'd be able to handle him, she thought furiously, but that's what she was and she hated him for taunting her with it.

She was wallowing so deep in silent offense, she moved automatically, leaving the elevator as the doors opened, barely taking in her surroundings until she heard her worst nightmare say, *"There she is."*

CHAPTER EIGHT

MIKOLAS WAS KICKING himself as the elevator came to a halt.

Viveka had been so beautiful when she had walked into the lounge, his heart had lurched. An unfamiliar lightheartedness had overcome him. It hadn't been the money spent on her appearance. It was the authentic beauty that shone through all the labels and products, the kind that waterfalls and sunsets possessed. You couldn't buy that kind of awe-inspiring magnificence. You couldn't ignore it, either, when it was right in front of you. And when you let yourself appreciate it, it felt almost healing…

He never engaged in rose smelling and sunset gazing. He lived in an armored tank of wealth, emotional distance and superficial relationships. His dates were formalities, a type of foreplay. It wasn't sexism. He invested even less in his dealings with men.

His circle never included people as unguarded as Viveka, with her defensive shyness and yearning for acceptance. Somehow that guilelessness of hers got through his barriers as aggression never would. She'd asked him why he'd saved her life and before he knew it, he was reliving the memory of pleading with everything in him for his grandfather—a stranger at the time—to save *him*.

Erebus hadn't.

Not right away. Not without proof.

Words such as *despair* and *anguish* were not strong enough to describe what came over him when he thought back to it.

She had had an idea what it was, though, without his having to say a word. He had seen more in her eyes than an offer of sex. Empathy, maybe. Whatever it was, it had been something so real, it had scared the hell out of him. He couldn't lie with a woman when his inner psyche was torn open that far. Who knew what else would spill out?

He needed escape and she needed to stay the hell back.

He was so focused on achieving that, he walked out of the elevator not nearly as aware of his surroundings as he should be.

As they came alongside the security desk, he heard, "There she is," and turned to see Grigor lunging at Viveka, nearly pulling her off her feet, filthy vitriol spewing over her scream of alarm.

"—think you can investigate me? I'll show you what murder looks like—"

Reflex took over and Mikolas had broken Grigor's nose before he knew what he was doing.

Grigor fell to the floor, blood leaking between his clutching fingers. Mikolas bent to grab him by the collar, but his security team rushed in from all directions, pressing Mikolas's Neanderthal brain back into its cave.

"Call the police," he bit out, straightening and putting his arm around Viveka. "Make sure you mention his threats against her life."

He escorted Viveka outside to his waiting limo, afraid, genuinely afraid, of what he would do to the man if he stayed.

As her adrenaline rush faded in the safety of the limo, Viveka went from what felt like a screaming pitch of tension to being a spent match, brittle and thin, charred and cold.

It wasn't just Grigor surprising her like that. It was how crazed he'd seemed. If Mikolas hadn't stepped in… But he had and seeing Grigor on the receiving end of the sickening thud of a fist connecting to flesh wasn't as satisfying as she had always imagined it would be.

She *hated* violence.

She figured Mikolas must feel the same, given his past. Those last minutes as they'd come downstairs kept replaying in her mind. She'd been filled with resentment as they'd left the elevator, hotly thinking that if saving a person's life didn't require repayment, why was he forcing her to go to this stupid party? He said she was under his protection, but it was more like she was under his thumb.

But the minute she was threatened, the very second it had happened, he had leaped in to save her. Again.

It was as ground-shaking as the first time.

Especially when the aftermath had him feeling the bones in his repaired hand like he was checking for fractures. His thick silence made her feel sick.

"Mikolas, I'm sorry," Viveka said in a voice that flaked like dry paint.

She was aware of his head swinging around but couldn't look at him.

"You know I only had Trina's interest at heart when I came to Greece, but it was inconsiderate to you. I didn't appreciate the situation I was putting you in with Grigor—"

"That's enough, Viveka."

She jolted, stung by the graveled tone. It made the blood congeal in her veins and she hunched deeper into her seat, turning her gaze to the window.

"That was my fault." Self-recrimination gave his voice

a bitter edge. "We signed papers for the merger today. I made sure he knew why I was squeezing him out. He tried to cheat me."

It was her turn to swing a surprised look at him. He looked like he was barely holding himself in check.

"I wouldn't have discovered it until after I was married to Trina, but your interference gave me a chance to review everything. I wound up getting a lot of concessions beyond our original deal. Things were quite ugly by the end. He was already blaming you so I told him I'd started an investigation. I should have expected something like this. I owe *you* the apology."

She didn't know what to say.

"You helped me by stopping the wedding. Thank you. I hope to hell the investigation puts him in jail," he added tightly.

He was staring at her intently, nostrils flared.

Her mouth trembled. She felt awkward and shy and tried to cover it with a lame attempt at levity. "Between Grigor and Hildy, I've spent most of my life being told I was an albatross of one kind or another. It's refreshing to hear I've had a positive effect for once. I thought for sure you were going to yell at me…" Her voice broke.

She sniffed and tried to catch a tear with a trembling hand before it ruined her makeup.

He swore and before she realized what he was doing, he had her in his lap.

"Did he hurt you? Let me see your arm where he grabbed you," he demanded, his touch incredibly gentle as he lightly explored.

"Don't be sweet to me right now, Mikolas. I'll fall apart."

"You prefer the goon from the lobby?" he growled, making a semihysterical laugh bubble up.

"You're not a goon," she protested, but obeyed the hard arms that closed around her and cuddled into him, numb fingers stealing under the edge of his jacket to warm against his steady heartbeat.

He ran soothing hands over her and let out a breath, tension easing from both of them in small increments.

She was still feeling shaky when they reached the Makricosta Olympus.

"I hate these things," he muttered as he escorted her to the brightly decorated ballroom. "We should have stayed in."

Too late to leave. People were noting their entrance.

"Do you mind if I…?" she asked as she spotted the ladies' room off to the right. She could only imagine how she looked.

A muscle pulsed in his jaw, like he didn't want her out of his sight, but after one dismayed heartbeat he said, "I'll be at the bar."

Reeling under an onslaught of gratitude and confusion and yearning, she hurried to the powder room and moved directly to the mirror to check her makeup. She felt like a disaster, but had only a couple of smudges to dab away.

"Synchórisi," the woman next to her said, gaze down as she fiddled with the straps on her shimmery black dress. Releasing a distinctly British curse she said, "My Greek is nonexistent. Is there any chance you speak English?"

Viveka straightened from the mirror, taking a breath to gather her composure. "I do."

"Oh, you're upset." The woman was a delicate blonde and her smile turned concerned. "I'm sorry. I shouldn't have bothered you."

"No, I'm fine," she dismissed with a wobbly smile. The woman was doing her a favor, not letting her dwell on all the mixed emotions coursing through her. "Not the bad kind of crying."

"Oh, did he do something nice?" she asked with a pleased grin. "Because husbands really ought to, now and again."

"He's not my husband, but…" Viveka thought of Mikolas saving her and thanking her for the wedding debacle. Her heart wobbled again and she had to swallow back a fresh rush of emotion. "He did."

"Good. I'm Clair, by the way." She offered her free hand to shake while her other hand stayed against her chest, the straps of her halter-style bodice dangling over her slender fingers.

"Viveka. Call me Vivi." Eyeing the straps, she guessed, "Wardrobe malfunction?"

"The worst! Is there any chance you have a pin?"

"I don't. Can you tie them?" She circled her finger in the air. "Turn around. Let's see what happened to the catch."

They quickly determined the catch was long gone and they were too short to tie.

"I bet a tiepin would hold it. Give me a minute. I'll ask Mikolas for his," Viveka offered.

"Good idea, but ask my husband," Clair said. "Then I won't have to worry about returning it."

Viveka chuckled. "Let me guess. Your husband is the man in the suit?" She thumbed toward the ballroom filled with a hundred men wearing ties and jackets.

Clair grinned. "Mine's easy to spot. He's the one with a scar here." She touched her cheek, drawing a vertical line. "Also, he's holding my purse. I needed two hands to keep myself together long enough to get in here or I would have texted him to come help me."

"Got it. I'll be right back."

* * *

Mikolas stood with the back of his hand pressed to a scotch on the rocks. So much for behaving mainstream and law-abiding, he thought dourly.

He was watching for Viveka, still worried about her. When she had apologized, he'd been floored, already kicking himself for bringing her downstairs at all. He could be at home making love to her, none of this having happened. Instead, he'd let her be terrorized.

There she was. He tried to catch her eye, but she scanned the room, then made for a small group in the far corner from the band.

Mikolas swore under his breath as she approached his target: Aleksy Dmitriev. The Russian magnate had logistics interests that crossed paths with his own from the Aegean through to the Black Sea. Dmitriev had never once returned Mikolas's calls and it grated. He hated being the petitioner and resented the other man for relegating him to that role.

Mikolas knew why Dmitriev was avoiding him. He was scrupulous about his reputation. He wouldn't risk sullying it by attaching himself to the Petrides name.

While Mikolas knew working with Dmitriev would be another seal of legitimacy for his own organization. That's why he wanted to partner with him.

Dmitriev stared at Viveka like she was from Mars, then handed her his drink. He removed his tiepin, handed it to her, then took back his glass. When she asked him something else, he nodded at a window ledge where a pocketbook sat. Viveka scooped it up and headed back to the ladies' room.

What the *hell*?

Viveka was thankful for the small drama that Clair had provided, but flashed right back to seesaw emotions when she returned to Mikolas's side. He stood out without trying. He wore that look of disinterest that alpha wolves wore with their packs, confident in his superiority so with nothing to prove.

A handful of men in sharp suits had clustered around him. They all wore bored-looking women on their arms.

Mikolas interrupted the conversation when she arrived. He took her hand and made a point of introducing her.

She smiled, but the man who'd been speaking was quick to dismiss her and continue what he was saying. He struck her as the toady type who sucked up to powerful men in hopes of catching scraps. The way the women were held like dogs on a leash was very telling, too.

Viveka let her gaze stray to the other groups, seeing the dynamic was very different in Clair's circle, where she was nodding at whoever was speaking, smiling and fully engaged in the conversation. Her husband was looking their way and she pressed a brief smile onto her mouth.

Nothing.

Mikolas had been right about invisible barriers.

"This must be your new bride if the merger has gone through," one of the other men broke in to say, frowning with confusion as he jumped his gaze between her and Mikolas.

I have a name, Viveka wanted to remind the man, but apparently on this side of the room, she was a "this."

"No," Mikolas replied, offering no further explanation.

Viveka wanted to roll her eyes. It was basic playground etiquette to act friendly if you wanted to be included in the games. That was what he wanted, wasn't it? Was this what he had meant when he had said it was her task to change how he was viewed?

"I stopped the wedding," she blurted. "He was supposed to marry my sister, but…" She cleared her throat as she looked up at Mikolas, laughing inwardly at the ridiculous claim she was about to make. "I fell head over heels. You weren't far behind me, were you?"

Mikolas wore much the same incredulous expression he had when he'd lifted her veil.

"Your sister can't be happy about that," one of the women said, perking up for the first time.

"She's fine with it," Viveka assured with a wave. "She'd be the first to say you should follow your heart, wouldn't she?" she prodded Mikolas, highly entertained with her embellishment on the truth. *Laugh with me*, she entreated.

"Let's dance." His grip on her hand moved to her elbow and he turned her toward the floor. As he took her in his arms seconds later, he said, "I cannot believe you just said that."

"Oh, come on. You said we should appear long-term. Now they think we're in love and by the way, your friends are a pile of sexist jerks."

"I don't have friends," he growled. "Those are people whose names I know."

His touch on her seemed to crackle and spark, making her feel sensitized all over. At the same time, she thought she heard something in his tone that was a warning.

Dancing with him was easy. They moved really well together right out of the gate. She let herself become immersed in the moment, where the music transmitted through them, making them move in unison. He held her in his strong arms and the closeness was deliciously stimulating. Her heart fluttered and she feared she really would tumble into deep feelings for him.

"They should call it heels over head," she said, trying to break the spell. "We're head over heels right now. It means you're upright."

He halted their dance, started to say something, but off to her right, Clair said, "Vivi. Let me introduce you properly. My husband, Aleksy Dmitriev."

Mikolas pulled himself back from a suffocating place where his emotions had knotted up. She'd been joking with all that talk of love, he knew she had, but even having a falsehood put out there to those vultures had made him uncomfortable.

He had been pleased to feel nothing for Trina. He would have introduced her as his wife and the presumption of affection might have been made, but it wouldn't have been true. It certainly wouldn't have been something that could be used to prey on his psyche, not deep down where his soul kept well out of the light.

Viveka was different. Her blasé claim of love between them was an overstatement and he ought to be able to dismiss it. But as much as he wanted to feel nothing toward her, he couldn't. Everything he'd done since meeting her proved to himself that he felt *something*.

He tried to ignore how disarmed that made him feel, concentrating instead on finding himself face-to-face with the man who'd been evading him for two years.

Dmitriev looked seriously peeved, mouth flat and the scar on his face standing out white.

It's the Viveka effect, Mikolas wanted to drawl.

Dmitriev nodded a stiff acknowledgment to Viveka's warm smile.

"Did you think you were being robbed?" Viveka teased him.

"It crossed my mind." Dmitriev lifted a cool gaze to Mikolas. *When I realized she was with you*, he seemed to say.

Mikolas kept a poker face as Viveka finished the introduction, but deep down he waved a flag of triumph over Dmitriev being forced to come to him.

It was only an introduction, he reminded himself. A hook. There was no reeling in this kind of fish without a fight.

"We have to get back to the children," Clair was saying. "But I wanted to thank you again for your help."

"My pleasure. I hope we'll run into each other in future," Viveka said. Mikolas had to give her credit. She was a natural at this role.

"Perhaps you can add us to your donor list," Mikolas said. *I do my homework*, he told Dmitriev with a flick of his gaze. Clair ran a foundation that benefited orphanages across Europe. Mikolas had been waiting for the right opportunity to use this particular door. He had no scruples about walking through it as Viveka's plus one.

"May I?" Clair brightened. "I would love that!"

Mikolas brought out one of his cards and a pen, scrawling Viveka's details on the back, mentally noting he should have some cards of her own printed.

"I'd give you one of mine, but I'm out," Clair said, showing hands that were empty of all but a diamond and platinum wedding band. "I've been talking up my fundraising dinner in Paris all night—oh! Would you happen to be going there at the end of next month? I could put you on that list, too."

"Please do. I'm sure we can make room," Mikolas said smoothly. *We, our, us.* It was a foreign language to him, but surprisingly easy to pick up.

"I'm being shameless, aren't I?" Clair said to her husband, dipping her chin while lifting eyes filled with playful culpability.

The granite in Dmitriev's face eased to what might pass for affection, but he sounded sincere as he contradicted her. "You're passionate. It's one of your many appealing qualities. Don't apologize for it."

He produced one of his own cards and stole the pen Mikolas still held, wordlessly offering both to his wife.

I see what you're doing, Dmitriev said with a level stare at Mikolas while Clair wrote. Dmitriev was of similar height and build to Mikolas. He was probably the only man in the room whom Mikolas would instinctively respect without testing the man first. He emanated the same air of self-governance that Mikolas enjoyed and had more than demonstrated he couldn't be manipulated into doing anything he didn't want to do.

He provoked all of Mikolas's instincts to dominate, which made getting this man's contact details that much more significant.

But even though he wasn't happy to be giving up his direct number, it was clear by Dmitriev's hard look that it was a choice he made consciously and deliberately—for his wife.

Mikolas might have lost a few notches of regard for the man if his hand hadn't still been throbbing from connecting with Grigor's jaw. Which he'd done for Viveka.

It was an uncomfortable moment of realizing it didn't matter how insulated a man believed himself to be. A woman—one for whom he'd gone heels over head—could completely undermine him.

Which was why Mikolas firmed himself against letting Viveka become anything more than the sexual infatuation she was. The only reason he was bent out of shape was because they hadn't had sex yet, he told himself. Once he'd had her, and anticipation was no longer clouding his brain, he'd be fine.

"That was what we came for," he said, after the couple

had departed. He indicated the card Viveka was about to drop into her pocketbook. "We can leave now, too."

Mikolas made a face at the card the doorman handed him on their way in, explaining he was supposed to call the police in the morning to make a statement. They didn't speak until they were in the penthouse.

"I've wanted Dmitriev's private number for a while. You did well tonight," he told her as he moved to pour two glasses at the bar.

"It didn't feel like I did anything," she murmured, quietly glowing under his praise. She yearned for approval more than most people did, having been treated as an annoyance for most of her early years.

"It's easy for you. You don't mind talking to people," he remarked, setting aside the bottle and picking up the glasses to come across and offer hers. "Do you take yours with water?"

"I haven't had ouzo in years," she murmured, trying to hide her reaction to him by inhaling the licorice aroma off the alcohol. "I shouldn't have had it when I did. I was far too young. *Yiamas.*"

Mikolas threw most of his back in one go, eyes never leaving hers.

"What, um…?" Oh, this man easily emptied her brain. "You, um, don't like talking to people? You said you hated those sorts of parties."

"I do," he dismissed.

"Why?"

"Many reasons." He shrugged, moving to set aside his glass. "My grandfather had a lot to hide when I first came to live with him. I was too young to be confident in my own opinions and didn't trust anyone with details about myself. As an adult, I'm surrounded by people who are so superficial, crying about ridiculous little trials, I can't summon any interest in whatever it is they're saying."

"Should I be complimented that you talk to me?" she teased.

"I keep trying not to." Even that was delivered with self-deprecation tilting his mouth.

Her heart panged. She longed to know everything about him.

His gaze fixed on her collarbone. He reached out to take her hair back from her shoulder. "You've had one sparkle of glitter here all night," he said, fingertip grazing the spot.

It was a tiny touch, an inconsequential remark, but it devastated her. Her insides trembled and she went very still, her entire being focused on the way he ever so lightly tried to coax the fleck off her skin.

Behind him, the lamps cast amber reflections against the black windows. The pool glowed a ghostly blue on the deck beyond. It made radiance seem to emanate from him, but maybe that was her foolish, dampening eyes.

Painful yearning rose in her. It was familiar, yet held a searing twist. For a long time she had wanted a man in her life. She wanted a confidant, someone she could kiss and touch and sleep beside. She wanted intimacy, physical and emotional.

She had never expected this kind of corporeal desire. She hadn't believed it existed, definitely hadn't known it could overwhelm her like this.

How could she feel so attracted and needy toward a man who was so ambivalent toward her? It was excruciating.

But when he took her glass and set it aside, she didn't resist. She kept holding his gaze as his hands came up to frame her face. And waited.

His gaze lowered to her lips.

They felt like they plumped with anticipation.

She looked at his mouth, not thinking about anything except how much she wanted his kiss. His lips were so beautifully shaped, full, but undeniably masculine. The tip of his tongue wet them, then he lowered his head, came closer.

The first brush of his damp lips against hers made her shudder in release of tension while tightening with anticipation. She gasped in surrender as his hands whispered down to warm her upper arms, then grazed over the fabric of her dress.

Then his mouth opened wider on hers and it was like a straight shot of ouzo, burning down her center and warming her through, making her drunk. Long, dragging kisses made her more and more lethargic by degrees, until he drew back and she realized her hand was at the back of his head, the other curled into the fabric of his shirt beneath his jacket.

He released her long enough to shrug out of his jacket, loosened his tie, then pulled her close again.

Her head felt too heavy for her neck, easily falling into the fingers that combed through her hair and splayed against her scalp. He kissed her again, harder this time, revealing the depth of passion in him. The aggression. It was scary in the way thunder and high winds and landslides were both terrifying and awe-inspiring. She clung to him, moaning in submission. Not just to him, but to her own desire.

They shuffled their feet closer, sealing themselves one against the other, trying to press through clothing and skin so their cells would weave into a single being.

The thrust of his aroused flesh pressed into her stomach and a wrench of conflict went through her. This moment was too perfect. It felt too good to be held like this, to ruin it with humiliating confessions about her defect and entreaties for special treatment. She felt too much toward him, not least gratitude and wonder and a regard that was tied to his compliments and his protection and his hand dragging her to the surface of the water before he'd even known her name.

She ached to share something with him, had since almost the first moment she'd seen him. *Be careful*, she told herself. Sex was powerful. She was already very susceptible to him.

But she couldn't make herself stop touching him. Her hands strayed to feel his shape, tracing him through his pants. It was a bold move for her, but she was entranced. Curious and enthralled. There was a part of her that desperately wanted to know she could please a man, *this* man in particular.

His breath hissed in and his whole body hardened. He gathered his muscles as if he was preparing to dip and lift her against his chest.

She drew back.

His arms twitched in protest, but he let her look at where his erection pressed against the front of his suit pants. He was really aroused. She licked her lips, not superconfident in what she wanted to do, but she wanted to do it.

She unbuckled his belt.

His hands searched under the fall of her hair. His touch ran down her spine, releasing the back of her dress.

As the cool air swirled from her waist around to her belly, her stomach fluttered with nerves. She swallowed, aware of her breasts as her bodice loosened and shifted against her bare nipples. She shivered as his fingertips stroked her bare back. Her hands shook as she pulled his shirt free and clumsily opened his buttons, then spread the edges wide so she could admire his chest.

Pressing her face to his taut skin, she rubbed back and forth and back again, absorbing the feel of him with her brow and lips, drawing in his scent, too moved to smile when he said something in a tight voice and slid his palm under her dress to brand her bottom with his hot palm.

Her mouth opened of its own accord, painting a wet path to his nipple. She explored the shape with her tongue, earned another tight curse, then hit the other one with a draw of her mouth. Foreplay and foreshadowing, she thought with a private smile.

"Bedroom," he growled, bringing his hands out of her dress and setting them on her waist, thumbs against her hip bones as he pressed her back a step.

Dazed at how her own arousal was climbing, Viveka smiled, pleased to see the glitter in his eyes and the flush on his cheeks. It increased her tentative confidence. She placed her hands on his chest and let her gaze stray past him to the armchair, silently urging him toward it.

Mikolas let her have her way out of sheer fascination. He refused to call it weakness, even though he was definitely under a spell of some kind. He had known there was a sensual woman inside Viveka screaming to get out. He hadn't expected this, though.

It wasn't manipulation, either. There were no sly smiles or knowing looks as she slid to her knees between his, kissing his neck, stroking down his front so his abdominals contracted under her tickling fingertips. She was focused and enthralled, timid but genuinely excited. It was erotic to be wanted like this. Beyond exciting.

As she finished opening his pants, his brain shorted

out. He was vaguely aware of lifting his hips so she could better expose him. The sob of want that left her was the kind of siren call that had been the downfall of ancient seamen. He nearly exploded on the spot.

He was thick and aching, so hot he wanted to rip his clothes from his body, but he was transfixed. He gripped the armrest in his aching hand and the back of the chair over his shoulder with the other, trying to hold on to his control.

He shouldn't let her do this, he thought distantly. His discipline was in shreds. But therein lay her power. He couldn't make himself stop her. That was the naked truth.

She took him in hand, her touch light, her pale hands pretty against the dark strain of his flesh. He was so hard he thought he'd break, so aroused he couldn't breathe, and so captivated, he could only hold still and watch through slitted eyes as her head dipped.

He groaned aloud as her hair slid against his exposed skin and her wet mouth took him in, narrowing his world to the tip of his sex. It was the most exquisite sensation, nearly undoing him between one breath and the next. She kept up the tender, lascivious act until he was panting, barely able to speak.

"I can't hold back," he managed to grit out.

Slowly her head lifted, pupils huge as pansies in the dim light, mouth swollen and shiny like he'd been kissing her for hours.

"I don't want you to." Her hot breath teased his wet flesh, tightening all his nerve endings, pulling him to a point that ended where her tongue flicked out and stole what little remained of his willpower.

He gave himself up to her. This was for both of them, he told himself. He would have staying power after this.

He'd make it good for her, as good as this. Nothing could be better, but at least this good—

The universe exploded and he shouted his release to the ceiling.

CHAPTER NINE

VIVEKA HUGGED THE front of her gaping dress to her breasts and could barely meet her own glassy eyes in the mirror. She was flushed and aroused and deeply self-conscious. She couldn't believe what she'd just done, but she had no regrets. She had enjoyed giving Mikolas pleasure. It had been extraordinary.

She had needed that for herself. She wasn't a failure in the bedroom after all. Okay, the lounge, she allowed with a smirk.

Her hand trembled as she removed the pins from her hair, pride quickly giving way to sexual frustration and embarrassment. Even a hint of desolation. If she wasn't such a freak, if she wasn't afraid she'd lose herself completely, they could have found release together.

Being selfless was satisfying in other ways, though. He might be thanking her for breaking up the wedding and saving him a few bucks, but she was deeply grateful for the way he had acknowledged her as worth saving, worth protecting.

The bathroom door that she'd swung almost closed pushed open, making her heart catch.

Mikolas took up a lazy pose that made carnal hunger clench mercilessly in her middle. The flesh that was hot with yearning squeezed and ached.

His open shirt hung off his shoulders, framing the light pattern of hair that ran down from his breastbone. His unfastened pants gaped low across his hips, revealing the narrow line of hair from his navel. His eyelids were heavy, disguising his thoughts, but his voice was gritty enough to make her shiver.

"You're taking too long."

The words were a sensual punch, flushing her with eager heat. At the same time, alarm bells—anxious clangs of performance anxiety—went off within her, cooling her ardor.

"For?" She knew what he meant, but she'd taken care of his need. They were done. Weren't they? If she'd ever had sex before, she wouldn't be so unsure.

"Finishing what you started."

"You did finish. You can't—" Was he growing hard again? It looked like his boxers were straining against the open fly of his pants.

She read. She knew basic biology. She knew he'd climaxed, so how was that happening? Was she really so incapable of gratifying a man that even oral sex failed to do the job?

"You can't… Men don't…again. Can they?" She trailed off, blushing and hating that his first real smile came at the expense of her inexperience.

"I'll last longer this time," he promised drily. "But I don't want to wait. Get your butt in that bed, or I'll have you here, bent over the sink."

Oh, she was never going to be that spontaneous. Ever. And for a first time? While he talked about lasting a *long* time?

"No." She hitched the shoulder of her dress and reached behind herself to close it. "You finished. We're done." Her face was on fire, but inside she was growing cold.

He straightened off the doorjamb. "What?"

"I don't want to have sex." Not entirely true. She longed to understand the mystique behind the act, but his talk of sink-bending only told her how far apart they were in experience. The more she thought about it, the more she went into a state of panic. Not him. Not tonight when she was already an emotional mess.

She struggled to close her zip, then crossed her arms, taking a step backward even though he hadn't moved toward her.

He frowned. "You don't want sex?"

Was he deaf?

"No," she assured him. Her back came up against the towel rail, which was horribly uncomfortable. She waved toward the door he was blocking. "You can go."

He didn't move, only folded his own arms and rocked back on his heels. "Explain this to me. And use small words, because I don't understand what happened between the lounge and here."

"Nothing happened." She couldn't stand that he was making her wallow in her inadequacy. "You...I mean, I *thought* I gave you what you wanted. If you thought—"

He didn't even want her. Not really. He would decide *if* and *when*, she recalled.

Good luck with that, champ. Her body made that decision for everyone involved, no matter what her head said.

Do not cry. Oh, she hated her body right now. Her stupid, dumb body that had made her life go so far sideways she didn't even understand how she was standing here having this awful conversation.

"Can you just go?" She glared at him for making this so hard for her, but her eyes stung. She bet they were red and pathetic looking. If he made her tell him, and he laughed— *"Please?"*

He stayed there one more long moment, searching her gaze, before slowly moving back, taking the door with him, closing it as he left. The click sounded horribly final.

Viveka stepped forward and turned the lock, not because she was afraid he'd come in looking for sex, but afraid he'd come in and catch her crying.

With a wrench of her hand, she started the shower.

Mikolas was sitting in the dark, nursing an ouzo, when he heard Viveka's door open.

He'd closed it himself an hour ago, when he'd gone in to check on her and found her on the guest bed, hair wrapped in a towel, one of his monogramed robes swallowing her in black silk. She'd been fast asleep, her very excellent legs bare to midthigh, a crumpled tissue in her lax grip. Several more had been balled up around her.

Rather than easing his mind, rather than answering any of the million questions crowding his thoughts, the sight had caused the turmoil inside him to expand, spinning in fresh and awful directions. Was he such a bad judge of a woman's needs? Why did he feel as though he'd taken advantage of her? She had pressed him into this very chair. She had opened his pants. She had gone down and told him to let go.

He'd been high as a kite when he had tracked her into her bathroom, certain he'd find her naked and waiting for him. Every red blood cell he possessed had been keening with anticipation.

It hadn't gone that way at all.

She'd felt threatened.

He was a strong, dominant man. He knew that and tried to take his aggressive nature down a notch in the bedroom. He knew what it was like to be brutalized by someone bigger and more powerful. He would never do that to the smaller and weaker.

He kept having flashes of slender, delicate Viveka looking anxious as she noticed he was still hard. He thought about her fear of Grigor. A libido-killing dread had been tying his stomach in knots ever since.

He couldn't bear the idea of her being abused that way. He'd punched Grigor tonight, but he wished he had killed him. There was still time, he kept thinking. He wasn't so far removed from his bloodline that he didn't know how to make a man disappear.

He listened to Viveka's bare feet approach, thinking he couldn't blame her for trying to sneak out on him.

She paused as she arrived at the end of the hall, obviously noticing his shadowed figure. She had changed into pajamas and clipped up her hair. She tucked a stray wisp behind her ear.

"I'm hungry. Do you want toast?" She didn't wait for his response, charging past him through to the kitchen.

He unbent and slowly made his way into the kitchen behind her.

She had turned on the light over the stove and kept her back to him as she filled the kettle at the sink. After she set the switch to Boil, she went to the freezer and found a frozen loaf of sliced bread.

Still keeping her back to him, she broke off four slices and set them in the toaster.

"Viveka."

Her slender back flinched at the sound of his voice.

So did he. The things he was thinking were piercing his heart. He'd been bleeding internally since the likeliest explanation had struck him hours ago. When someone reacted that defensively against sexual contact, the explanation seemed really obvious.

"When you said Grigor abused you..." He wasn't a coward, but he didn't want to speak it. Didn't want to hear it. "Did he...?" His voice failed him.

Viveka really wished he hadn't still been up. In her perfect world, she never would have had to face him again, but as the significance of his broken question struck her, she realized she couldn't avoid telling him.

She buried her face in her hands. "No. That's not it. Not at all."

She *really* didn't want to face him.

But she had to.

Shoulders sagging, she turned and wilted against the cupboards behind her. Her hands stayed against her stinging cheeks.

"Please don't laugh." That's what the one other man she'd told had done. She'd felt so raw it was no wonder she hadn't been able to go all the way with him, either.

She dared a peek at Mikolas. He'd closed a couple of buttons, but his shirt hung loose over his pants. His hair was ruffled, as though his fingers had gone through it a few times. His jaw was shadowed with stubble and he looked tired. Troubled.

"I won't laugh." He hadn't slept, even though it was past two in the morning. For some reason that flipped her heart.

"I wasn't a very happy teenager, obviously," she began. "I did what a lot of disheartened young girls do. I looked for a boy to save me. There was a nice one who didn't have much, but he had a kind heart. I can't say I loved him, not even puppy love, but I liked him. We started seeing each other on the sly, behind Grigor's back. After a while it seemed like the time to, you know, have sex."

The toaster made a few pinging, crackling noises and

the kettle was beginning to hiss. She chewed her lip, fully grown and many years past it, but still chagrined.

"I mean, fourteen is criminally young, I realize that. And not having any really passionate feelings for him… It's not a wonder it didn't work."

"Didn't work," he repeated, like he was testing words he didn't know.

She clenched her eyes shut. "He didn't fit. It hurt too much and I made him stop. Please don't laugh," she rushed to add.

"I'm not laughing." His voice was low and grave. "You're telling me you're a virgin? You never tried again?"

"Oh, I did," she said to the ceiling, insides scraped hollow.

She moved around looking for the tea and butter, trying to escape how acutely humiliating this was.

"My life was a mess for quite a while, though. Grigor found out I'd been seeing the boy and that I'd gone to the police about Mum. He kicked me out and I moved to London. *That* was a culture shock. The weather, the city. Aunt Hildy had all these rules. It wasn't until I finished my A levels and was working that I started dating again. There was a guy from work. He was very smooth. I realize now he was a player, but I was quite taken in."

The toast popped and she buttered it, taking her time, spreading right to the edges.

"He laughed when I told him why I was nervous." She scraped the knife in careful licks across the surface of the toast. "He was so determined to be The One. We fooled around a little, but he was always putting this pressure on me to go all the way. I *wanted* to have sex. It's supposed to be great, right?"

Pressure arrived behind her eyes again. She couldn't look at him, but she listened, waiting for his confirmation that yes, all the sex he'd had with his multitude of lovers had been fantastic.

Silence.

"Finally I said we could try, but it really hurt. He said it was supposed to and didn't want to stop. I lost my temper and threw him out. We haven't spoken since."

"Do you still work with him?"

"No. Old job. Long gone." The toast was buttered before her on two plates, but she couldn't bring herself to turn and see his reaction.

She was all cried out, but familiar, hopeless angst cloaked her. She just wanted to be like most people and have sex and like it.

"Are you laughing?" Her voice was thready and filled with the embarrassed anguish she couldn't disguise.

"Not at all." His voice sounded like he was talking from very far away. "I'm thinking that not in a thousand years would I have guessed that. Nothing you do fits with the way other people behave. It didn't make sense that you would give me pleasure and not want anything for yourself. You respond to me. I couldn't imagine why you didn't want sex."

"I *do* want sex," she said, flailing a frustrated hand. "I just don't want it to *hurt*." She finally turned and set his plate of toast on the island, avoiding his gaze.

The kettle boiled, giving her breathing space as she moved to make the tea. When she sat down, she went around the far end of the island and took the farthest stool from where he stood ignoring the toast and tea she'd made for him.

She couldn't make herself take a bite. Her body was hot and cold, her emotions swinging from hope to despair to worry.

"You're afraid I wouldn't stop if we tried." His voice

was solemn as he promised, "I would, you know. At any point."

A tentative hope moved through her, but she shook her head. "I don't want to be a project." Her spoon clinked lightly as she stirred the sugar into her tea. "I can't face another humiliating attempt. And yes, I've been to a doctor. There's nothing wrong. I'm just…unusually…" She sighed hopelessly. "Can we stop talking about this?"

He only pushed his hands into his pockets. "I wasn't trying to talk you into anything. Not tonight. Unless you want to," he said in a wry mutter, combing distracted fingers through his hair. "I wouldn't say no. You're not a project, Viveka. I want you rather badly."

"Do you?" She scoffed in a strained voice, reminding him, "You said *you* would decide if and when. That *I* was the only one who wanted sex. I can't help the way I react to you, you know. I might have tried with you tonight if I'd thought it would go well, but…"

Tears came into her eyes. It was silly. She was seriously dehydrated from her crying jags earlier. There shouldn't be a drop of moisture left in her.

"I wanted you to like it," she said, heart raw. "I wanted to know I could, you know, *satisfy* a man, but no. I didn't even get that right. You were still hard and—"

He muttered something under his breath and said, "Are you really that oblivious? You *did* satisfy me. You leveled me. Blew my mind. Reset the bar. I don't have words for how good that was." He sounded aggrieved as he waved toward the lounge. "My desire for you is so strong I was aroused all over again just thinking about doing the same to you. *That's* why I was hard again."

If he didn't look so uncomfortable admitting that, she might have disbelieved him.

"When we were on the yacht, you said you thought it

was exciting that I respond to you." Her chest ached as she tried to figure him out. "If the attraction is just as strong for you, why don't you want me to know? Why do you keep—I mean, before we went out tonight, you acted as if you could take it or leave it. It's *not* the same for you, Mikolas. That's why I don't think it would work."

"I never like to be at a disadvantage, Viveka. We had been talking about some difficult things. I needed space."

"But if we're equal in feeling *this* way…? Attracted, I mean, why don't you want me to know that?"

"That's not an advantage, is it?"

His words, that attitude of prevailing without mercy, scraped her down to the bones.

"You'll have to tell me sometime what that's like," she said, dabbing at a crumb and pressing it between her tight lips. "Having the advantage, I mean. Not something I've ever had the pleasure of experiencing. Not something I should want to go to bed with, frankly. So *why do I*?"

He did laugh then, but it was ironic, completely lacking any humor.

"For what it's worth, I feel the same." He walked out, leaving his toast and tea untouched.

Mikolas was trying hard to ignore the way Viveka Brice had turned his life into an amusement park. One minute it was a fun house of distorted mirrors, the next a roller coaster that ratcheted his tension only to throw him down a steep valley and around a corner he hadn't seen.

Home, he kept thinking. It was basic animal instinct. Once he was grounded in his own cave, with the safety of the familiar around him, all the ways that she'd shaken up his world would settle. He would be firmly in control again.

Of course he had to keep his balance in the dizzying teacup of her trim figure appearing in a pair of hip-hugging jeans and a completely asexual T-shirt paired with the doe-eyed wariness that had crushed his chest last night.

He couldn't say he was relieved to hear the details of her sexual misadventures. The idea of her lying naked with other men grated, but at least she hadn't been scarred by the horrifying brutality he'd begun to imagine.

On the other hand, when she had finally opened up, the nakedness in her expression had been difficult to witness. She was tough and brave and earnest and too damned sensitive. Her insecurity had reached into him in a way that antagonism couldn't. The bizarre protectiveness she already inspired in him had flared up, prompting him to assuage her fears, reassure her. He had wound up revealing himself in a way that left him mistrustful and feeling like he'd left a flank unguarded.

Not a comfortable feeling at all.

He hadn't been able to sleep. Much of it had been the ache in his body, craving release in hers. He yearned to *show* her how it could be between them. At the same time, his mind wouldn't stop turning over and over with everything that had happened since she had marched into his life. At what point would she quit pulling the rug out from under him?

"Are you taking me back in time? What is that?" She was looking out the window of the helicopter.

He leaned to see. They were approaching the mansion and the ruins built into the cliff below it.

"That is the tower where you will be imprisoned for the rest of your life." *There* was a solution, he thought.

"Don't quit your day job for comedy."

Her quick rejoinder made humor tug at the corner of his mouth. He was learning she used jokes as a defense, similar to how he was quick to pull rank and impose his control over every situation. The fact she was being cheeky now, when he was in her space, told him she was shoring up her walls against him. That niggled, but wasn't it what he wanted? Distance? Barriers?

"The Venetians built it." He gazed at her clean face so close to his, her naked lips. She smelled like tea and roses and woman. He wanted to eat her alive. "See where the stairs have been worn away by the waves?"

Viveka couldn't take in anything as she felt the warmth off the side of his face and caught the smell of his aftershave. She held herself very still, trying not to react to his closeness, but her lips tingled, longing to graze his jaw and find his mouth. Lock with him in a deep kiss.

"We preserved the ruins as best we could. Given the fortune we spent, we were allowed to build above it."

She forced her gaze to the view, instantly enchanted. What little girl hadn't dreamed of being spirited away to an island castle like in a fairy tale?

The modern mansion at the top of the cliff drew her eye unerringly. The view was never-ending in all directions and the ultracontemporary design was unique and fascinating, sprawling in odd angles that were still perfectly balanced. It was neither imposing nor frivolous. It was solid and sophisticated. Dare she say elegant?

She noticed something on the roof. "Are those solar panels?"

"*Naí.* We also have a field of wind turbines. You can't see them from here. We're planning a tidal generator, too. We only have to finalize the location."

"How ecologically responsible of you." She turned her face and they were practically nose to cheekbone.

He sat back and straightened his cuff.

"I like to be self-sufficient." A tick played at the corner of his mouth.

Under no one's power but his own. She was seeing that pattern very clearly. Should she tell him it made him predictable? she wondered with private humor.

A few minutes later, she followed him into an interior she hadn't expected despite all she'd seen so far of the way he lived. The entrance should have struck her as over the top, with its smooth marble columns and split staircase that went up to a landing overlooking, she was sure, the entire universe.

The design remained spare and masculine, however, the colors subtle and golden in the midday light. Ivory marble and black wrought iron along with accents of Hellenic blue made the place feel much warmer than she expected. As they climbed the stairs, thick fog-gray carpet muffled their steps.

The landing looked to the western horizon.

Viveka paused, experiencing a strange sensation that she was looking back toward a life that was just a blur of memory, no longer hers. Oddly, the idea slid into her heart not like a blade that cut her off from her past, but more like something that caught and anchored her here, tugging her from a sea of turbulence to pin her to this stronghold.

She rubbed her arms at the preternatural shiver that chased up her entire body, catching Mikolas's gaze as he waited for her to follow him up another level.

The uppermost floor was fronted by a lounge that was surrounded by walls of glass shaded by an overhang to keep out the heat. They were at the very top of the world here. That's how it felt. Like she'd arrived at Mount Olympus, where the gods resided.

There was a hot tub on the veranda along with lounge chairs and a small dining area. She stayed inside, glancing around the open-plan space of a breakfast nook, a sitting area with a fireplace and an imposing desk with two flat monitors with a printer on a cabinet behind it, obviously Mikolas's home office.

As she continued exploring, she heard Mikolas speaking, saying her name. She followed to an open door where a uniformed young man came out. He saw her, nodded and introduced himself as Titus, then disappeared toward the stairs.

She peered into the room. It was Trina's boudoir. Had to be. There were fresh flowers, unlit candles beside the bucket of iced champagne, crystal glasses, a peignoir set draped across the foot of the white bed, and a box of chocolates on a side table. The exterior walls were made entirely out of glass and faced east, which pleased her. She liked waking to sun.

Don't love it, she cautioned herself, but it was hard not to be charmed.

"Oh, good grief," she gasped as Mikolas opened a door to what she had assumed was a powder room. It was actually a small warehouse of prêt-à-porter.

"Did you buy all of Paris for her?" She plucked at the cuff of a one-sleeved evening gown in silver-embroidered lavender. The back wall was covered in shoes. "I hate to tell you this, but my foot is a full size bigger than Trina's."

"One of your first tasks will be to go through all of this so the seamstress can alter where necessary. The shoes can be exchanged." He shrugged one shoulder negligently.

The closet was huge, but way too small with both of them in it.

She tried to disguise her self-consciousness by picking up a shoe. When she saw the designer name, she gently rubbed the shoe on her shirt to erase her fingerprint from the patent leather and carefully replaced it.

"Change for lunch with my grandfather. But don't take too long."

"Where are you going?" she asked, poking her head out to watch him cross to a pair of double doors on the other side of her room, not back to the main part of the penthouse.

"My room." He opened one of the double doors as he reached it, revealing what she thought at first was a private sitting room, but that white daybed had a towel rolled up on the foot of it.

Drawn by curiosity, she crossed to follow him into the bathroom. Except it was more like a high-end spa. There was an enormous round tub set in a bow of glass that arched outward so the illusion for the bather was a soak in midair.

"Wow." She slowly spun to take in the extravagance, awestruck when she noted the small forest that grew in a rock garden under a skylight. A path of stones led through it to a shower *area* against the back wall. Nozzles were set into the alcove of tiled walls, ready to spray from every level and direction, including raining from the ceiling.

She clapped her hand over her mouth, laughing.

The masculine side of the room was a double sink and mirror designed along the black-and-white simplistic lines Mikolas seemed to prefer, bracketed by a discreet door to a private toilet stall that also gave access to his bedroom. Her side was a reflection of his, with one sink removed to make way for a makeup bench and a vanity of drawers already filled with unopened cosmetics.

"You live like this," she murmured, closing the drawer.

"So do you. Now."

Temporarily, she reminded herself, but it was still like trying to grasp the expanse of the universe. Too much to comprehend.

A white robe that matched the black ones she'd already worn hung on a hook. She flipped the lapel enough to see the monogram, expecting a T and finding an M. She sputtered out another laugh. He was so predictably possessive!

"Can you be ready in twenty minutes?"

"Of course," she said faintly. "Unless I get lost in the forest on the way back to my room."

My room. Freudian slip. She dropped her gaze to the mosaic in the floor, then walked through her water closet to her room.

It was only as she stood debating a pleated skirt versus a sleeveless floral print dress that the significance of that shared bathroom struck her: he could walk in on her naked. Anytime.

CHAPTER TEN

VIVEKA WASN'T SURE what she expected Mikolas's grandfather to look like. A mafia don from an old American movie? Or like many of the other retired Greek men who sat outside village *kafenions*, maybe wearing a flat cap and a checked shirt, face lined by sun and a hard life in the vineyard or at sea?

Erebus Petrides was the consummate old-world gentleman. He wore a suit as he shared a drink with them before they dined. He had a bushy white mustache and excellent posture despite his stocky weight and the cane he used to walk. He and Mikolas didn't look much alike, but they definitely had the same hammered silver eyes and their voices were two keys of a similar strong, commanding timbre.

Erebus spoke English, but preferred Greek, stretching her to recall a vocabulary she hadn't tested in nine years—something he gently reproached her over. It was a pleasant meal that could have been any "Meet the Parents" occasion as they politely got to know each other. She had to keep reminding herself that the charismatic old man was actually a notorious criminal.

"He seems very nice," she said after Erebus had retired for an afternoon rest.

Mikolas was showing her around the rest of the house.

They'd come out to the pool deck where a cabana was set up like a sheikh's tent off to the side and the Ionian Sea gleamed into the horizon.

Mikolas didn't respond and she glanced up to see his mouth give a cynical twitch.

"No?" she prompted, surprised.

"He wouldn't have saved me if I hadn't proven to be his grandson."

Her heart skipped and veered as she absorbed that none of this would have happened. She wouldn't be here and neither would he. They never would have met. *What would have become of that orphaned boy?*

"Do you wish that your mother had told your father about you?"

"She may have. My father was no saint," he said with disparagement. "And there is no point wishing for anything to be different. Accept what is, Viveka. I learned that long ago."

It wasn't anything she didn't see in a pop philosophy meme on her newsfeed every day, but she always resisted that fatalistic view. She took a few steps away from him as though to distance herself from his pessimism.

"If I accepted what I was given, I would still be listening to Grigor call me ugly and useless." She didn't realize her hands became tight fists, or that he had come up behind her, until his warm grip gently forced her to bend her elbow as he lifted her hand.

He looked at her white knuckles poking like sharp teeth. His thumb stroked along that bumpy line.

"You've reminded me of something. Come." He smoothly inserted his thumb to open her fist and kept her hand as he tugged her into the house.

"Where?"

He only pulled her along through the kitchen and down

the service stairs into a cool room where he turned on the lights to reveal a gym.

Perhaps the original plans had drawn it up as a wine cellar, but it was as much a professional gym as any that pushed memberships every January. Bike, tread, elliptical. Every type of weight equipment, a heavy bag hanging in the corner, skipping ropes dangling from a hook and padded mats on the floor. It was chilly and silent and smelled faintly of leather and air freshener.

"You'll meet me here every morning at six," he told her.

"Pah," she hooted. "Not likely."

"Say that again and I'll make it five."

"You're serious?" She made a face, silently telling him what she thought of that. "For heaven's sake, why? I do cardio most days, but I prefer to work out in the evening."

"I'm going to teach you to throw a punch. This—" he lifted the hand he still held and reshaped it into a fist again "—can do better. And this—" he touched under her chin, lifting her face and letting his thumb tag the spot on her lip where Grigor's mark had been "—won't happen again. Not without your opponent discovering very quickly that he has picked a fight with the wrong woman."

She had been trying to pretend she wasn't vitally aware of her hand in his. Now he was touching her face, looking into her eyes, standing too close.

Somehow she had thought that giving him pleasure would release some of this sexual tension between them. Now everything they'd confessed made it so much worse. The pull was so much *deeper*. He knew things about her. Intensely personal things.

She drew away, breaking all contact, trying to keep a grip on herself as she took in what he was saying.

"You keep surprising me. I thought you were a hardened..." She cut him a glance of apology. "Criminal.

You're actually quite nice, aren't you? Wanting to teach me how to defend myself."

"Everyone who surrounds me is a strength, not a liability. That's all this is."

"Liability." The label winded her, making her look away. It was familiar, but she had hoped there was a growing regard between them. But no. He might be attracted to her sexually, last night might have changed her forever, but she was still that thing he was saddled with.

"Right. Whatever you need me to be, wherever." She fought not to let her smarting show, but from her throat to her navel she burned.

"Do you like feeling helpless?" he demanded.

"No," she choked. This feeling of being at *his* mercy was excruciating.

"Then be here at six prepared to work."

What had he been thinking? Mikolas asked himself the next morning. This was hell.

Viveka showed up in a pair of clinging purple pants that ended below her knees. The spandex was shiny enough to accent every dip and curve of her trim thighs. Her pink T-shirt came off after they'd warmed up with cardio, revealing the unique landscape of her abdomen. Now she wore only a snug blue sports bra that flattened her modest breasts and showed off her creamy shoulders and chest and flat midriff.

He was so distracted by lust, he would get his lights blacked out for sure.

He would deserve it. And he couldn't even make a pass to slake it. He'd told two of his guards who had come in to use the gym that they could stay. They were spotting each other, grunting over the weights, while Mikolas put his hands on Viveka to adjust her stance and coached her through stepping into a punch. She smelled like shampoo and woman sweat. Like they'd been petting each other into acute arousal.

"You're holding back because you're afraid you'll hurt yourself," he told her when she struck his palm. He stopped her to correct her wrist position and traced up the soft skin of her forearm. "Humans have evolved the bone structure in here to withstand the impact of a punch."

"My bones aren't as big as yours," she protested. "I *will* hurt myself in a real fight. Especially if I don't have this." She held up her arm to indicate where he'd wrapped her hands to protect them.

"You might even break your hand," he told her frankly. "But that's better than losing your life, isn't it? I want you on the heavy bag twice a day for half an hour. Get used to how it feels to connect so you won't hesitate when it counts. Learn to use your left with as much power as the right."

Her brow wrinkled with concentration as she went back to jabbing into his palms. She was taking this seriously, at least.

That earnestness worried him, though. It would be just like her to take it to heart that *she* should protect *him*. He'd blurted out that remark about liability last night because he hadn't wanted to admit that her inability to protect herself had been eating at him from the moment he'd seen Grigor throw her around on the deck of a stranger's yacht.

He'd hurt her feelings, of course. She'd made enough mentions of Grigor's disparagement and her aunt's indifference that he understood Viveka had been made to feel like a burden and was very sensitive to it. That heart of hers was so easily bruised!

The more time he spent with her, the more he could

see how utterly wrong they were for each other. He could wind up hurting her quite deeply.

I do want sex. I just don't want it to hurt.

Her jab was off-center, glancing off his palm so she stumbled into him.

"Sorry. I'm getting tired," she said breathlessly.

"I wasn't paying attention," he allowed, helping her find her feet.

Damn it, if he didn't keep his guard up, they were both going to get hurt.

Viveka was still shaking from the most intense workout of her life. Her arms felt like rubber and she needed the seamstress's help to dress as they worked through the gowns in her closet. She would have consigned Mikolas firmly to hell for this morning's punishment, but then his grandfather's physiotherapist arrived on Mikolas's instruction to offer her a massage.

"He said you would need one every day for at least a week."

Viveka had collapsed on the table, groaned with bliss and went without prompting back to the gym that afternoon to spend another half hour on the wretched heavy bag.

"You'll get used to it," Mikolas said without pity at dinner, when she could barely lift her fork.

"Surely that's not necessary, is it?" Erebus admonished Mikolas, once his grandson had explained why Viveka was so done in.

"She wants to learn. Don't you?" Mikolas's tone dared her to contradict him, but he wasn't demanding she agree with him in front of his grandfather. He was insisting on honesty.

"I do," she admitted with a weighted sigh, even though

the very last thing she ever wanted was to engage in a fistfight. She couldn't help wondering if Grigor would have been as quick to hit her if she'd ever hit him back, though. She'd never had the nerve, fearing she'd only make things worse.

Mikolas's treatment of her in the gym, as dispassionate as it had been, had also been heartening. He seemed to have every confidence in her ability to defend herself if she only practiced. That was an incredibly compelling thought. Empowering.

It made her grateful to him all over again. And yes, deep down, it made her want to make him proud. To show him what she was capable of. Show herself.

Of course, the other side of that desire to be plucky and capable was a churning knowledge that she was being a coward when it came to sex. She wanted to be proficient in that arena, too.

The music was on low when they came into the lounge of his penthouse later, the fire glowing and a bottle of wine and glasses waiting. Beyond the windows, stars sparkled in the velvet black sky and moonlight glittered on the sea.

Had he planned this? To seduce her?

Did she want to be seduced?

She sighed a little, not sure what she wanted anymore.

"Sore?" he asked, moving to pour the wine.

"Hmm? Oh, it's not that bad. The massage helped. No, I was just thinking that I'm stuck in a holding pattern."

He lifted his brows with inquiry.

"I thought once Hildy was sorted, I would begin taking my life in hand. Trina was supposed to come live with me. I had some plan that we would rent a flat and take online quizzes, choose a career and register for classes…" She had been looking forward to that, but her sister's life had skewed off from hers and she didn't even have the worry of Hildy any longer. "Instead, my future is a blank page."

On Petrides letterhead, she thought wryly.

"I'll figure it out," she assured herself. "Eventually. I won't be here forever, right?"

That knowledge was the clincher. If it had taken her twenty-three years to find a man who stirred her physically, how long would it take to find another?

She looked over to him.

Whatever was in her face made him set down the bottle, corkscrew angled into the unpopped cork.

"I keep telling myself to give you time." His voice was low and heavy, almost defeated. "But bringing you into my bed is all I can think about. Will you let me? I just want to touch you. Kiss you. Give you what you gave me."

Her belly clenched in anticipation. She couldn't imagine being *that* uninhibited, but she couldn't imagine *not* going to bed with him. She wanted him *so much* and she honestly didn't know how to resist any longer.

Surrender happened with one shaken, "Yes."

He kind of jolted, like he hadn't expected that. Then he came across and took her face in his two hands, covering her lips with his hot, hungry mouth. They kissed like lovers. Like people who had been separated by time and distance and deep misunderstanding. She curled her arms around his neck and he broke away long enough to scoop her up against his chest, then kissed her again as he carried her to his bedroom.

She waited for misgivings and none struck. Her fingers went into his hair as she kissed him back.

He came down on the mattress with her and she opened her eyes only long enough to catch an impression of monochromatic shades lit by the bluish half-moon. The carpet was white, the furniture silver-gray, the bedspread black.

Then Mikolas tucked her beneath him and stroked without hurry from her shoulder, down her rib cage, past her waist and along her hip.

"You can—" she started to say, but he brushed another kiss over her lips, lazy and giving and thorough.

"Don't worry," he murmured and kissed her again. "I just want to touch you." Another soft, sweet, lingering kiss. "I'll stop if you tell me to." Kissing and kissing and kissing.

It was delicious and tender and not the least bit threatening with his heavy hand only making slow, restless circles where her hip met her waist.

She wanted more. She wanted sex. It wasn't like the other times she'd wanted sex. Then it had been something between an obligation and a frustrating goal she was determined to achieve.

This was nothing like that. She wanted *him*. She wanted to share her body with Mikolas, feel him inside her, feel close to him.

Make love to me, she begged him with her lips, and ran her hands over him in a silent message of encouragement. When she rolled and tried to open the zip on her dress, he made a ragged noise and found it for her, dragging it down. He lifted away to draw her sleeve off her arm, exposing her bra. One efficient flick of his fingers and the bra was loose.

With reverence, he eased the strap down her arm, dislodging the cup so her breast thrust round and white, nipple turgid with wanton need.

Insecurity didn't have time to strike. He lowered his head and tongued lightly, cupped with a warm hand, then with another groan of appreciation, opened his mouth in a hot branding, letting her get used to the delicate suction before pulling a little harder.

Her toes curled. She wanted to speak, to tell him this was good, that he wouldn't have to stop, but sensation rocked her, coiling in her abdomen, making her loins weep with need. When his hand stroked to rub her bottom, she dragged at her skirt herself, earning a noise of approval as she drew the ruffled fabric out of the way.

He teased her, tracing patterns on her bare thighs, lifting his head to kiss her again and give her his tongue as he made her wait and wait.

"Mikolas," she gasped.

"This?" He brought his hand to the juncture of her thighs and settled his palm there, letting her get used to the sensation. The intimacy. "I want that, too," he breathed against her mouth.

She bit back a cry of pure joy as the weight of his hand covered her, hot and confident. He rocked slowly, increasing the pressure in increments, inciting her to crook her knee so she was open to his touch. Eyes closed, she let herself bask in this wonderful feeling, tension climbing.

When he lifted his hand, she caught her breath in loss, opening her eyes.

He was watching her while his fingertips traced the edge of her knickers, then began to draw them down her thighs.

The friction of lace against her sensitized skin made her shiver. As the coolness of the room struck her damp, eager flesh, she became starkly aware of how her clothing was askew, her breast exposed, her sex pouted and needy, her body trembling with ridiculously high desire.

For a moment anxiety struck. She wanted to rush past this moment, rush through the hard part, have done with this interminable impasse. She lifted her hips so he could finish skimming them away, but when he came down beside her again, he only combed her hair back from her face.

"I just want to feel you. I'll be gentle," he promised, and kissed her lightly.

Yes, she almost screamed.

Embarrassment ought to be killing her, but arousal was pulsing in her like an electrical current. And when he cradled her against him this way, she felt very safe.

They kissed and his hand covered her again. This time she was naked. The sensation was so acute she jolted under his touch.

"Just feel," he cajoled softly. "Tell me what you like. Is that good?"

He did things then that were gorgeous and honeyed. She knew how her body worked, but she had never felt this turned on. She didn't let herself think, just floated in the deep currents of pleasure he swirled through her.

"Like that?" He kept up the magical play, making tension coil through her so she moaned beneath his kiss, encouraging him. Yes, like that. Exactly like that.

He pressed one finger into her.

She gasped.

"Okay?" he breathed against her cheek.

She clasped him with her inner muscles, loving the sensation even though it felt very snug. She was so aroused, so close, she covered his hand with her own and pressed. She rocked her hips as he made love to her with his hand and shattered into a million pieces, cries muffled by his smothering kiss.

CHAPTER ELEVEN

THEY WERE GOING to kill each other.

Mikolas was fully clothed and if she shaped him through his pants right now, he would explode.

But oh, she was amazing. He licked at her panting lips, wanting to smile at the way she clung to his mouth with her own, but weakly. She was still shivering with the aftershocks of her beautiful, stunning orgasm.

He caressed her very, very gently, coaxing her to remain aroused. He wanted to do that to her again. Taste her. Drown in her.

She made a noise and kissed him back with more response, restless hands picking at his shirt, looking for the buttons.

He broke them open with a couple of yanks, then shrugged it off and discarded it, too hot for clothes. On fire for her.

She pulled her other arm free of her dress and held up her arms for him to come back. Soft curves, velvety skin. He loved the feel of her against his bare chest and biceps. Delicate, but spry. So warm, smelling of rain and tea and the drugging scent of sexual fulfillment.

Her smooth hands traced over his torso and back, making him groan at how good it felt on skin that was taut and sensitized. She tasted like nectarines, he thought, opening his mouth on the swell of her breast. He tongued her nipple, more aggressive than he had been the first time.

She arched for more.

He was going too fast, he cautioned himself, but he wanted to consume her. He wanted her dress out of the way, he wanted her hands everywhere on him—

She arched to strip the garment down.

He slid down the bed as he whisked the dress away, pressing his lips to her quivering belly, blowing softly on the fine hairs of her mound, laughing with delight at finally being here. He was so filled with desire his heart was slamming, pulse reverberating through his entire body.

"Mikolas," she breathed.

Her fingers were in his hair like she was petting a wolf, tugging hard enough to force him to lift his head before he'd barely nuzzled her.

"Make love to me."

A lightning rod of lust went through him. He steeled himself to maintain his control when all he wanted was to push her legs apart and rise over her.

"I am." He was going to make her scream with release.

"I mean really." Her hand moved to cradle his jaw, her touch light against the clenched muscle in his cheek. Entreaty filled her eyes. "Please."

She had come into his life to destroy him in the most subversive yet effective way possible.

He could barely move, but he drew back, coming up on an elbow, trying to hold on to what shreds of gentlemanly conduct he possessed.

"Do you ever do what's expected of you?"

"You don't want to?" The appalled humiliation that crept into her tone scared the hell out of him.

"Of course I *want* to." He spoke too harshly. He was barely hanging on to rational thought over here.

She tensed, wary.

He set his hand on her navel, breathed, tried to find something that passed for civilized behavior, but found only the thief he had once been. His hand stole lower, unable to help himself. His thumb detoured along her cleft, finding her slick and ready. Need pearled into one place that made her gasp raggedly when he found it, circling and teasing.

Her thighs relaxed open. She arched to his touch. “Please,” she begged. “I want to know how it feels.”

He was only human, not a superhero. He pulled away, hearing her catch back a noise of injury.

Her breath caught in the next instant as she saw he was rising to open his pants. He stripped in jerky, uncoordinated movements, watching her swallow and bite her bottom lip. He made himself take his time retrieving the condom so she had lots of opportunity to change her mind.

“I’ll stop if you want me to,” he promised as he covered himself, then settled over her. He would. He didn’t know how, but he would.

Please don’t make me stop.

It would really happen this time. Viveka’s nerves sizzled as Mikolas covered her. He was such a big person compared with her. He *loomed.* She skimmed her fingertips over his broad shoulders and was starkly aware of how much space his hips and thighs took up as he settled without hesitation between her own.

She tensed, nervous.

He kissed her in abbreviated catches of her mouth that didn’t quite satisfy before he pulled away, then did it again.

She made a noise of impatience and wiggled beneath him. “I want—”

“Me, too,” he growled against her mouth. Then he lifted

to trace himself against her folds. "You're sure?" he murmured, looking down to where they touched.

So sure. "Yes," she breathed.

He positioned himself and pressed.

It hurt. So much. She fought her instinctive tension, tried to make herself relax, tried not to resist, but the sting became more and more intense. He seemed huge. Tears came into her eyes. She couldn't hold back a throaty noise of anxiety.

He stilled, shuddering. The sting subsided a little.

"Viveka." His voice was ragged. "That's just the tip—" He hung his head against her shoulder, forehead damp with perspiration, big body shaking.

"Don't stop." She caught her foot behind his thigh and tried to press him forward.

"*Glykia mou*, I don't want to hurt you." He lifted his face and wore a tortured expression.

"That's why it's okay if you do." Her mouth quivered, barely able to form words. It still hurt, but she didn't care. "I trust you. Please don't make me do this with someone else."

He bit out a string of confounded curses, looking into the shadows for a moment. Then he met her gaze and carefully pressed again.

She couldn't help flinching. Tensing. The stretch hurt a lot. He paused again, looked at her with as much frustration as she felt.

"Don't try to be gentle. Just do it," she told him.

He wavered, then made a tight noise of angst, covered her mouth, gathered himself and thrust deep.

She arched at the flash of pain, crying out into his mouth.

They both stayed motionless for a few hissing breaths.

Slowly the pain eased to a tolerable sting. She moved her lips against his and he kissed her gently. Sweetly.

"Do you hate me?" His voice was thick, his brow tense as he set it against hers. His expression was strained.

He didn't move, letting her get used to the feel of a man inside her for the first time. And he held her in such protective arms, her eyes grew wet from the complete opposite of pain: happiness.

She returned his healing kiss with one that was a little more inciting.

"No," she answered, smiling shakily, feeling intensely close to him. She let her arms settle across his back and traced the indent of his spine, enjoying the way he reacted with a shiver.

"Want to stop?" he asked.

"No." Her voice was barely there. Tentatively she moved a little, settling herself more comfortably beneath him. "I'm not sure I want you to move at all," she admitted wryly. "Ever."

His breath released on a jagged chuckle. "You are going to be the death of me."

Very carefully, he shifted so he was angled on his elbow, then he made a gentling noise and touched where they were joined.

"You feel so good," he crooned in Greek, gently soothing and stimulating as he murmured compliments. "I thought nothing could be better than the way you took me apart with your mouth, but this feels incredible. You're so perfect, Viveka. So lovely."

The noise that escaped her then was pure pleasure. He was leading her down the road of stirred desire to real excitement. It felt strange to have him lodged inside her while her arousal intensified. Part of her wanted him to move, but she was still wary of the pain and this felt so good. The way he stretched her accentuated the sensations. She grew taut and deeply aroused. Restless and—

"Oh, Mikolas. Please. Oh—" A powerful climax rocked her. Her sheath clenched and shivered around his hard shape with such power she could hardly breath. Stars imploded behind her eyes and she clung to him, crying out with ecstasy. It was beautiful and selfish and heavenly.

As the spasms faded, he began to pull away. The friction felt good, except sharp. She wasn't sure she could take that in a prolonged way, but then he was gone from her body and she was bereft.

"You didn't, did you?" She reached to find his thick shaft, so hard and hot, obviously unsatisfied.

He folded his hand over hers and pumped into her fist. Two, three times, then he pressed a harsh groan into her shoulder, mouth opening so his teeth sat against her skin, not quite biting while he shuddered and pulsed against her palm.

Shocked, but pleased, she continued to pleasure him until he relaxed and released her. He removed the condom with a practiced twist, then rolled away and sat up to discard it. Before he came back, he dragged the covers down and pulled her with him as he slid under them.

"Why did you do that?" she asked as he molded her to his front, stomach to stomach.

"So we won't be cold while we sleep." He adjusted the edge of the sheet away from her face.

"You know what I mean." She pinched his chest, unable to lie still when it felt so good to rub her naked legs against his and nuzzle his collarbone with her lips.

"Learn to speak plainly when we're in bed," he ordered.

"Or what?" She was giddy, so happy with being his lover she felt like the sun was lodged inside her.

"Or I may not give you what you want."

They were both silent a moment, bodies quieting.

"You did," she said softly, adjusting her head against his shoulder. "Thank you."

He didn't say anything, but his hand moved thoughtfully in her hair.

A frozen spike of insecurity pierced her. "Did *you* like it?"

He snorted. "I have just finessed my way through initiating a particularly delicate virgin. My ego is so enormous right now, it's a wonder you fit in the bed."

Viveka woke to an empty bed, couldn't find Mikolas in the penthouse, realized she was late for the gym and decided she was entitled to a bath. She was climbing out of it, a thick white towel loosely clutched around her middle, when he strolled in wearing his gym shorts and nothing else.

"Lazy," he stated, pausing to give her a long, appreciative look.

"Seriously?" Before that bath, she had ached *everywhere.*

His mouth twitched and he came closer, gaze skimming down her front. "Sore?"

She shrugged a shoulder, instantly so shy she nearly couldn't bear it. The things they'd done!

She blushed, aware that her gaze was coveting the hard planes of his body, and instantly wanted to be close to him. Touch, feel, kiss…more.

She wasn't sure how to issue the invitation across the expanse of the spa-like bathroom, but he wasn't the novice she was. He took the last few laconic steps to reach her, spiky lashes lowering as he stared at her mouth. When his head dipped, she lifted her chin to meet his kiss. Her free hand found his stubbled cheek while her other kept her towel in place.

"Mmm..." she murmured, liking the way he didn't rush, but kissed her slowly and thoroughly.

He drew back and tried taking the towel in his two hands.

She hesitated.

"I only want a peek," he cajoled.

"It's daylight," she argued.

"Exactly."

If she had feared that having sex would weaken her will around him, the fear was justified. She wanted to please him. She wanted to offer her whole self and plead with him to cherish her. Her fingers relaxed under the knowledge she was giving up more than control of a towel.

As he opened it, however, and took a long eyeful of her sucked-in stomach and thrust-out breasts, she saw desire grip him with the same lack of mercy it showed her. He swallowed, body hardening, jaw clenched like he was under some kind of deep stress.

"I was only going to kiss you," he said, lifting lust-filled eyes to hers. "But if you—"

"I do," she assured him.

He let the towel drop and she met him midway, moaning with acquiescence as he pressed her onto the daybed. Her inhibitions about the daylight quickly burned up as his stubble slid down her neck to her breast where he sucked and made her writhe. When he slid even lower, scraping her stomach then her thighs as he knelt on the floor, she threw her arm across her eyes and let him do whatever he wanted.

Because it was what she wanted. Oh, that felt exquisite.

"Don't stop," she pleaded when he lifted his head.

"Can you take me?" he growled, scraping his teeth with mock threat along her inner thigh.

She nodded, little echoes of wariness threatening, but

she couldn't take her eyes off his form as he rose and moved to the mirror over his sink, found a condom and covered himself.

When he came back and stood over her, she stayed exactly as he'd left her, splayed weakly with desire, like some harem girl offered for his pleasure.

His hands flexed like he was struggling against some kind of internal pain.

"Mikolas," she pleaded, holding out her arms.

He made a noise of agony and came down over her, heavy and confident, thighs pressing hers wide as he positioned himself. "I don't want to hurt you." His hand tangled in her hair. "But I want you so damned much. Stop me if it hurts."

"It's okay," she told him, not caring about the burn as she arched, inviting him to press all the way in. It hurt, but his first careful thrusts felt good at the same time. The friction of him moving inside her made the connection that much more intense. She rose to the brink very quickly, climaxing with a sudden gasp, clinging to him, shocked at her reaction.

He shuddered, lips pressed into her neck, and hurried to finish with her, groaning fulfillment against her skin.

She was disappointed when he carefully disengaged and sat up, his back to her.

She started to protest that it was okay, holding him in her didn't hurt anymore, but she was distracted by the marks on his back. They were pocked scars that were visible only because the light was so bright. She'd seen his back on the yacht, but in lamplight she hadn't noticed the scars. They weren't raised, but there were more than a dozen.

"What happened to your back?" she asked, puzzled.

Mikolas rose and walked first to his side of the room,

where he scanned around his sinks, then went across to her vanity, where he found the remote for the shower.

"We should set some ground rules," he said.

"Leave the remote on your side?" she guessed as she rose. She walked past her discarded towel for her white robe, wondering why she bothered when she was thinking of joining him in the shower. She wanted to touch him, to close this distance that had arisen so abruptly between them.

"That," he agreed. "And we'll only be together for a short time. Call me your lover if you want to, but do not expect us to fall in love. Keep your expectations low."

She fell back a step as she tied her robe, giving it a firm yank like the action could tie off the wound he'd just inflicted.

But what did she think they were doing? Like fine weather, they were enjoying each other because they were here. That was all.

"I wasn't fishing for a marriage proposal," she defended.

"So long as we're clear." He aimed the remote and started the shower jets.

Scanning his stiff shoulders, she said, "Is this because I asked about your back? I'm sorry if that was too personal, but I've told you some really personal things about me."

"Talk to me about whatever you want. If I don't want to tell you something, I won't." He spoke with aloof confidence, but his expression faltered briefly, mouth quirking with self-deprecation.

Because he had already shared more than made him comfortable?

"There's nothing wrong with being friends, is there?"

He glanced at her, his expression patient, but resolute.

"You don't have friends," she recalled from the other

night, thinking, *I can see why.* "What's wrong with friendship? Don't you want someone you can confide in? Share jokes with?"

His rebuff was making her feel like a houseguest who had to be tolerated. Surely they were past that! He'd just enjoyed *her* hospitality, hadn't he?

"They're cigar burns," he said abruptly, rattling the remote control onto the space behind the sink. "I have more on the bottoms of my feet. My captors used to make me scream so my grandfather could hear it over the phone. *There was more than one call.* Is that the sort of confiding you're looking for, Viveka?" he challenged with antagonism.

"Mikolas." Her breath stung like acid against the back of her throat. She unconsciously clutched the robe across her shattered heart.

"That's why I don't want to share more than our bodies. There's nothing else worth sharing."

Mikolas had been hard on Viveka this morning, he knew that. But he'd been the victim of forces greater than himself once before and already felt too powerless around her. The way she had infiltrated his life, the changes he was making for her, were unprecedented.

Earlier that day, he had risen while she slept and spent the morning sparring, trying to work his libido into exhaustion. She had to be sore. He wasn't an animal.

But one glance at her rising from the bath and all his command over himself had evaporated. At one point, he'd been quite sure he was prepared to beg.

Begging was futile. He *knew* that.

But so was thinking he could treat Viveka like every other woman he'd slept with. Many of them had asked about his back. He'd always lied, claiming chicken pox had caused the scars. For some reason, he didn't want to lie to Viveka.

When he had finally blurted out the ugly truth, he'd seen something in her expression that he outwardly rejected, but inwardly craved: agony on his behalf. Sadness for that dark time that had stolen his innocence and left him with even bigger scars that no one would ever see.

Damn it, he was self-aware enough to know he used denial as a coping strategy, but there was no point in raking over the coals of what had been done to him. Nothing would change it. Viveka wanted a jocular companion to share opinions and anecdotes with. He was never going to be that person. There was too much gravity and anger in him.

So he had schooled her on what to expect, and it left him sullen through the rest of the day.

She wasn't much better. In another woman, he would have called her subdued mood passive-aggressive, but he already knew how sensitive Viveka was under all that bravado. His churlish behavior had tamped down her natural cheerfulness. That made him feel even more disgusted with himself.

Then his grandfather asked her to play backgammon and she brightened, disappearing for a couple of hours, coming back to the penthouse only to change for the gym.

Why did that annoy him? He wanted her to be self-sufficient and not look to him to keep her amused. Later that evening, however, when he found her plumping cushions in the lounge, he had to ask, "What are you doing?"

"Tidying up." She carried a teacup and plate to the dumbwaiter and left it there.

"I pay people to do that."

"I carry my weight," she said neutrally.

He pushed his hands into his pockets, watching her

click on a lamp and turn off the overhead light, then lift a houseplant—honest to God, she checked a plant to see if it needed water rather than look at him.

"You're angry with me for what I said this morning."

"I'm not." She sounded truthful and folded her arms defensively, but she finally turned and gave him her attention. "I just never wanted to be in this position again."

The bruised look in her eye made him feel like a heel.

"What position?" he asked warily.

"Being forced on someone who doesn't really want me around." Her tight smile came up, brave, but fatalistic.

"It's not like that," he ground out. "I told you I want you." Admitting it still made him feel like he was being hung by his feet over a ledge.

"Physically," she clarified.

Before the talons of a deeper truth had finished digging into his chest, she looked down, voice so low he almost didn't hear her.

"So do I. That's what worries me," she continued.

"What do you mean?"

She hugged herself, shrugging. Troubled. "Not something worth sharing," she mumbled.

Share, he wanted to demand, but that would be hypocritical. Regret and apology buzzed around him like biting mosquitoes, annoying him.

It had taken him years to come to this point of being completely sure in himself. A few days with this woman, and he was second-guessing everything he was or had or did.

"Can we just go to bed?" Her doe eyes were so vulnerable, it took a moment for him to comprehend what she was saying. He had thought they were fighting.

"Yes," he growled, opening his arms. "Come here."

She pressed into him, her lips touching his throat. He sighed as the turmoil inside him subsided.

Every night, they made love until Viveka didn't even remember falling asleep, but she always woke alone.

Was it personal? she couldn't help wondering. Did Mikolas not see anything in her to like? Or was he simply that removed from the normal needs of humanity that he genuinely didn't want any closer connections? Did he realize his behavior was hurtful? Did he know and not *care*?

Whenever she had dreamed of being in an intimate relationship with a man, it had been intimacy across the board, not this heart-wrenching openness during sex and a deliberate distance outside of it. Was she saying too much? *Asking* too much?

She became hypersensitive to every word she spoke, trying to refrain from getting too personal. The constant weighing and worrying was exhausting.

It was harder when they traveled. At least with his grandfather at the table, the conversation flowed more naturally. As Mikolas dragged her to various events across Europe, she had to find ways to talk to him without putting herself out there too much.

"I might go to the art gallery while you're in meetings this morning. Unless you want to come? I could wait until this afternoon," was a typical, neutral approach. She loved spending time with him, but couldn't say *that*.

"I can make myself available after lunch."

"It's an exhibition of children's art," she clarified. "Is that something you'd want to see?" Now she felt like she was prying. Her belly clenched as she awaited rejection.

He shrugged, indifferent. "Art galleries aren't something I typically do, but if you want to see it, I'll take you."

Which made her feel like she was imposing on his time,

but he was already tapping it into his schedule. Later he paced around the place, not saying much, while she held back asking what he thought. She wanted to tell him about her early aspirations and point to what she liked and ask if he'd ever messed around with finger paints as a child.

She actually found herself speaking more freely to strangers over cocktails than she did with him. He always listened intently, but she didn't know if that was for show or what. If he had interest in her thoughts or ambitions, she kept thinking, he would ask her himself, but he never did.

Tonight she was revealing her old fascination with art history and Greek mythology. It felt good to open up, so she shared a little more than she normally would.

"I actually won an award," she confided with a wrinkle of her nose. "It was just a little thing for a watercolor I painted at school. I was convinced I'd become a world-famous artist," she joked. "I've always wanted to take a degree in art, but there's never been the right time."

It was small talk. They were nice people, owners of a hotel chain whom she'd met more than once.

Deep down, she was congratulating herself on performing well at these events, remembering the names of children and occasionally going on shopping dates. Tonight she had found herself genuinely interested in Adara Makricosta's plans for her hotels. That's how her own career goals had come up. Adara Makricosta was the CEO of a family-owned chain and had asked Viveka about her own work.

Viveka sidestepped the admission she was merely a mistress whose job it was to create this warming trend Mikolas was enjoying among the world's most rich and powerful.

"Why didn't you tell me that before?" Mikolas asked

when Adara and Gideon had moved on. "About wanting to study art," he prompted when she only looked at him blankly.

Viveka's heart lurched and she almost blurted out, *Because you wouldn't care.* She swallowed.

"It's not practical. I thought about taking evening classes around my day job, but I always had Hildy to look after. And I knew once I was in this position, looking to my own future, I would need to devote myself to a proper career, not dabble in something that will never pay the bills."

She ought to be thinking harder about that, not using up all her brain space trying to second-guess the man in front of her.

"You don't have bills now. Sign up for something," he said breezily.

"Where? To what end?" Her throat tightened. "We're constantly on the move and I don't know how long I'll be with you. No. There's no point." It would hurt to see that phoenix of a dream rise up from the ashes only to fly away.

Or was he implying she would be with him for the long term?

She did the unthinkable and searched his expression for some sign that he had feelings for her. That they had a future.

He receded behind a remote mask, horribly quiet for the rest of the night and even while they traveled back to Greece, adding an extra layer of tension to their trip.

Viveka was still smarting over Mikolas's behavior when she woke in his bed the next morning. They were sleeping late after arriving in the wee hours. She stayed motionless, naked in the spoon of his body, not wanting to move and wake him. She often fell asleep in his arms, but she never woke in them. This was a rare moment of closeness.

It was the counterfeit currency that all women—like mother like daughter—too often took in place of real regard.

Because, no matter how distanced she felt from Mikolas during the day, in bed she felt so integral to him it was a type of agony to be anywhere else. When he made love to her, it felt like love. His kisses and caresses were generous, his compliments extravagant. She warmed and tingled just thinking about how good it felt to join with him, but it wasn't just physical pleasure for her. Lying with him, naked and intimate, was emotionally fulfilling.

She was falling for him.

His breathing changed. He hardened against her backside and she bit her lip, heartened by the lazy stroke of his hand and the noise of contentment he made, like he was pleased to wake with her against him.

Such happiness brimmed in her, she couldn't help but wriggle her butt into his hardness, inviting the only affection he seemed to accept, wanting to hold on to this moment of harmony.

His mouth opened on her shoulder and his hand drifted down her belly into the juncture of her thighs. He made a satisfied noise when he found her wet and ready.

She gasped, stimulated by his lazy touch. She stretched her arm to the night table, then handed a condom over her shoulder as she nestled back against him, eager and needy. He adjusted her position and a moment later thrust in, sighing a hot breath against her neck, setting kisses against her nape that were warm and soft. Caring. Surely he cared?

She took him so easily now. It was nothing but pleasure, so much pleasure. She hadn't known her body could be like this: buttery and welcoming. It was almost too good. She was so far ahead of him, having been thinking about this while he slept against her, she soared over the top in moments. She cried out, panting and damp with sweat, overcome and floating, speechless in her orgasmic bliss.

"Greedy," he said in a gritty morning voice, rubbing his mouth against her skin, inhaling and calling her beautiful in Greek. Exquisite. Telling her how much he enjoyed being inside her. How good she made him feel.

He came up on his elbow so he could thrust with more power. His hand went between her legs again, ensuring her pleasure as he moved with more aggression.

She didn't mind his vigor. She was so slick, still so aroused, she reveled in the slap of his hips into her backside, hand knotting in the bottom sheet to brace herself to receive him, making noises close to desperation as she felt a fresh pinnacle hover within reach.

"Don't hold back," he ground out. "Come with me. *Now.*"

He pounded into her, the most unrestrained he'd ever been. She cried out as her excitement peaked. An intense climax rolled through her, leaving her shattered and quaking in ecstasy.

He convulsed with equal strength, arms caging her, hoarse shout hot against her cheek. He jerked as she clenched, continuing to push deep so she was hit by wave after wave of aftershocks while he thrust firmly into her, like he was implanting his essence into her core.

As the sensual storm battered them, he remained pressed over her, crushing her beneath his heavy body. Finally, the crisis began to subside and he exhaled raggedly as he slid flat, his one arm under her neck bending so he could cradle her into his front. They were coated in perspiration. It adhered her back to his front and she could feel his heart still pounding unsteadily against her shoulder blade. Their legs were tangled, their bodies still joined, their breaths slowing to level.

It was the most beautifully imperfect moment of her life. She loved him. Endlessly and completely. But he didn't love her back.

Mikolas had visited hell. Then his grandfather had accepted him and he had returned to the real world, where there were good days and bad days. Now he'd found what looked like heaven and he didn't trust it. Not one little bit.

But he couldn't turn away from it—*from her*—either.

Not without feeling as though he was peeling away his own skin, leaving him raw and vulnerable. He was a molting crab, losing his shell every night and rebuilding it every day.

This morning was the most profound deconstruction yet. He always tried to leave before Viveka woke so he wouldn't start his day impacted by her effect on him, but the sweet way she'd rubbed herself into his groin had undone him. She had gone from a tentative virgin to a sensual goddess capable of stripping him down to nothing but pure sensation.

How could he resist that? How could he not let her press him into service and give himself up to the joy of possessing her. It had been all he could do to hold back so she came with him. Because she owned him. Between the sheets, she completely owned him. Right now, all he wanted in life was to stay in this bed, with her body replete against his, her fingertips drawing light patterns on the back of his hand.

Don't *want*.

He made himself roll away and sit up, to prove himself

master over whatever this thing was that threatened him in a way nothing else could.

She stayed inside him, though. In his body as an intoxicant, and in his head as an unwavering awareness. And because he was so attuned to her, he heard the barely discernible noise she made as he pushed to stand. It was a sniff. A lash. A cat-o'-nine-tails that scored through his thick skin into his soul.

He swung around and saw only the bow of her back, still curled on her side where he'd left her. He dropped his knee into the mattress and caught her shoulder, flattening her so he could see her face.

She gasped in surprise, lifting a hand to quickly try to wipe away the tears that stood in her eyes. Self-conscious agony flashed in her expression before she turned her face to hide it.

His heart fell through the earth.

"I thought you were with me." He spoke through numb lips, horrified with himself. He could have sworn she had been as passionately excited as he was. He had felt her slickness, the ripples of her orgasm. Was he kidding himself with how well he thought he knew her?

"You have to tell me if I'm being too rough," he insisted, his usual command buried in a choke of self-reproach.

"It's not that." Her expression spasmed with dismay. She pushed the back of her wrist across her eye, then brushed his hand off her shoulder so she could roll away and sit up. "I used to be so afraid of sex. Now I like it."

She rubbed her hands up and down her arms, the delicacy of her frame striking like a hammer between his eyes. Her nude body pimpled at the chill as she rose.

"I'm grateful," she claimed, turning to offer him a smile, but her lashes were still matted. "Take a bow. Let me know what I owe you."

Those weren't tears of gratitude.

His heart lurched as he found himself right back in that moment where he had impulsively told her to pursue her interests and she had searched for reassurance that she would be with him for the long haul.

I don't know how long I'll be with you.

It had struck him at that moment that at some point she would leave and he hadn't been able to face it. He skipped past it now, only saying her name.

"Viveka." It hurt his throat. "I told you to keep your expectations low," he reminded, and felt like a coward, especially when her smile died.

She looked at him with betrayal, like he'd smacked her.

"Don't," he bit out.

"Don't what? Don't like it?"

"Don't be hurt." He couldn't bear the idea that he was hurting her. "Don't feel *grateful*."

She made a choking noise. "Don't tell me what to feel. That is where you control what I feel." She pointed at the rumpled sheets he knelt upon, then tapped her chest and said on a burst of passion, "In here? This is mine. I'll feel whatever the hell I want."

Her blue eyes glowed with angry defiance, but something else ravaged her. Something sweet and powerful and pure that shot like an arrow to pierce his breastbone and sting his heart. He didn't try to put a name to it. He was afraid to, especially when he saw shadows of hopelessness dim her gaze before she looked away.

"I'm not confusing sex with love, if that's what you're worried about." She moved to the chair and pulled on his shirt from the night before, shooting her arms into it and folding the front across her stomach. She was hunched as though bracing for body blows. "My mother made that mistake." Her voice was scuffed and desolate. "I won't. I know the difference."

Why did that make him clench his fist in despair? He ought to be reassured.

He almost told her this wasn't just sex. When he walked into a room with her hand in his, he was so proud it was criminal. When she dropped little tidbits about her life before she met him, he was fascinated. When she looked dejected like that, his armored heart creaked and rose on quivering legs, anxious to show valor in her name.

Instead he stood, saying, "I'll send an email today. To ask how the investigation is coming along. On your mother," he clarified, when she turned a blank look on him.

She snorted, sounding disillusioned as she muttered, "Thanks."

"Your head is not in the game today," Erebus said, dragging Viveka's mind to the *távli* board, where he was placing one of his checkers on top of hers.

Were they at *plakoto* already? Until a few weeks ago, she hadn't played since she and Trina were girls, but the rules and strategies had come back to her very quickly. She sat down with Erebus at least once a day if she was home.

"Jet lag," she murmured, earning a *tsk*.

"We don't lie to each other in this house, *poulaki mou*."

Viveka was growing fond of the old man. He was very well-read, kept up on world politics and had a wry sense of humor. At the same time, he was interested in *her*. He called her "my little birdie" and always had something nice to say. Today it had been, *"I wish you weren't leaving for Paris. I miss you when you're traveling."*

She'd never had a decent father figure in her life and

knew it was crazy to see this former criminal in that light, but he was also sweetly protective of her. It was endearing.

So she didn't want to offend him by stating that his grandson was tearing her into little pieces.

"I wonder sometimes what Mikolas was like as a child," she prevaricated.

She and Erebus had talked a little about her aunt and he'd shared a few stories from his earliest years. She was deeply curious how such a kind-seeming man could have broken the law and fathered an infamous criminal, but thought it better not to ask.

He nodded thoughtfully, gesturing for her to shake the cup with the dice and take her turn.

She did and set the cup within his reach, but he was staring across the water from their perch outside his private sitting room. In a few weeks it would be too hot to sit out here, but it was balmy and pleasant today. A light breeze moved beneath the awning, carrying his favorite *kantada* folk music with it.

"Pour us an ouzo," he finally said, two papery fingers directing her to the interior of his apartment.

"I'll get in trouble. You're only supposed to have one before dinner."

"I won't tell if you don't," he said, making her smile.

He came in behind her as she filled the small glasses. He took his and canted his head for her to follow him.

She did, slowly pacing with him as he shuffled his cane across his lounge and into his bedroom. There he sat with a heavy sigh into a chair near the window. He picked up the double photo frame on the side table and held it out to her.

She accepted it and took her time studying the black-and-white photo of the young woman on the one side, the boy and girl sitting on a rock at a beach in the other. They were perhaps nine and five.

"Your wife?" she guessed. "And Mikolas's father?"

"Yes. And my daughter. She was… Men always say they want sons, but a daughter is life and light. A way for your wife to live on. Daughters are love in its purest form."

"That's a beautiful thing to say." She wished she knew more about her own father than a few barely recollected facts from her mother. He'd been English and had dropped out of school to work in radio. He'd married her mother because she was pregnant and died from a rare virus that had got into his heart.

She sat on the foot of Erebus's bed, facing him. "Mikolas told me you lost your daughter when she was young. I'm sorry."

He nodded, taking back the frame and looking at it again. "My wife, too. She was beautiful. She looked at me the way you look at Mikolas. I miss that."

Viveka looked into her drink.

"I failed them," Erebus continued grimly. "It was a difficult time in our country's history. Fear of communism, martial law, censorship, persecution. I was young and passionate, courting arrest with my protests. I left to hide on this island, never thinking they would go after my wife."

His cloudy gray eyes couldn't disguise his stricken grief.

"The way my son told me, my daughter was crying, trying to cling to their mother as the military police dragged her away for questioning. They knocked her to the ground. Her ear started bleeding. She never came to. Brain injury, perhaps. I'll never know. My wife died in custody, but not before my son saw her beaten unconscious for trying to go back to our daughter."

Viveka could only cover her mouth, holding back a cry of protest.

"By the time I was reunited with him, my son was twisted beyond repair. I was warped, too. The law? How could I have regard for it? What I did then, bribes, theft, smuggling… None of that sits on my conscience with any great weight. But what my son turned into…"

He cleared his throat and set the photo frame back in its place. His hands shook and he took a long time to speak again.

"My son lost his humanity. The things he did… I couldn't make him stop, couldn't bring him back from that. It was no surprise to me that he was killed so violently. It was the way he lived. When he died I mourned him, but I also mourned what should have been. I was forced to face my many mistakes. The things I had done caused me to outlive my children. I hated the man I had become."

His pain was tangible. Viveka ached for him.

"Into this came a ransom demand. A street rat was claiming to be my grandson. Some of my son's rivals had him."

Her heart clenched. She was listening intently, but was certain she wouldn't be able to bear hearing this.

"You want to know what Mikolas was like as a child? So do I. He came to me as an empty shell. Eyes this big." He made a circle with his finger and thumb. "Thin. Brittle. His hand was crushed, some of his fingernails gone. Three of his teeth gone. He was *broken*." He paused, lined face working to control deep pain, then he admitted, "I think he hoped I would kill him."

She bit her lip, eyes hot and wet, a burn of anguish like a pike spreading from her throat to the pit of her stomach.

"He said that if the blood test hadn't been positive, you

wouldn't have helped him." She couldn't keep the accusation, the blame, out of her voice.

"I honestly can't say what I would have done," Erebus admitted, eyes rheumy. "Looking back from the end of my life, I want to believe my conscience would have demanded I help him regardless, but I wasn't much of a man at the time. They showed me a picture and he looked a little like my son, but..."

His head hung heavy with regret.

"He begged me to believe he was telling the truth, to accept him. I took too long." He took a healthy sip of his ouzo.

She'd forgotten she was holding one herself. She sipped, thinking how forsaken Mikolas must have felt. No wonder he was so impermeable.

"He thinks I want him to redeem the Petrides name, but *I* need redemption. To some extent I have it," Erebus allowed with deep emotion. "I'm proud of all he's accomplished. He's a good man. He told me why he brought you here. He did the right thing."

She suppressed a snort. Mikolas's reasons for keeping her and her reasons for staying were so fraught and complex, she didn't see any way to call them wholly right or wrong.

"He has never recovered his heart, though. All the things he has done? It hasn't been for me. He has built this fortress around himself for good reason. He trusts no one, relies on no one."

"Cares about no one," she murmured despondently.

"Is that what puts that hopeless expression on your face, *poulaki mou*?"

She knocked back her drink, giving a little shiver as the sweet heat spread from her tongue to the tips of her limbs. Shaking back her hair, she braced herself and said, "He'll never love me, will he?"

Erebus didn't bother to hide the sadness in his eyes. Because they didn't lie to each other.

Slowly the glow of hope inside her guttered and doused.

"We should go back to our game," he said.

CHAPTER TWELVE

MIKOLAS GLANCED UP as Viveka came out of the elevator. She never used it unless she was coming from the gym, but today she was dressed in the clothes she'd worn to lunch.

She staggered and he shot to his feet, stepping around his desk to hurry toward her. "Are you all right?"

"Fine." She set a hand on the wall, holding up the other to forestall him. "I just forgot that ouzo sneaks up on you like this."

"You've been *drinking*?"

"With your grandfather. Don't get mad. It was his idea, but I'm going to need a nap before dinner. That's what he was doing when I left him."

"This is what you two get up to over backgammon?" He took her arm, planning to help her to her room.

"Not usually, no." Her hand came to his chest. She didn't move, just stared at her hand on his chest, mouth grave, brow wearing a faint pleat. "We were talking."

That sounded ominous. She glanced up and anguish edged the blue of her irises.

Instinctively, he swallowed. His hand unconsciously tightened on her elbow, but he took a half step back from her. "What were you talking about?"

"He loves you, you know." Her mouth quivered, the corners pulling down. "He wishes you could forgive him."

He flinched, dropping his hand from her arm.

"He understands why you can't. Even if you did reach out to him, I don't think he would forgive himself. It's just…sad. He doesn't know how to reach you and—" She rolled to lean her shoulders against the wall, swallowing. "You won't let anyone in, ever, will you? Is this really all you want, Mikolas? Things? Sex without love?"

He swore silently, lifting his gaze to the ceiling, hands bunching into fists, fighting a wave of helplessness.

"I lied to you," he admitted when he trusted his voice. "That first day we met, I said my grandfather gave me anything I wanted." He lowered his gaze to her searching one. "I didn't want any of those things I asked for."

He had her whole attention.

"It was my test for him." He saw now the gifts had been his grandfather's attempts to earn his trust, but then it had been a game. A deadly, terrifying one. "I asked him for things I didn't care about, to see if he would get them for me. I never told him what I really wanted. I never told anyone."

He looked at his palm, rubbed one of the smooth patches where it had been held against a hot kettle, leaving shiny scar tissue.

"I never tell anyone. Physical torture is inhuman, but psychological torture…" His hand began shaking.

"Mikolas." Her hand came into his. He started to pull away, but his fingers closed over hers involuntarily, holding on, letting her keep him from sinking into the dark memories.

His voice felt like it belonged to someone else. "They would ask me, 'Do you want water?' 'Do you want the bathroom?' 'Do you want us to stop?' Of course I said yes. They never gave me what I wanted."

Her hand squeezed his and her small body came into

the hollow of his front, warm and anxious to soothe, arms going around his stiff frame.

He set his hands on her shoulders, resisting her offer of comfort even though it was all he wanted, ever. He resisted *because* it was what he wanted beyond anything.

"I can't—I'm not trying to hurt him. But if I trust him, if I let him mean too much to me, then what? He's not in a position to be my savior again. He's a weakness to be used against me. I can't leave myself open to that. Can you understand that?"

Her arms around him loosened. For a moment her forehead rested in the center of his chest, then she pressed herself away.

"I do." She took a deep, shaken breath. "I'm going to lie down."

He watched her walk away while two tiny, damp stains on his shirt front stayed cold against his skin.

"Vivi!" Clair exclaimed as she approached with her husband, Aleksy.

Viveka found a real smile for the first time all night. In days, really. Things between her and Mikolas were more poignantly strained than ever. She loved him so much and understood now that he was never going to let himself love her.

"How's the dress?" Viveka teased, rallying out of despondency for her hostess.

"I've taken to carrying a mending kit." Clair ruefully jiggled her pocketbook.

"I've been looking forward to seeing you again," Viveka said sincerely. "I've had a chance to read up on your foundation. I'm floored by all you do! And I have an idea for a fund-raiser that might work for you."

Mikolas watched Viveka brighten for the first time in

days. Her smile caused a pang in his chest that was more of a gong. He wanted to draw that warmth and light of hers against the echoing discord inside him, finally settling it.

"I saw a children's art exhibit when we were in New York. I was impressed by how sophisticated some of it was. It made me think, what if some of your orphans painted pieces for an auction? Here, let me show you." She reached into her purse for her phone, pausing to listen to something Clair was saying about another event they had tried.

Beside him, Aleksy snorted.

Mikolas dragged his gaze off Viveka, lifting a cool brow of inquiry. He had let things progress naturally between the women, not pursuing things on the business front, willing to be patient rather than rush fences and topple his opportunity with the standoffish Russian.

"I find it funny," Aleksy explained. "You went to all this trouble to get my attention, and now you'd rather listen to her than speak to me. I made time in my schedule for you tomorrow morning, if you can tear yourself away…?"

Mikolas bristled at the supercilious look on the other man's face.

Aleksy only lifted his brows, not intimidated by Mikolas's dark glare.

"When we met in Athens, I wondered what the hell you were doing with her. What *she* was doing with *you*. But…" Aleksy's expression grew self-deprecating. "It happens to the best of us, doesn't it?"

Mikolas saw how he had neatly painted himself into a corner. He could dismiss having any regard for Viveka and undo all her good work in getting him this far, or he could suffer the assumption that he had a profound weakness: *her*.

Before he had to act, Viveka said, "Oh, my God," and

looked up from her phone. Her eyes were like dinner plates. “Trina has been trying to reach me. Grigor had a heart attack. He’s dead.”

Mikolas and Viveka left the party amid expressions of sympathy from Clair and Aleksy.

Viveka murmured a distracted “thank you,” but they were words that sat on air, empty of meaning. She was in shock. Numb. She wasn’t *glad* Grigor was dead. Her sister was too torn up about the loss when she rang her, expressing regret and sorrow that a better relationship with her father would never manifest. Viveka wouldn’t wish any sort of pain on her little sister, but she felt nothing herself.

She didn’t even experience guilt when Mikolas surmised that Grigor had been under a lot of stress due to the inquiries Mikolas had ordered. He hadn’t had much to report the other day, but ended a fresh call to the investigator as they returned to the hotel.

“The police on the island were starting to talk. They could see that silence looked like incompetence at best, bribery and collusion at worst. Charges were sounding likely for your mother’s murder and more. My investigator is preparing a report, but without a proper court case, you’ll probably never have the absolute truth on how she died. I’m sorry.”

She nodded, accepting that. It was enough to know Grigor had died knowing he hadn’t got away with his crimes.

“Trina will need me.” It felt like she was stating the obvious, but it was the only concrete thought in her head. “I need to book a flight.”

“I’ve already messaged my pilot. He’s doing his preflight right now. We’ll be in the air as soon as you’re ready.”

She paused in gathering the things that had been unpacked into drawers for her.

"Didn't I hear Aleksy say something about holding an appointment for you tomorrow?" She looked at the clothes she'd brought to Paris. "Not one thing suitable for a funeral," she murmured. "Would Trina understand if I wore that red gown, do you think?" She pointed across the room to the open closet.

No response from Mikolas.

She turned her head.

He looked like he was trying to drill into her head with his silvery eyes. "I can rebook with Aleksy."

So careful. So watchful. His remark about coming with her penetrated.

"Do you need to talk to Trina?" she asked, trying to think through the pall of details and decisions that would have to be made. "Because she inherits? Does his dying affect the merger?"

Something she couldn't interpret flickered across his expression. "There will be things to discuss, yes, but they can wait until she's dealt with immediate concerns."

"I wonder if he even kept her in his will," she murmured, setting out something comfortable to travel in, then pulling off her earrings. Gathering her hair, she moved to silently request he unlatch the sapphire necklace he'd given her this evening. "Trina told me he blamed me for everything, not her, so I hope he didn't disinherit her. Who else would he leave his wealth to? Charity? Ba-ha-ha. Not."

The necklace slithered away and she fetched the velvet box, handing it to him along with the earrings, then wormed her way out of her gown.

"Trina better be a rich woman, after everything he put her through. It doesn't seem real." She knew she was babbling. She was processing aloud, maybe because she was afraid of what *would* be said if she wasn't already doing the talking. "I've never been able to trust the times when I've thought I was rid of him. Even after I was living with Hildy, things would come up with Trina and I'd realize he was still a specter in my life. I was so sure the wedding was going to be *it*. Snip, snip, snip."

She made little scissors with her fingers, cutting ties to her stepfather, then bounced her butt into the seat of her jeans and zipped. Her push-up bra was overkill, but she pulled a T-shirt over it, not bothering to change into a different one.

"Now it's really here. He's dead. No longer able to wreck my life."

She made herself face him. Face *it*. The truth she had been avoiding.

"I'm finally safe from him."

Which meant Mikolas had no reason to keep her.

Mikolas was a quick study, always had been. He had seen the light of the train coming at him from the end of the tunnel the moment her lips had shaped the words, *He's dead.*

He had watched her pack and change and had listened to her walk herself to the platform and he still wasn't ready when her pale, pale face tilted up to his to say goodbye.

I can rebook with Aleksy. That was as close as he could come to stating that he was willing to continue their affair. He wasn't offering her solace. She wasn't upset beyond concern for her sister. God knew she didn't need *him*. He had deliberately stifled that expectation in her.

She looked down so all he could see of her expression was her pleated brow. "If you could give me some time to work out how to manage things with Aunt Hildy—"

He turned away, instantly pissed off. *So* pissed off. But he was unable to blame anyone but himself. He was the one who had fought letting ties form between them. He'd called what they had chemistry, sexual infatuation, protection.

"We're square," he growled. "Don't worry about it."

"Hardly. I'll get her house on the market as soon as I can—"

"I have what I wanted," he insisted, while a voice in his head asked, *Do you?* "I'm in," he continued doggedly. "None of the contacts I've made can turn their backs on me now."

"Mikolas—" She lowered to the padded bench in front of the vanity, inwardly quailing. *Don't humiliate yourself*, she thought, but stumbled forward like a love-drunk fool. "I care for you." Her voice thickened. "A lot." She had to clear her throat and swallow. Blink. Her fingers were a tangled mess against her knees. "If you would prefer we stay together…just say it. I know that's hard for you, but…" She warily lifted her gaze.

He was a statue, hands fisted in his pockets, immobile. Unmoved.

Her heart sank. "I can't make an assumption. I would feel like I'm still something you took on. I have to be something…" *You want.* Her mouth wouldn't form the words. This was hopeless. She could see it.

Mikolas's fists were so tight he thought his bones would crack. The shell around his heart was brittle as an egg's, threatening to crack.

"It's never going to work between us," he said, speaking as gently as he could, trying so hard not to bruise her. "You want things that I don't. Things I can't give you."

He was trying to be *decent*, but he knew each word was a splash of acid. He felt the blisters forming in his soul. "It's better to end it here."

It happens to the best of us.

What about the worst? What about the ones who pushed it away before they knew what they were refusing?

What about the ones who were afraid because it meant succumbing to something bigger than themselves? Because it meant handing someone, *everyone*, the power to hurt him?

The room seemed to dim and quiet.

She nodded wordlessly, lashes low. Her gorgeous, kissable mouth pursed in melancholy.

And when she was gone, he wondered why, if the threat of Grigor was gone, he was still so worried about her. If he feared so badly that she would hurt him, why was her absence complete agony?

If all he had wanted from her was a damned business contact, why did he blow off his appointment with Aleksy the next morning and sit in a Paris hotel room all day, staring at sapphire jewelry he'd bought because the blue stones matched her eyes, willing his phone to ring?

"You're required to declare funds over ten thousand euros," the male customs agent in London said to Viveka as they entered a room that was like something off a police procedural drama. There was a plain metal table, two chairs, a wastebasket and a camera mounted in the ceiling. If there was a two-way mirror, she couldn't see it, but she felt observed all the same.

And exhausted. The charter from the island after Grigor's funeral had been delayed by weather, forcing her to miss her flight out of Athens. They had rebooked her, but on a crisscross path of whichever flight left soonest in the general direction of London. She hadn't eaten or slept and was positively miserable.

"I forgot I had it," she said flatly.

"You forgot you're carrying twenty-five thousand euros?"

"I was going to put it in the bank in Athens, but I had already missed my connection. I just wanted to get home."

He looked skeptical. "How did you come by this amount of cash?"

"My sister gave it to me. For my aunt."

His brows tilted in a way that said, *Right*.

She sighed. "It's a long story."

"I have time."

She didn't. She felt like she was going to pass out. "Can I use the loo?"

"No." Someone knocked and the agent accepted a file, glancing over the contents before looking at her with more interest. "Tell me about Mikolas Petrides."

"Why?" Her heart tripped just hearing his name. Instantly she was plunged into despair at having broken off with him. When she had left Paris, she had told herself her feelings toward Mikolas were tied up in his protecting her from Grigor, but as the miles between them piled up, she kept thinking of other things: how he'd saved her life. How he'd brought her a life jacket, and said all the right things that night in Athens. How he'd taught her to fight. And make love.

Tears came into her eyes, but now was not the time.

"It looks like you've been traveling with him," the agent said. "That's an infamous family to truck with."

"The money has nothing to do with him!" That was a small lie. Once Viveka had spilled to her sister how she had come to be Mikolas's mistress, Trina had gone straight to her father's safe and emptied it of the cash Grigor had kept there.

Use this for Hildy. She's my aunt, too. I don't want you in his debt.

Viveka had balked, secretly wanting the tie to Mikolas. Trina had accused her of suffering from Stockholm syndrome. Her sister had matured a lot with her marriage and the death of Grigor. She had actually invited Viveka to live with them, but Viveka didn't want to be in that house, on that island, with newlyweds being tested by Trina's reversal of fortunes, since Grigor had indeed left Trina a considerable amount of money. Truth be told, Trina and Stephanos had a lot to work through.

So did Viveka. The two weeks with her sister had been enormously rejuvenating, but now it was time to finally, truly, take the wheel on her own life.

"Look." She sounded as ragged as she felt. "My half sister came into some money through the death of her father. My aunt is in a private facility. It's expensive. My sister was trying to help. That's all."

"Are you sure you didn't steal the money from Petrides? Because your flight path looks like a rabbit trying to outrun a fox."

"He wouldn't care if I did," she muttered, thinking about how generous he'd always been.

The agent's brows went up.

"I'm kidding! Don't involve him." All that work on his part—a lifetime of building himself into the head of a legitimate enterprise—and she was going to tumble it with one stupid quip? *Nice job, Viveka.*

"Tell me about your relationship with him."

"What do you mean?"

"You slept with him?"

"Yes. And no," she rushed on, guessing what he was going to say next. "Not for twenty-five thousand euros."

"Why did you break it off?"

"Reasons."

"Don't be smart, Ms. Brice. I'm your only friend right now. What was the problem? A lover's tiff? And you helped yourself to a little money for a fresh start?"

"There was no tiff." He didn't love her. That was the tiff. He would never love her and *she loved him so much.* "I'm telling you, the money has nothing to do with him. *I* have nothing to do with him. Not anymore."

She was going to cry now, and completely humiliate herself.

Mikolas was standing at the head of a boardroom table when his phone vibrated.

Viveka's picture flashed onto the screen. It was a photo he'd taken stealthily one day when creeping up on her playing backgammon with his grandfather. He'd perfectly caught her expression as she'd made a strong play, excited triumph brightening her face.

"Where's Vivi?" his grandfather had asked when Mikolas returned from Paris without her.

"Gone."

Pappoús had been stunned. Visibly heartbroken, which had concerned Mikolas. He hadn't considered how Viveka's leaving would affect his grandfather.

Pappoús had been devastated for another reason. "Another broken heart on my conscience," he'd said with tears in his eyes.

"It's not your fault." *He* was the one who had forced her to stay with him. He'd seduced her and tried not to lead her on, but she'd been hurt all the same. "She liked you," he tried to mollify. "If anything, you gave her some of what I couldn't."

"No," his grandfather had said with deep emotion. "If I hadn't left you suffering, you would not be so damaged. You would be able to love her as she's meant to be loved."

The words stung, but they weren't meant to be cruel. The truth hurt.

"You have never forgiven me and I wouldn't deserve it if you did," Pappoús went on. "I allowed your father to become a monster. He gave you nothing but a name that put you through hell. That is my fault." His shaking fist struck his chest.

He was so white and anguished, Mikolas tensed, worried his grandfather would put himself into cardiac arrest.

"I wasn't a fit man to take you in, not when you needed someone to heal you," Pappoús declared. "My love came too late and isn't enough. You don't trust it. So you've rejected her. She doesn't deserve that pain and it comes back to me. It's my fault she's suffering."

Mikolas had wanted to argue that what Viveka felt toward him wasn't real love, but if anyone knew how to love, it was her. She loved her sister to the ends of the earth. She experienced every nuance of life at a level that was far deeper than he ever let himself feel.

"She'll find love," Mikolas had growled, and was instantly uncomfortable with the idea of another man holding her at night, making her believe in forever. He hated the invisible man who would make her smile in ways he never had, because she finally felt loved in return.

"Vivi is resilient," his grandfather agreed with poignant pride.

She was very resilient.

When Mikolas had received the final report on Grigor's responsibility for her mother's death, he had been humbled. The report had compiled dozens of reports of assault and other wrongdoings across the island, but it was the unearthed statement made by Viveka that had destroyed him.

How much difference was there between one man pulling his tooth and another bruising a girl's eye? Mikolas had lost his fingernails. Viveka had lost her *mother*. He had been deliberately humiliated, forced to beg for air and water—death even—until his DNA had saved him. She had made her way to a relative who hadn't wanted her and had kept enough of a conscience to care for the woman through a tragic decline.

Viveka would find love because, despite all she had endured, she was *willing* to love.

She wasn't a coward, ducking and weaving, running and hiding, staying in Paris, saying, *It's better that it ends here.*

It wasn't better. It was torment. Deprivation gnawed relentlessly at him.

But the moment her face flashed on his phone, respite arrived.

"I have to take this," Mikolas said to his board, voice and hand trembling. He slid his thumb to answer, dizzy with how just anticipating the sound of her voice eased his suffering. "Yes?"

"I thought I should warn you," she said with remorse. "I've kind of been arrested."

"Arrested." He was aware of everyone stopping their murmuring to stare. Of all the things he might have expected, that was the very last. But that was Viveka. "Are you okay? Where are you? What happened?"

Old instincts flickered, reminding him he was revealing too much, but in this moment he didn't care about himself. He was too concerned for her.

"I'm fine." Her voice was strained. "It's a long story and Trina is trying to find me a lawyer, but they keep bringing up your name. I didn't want to blindside you if it winds up in the papers or something. You've worked so hard to get everything just so. I hate to cast shadows. I'm really sorry, Mikolas."

Only Viveka would call to forewarn him and ask nothing for herself. How in the world had he ever felt so threatened by this woman?

"Where are you?" he repeated with more insistence. "I'll have a lawyer there within the hour."

CHAPTER THIRTEEN

MIKOLAS'S LAWYER LEFT Viveka at Mikolas's London flat, since it was around the corner from his own. She was on her very last nerve and it was two in the morning. She didn't try to get a taxi to her aunt's house. She didn't have the key and would have to ask the neighbor for one tomorrow.

So she prevailed upon Mikolas *again* and didn't bother trying to find bedding for his guest room. She threw a huge pity party for herself in the shower, crying until she couldn't stand, then she folded Mikolas's black robe into a firm hug around her and crawled into his bed with a box of tissues that she dabbed against her leaking eyes.

Sleep was her blessed escape from feeling like she'd only alienated him further with this stupid questioning. The customs agents were hanging on to the money for forty-eight hours, because they could, but the lawyer seemed to think they'd give it up after that. She really didn't care, she was just so exhausted and dejected and she missed Mikolas so bad…

A weight came onto the mattress beside her and a warm hand cupped the side of her neck. The lamp came on as a man's voice said, "Viveka."

She jerked awake, sitting up in shock.

"Shh, it's okay," he soothed. "It's just me. I was trying not to scare you."

She clutched her hand across her heart. "What are you doing here?"

His image impacted her. Not just his natural sex appeal in a rumpled shirt and open collar. Not just his stubbled cheeks and bruised eyes. There was such tenderness in his gaze, her fragile composure threatened to crumple.

"Your lawyer said you were in Barcelona." She had protested against Mikolas sending the lawyer, insisting she was just informing him as a courtesy, but he'd got most of the story out of her before her time on the telephone had run out.

"I was." His hooded lids lowered to disguise what he was thinking and his tongue touched his lip. "And I'm sorry to wake you, but I didn't want to scare you if I crawled in beside you."

She followed his gaze to the crushed tissues littering the bed and hated herself for being so obvious. "I was being lazy about making up the other bed. I'll go—"

"No. We need to talk. I don't want to wait." He tucked her hair back from her cheek, behind her ear. "Vivi."

"Why did you just call me that?" She searched his gaze, her brow pulled into a wrinkle of uncertainty, her pretty bottom lip pinched by her teeth.

"Because I want to. I have wanted to. For a long time." It wasn't nearly so unsettling to admit that as he'd feared. He had expected letting her into his heart would be terrifying. Instead, it was like coming home. "Everyone else does."

A tentative hope lit her expression. "Since when do you want to be like everyone else?"

He acknowledged that with a flick of his brow, but the tiny flame in his chest grew bigger and warmer.

"Since when do I tell you or anyone what I want? Is

that what you're really wondering?" He wanted so badly to hold her. Gather all that healing warmth she radiated against him and close up the final gaps in his soul. He made himself give her what she needed first. "I want *you*, Vivi. Not just for sex, but for things I can't even articulate. That scares me to say, but I want you to know it."

She sucked in a breath and covered her mouth with both hands.

This can't be real, Viveka thought, blinking her gritty eyes. She pinched herself and he let out a husk of a laugh, immediately trying to erase the sting with a gentle rub of his thumb.

His hand stayed on her arm. His gaze lifted to her face while a deeply tender glow in his eyes went all the way through her to her soul.

"I was terrified that if I let myself care for you, someone would use that against me. So what did I do? I pushed you away and inflicted the pain on myself. I was right to fear how much it would hurt if you were out of my reach. It's unbearable."

"Oh, Mikolas." Her mouth trembled. "You inflicted it on both of us. I want to be with you. If you want me, I'm right here."

He gathered her up, unable to help himself. For a long time he held her, just absorbing the beauty of having her against him. He was aware of a tickling trickle on his cheek and dipped his head to dry his cheek against her hair.

"Thank you for saying you want me," she said. Her slender arms tightened until she pressed the breath from his lungs. "It's enough, you know." She lifted her red eyes to regard him. "I won't ask you to say you love me. But I should have said it myself before I left Paris. I've been sorry that I didn't. I was trying to protect myself from being more hurt than I was. It didn't work," she said ruefully. "I love you so much."

"You're too generous." He cupped her cheek, wiping away her tear track with the pad of his thumb, humbled. "I want your love, Vivi. I will pay any price for that. Don't let me be a coward. Make me give you what you need. Make me say it and mean it."

"You're not a coward." Fresh tears of empathy welled in her eyes, seeping into all those cracks and fissures around his heart, widening them so there was more room for her to come in.

"I was afraid to tell you I was coming," he admitted. "I was afraid you wouldn't be here if you knew. That you wouldn't let me try to convince you to stay with me."

Viveka's heart was pattering so fast she could hardly breathe. "You only have to ask," she reminded.

"Ask." Mikolas smoothed her hair back from her face, gazing at her, humbly offering his heart as a flawed human being. "I can't insult you by asking you to *stay* with me. I must ask you the big question. Will you be my wife?"

Viveka's heart staggered and lurched. "Are you serious?"

"Of course I'm serious!" He was offended, but wound up chuckling. "I will have the right woman under the veil this time, too. Actually," he added with a light kiss on her nose, "I did the first time. I just didn't know it yet."

Tears of happiness filled her eyes. She threw her arms around his neck, needing to kiss him then. To hold him and *love* him. "Yes. Of course I'll marry you!"

Their kiss was a poignant, tender reunion, making all of her ache. The physical sparks between them were stronger than ever, but the moment was so much more than that, imbued with trust and openness. It was expansive and scary and uncharted.

Beautiful.

"I want to make love to you," he said, dragging his mouth to her neck. "*Love*, Vivi. I want to wake next to you and make the best of every day we are given together."

"Me, too," she assured him with a catch of joy in her voice. "I love you."

EPILOGUE

"Papa, I'm cold."

Viveka heard the words from her studio. She was in the middle of a still life of Callia's toys for the advanced painting class she'd been accepted into. Three years of sketching and pastels, oils and watercolors, and she was starting to think she wasn't half bad. Her husband was always quick to praise, of course, but he was shamelessly biased.

She wiped the paint off her fingers before she picked up the small pink jumper her daughter had left there on the floor. When she came into the lounge, however, she saw that it was superfluous. Mikolas was already turning from his desk to scoop their three-year-old into his lap.

Callia stood on his thigh to curl her arms around his neck before bending her knees and snuggling into his chest, light brown curls tucked trustingly against his shoulder. "I love you," she told him in her high, doll-like voice.

"I love you, too," Mikolas said with the deep timbre of sincerity that absolutely undid Viveka every time she heard it.

"I love Leo, too," she said in a poignant little tone, mentioning her cousin, Trina's newborn son. She had cried when they'd had to come home. She looked up at Mikolas. "Do you love Leo?"

"He spit up on my new shirt," Mikolas reminded drily, then magnanimously added, "But yes, I do."

Callia giggled, then began turning it into a game. "Do you love Theítsa Trina?"

"I've grown very fond of her, yes."

"Do you love Theíos Stephanos?"

"I consider him a good friend."

"Did you love Pappoús?" She pointed at the photo on his desk.

"I did love him, very much."

Callia didn't remember her great-grandfather, but he had held her swaddled form, saying to Viveka, *She has your eyes*, and proclaiming Mikolas to be a very lucky man.

Mikolas had agreed wholeheartedly.

Losing Erebus had been hard for him. For both of them, really. Fortunately, they'd had a newborn to distract them. Falling pregnant had been a complete surprise to both of them, but the shock had quickly turned to excitement and they were so enamored with family life, they were talking of expanding it even more.

"Do you love Mama?" Callia asked.

Mikolas's head came up and he looked across at Viveka, telling her he'd been aware of her the whole time. His love for her shone like a beacon across the space between them.

"My love for your mother is the strongest thing in me."

* * * * *

THE GREEK'S READY-MADE WIFE

JENNIFER FAYE

For Karen.

Thanks for being such a wonderful, supportive friend and big sis. May your future bring you many amazing adventures both near and far. In case your travels don't take you to Greece, here's an armchair vacation for you.

CHAPTER ONE

"MARRY ME."

Kyra Pappas's breath caught in her throat. She hovered in the doorway of the Governor's suite of the Blue Tide Resort, the housekeeping pass card still clutched in one hand and a pink feather duster in the other. Had she heard correctly? Did someone just utter a marriage proposal?

Talk about bad timing on her part. Still, being a romantic at heart, she couldn't resist trying to catch a quick glimpse of the happy couple before making a hasty exit. Her gaze scanned the room until she stumbled across the most gorgeous man wearing a gray tailored suit, sans the tie.

Wait. She recognized him. Yesterday, he'd returned to this suite just as she'd finished freshening everything. They'd chatted briefly about her being American. He'd inquired whether she enjoyed working at the resort. As their conversation had progressed, he'd mentioned some local sites she should visit while in Greece. He'd certainly seemed nice enough.

But right now, he was staring directly at her. Why would he be looking at her when he was in the middle of a marriage proposal? Kyra glanced around. They were alone. And the television was turned off. How could that be?

And then a thought struck her. Surely he wasn't posing the question to her. The breath caught in her throat. No. Impossible.

Her puzzled gaze studied the man with the tanned face. She could stare at him for hours. His dark wavy hair made her long to run her fingers through it, while his startling azure-blue eyes seemed to see all. He kept staring at her as though he expected her to respond. Perhaps she hadn't heard him correctly.

"I'm sorry. What did you say?"

His dark brows drew together as his forehead wrinkled. "I...asked if you'd marry me."

He really had proposed. This stranger wanted to marry her? To say she was caught off guard was akin to saying the Hope diamond was just another trinket.

For just the briefest moment, she imagined what it'd be like if he was serious. Until now, no one had spoken those words to her. On those occasional Saturday nights when she was home alone, she wondered if she'd ever fall in love. But she wasn't desperate enough to fall for the charming words of a stranger—however sexy he may be.

Besides, the last thing she wanted was to be tied down—not now when she'd just embarked on an adventure to find her extended family. She had other priorities and love wasn't one of them. It wasn't even on her lengthy to-do list.

She studied the serious expression on the man's face. He certainly didn't seem to be making light of his proposal. So then why had he proposed marriage to a total stranger? Was he delusional? Or had he made some sort of ridiculous wager with his buddies?

"Are you feeling all right, sir?" Her gaze panned the room again, this time a bit more slowly, looking for an open liquor bottle or a hidden camera. Anything to explain his odd behavior.

"I...I'm not exactly handling this well." He rubbed a hand over his clean-shaven jaw. "I must admit that I've never proposed to anyone before."

"Is this some sort of bet? A joke?"

His face turned gravely serious. "Certainly not. This is a serious business proposition. One that could benefit you handsomely."

Which was it? A marriage proposal? Or a business proposition? Kyra's mouth opened but nothing came out. Perhaps it was for the best. The man must have started drinking early that day even though she couldn't find any signs of it. The best thing she could do was beat a hasty retreat. She took a step back.

"Don't look so scared. I'm really not that bad." He sent her a lazy smile that made her stomach quiver. "I'm usually so much better at these things. Give me a moment to explain."

"I have work to do." She'd heard about rich people having weird tendencies. She kept a firm eye on him as she took another step back. "I…I'll stop back later and…um, freshen up your room."

"Please, don't go." He took a few quick steps toward her.

She held up a hand to stop him. "Don't come any closer or I'll scream."

"Relax. I won't hurt you. I promise." He rubbed the back of his neck. "I'm sorry. I'm really making a mess of things. I guess I should be relieved this isn't a real proposal."

She eyed him up to see if at last he was being on the level. The guilty puppy look on his face was so cute and tugged at her sympathies. He must be in a real bind to suggest something so preposterous. "Apology accepted. Now I really should get back to work."

"Aren't you at least curious about my proposal?"

Of course she was. Who wouldn't be? She studied the man a little more, noticing how the top couple of buttons on his slate blue button-down shirt were undone. It gave her the slightest hint of his muscular chest. She swallowed hard. To keep from staring, she diverted her gaze. On his arm, she spotted a fancy wristwatch. She wouldn't be surprised to find it was a Rolex.

He looked every inch a successful businessman right down to his freshly polished shoes. A man who was used to getting what he wanted. A man who made calculated decisions. And somehow he'd decided she would do for his plan. Interesting.

"Yes, I'm curious." She crossed her arms to keep from fidgeting. What would it hurt to hear him out? "Go ahead. I'm listening."

"Wouldn't you rather come inside and have a seat where you'll be more comfortable?"

"I'm good here." Until she had a clue what was going on, she was staying close to the open door. After all, she grew up in New York City. Her mother taught her at an early age not to trust strangers. Although, she didn't know if her mother would extend that warning to dashing billionaires or not, but Kyra didn't find wealth and class as important as her mother did.

He shifted his weight from one foot to the other. "I realize we don't know each other very well. But I enjoyed our conversation yesterday. You seem like a very interesting young woman, and you have a way of putting people at ease."

She did? She'd never been told that before. "Thank you. But I don't understand why you're, uh, proposing to me."

"I'm trying to secure a very important business deal. The problem is the seller is an older gentleman and a traditionalist. He has certain expectations that I currently fail to meet. Such as being a family man."

He wants to play house with me?

No way. She wasn't doing this. She didn't even know his name. "I'm not the right person."

"You're exactly who I need." His eyes gleamed with excitement.

She made an obvious point of glancing at the time on her phone. "I really need to get going. I have a lot of rooms to clean today."

"You don't have to worry. I'll vouch for you."

What an odd thing to say, but then again, this whole episode could easily be classified as bizarre. Just so she knew who to avoid in the future, she asked, "Who are you?"

His dark brows rose. "You don't know?"

She shook her head. The only thing she knew about him was that no one had a right to look that sexy. "Would I have asked if I knew?"

"True. Allow me to introduce myself. My name is Cristo Kiriakas."

His name did ring a bell—a very loud bell. It took a moment until she was able to place it. Kyra gasped. He was her boss—the owner of the Glamour Hotel and Casino chain that included the newly built Blue Tide Resort. She would have known it was him if only she'd done her homework. This was, after all, the Governor's suite—the best in the resort.

"Nice to meet you, Mr. Kiriakas. I…I'm Kyra Pappas. I didn't recognize you."

"Don't look so worried." He spoke in a calm, soothing tone. "I didn't expect you to recognize me. And please, call me Cristo. My father insists on going by Mr. Kiriakas. So every time you say that name, I'll be looking over my shoulder for my father."

"Sorry, sir. Um. Cristo. You can call me Kyra." At this particularly awkward juncture, she supposed the wisest thing to do regarding her employment while in a foreign country was to reason with the man. "Does my job hinge on me playing along with your wedding plans?"

"No, it doesn't. You don't have to worry. Your job is safe."

She wasn't sure about that. "Surely you have a girlfriend—someone close to you—to marry."

His jaw tensed and a muscle in his cheek twitched. "Yes, I could find someone to marry for real, but the truth is I don't want to be married. Not for keeps."

"Then why jump through all of these hoops? You seem rich enough to do as you please."

"I wish it were as easy as that. But having money doesn't mean things come to you any easier. Some things are still unobtainable without help."

Kyra had lived with money and without money. She found that both lifestyles had their positives and negatives. But she didn't know that other people had similar opinions. Her mother seemed to think that having money was the only important thing in life. And if you no longer had money, like her and her mother, then you pretended as if you did. Kyra didn't subscribe to that way of thinking, but after going round and round with her mother, she knew trying to change her mother's mind was a waste of time.

Kyra eyed up Cristo. "And you want my help to create a paper marriage so you can conclude a business deal?" She struggled to get this all straight in her mind. "And when the deal's complete, we'll go our separate ways?"

"Yes." He smiled as though relieved that she finally grasped what he was saying. "But it's not just any business deal. It'll be the biggest of my career. It'll change everything."

The conviction in his voice surprised her. Even though she didn't quite understand the importance of this deal, she felt bad for him. Why would anyone have to propose to a stranger in order to do business? No one should marry someone they didn't love heart, body and soul. For any reason.

Perhaps he needed a bit of coaxing in order to see things clearly. "There has to be another way."

He shook his head. "If there was, trust me, I would have done it by now."

She paused for a moment and gave his predicament a bit of thought. "Well, if marriage is so important, why can't you just have a fake fiancée? Wouldn't that save you a lot of trouble?"

Not that she was applying for the position—even though his blue eyes were mesmerizing and his mouth looked as though it could do the most delicious things. The fact was she'd come to Greece with her own agenda. And getting caught up in someone else's drama would only delay making life better for her and her mother.

This lady was sharp.

That was a definite bonus.

Cristo smiled. He knew from the moment he'd met Kyra that there was something special about her. And it went much deeper than her silky dark hair with long bangs that framed her big brown eyes. The rest of her hair was pulled back in a ponytail. He imagined how seductive she'd look with her hair loose and flowing over her shoulders.

However, his interest in her went beyond her good looks. From the moment they'd met, he'd noticed the warmth in her smile and the ease in her manner. Who knew she'd end up being the answer to his problems? He hadn't—not until this morning when he submitted his final proposal to the Stravos Trust to purchase its hotel chain. It had been summarily rejected without review.

He knew then and there that he was going to have to play by the off-the-wall rules laid out by the reclusive billionaire Nikolaos Stravos, whether he liked it or not. And he most certainly did not like having his business deals hinge on his personal life.

Although, Kyra's suggestion of an engagement might make the arrangement a bit more tolerable. An engagement wouldn't necessitate the use of attorneys and an ironclad prenuptial agreement. It'd be all very neat and tidy.

His gaze met and held hers. He needed more information in order to make this work. "How long have you been working at the Blue Tide? I don't remember seeing you around here before yesterday."

"That's because yesterday was my first day. I used to work in the New York hotel."

"Did you work there long?"

"A few years."

"And it was in housekeeping?"

She nodded, but the way she worried her bottom lip was a dead giveaway that she was leaving something out. If he was going to trust her with this important deal, he had to know what she was leaving out. "What aren't you saying?"

Her gaze met his as though deciding if she should trust him or not. After a few seconds, she said, "I'm currently taking online courses in international hotel management."

"I don't understand. Why would you be hesitant to tell me that?"

She laced her fingers together. "I didn't want you to think I was ungrateful for my current position."

He smiled at her, hoping to ease her obvious discomfort. "The thought never would have crossed my mind. I encourage all of my employees to further themselves. In fact, we have in-house training sessions periodically."

"I know. I checked into them."

Again, she was leaving something out, but he was pretty sure of what she was hesitant to say. "But we don't offer the classes you are interested in. And if you don't mind me asking, what might that be?"

She straightened her thin shoulders and tilted up her chin. "Property manager."

Of course. He should have known. There was a get-it-done spirit to her. "I have no doubt that you will succeed."

Her lips lifted into a warm smile. "Thank you."

So she had drive. He respected that. But there was still so much that he didn't know about her. The cautious side of him said to pull her personnel file, but there wasn't time. However, his manager made a practice of thoroughly investigating prospective employees. She must have a clean history or she wouldn't be here.

"I enjoyed our conversation yesterday. You're a very insightful young woman. And I would consider it a huge favor if you were to help me out with my business issue."

The panic vacated her eyes as her rigid stance eased. "I

really do like my job with housekeeping. It allows me time to, uh…sightsee and stuff."

"Will you at least consider my proposition?"

"I have. And the answer is no. I'm sorry, but you'll have to find yourself someone else to play the part." She started out the door.

"Please think it over." He threw out an outrageous dollar figure that put a pause in her step. "I really need your assistance."

He was running out of time.

And options.

CHAPTER TWO

THE MOST LOGICAL thing to do right now was to keep walking.

Yet there was that note of desperation in Cristo's voice. Something told her that he didn't say please very often.

Kyra hesitated, her back still to him. Why was this most bizarre plan so important to him? What secrets was he holding back? And why did she care? This wasn't her problem.

"If I didn't really need your help, I wouldn't have proposed this arrangement. I swear." Weariness laced his every syllable. "I will make it worth your while. If that wasn't enough money, name your price."

Why did it always come back to money? "I'm not for sale."

She headed straight for her cart of cleaning supplies. She dropped the feather duster back in its proper spot. Her curiosity got the best of her. She glanced over her shoulder to see if Cristo had followed her into the hallway.

He hadn't. She breathed easier. What in the world did they put in the water around here? Because there was no way that whole scene was normal. After all, they were strangers. No one would ever believe they were a couple.

As she prepared to push her cart to the next suite, she recalled the large dollar figure he'd named and the offer to make it bigger if necessary. Okay, she may not be a gold digger, but that didn't mean she'd turn her nose up at some extra income. But could she really play the part of his fiancée?

Could she pretend to be something she wasn't?

Wouldn't that make her a hypocrite?

Kyra paused in front of the next suite. She recalled how

many times she'd gone round and round with her mother in the past year since her father's death about putting on a show for her mother's country-club friends. When her father had died, so had their silver-spoon lifestyle.

Kyra felt sorry for her mother—first losing the love of her life and then having to go back to work after twenty-plus years as a stay-at-home mom. With her mother buried beneath a mountain of debt, Kyra had moved back in to help meet the mortgage payments. And though this new position in Greece took her away from home, Kyra reconciled it with the fact that it paid more so she could send more money home.

The one other reason Kyra had taken the position was to help her mother—even if her mother swore she didn't need help. With her father gone, her mother was depressed and lonely as her country-club friends had less and less to do with her. With no other family in New York, Kyra had hoped to locate her father's extended family. If she could forge bonds with them, maybe she could make a life for her and her mother here in Greece. By once again being part of a warm, supportive family, perhaps her mother wouldn't feel so alone.

One thought after the next rolled around in Kyra's mind as she cleaned the remaining suites on the floor. All the while, her thoughts moved back and forth between doing what she felt was right and earning enough money to help her mother, who had always been there for her. Did Kyra's principles outweigh her duty to help her mother?

And the fact she was in Greece gave her the freedom to make decisions she wouldn't normally make. Being thousands of miles from New York City meant her chance of running into anyone she knew was slim to none. Well, there was one person at the Blue Tide that knew her, her best friend, Sofia Moore. But Sofia would keep her secret.

Speaking of her best friend, Kyra could really use some advice right now. If anyone could make sense of this very odd opportunity, it would be Sofia. Once the last suite on the floor had been put to rights, Kyra paused next to the large window overlooking the private cove. She pulled out her phone. Her fingers moved rapidly over the screen.

Mop&Glow007 (Kyra): Hey, you're never going to believe this. I met someone.

She just couldn't bring herself to admit that she'd been proposed to by a stranger, only to learn later it was their boss. Somehow, it sounded desperate on his part. And she felt sorry for Cristo.

Seconds turned into a minute, then two, and still no response. Where was Sofia? Probably still cleaning the exclusive bungalows that lined the beach. But Sofia always had her phone close at hand.

MaidintheShade347 (Sofia): As in a guy?

Mop&Glow007 (Kyra): Yes.

MaidintheShade347 (Sofia): What? But how? You swore off guys.

Mop&Glow007 (Kyra): I know. But he found me.

MaidintheShade347 (Sofia): And it was love at first sight?

Mop&Glow007 (Kyra): Not quite. More like a business deal.

MaidintheShade347 (Sofia): He offered to pay you to be his girlfriend?

Mop&Glow007 (Kyra): Yep. A bundle.

MaidintheShade347 (Sofia): You can't be serious. Is this a joke?

Mop&Glow007 (Kyra): No joke.

MaidintheShade347 (Sofia): Is he cute?

Mop&Glow007 (Kyra): Very.

MaidintheShade347 (Sofia): Is he rich?

Mop&Glow007 (Kyra): Very.

MaidintheShade347 (Sofia): And you accepted?

Mop&Glow007 (Kyra): Not yet.

MaidintheShade347 (Sofia): Why not?

Mop&Glow007 (Kyra): You think I should really consider this idea?

MaidintheShade347 (Sofia): Sure. It's not like you have anything better waiting in the wings.

Mop&Glow007 (Kyra): Thx for making me sound so pathetic.

MaidintheShade347 (Sofia): Oops! My bad. Go for it. Gotta run. Talk soon.

Kyra blinked and read Sofia's last message again. *Go for it.* Was she serious? Then again, ever since Sofia had caught her boyfriend in bed with another woman, Sofia's attitude had changed drastically. When it came to men, she didn't trust them and she refused to get serious, but she was open to having a good time. Kyra was happy that Sofia had regained her spirit and was getting out there and trying different things. But should Kyra do the same? Then again, wasn't that part of the reason for this trip to Greece? Trying something different?

Maybe it was time she quit living life so conservatively. Maybe it wouldn't hurt to color outside the lines, just a little. Mr. Kiriakas's tanned, chiseled face formed in her mind. It certainly wouldn't be so bad being his fiancée for a night or two. She had enjoyed talking to him the other day, and when he smiled, it made her stomach quiver. Sofia was right. She had nothing to lose. It might actually be fun.

Before she could chicken out, she turned in her supplies and rushed to the small apartment she shared with Sofia in the employee housing. Once she had showered and changed into yellow capris and a pink cotton top, she rushed to his suite. She didn't have any idea if he'd still be there.

Her knuckles rapped on the door. She hadn't been this nervous since she came home from school with a below average grade on her report card. She didn't know why she was so jittery. Cristo certainly was nice enough. Besides, this whole thing was his idea.

The door swung open and there before her stood her almost-fiancé, all six foot plus of toned muscle. She tilted her chin upward in order to meet his gaze. "I…I thought over what you said earlier, and I have a few questions for you."

He hesitated and then swung the door open. "Come in."

She glanced around, making sure they were alone. As she did so, she took in the difference in decor between this suite and the other units. For one thing, the standard black upholstered furniture was leather in this suite. The art on the walls consisted of prints in the other suites, but in here everything was original, one-of-a-kind paintings. And lastly, the suite definitely had a lived-in feel—a sense of hominess to it.

Behind her, she could hear the door snick shut. It was

just the two of them, alone. Suddenly Kyra didn't feel quite so confident, so ready to strike a business deal. Right now, even the memory of Sofia's encouraging words sounded foolish. After all, she didn't go out on limbs and take big risks. She liked to play it safe.

Cristo cleared his throat. "Should I take your presence to mean you've changed your mind about my offer?"

She forced her gaze to meet his. "It depends on your answers to my questions."

"What would you like to know?"

Comfortable that she'd left herself an out, should she need it, she leveled her shoulders. "The pretense of being your fiancée, it would only be a show for others, right? You don't want me to, um…sleep with you?"

"No. No. Nothing like that."

She breathed a little easier. "And how long would I have to pretend to be your fiancée?"

"I'll be honest with you. I'm not sure."

"So this is going to take longer than a day or two?"

He hesitated. "Yes, it will. But only until my business deal is concluded. It could be a few weeks or as long as a couple of months—"

"Months?" Kyra shook her head. *No way.* He was simply asking too much of her. "That's not possible. I can't pretend to be your fiancée for that long."

"Are you planning to return to the States before then?"

The easiest way out of this mess was to say yes, but in truth she wasn't leaving Greece until she had a chance to track down her father's family. And since she didn't have a starting point, she didn't know how long that would take her. "No. I'm not leaving yet. I…I have things to do here."

"Anything I can help you with?" When she cast him a skeptical look, he rushed to add, "There are no strings attached to that offer. I like you. You make me smile, and it's been a while since anyone did that. Whether you agree to this plan or not, I'd like to help you out, if I can."

Now, why did he have to go and do that? It would have been so much easier to say no to a man who was pushy and arrogant. None of those descriptions quite fit Cristo Kiriakas. He was more like a really hot, Grecian…gentleman.

"Thank you. That's very kind of you. But not necessary."

"It may not be necessary, but I'd like to help. What has you here in Greece?"

His eyes told her that he was serious. He was really interested in her. So what would it hurt to open up and share a little with him?

"I'm here to find my extended family, or what's left of it." Cristo's brows rose with surprise, encouraging her to continue. "My father passed away a little more than a year ago. He'd always wondered about his extended family and had promised one day we'd take a trip here to see what we could learn. Now that he can't finish our research, I'm taking up where he left off."

"It sounds important."

"It is. For me, that is. My mother doesn't understand my need to do this." In fact, her mother had done everything in her power to curtail Kyra's trip, from pleading to offering up excuse after excuse until she finally resorted to a big guilt trip.

"I know some people who go by the name Pappas—"

"You do?" Could it really be this simple? "How do I find them?"

He held up a hand. "Slow down. Pappas isn't exactly a unique name."

"Oh." She'd known that from her research, but after hitting so many dead ends, she just wanted some hope.

"Do you have much family in the States?" Cristo's voice halted her thoughts.

"There's just me and my mother. The rest of my mother's family, small as it was, passed away. I thought my mother would understand my need to find out more about my past, especially after losing my father. But all she did was get angry and resentful any time I brought up a trip to Greece. Finally, I just stopped trying to make her understand."

"So you thought by taking a job here that you would have the perfect excuse to investigate your family's roots?"

She nodded. At the same time, her phone chimed. Expecting it to be Sofia, she grabbed it from her pocket. The caller ID said Mom. Kyra forwarded the call to her voice mail before slipping the phone back in her pocket.

"If you need to answer that, go ahead."

"It's not important. I'll get it later." The last thing Kyra needed right now was to talk to her mother in front of Cristo—a man who had a way of short-circuiting her thoughts with just a look. No man had ever had that kind of power over her. And she wasn't sure she liked it, but another part of her found him exciting—exhilarating—unlike any man she'd ever known.

"Suit yourself." He moved to the fully stocked refrigerator and removed a bottle of water. He glanced over his shoulder at her. "Would you care for one, too?"

What would it hurt? After all, he was being nice enough and she was a bit thirsty. "Yes. Thank you."

Her phone chimed again. It wasn't like her mother to call right back. Kyra did a quick time change in her head and realized that her mother should be at her second part-time job. Perhaps she was just checking in on one of her breaks.

When Cristo handed over the bottle, their fingers brushed. Their gazes met and held. The breath caught in her throat. She'd never gazed into eyes so intense, so full of energy. She'd heard people talk about instant attraction but she hadn't really known what they were talking about until now. Sure, she'd noticed some really good-looking guys, but they'd always been easily forgotten. Something told her that Cristo would not be so easily dismissed.

He stepped back. "If you'd like something to eat, I could order from the restaurant downstairs."

"No, thanks. I'm fine." With the flutter of nerves in her stomach, there was no way she could eat a bite of anything. "About the arrangement. Will we have to be seen in public together?"

"Definitely." His gaze narrowed. "Will that be a problem? Do you have a boyfriend?"

"No. No boyfriend." She glanced down at her casual clothes and then at his designer suit. "But I don't have anything appropriate in my wardrobe."

"No worries. A new wardrobe and accessories will be part of your benefits package."

Just like that he could arrange for a new, designer wardrobe without even a thought. Wow. How much was this man worth?

With a slight tremor in her hand, she pressed the cold bottle to her lips and took a small sip. She tried to recall the other questions she'd wanted to ask, but her mind drew a blank. At least she'd asked the important ones.

He walked over and placed his bottle on the bar. "I know this is rushing things, but I really need to know your answer to my offer."

"You definitely don't give a girl much time to weigh her options."

His voice grew deeper. "Maybe I just don't want to give you time to find an excuse to back out on me. I can already tell you're going to make my life interesting. You, my dear, are quite intriguing. And I find that refreshing."

"Is that all you find attractive?" The flirtatious words slipped over her lips before they registered in her mind.

His eyes lit up as the heat of embarrassment swirled in her chest and rose up her neck. What was she doing? She barely even knew this man. And yet, she was drawn to him like a moth to a flame, but if she wasn't cautious, she'd get burned.

"It's definitely not the only attractive aspect of this arrangement. Not even close—"

"The money you offered, is it still part of the deal?"

He nodded.

"And can you pay me weekly?" She wanted to pay down the mortgage as soon as possible.

His brows rose. "If that's what you'd like."

"It is."

She made the mistake of gazing into his eyes and noting that he looked at her with genuine interest. Did she really intrigue him? Her heart fluttered. Would it be so bad to have a gorgeous fiancé for just a bit? After all, you only live once. What did it hurt to have a little adventure?

And aside from the money, he'd mentioned helping her to search for her family roots. Now she had to make certain it was part of the deal. "And you agree to assist me in the search for my extended family?"

"I do."

She stepped up to him and extended her hand. "You have yourself a fiancée."

Instead of accepting her hand and shaking it, he lifted it to his lips. His feathery light kiss sent waves of delicious sensations coursing through her body. Much too soon he released her.

"When, um…do we start?" She hoped her voice sounded calmer than she felt at the moment.

"Right now. You have a wedding to plan and we need to get to know each other much better if we are going to convince others that we're a genuine couple."

Her phone chimed. It was her mother again. Something was definitely wrong. Kyra couldn't deny it any longer. "Excuse me for a moment while I answer this."

He nodded in understanding.

Kyra moved toward the wall of windows that overlooked the white sandy beach and aquamarine water. She pressed the phone to her ear. Before she could utter a word, she heard her mother's voice.

"Kyra, why didn't you answer your phone? I didn't call

to talk to your voice mail. Do you even listen to your messages? If you had, you'd know this is important—"

"Mom, stop. Take a breath and then tell me what's the matter."

"Everything."

Her mother had a way of blowing things out of proportion. *Please let this be one of those times.* "Mom, are you all right? You aren't in the hospital, are you?"

"The hospital? Why would I be there?"

Kyra exhaled a relieved sigh. "Just tell me what's wrong."

"My life. It's over. You have to come home."

Not melodramatic at all. "I'm sure it's not that bad."

"How would you know? You don't even know what's the matter."

Kyra fully expected this would be another engineered guilt trip. "Mom, just tell me."

"I would if you'd quit interrupting."

Keeping her back to Cristo, Kyra rolled her eyes. Why did talking to her mother always have to be an exercise in patience? Her father must have had more patience than a saint. "I'm listening now."

"They let me go. Can you believe that? After all I did for them. Is there no longer any such thing as loyalty and respect?"

"Who let you go?"

"The cleaning company. They said they lost some contracts and had to downsize. How can they do that? Don't they know I have bills to pay?" Her mother's voice cracked with emotion. "Kyra, you have to come home right away. I need you."

She should have known it'd come round to this. "I can't. I have a job to do."

"But we're going to lose our home." There was an awkward pause. "I don't know what I'm going to do. I'm all alone."

"Don't worry." Kyra may not agree with everything her

mother said and did, but she still loved her. And her mother didn't deserve to lose her home—no one did. "You won't lose your home. I'll help you."

Kyra, realizing that she'd said too much in front of Cristo, wound up the phone conversation. She promised to call her mother back soon.

Not sure how much Cristo had overheard, her body tensed. Her mother always did have the most amazing timing. Still, there was no undoing what had been done.

She turned to him. He was staring at her with questions reflected in his eyes. She couldn't blame him. If the roles had been reversed, she would have been curious, as well. "Sorry. That was my mother."

"I take it there's a problem."

Kyra really didn't want to get into this with him. "There is, but it's nothing I can't deal with."

He arched a dark brow. "Are you sure about that? I mean, if you have to leave Greece, it's best that we end our arrangement now—"

"No. That won't be necessary." And she didn't add that the money he'd been willing to pay her for her time would be a huge help with her mother's plight. Her doubts about whether she really wanted to move forward with this plan had just been overturned. She owed this to her mother. "I'm all yours—so to speak."

CHAPTER THREE

KYRA WAS ALL HIS.

Cristo couldn't deny that he liked the sound of those words. In fact, that wasn't the only thing he could imagine passing by that tempting mouth.

Cristo gave himself a mental shake. What was he doing daydreaming about this woman? He knew better than to think of romance. He'd witnessed firsthand what happened when the romance turned cold. His parents were like the king and queen of Frostville. He got frostbite every time they were in the same room. He refused to end up unhappy like them.

Cristo cleared his throat. "Maybe we should start this relationship over." He held out his hand to her. "Hi. I'm Cristo."

She slipped her slender hand in his. He immediately noticed the coolness of her skin. She was undeniably nervous. That was good because he was, too.

Her fingers tightened around his hand. "Hi. My name's Kyra. I have the feeling this is going to be quite an adventure."

He had the same feeling but for other reasons, none that he wanted to delve into at the moment. "Let me know whatever you'll need to make this arrangement as pleasant as possible."

As she pulled her hand away, surprise reflected in her eyes. "You make it sound like I've just released the genie from the magic lantern."

"Not exactly. But I do want you to be comfortable during our time together." Cristo knew how thorough Stravos was with his background checks of potential business associates. "I need this engagement to be as authentic as possible. Don't spare any detail or expense."

"What expense?"

"For our wedding."

"You're serious? You really want me to plan a wedding that's never going to happen?"

He nodded. "You have no idea what type of man I'm dealing with. Nikolaos Stravos is sharp and thorough."

"But if people know about this engagement, how are you going to explain it when we break up?"

"I thought about it and we'll handle it just like everyone else who calls off their wedding. We'll tell people it's an amicable split and we'd appreciate everyone respecting our privacy during this difficult time."

"That may be fine for the public but not for close friends and relatives."

"I've thought of that, too." He smiled, liking having all of the answers. "We'll tell them we couldn't agree on kids. You want a couple and I want none."

"Are you serious?"

He nodded. "It's a legitimate reason with no associated scandal. We won't be the first couple to break up over the subject."

She paused as though giving the subject serious consideration. "I suppose it'll work."

He cleared his throat. "It's the truth, at least partially. I'm too busy for a family." That wasn't the only reason he'd written off being a father, but it was all he was willing to share at the moment. "If we're going to do this, we have to make the relationship authentic to hold up under scrutiny. Starting with you moving in here."

"But…but I can't. I told you I'm not sleeping with you."

"And I don't expect you to. But if people are supposed to believe we're getting married, then they'll expect us to be intimate." When she opened her mouth to protest, he held up his hand silencing her. "We only have to give people the impression. Nothing more. Is that going to be a problem?"

Her worried gaze met his. He couldn't blame her for hesitating. He knew he was asking a lot of her. But he was stuck between the proverbial rock and a hard place. She'd been a really good sport, until now.

He had to give her an out. He owed her that much. "It's okay if you want to back out. I will totally understand."

For a moment, he thought she had indeed changed her mind—that she was going to head for the door and never look back. His body tensed. He didn't have a plan B. He'd only devised this plan, such as it was, on the spur of the moment.

When she spoke, her voice was surprisingly calm and held a note of certainty. "You're right. People will grow suspicious if we don't act like a normal engaged couple. But won't people talk about me being a maid?"

He shook his head. "You've only been on the job for two days, and I'm guessing you haven't met many guests."

"No. Not really."

"Good. I wouldn't worry." She glanced around the suite as though trying to decide how they would coexist. He could ease her mind. "Don't worry. There's a guest room with a lock on the door. But I'm sure you probably already know that."

She nodded. "When do you want me to move in?"

"Now. I'll send someone to gather your stuff. It'll be less obvious if you aren't lugging around your suitcases. Are you staying in the employee accommodations?"

She gave him the unit number. "But I…I need to tell my friend."

"Remember, this arrangement has to be kept strictly between us. You can't tell anyone about it or it'll never work. Nikolaos Stravos has contacts everywhere."

"Understood."

"Good. You stay here and I'll have your luggage delivered to you." Her mouth opened, then closed. "Is there a problem?"

She shook her head. "I'll have Sofia toss my things together."

"Good. Because we have big plans tonight."

Was this really happening?

Dressed in a maroon designer dress from the overpriced boutique in the lobby, Kyra held on to Cristo's arm. She was glad to have something to steady her as her knees felt like gelatin. Her hair had been professionally styled and her makeup had been applied by a cosmetologist. It was certainly a lot of fuss for a dinner date. What was Cristo up to?

She highly doubted she'd be able to eat a bite. Her stomach was a ball of nerves. They paused at the entrance of the resort's High Tide Restaurant. The place was dimly lit with candles on each table. Gentle, soothing music played in the background, but it wasn't having any effect on Kyra.

Numerous heads turned as the maître d' escorted them to a corner table. Cristo made a point of greeting people. It was like being on the arm of royalty as everyone seemed to know him. At last at their table, Cristo pulled out her chair. Quite the gentleman. She was impressed.

He took the seat across from her. "Relax. You look beautiful."

Heat warmed her cheeks. She knew she shouldn't let his words get to her. Everything he said and did tonight was all an act. "You look quite handsome yourself."

"Thank you." He sat up a little straighter as a smile reflected in his eyes. "Can I order you some wine? Maybe it'll help you relax."

"Is it that obvious?" She worried her bottom lip while fidgeting with the silverware.

He reached out to her. His hand engulfed hers, stilling it. "Just a little."

Her gaze met his before glancing down at their clasped

hands. She attempted to pull away, but he tightened his grip and stroked the back of her hand with his thumb, sending wave after wave of delicious sensations coursing through her body.

She struggled to come up with a coherent thought. "What are you doing?"

"Trying to get my fiancée to relax and enjoy herself. We don't want anyone wondering why you look so unhappy, do we?"

"Oh." She glanced around, making sure they weren't being watched. Thankfully, no one seemed to notice the bumpy start to their evening. Cristo was right, she needed to do better at holding up her end of this deal—no matter how unnerving it was being in this dimly lit restaurant at a candlelit table with the most handsome man in the room while trying to remain detached.

After making sure the server wasn't within earshot, she said softly, "Would you mind releasing my hand?"

Cristo's brows lifted, but he didn't say a word as he pulled away. She immediately noticed the coldness where he'd once been touching her. She shoved the unsettling thought aside as she picked up the menu. *Just act normal.*

"Would you like me to recommend something?"

Her gaze lifted over the edge of the menu, which was written in both Greek and English. "Do you have it memorized?"

"Would it be bad if I said I did?"

"Really?" He nodded and she added, "You take a hands-on boss to a whole new level."

His eyes twinkled as his smile grew broader and she suddenly realized that her words could be taken out of context. It'd been a total slip of the tongue. Hadn't it?

"The chef's specialty is seafood."

She forced her gaze to remain on the menu instead of continuing to stare into Cristo's eyes. Though her gaze focused on the scrolled entrées, none of it registered in her mind. "I'm not really a seafood fan."

"Beef? Salad? Pasta—"

"Pasta sounds good." Especially on a nervous stomach.

Cristo talked her through the menu. His voice was soothing and little by little she began to relax. She decided on chicken Alfredo and Cristo surprised her by ordering the same thing.

"You didn't have to do that."

His brows drew together. "Do what?"

"Order the same thing just to make me feel better."

A smile warmed his face. "Perhaps we just have similar tastes."

Perhaps they did. Now, why did that warm a spot in her chest? It wasn't as if this was a real date. Everything was a case of make-believe. Did that include his words?

He didn't give her time to contemplate the question as he continued the conversation, moving on to subjects such as how the weather compared to New York, and the differences between the Blue Tide Resort and his flagship business, the Glamour Hotel in New York City, where she'd previously worked.

She appreciated that he was trying so hard to put her at ease. It was as though they were on a genuine date. He even flirted with her, making her laugh. Kyra was thoroughly impressed. She didn't think he would be this patient or kind. She had to keep reminding herself that it was all a show. But the more he talked, the harder it was to remember this wasn't a date.

Much later, the meal was over and Cristo stared at her in the wavering candlelight. "How about dessert?"

She shook her head as she pressed a hand to her full stomach. "Not me. I'm going to have to run extra long tomorrow just to wear off a fraction of these calories."

He pressed his elbows to the table and leaned forward.

"You don't have to worry. You look amazing. Enjoy tonight. Consider it a new beginning for both of us."

A new beginning? Why did it seem as though he was trying to seduce her tonight? Maybe because he was. She was going to have to be extra careful around this charmer.

"The dinner was great. Thank you so much. But I honestly can't eat another bite."

A frown pulled at his lips. "I have something special ordered just for you."

"You do?" No one had ever gone to this much trouble for her, pretend or real.

He nodded. "Will you at least sample it? I wouldn't want the chef to be insulted."

"Of course." Then she had an idea. "Why don't you share it with me?"

"You have a deal." He signaled to the waiter that they were ready for the final course. It seemed almost instantaneous when the waiter appeared. He approached with a solitary cupcake.

It wasn't until the waiter had placed the cupcake in front of her that she realized there was a diamond ring sitting atop the large dollop of frosting. The jewel was big. No, it was huge.

Kyra gasped.

The waiter immediately backed away. Cristo moved from his chair and retrieved the ring. What was he up to? Was it a mistake that he was going to correct? Because no one purchased a ring that big for someone who was just their fake fiancée. At least no rational person.

Cristo dropped to his knee next to her chair. Her mouth opened but no words came out. Was he going to propose to her? Right here? In front of everyone?

A noticeable silence fell over the room as one by one people turned and stared at them. The only sound now was the quickening beat of her heart.

Cristo gazed into her eyes. "Kyra, you stumbled into my

life, reminding me of all that I'd been missing. You showed me that there's more to life than business. You make me smile. You make me laugh. I can only hope to make you nearly as happy. Will you make me the happiest man in the world and marry me?"

The words were perfect. The sentiment was everything a woman could hope for. She knew this was where she was supposed to say *yes*, but even though her jaw moved, the words were trapped in her throat. Instead, she nodded and blinked back the involuntary rush of emotions. Someday she hoped the right guy would say those words to her and mean them.

Cristo took her hand in his. She was shaking and there wasn't a darn thing she could do at that moment to stop it. Perhaps she should have realized he had this planned all along, what with her fancy dress and the stylist. If he wanted a surprised reaction, he got it.

Who'd have thought Cristo had a romantic streak? He'd created the most amazing evening. Something told her she would never forget this night. She couldn't wait to tell Sofia. She was going to be so upset that she missed it.

Cristo stood and then helped Kyra to her feet. As though under a spell, she leaned into him. There was an intensity in his gaze that had her staring back, unable to turn away. Her pulse raced and her heart tumbled in her chest.

When his gaze dipped to her mouth, the breath caught in her throat. He was going to kiss her. His hands lifted and cupped her face. Their lips were just inches apart.

She should pull back. Turn away. Instead, she stood there anxiously waiting for his touch. Would it be gentle and teasing? Or would it be swift and demanding?

"You complete me." Those softly spoken words shattered her last bit of reality. She gave in to the fantasy. He was her Prince Charming and for tonight she was his Cinderella.

The pounding in her chest grew stronger. She needed

him to kiss her. She needed to see if his lips felt as good against hers as they'd felt on her hand.

"How did I get so lucky?" His voice crooned. Yet his voice was so soft that it would be impossible for anyone to hear—but her.

If he expected her to speak, he'd be waiting a long time. This whole evening had spiraled beyond anything she ever could have imagined. She was truly speechless, and that didn't happen often.

His head dipped. This was it. He was really going to do it. And she was really going to let him. Her body swayed against his. Her soft curves nestled against his muscular planes.

She lifted on her tiptoes, meeting him halfway. Her eyelids fluttered closed. His smooth lips pressed to hers. At first, neither of them moved. It was as though they were both afraid of where this might lead. But then the chemistry between them swelled, mixed and bubbled up in needy anticipation.

Kyra's arms slid up over his broad shoulders and wrapped around his neck. Her fingers worked their way through the soft, silky strands of his hair. This wasn't so bad. In fact, it was…amazing. Her lips moved of their own accord, opening and welcoming him.

He was delicious, tasting sweet like the bottle of bubbly he'd insisted on ordering. She'd thought it'd just been to celebrate their business arrangement. She had no idea it was part of this seductive proposal. This man was as dangerous to her common sense as he was delicious enough to kiss all night long.

When applause and whistles filled the restaurant, it shattered the illusion. Kyra crashed back to earth and reluctantly pulled back. Her gaze met his passion-filled eyes. He wanted her. That part couldn't be faked. So that kiss had been more than a means to prove to the world that their relationship was real. The kiss had been the heart-pounding, soul-stirring genuine article.

Her shaky fingers moved to her lips. They still tingled. Realizing she was acting like someone who hadn't been kissed before, she moved her hand. Her gaze landed upon her hand and the jaw-dropping rock Cristo had placed there. The large circular diamond had to be at least four, no make that five, carats. It was surrounded by a ring of smaller diamonds. The band was a beautiful rose gold with tiny diamonds adorning the band. She was in love—with the ring, of course.

"Do you like it?" Cristo moved beside her and gazed down at the ring.

"It's simply stunning. But it's far too much."

Cristo leaned over and whispered, "The ring quite suits you even if it can't compare to your beauty. How about we take our cupcake upstairs?"

CHAPTER FOUR

KYRA'S HEART BEAT out a rapid *tap-tap-tap.*

Why was Cristo staring at her as though she was the dessert?

He leaned close and spoke softly. "You're enjoying the evening, aren't you?"

The wispy feel of his hot breath on her neck sent a wave of goose bumps cascading down her arms. "I…I am. It's magical."

"Good. It's not over yet."

This evening had been so romantic that she couldn't help but wonder if he'd almost gotten caught up in the show. Would he kiss her again? Her gaze shifted to his most tempting lips. Did she want him to?

He extended his arm to her and she accepted the gesture. Before they exited the restaurant, she glanced back at the table to make sure she hadn't forgotten anything. "What about the cupcake?"

"It'll be delivered to our suite along with another bottle of champagne." He turned to the waiter to make the arrangements.

Our suite. It sounded so strange. She wasn't sure how she felt about being intimately linked with Cristo—even if it was all a show.

On their way to the elevator, people stopped to congratulate them. Kyra smiled and thanked them, but inside she felt like such a fraud. A liar. Once again her life had become full of lies and innuendos, but this time instead of being a casual observer of her mother's charade, Kyra was the prime star. She didn't like it…but then again, she glanced at Cristo, there were some wonderful benefits. Not that she was confusing fiction with fact, but there was this tiny moment of *what-if* that came over her.

Once inside the elevator, it was just the two of them. He pressed the button for the top floor and swiped his keycard. She knew this was the end of her fairy-tale evening. She needed to get control of her meandering thoughts. It'd help if he wasn't touching her, making her pulse do frantic things. When she tried to withdraw her hand, he placed his other hand over hers.

What in the world?

She turned a questioning glance his way only to find desire reflected in his eyes. Her heart slammed into her chest. Had he forgotten the show was over? They were alone now. But he continued to gaze deep into her eyes, turning her knees to gelatin.

Was it possible he intended to follow up that kiss in the restaurant with another one? Blood pounded in her ears. Was it wrong that she wanted him to do it—to press his mouth to hers? The breath caught in her lungs. She tilted her chin higher. *Do it. I dare you.*

He turned and faced forward. *Wait. What happened?* Had she misread him? She inwardly groaned. This arrangement was going to be so much harder than she ever imagined.

The elevator doors slid open. Another couple waited outside. The young woman was wrapped in her lover's arms. They were kissing and oblivious to everything around them. Caught up in their own world, the elevator doors closed without them noticing. Now, that was love.

It definitely wasn't what had been going on between her and Cristo. That had been—what—lust? Curiosity? Whatever it was, it wasn't real. And now it was over.

Cristo grew increasingly quiet as he escorted her to their suite. He opened the door for her—forever the gentleman. It'd be so much easier to keep her distance from him if he'd just act like one of the self-centered, self-important jerks that her mother insisted on setting her up with because they had a little bit of money and prestige. Her mother never understood those things weren't important to Kyra.

She stopped next to one of the couches and turned back to him. "Thank you for such a wonderful evening." Before she forgot, she slipped the diamond ring from her finger and held it out to him. "Here. You'd better take this. I don't want anything to happen to it."

He shook his head. "No. It's yours."

"But I can't keep it. It's much too valuable." And held far too many innuendos of love and forever. Things that didn't apply to them.

Cristo frowned. "Now, how would it look if my fiancée went around without a ring on her finger?"

"You're serious? You really want me to wear this? What if something happens to it?"

"Yes, I'm serious. And nothing will happen to it. Besides, I like the way it looks on your hand." He slipped his phone from his pocket and started to flip through messages. "Now, if you'll excuse me, I've got some business to attend to."

"Now? But it's getting late."

His forehead wrinkled as though he was already deep in thought. "It's never too late for work."

And just like that, her carriage turned back into a pumpkin—her prince was more interested in his phone than in her. She felt so foolish for getting caught up in the illusion. Why did she think he'd be any different from the other guys in suits that she'd dated?

"No problem. I'll just go to my room."

There was a knock at the door.

Cristo moved to the door and swung it open. "You're just in time. We were getting thirsty." He turned to her with a warm smile. "Darling, dessert is here. Why don't you go get comfortable and I'll bring it in."

A server rolled in a cart with a cupcake tree and a bottle

of bubbly on ice. The man sent her a big smile as though he knew what she would be up to that evening. Wouldn't he be surprised to know that she was going to bed alone?

Kyra was more than happy to head toward the bedroom. Her strides were short but quick. The evening's show had left her emotionally and physically drained. All she wanted to do now was slip into something comfortable and curl up in bed.

"Kyra, you can come back." Cristo turned to her. "Would you like me to open the wine for you?"

She didn't want to return to the living room. And she certainly didn't need any more bubbly. She needed time to sort her thoughts. But on second thought, it was better she went to him rather than having him seek her out.

Reluctantly she strolled back into the living room. "I think I'll turn in early tonight."

"It's probably a good idea. You have a lot to do tomorrow. Good night." He moved to the study just off the living room and pushed the door closed behind him.

How could he turn the charm off and on so casually?

With a sigh, Kyra headed for her bedroom, which was situated across the hall from his. This hotel suite was quite spacious, resembling a penthouse apartment. She should really snap some pictures to show her mother, but Kyra's heart just wasn't in it. Maybe tomorrow.

Her phone chimed with a new message. Still in her fancy dress, she flounced down on the bed with her phone in hand.

MaidintheShade347 (Sofia): Don't keep me hanging. How'd the date go???

Kyra stared at the glowing screen, wondering what in the world to tell her friend. That the night was amazing, magical, romantic…or the truth, it was a mistake. Plain and simple. She shouldn't have agreed to this arrangement. She wasn't an actress. It was just too hard putting on a show. And worst of all, she was getting caught up in her own performance.

Still, she had to respond to Sofia. Her mind raced while her fingers hovered over the screen.

Mop&Glow007 (Kyra): It was nice.

Immediately a message pinged back as though Sofia had been sitting there waiting to hear a detailed report.

MaidintheShade347 (Sofia): Nice? Was it that bad?

Mop&Glow007 (Kyra): It was better than nice.

MaidintheShade347 (Sofia): That's more like. Now spill.

Mop&Glow007 (Kyra): I wore the most amazing dress. We dined downstairs in the High Tide Restaurant.

MaidintheShade347 (Sofia): Good start. So why are you messaging me?

Mop&Glow007 (Kyra): Why not? You messaged me first.

MaidintheShade347 (Sofia): And I'm not with a hot guy.

Mop&Glow007 (Kyra): Neither am I.

MaidintheShade347 (Sofia): You mean the evening is over already?

Mop&Glow007 (Kyra): He's working.

MaidintheShade347 (Sofia): What did you do wrong?

Her? Why did she have to do something wrong? It's not as if they had gone out tonight with romance in mind. The night ended just the way she expected—though she really had thought at some point over dinner that he was truly into her. The man had given an Oscar-winning performance.

Mop&Glow007 (Kyra): I've got a headache. I'm calling it a night. Talk tomorrow.

She kicked off her shoes and stretched her toes. It'd been a long time since she'd spent an evening in heels. She thought she'd left this kind of life back in New York.

Something told her that sleep would be a long way off. She had too much on her mind—a man with unforgettable blue eyes and a laugh that warmed her insides. How in the world was she going to stay focused on finding her family when Cristo was pulling her into his arms and passionately kissing her?

Where was she?

Cristo refilled his coffee mug for the third time that morning and took a long slow sip of the strong brew. He stared across the spacious living room toward the short hallway leading to Kyra's bedroom. Maybe he should go check on her. He started in that direction when her door swung open. He quickly retreated back to the bar, where he made a point of topping off his coffee.

Kyra leisurely strolled into the living room wearing a neon pink, lime green and black tank top. His gaze drifted down to find a pair of black running shorts that showed off her toned legs. Maybe he should have chosen someone who was less distracting to play the part of his fiancée.

When he realized he was staring, he moved his gaze back to her face. "Good morning."

"Morning." She stretched, revealing the flesh of her flat stomach. Cristo swallowed hard. She yawned and then sent him a sheepish look. Her gaze swept over him from head to foot and then back again. "How long have you been awake?"

He glanced at his watch, finding it was a couple of minutes past seven. "A couple of hours."

Her beautiful eyes widened. "You certainly don't believe in sleeping in, do you?"

He shook his head. "Not when there's work to be done. Would you like some coffee?"

"I'd love some."

He grabbed another mug. "Do you take cream and sugar?"

"Just a couple packs of sweetener."

"Which color do you prefer? Pink? Blue? Yellow?"

"Yellow."

He added the sweetener and gave it a swirl. "If you want to make another pot of coffee, you'll find all of the supplies in the cabinet." He gestured below the coffeemaker. "Make yourself at home."

"You won't be here today?"

He handed over the cup. "I have some meetings in the city that I need to attend. Besides, you'll be so busy that you'll never notice my absence."

"Busy? Doing what?"

"You haven't changed your mind about our arrangement, have you?" He noticed how she fidgeted with the ring on her finger. He hadn't been lying last night when he said it looked perfect on her. In fact, if he hadn't made a hasty exit last night, he would have followed up their kiss with so much more than either of them was ready for at this juncture.

"No. I… I haven't changed my mind."

"Good. Because we made the paper." He grabbed the newspaper from the end of the bar and handed it to her.

"We did. But how?" When she turned to the society page, she gasped.

He had to admit that he'd been a bit shocked when he'd

seen the picture of them in a steamy lip-lock. He'd meant for it to look real, but he never imagined it'd be quite so steamy. Had she really melted into his arms so easily—so willingly?

And for a moment, he'd forgotten that it was all pretend. He'd wanted her so much when they'd returned to the suite that it was all he could do to keep his hands to himself. Thank goodness he had the handy excuse of work waiting for him, because a few more minutes around her and his good intentions might have failed him.

"I didn't realize it'd be in the papers." Kyra tossed aside the paper. "This wasn't part of our agreement. This is awful. My mother isn't going to understand. She…she's going to think we're really a couple. That you and I— That we're actually going to get married. This is a mess. What am I going to tell her? How do I explain this?"

"Calm down. You don't have to tell her anything—"

"Of course I do. When she sees that photo, she'll jump to the obvious conclusion. She'll tell all of her friends. It'll be a nightmare to straighten out."

"No, it won't. Trust me." His soft tones eased her rising anxiety.

"Why should I trust you?"

"Because I made sure this photo was just for the papers here in Athens. Nothing will be printed in New York."

Her gaze narrowed in on him. "Are you absolutely certain?"

He nodded. "I am. Trust me. I have this planned out. We may not be on the front page, but we did make a big headline in the society section. Hopefully it'll be enough to garner Stravos's attention."

"Why would you think this man would look at the society section? Isn't that geared more toward women?"

"Trust me. Nothing gets past this man, especially when he's considering doing business with a person. I'm sure he doesn't stay on top of everything himself, but he has plenty of money to pay people to do the research. But since Stravos is a bit of a hermit living here in Greece on an isolated estate, there's no need for our engagement to be announced in the American papers."

"You're sure?"

"I am."

The rigid line of her shoulders eased and she dropped down on the arm of a couch. "The next time, you might want to mention that part first."

"Would it really be so bad if your mother thought you and I were a couple?"

Kyra immediately nodded. "You have no idea how bad it would be. Until recently, my mother had made it her life's mission to marry me off to one of her friends' sons."

"And you're opposed to getting married?"

"No." Her voice took on a resolute tone. "What I'm opposed to is being someone's arm decoration. I don't want to be someone they drag out for appearances and then forget about the rest of the time."

"I can't believe a man could forget about you."

There was a distinct pause. "It's not worth talking about."

She was one of those women Cristo tried to avoid—the ones who didn't understand the importance of business. He didn't want someone dictating to him when he could and couldn't work. His email constantly needed attention. Almost every bit of correspondence was marked urgent. He didn't want to have to choose between his work and a significant other. Because in the end, his work would win. Work was what he could count on—it wouldn't let him down.

And he didn't imagine there was a man alive who could ignore Kyra. Himself included. He didn't think it was humanly possible. Her presence dominated a room with her beauty and elegance. Even he had gotten carried away the prior evening.

If he was honest with himself, the reason he avoided a

serious relationship was because he could never live up to certain expectations. He'd promised himself years ago that he'd never become a father. He'd learned firsthand how precious and fleeting life could be. All it took was one flawed decision, one moment of distraction, and then tragedy strikes.

The dark memories started to crowd in, but Cristo willed them away. He wasn't going to get caught up in the past and the weighty guilt—not now.

Kyra sighed. "My father was a workaholic. He loved us, but I think he loved his work more. My mother would never admit that. For her, he was the love of her life. But I sometimes wonder if she realizes all she missed out on."

"So you want someone who is the exact opposite of your father?" Cristo wasn't quite sure how that would work. What sort of man didn't get caught up in his work?

She shrugged. "Let's just say I'm not interested in getting involved with anyone at this point in my life. But if I were, I'd want to come first. When we're out to dinner, I'd want his attention focused on me and our conversation, not on his phone."

"That sounds fair." He wondered if she was recalling their dinner the prior evening. His full attention had been on her. He wanted to convince himself that it was because he needed to put on a believable show for the public—a besotted lover and all that it entailed. But the truth was the more Kyra had talked, the more captivated he'd become with her. He swallowed hard, stifling his troubling thoughts. "I've left you some information to get you started with the wedding plans. There's every bridal magazine available, the phone numbers of all the local shopkeepers and a credit card to make whatever purchases are necessary."

"You don't mind if I go for a quick run before I start, do you?"

He glanced at her formfitting outfit. It looked good on her. Really good. "Make your own schedule. But just so you know, the wedding is in six weeks. You don't have a lot of time to spare."

"Six weeks?" Her brown eyes opened wide. "You sure don't give a girl much time to plan. It's a good thing this wedding isn't really going to take place. I'm not sure I could work out all of the details in time."

"But you must. There can't be any cutting corners. Nothing that gives the slightest hint this wedding is anything other than genuine."

"I'll try my best." She frowned as she made her way over to the desk to examine the aforementioned items. "How will I know what to spend? Is there a budget?"

"No budget. Use your best judgment. But remember, this wedding is meant to impress important people. Spare no expense in planning our lavish, yet intimate nuptials."

"This is all still pretend, right? You aren't actually planning to go through with the wedding, are you?"

"Of course not."

She sent him a hesitant look as though trying to figure out if he was on the level or not. "I'll do my best. I don't have much experience with wedding planning."

"I'm sure you'll do fine." He grabbed his briefcase and headed for the door, knowing he had lingered longer than was wise. He paused and glanced over his shoulder. "My cell number is on the desk. If you need me, feel free to call. Otherwise, I'll see you for dinner."

"Not so fast. We aren't finished."

CHAPTER FIVE

CRISTO STOPPED IN his tracks.

What could he have forgotten? He thought he'd accounted for everything.

He turned back to Kyra. "Is there something else you need?"

She nodded. "We had an agreement. You said you would help me search for my extended family."

And so he had. But the last thing he had time for at this critical juncture was to go climbing through Kyra's family tree. "Have you tried doing some research online?"

"Yes. But I couldn't figure out how to narrow my search. I thought a trip to a library or somewhere with records of past residents of the area would be helpful."

"Your family, they're from Athens?"

"I'm not sure. I know my grandparents set sail for the States from here."

A frown pulled at his lips. He didn't have time to waste running around on some genealogy project when he had a billion-dollar deal to secure. He'd risked everything on this venture…from his position as CEO of Glamour Hotel and Casino to his tenuous relationship with his father.

Cristo clearly remembered how his father had scoffed at the idea of taking the already successful hotel and casino chain and making it global. Cristo knew if the chain was allowed to become static, that its visitors would find the hotels limited and stale. The Glamour chain would ultimately begin to die off. He refused to let that happen.

Cristo adjusted his grip on his briefcase. "I'll have a car at your disposal. Feel free to visit any of the local villages or the library in Athens."

She pressed her hands to her hips. "I thought you'd be accompanying me. You know, to help search for my family."

He recalled saying something along those lines, but he just didn't have time today. "Sorry. I've got a meeting in the city with a banker."

"And tomorrow?"

Tomorrow he had more meetings planned. He couldn't even get away from the demands on his time in this fake relationship. It just made him all the more determined to retain his independence.

"Cristo?"

"Fine. I'll check my calendar and get back to you after today's meeting."

She nodded.

Before he walked away, he might as well find out what this venture would entail. "What information do you have to go on?" His phone buzzed. "Hold on." He checked the screen. "My car is here. I must go. I'll look at what you have this evening."

As he rushed out the door, his thoughts circled back around to the sight of Kyra in those black shorts that showed off her tanned legs. Even her toenails had been painted a sparkly pink. And then there was that snug tank top that showed off her curves.

His footsteps hesitated. Maybe he should have offered to go running with her. Almost as soon as the thought crossed his mind, he inwardly groaned. He couldn't—he wouldn't—let his beautiful new fiancée distract him from achieving his goal.

He was so close to forging a deal to purchase the Stravos Star Hotels. It was just a matter of time until he heard back from Nikolaos Stravos about that invitation Cristo had extended for a business meeting. That steamy kiss in the newspaper, with the headline of Cristo Kiriakas is Off the Market, should have done the trick.

* * *

Her lungs strained.

Her muscles burned.

At last Kyra stopped running. Each breath came in rapid succession.

She leaned back against the stone wall lining the walkway in front of the resort. She knew she should have run first thing that morning instead of putting it off. But she'd become so engrossed with the wedding magazines that she'd found herself flipping through one glossy page after the next. When she got to the tuxes, she imagined Cristo in each of them. The man was so handsome that he would look good in most anything. She wasn't quite so fortunate with her broad hips and short legs. It took a certain kind of dress to hide her imperfections.

By late that afternoon, she'd felt pent-up and her head ached. She had more questions about the wedding than answers. What she needed was to talk with Cristo. She knew the wedding would never actually take place, but he'd insisted they were going for authenticity and to pull that off she needed some answers.

When she made her way back to the suite, she called out to him, "Cristo? Cristo, are you here?"

There wasn't a sound. *Drat.*

She moved to the bar where he'd left her his cell number. She entered it in her phone in order to send him a text message.

Mop&Glow007 (Kyra): I have some questions about the wedding. Will you be home soon?

She figured it wouldn't be too long before he responded as he seemed to have his phone glued to his palm. She imagined him falling asleep with it in his hands. Then again, she could easily imagine something else in his hands…um, make that someone else in his very capable hands. And this time, they wouldn't be putting on a show.

She jerked her thoughts to a halt. She was already hot and sweaty from her run. No need to further torture herself.

Her phone chimed.

CristoKiriakasCEO: Meeting has turned into dinner. Will be late. Don't wait up.

Just like that she'd been dismissed. Forgotten. Frustration bubbled in her veins. Cristo was just like the other men her mother had paraded through her life.

Mop&Glow007 (Kyra): Don't worry. I won't.

Her finger hovered over the send button. But then she realized she was being childish. It wasn't as if they were a real couple. This was all make-believe, thankfully. Her heart went out to any poor woman who actually fell for Cristo's stunning good looks and charming smile. He would forget her, too.

Kyra deleted her heated comment and instead wrote, Have a good night.

She told herself she should be happy. It'd give her quiet time to study for her hotel management accreditation. She hated to admit it, but she was woefully behind. Getting ready to move across the Atlantic had been her priority and then she'd been focused on learning her new position at the Blue Tide Resort.

After a quick shower, she made herself comfortable on the couch. Her assignment was to read four chapters and then complete the online questions.

Before she had time to do more than read one chapter, her phone chimed. Was it Cristo? Kyra anxiously searched the couch for her misplaced phone. Had he had a change of heart? Was he in fact different than the men she'd known? He certainly kept her guessing.

MaidintheShade347 (Sofia): What are you doing?

A wave of disappointment washed over Kyra. She had to quit thinking Cristo would surprise her by being anything other than a workaholic. Soon their arrangement would be over and she could get on with her own life.

Mop&Glow007 (Kyra): Studying.

MaidintheShade347 (Sofia): What? You land a really hot, really rich guy and you're studying???

Mop&Glow007 (Kyra): Cristo isn't here.

MaidintheShade347 (Sofia): He bailed on you for dinner?

So Kyra wasn't the only one with that thought.

Mop&Glow007 (Kyra): His meeting ran late. He won't be back for hours.

MaidintheShade347 (Sofia): Oh, good. My date bailed on me. I'll be right over.

Kyra glanced at the unread material on her e-reader and then back at her phone. Maybe some company was exactly what she needed. It'd help get her head screwed on straight. She'd study later. Satisfied Sofia would put normalcy back into her life, Kyra smiled.

Mop&Glow007 (Kyra): See you soon.

And Sofia wasn't kidding. Within a few minutes, there was a knock at the door. At last the evening was starting to look up. She rushed to the door.

Sofia was a couple of inches shorter than her and wore her dark hair in a pixie cut, which worked well with her heart-shaped face. She strolled into the living room and gazed all around. "So this is your," she said, using air quotes for the next word, "'boyfriend's' place?"

Kyra nodded. "I told you he's rich."

"You didn't say *how* rich. This place is really decked out. It's fancier than those exclusive bungalows I clean." Sofia stopped next to one of the couches and glanced down. "Hey, what's this?"

Oh, shoot. Kyra had totally forgotten to put the bridal magazines away. Now she had a lot of explaining to do.

"Are these yours?" Sofia's puzzled gaze met hers. When Kyra nodded, Sofia asked, "But I thought you were paid to be his girlfriend? You didn't mention anything about marrying him. I would have remembered that."

"I'm not marrying him."

Sofia glanced at the open magazine on the glass coffee table. "Looks like you are to me."

"Well, I'm not. I…I'm planning a wedding."

"For whom?"

"Um…so what do you want to eat?" Kyra moved to the desk to retrieve the menus from the drawer. She'd found them earlier at lunchtime. "We could get a pizza."

"Don't go changing the subject. Are you really marrying some guy you hardly know?"

Why did this whole arrangement sound so terribly wrong when Sofia said it? "Hey, I thought you said I should go for it and enjoy an adventure."

"But I didn't say to marry the dude."

Kyra knew she'd promised Cristo that she wouldn't tell anyone about their arrangement, but Sofia wasn't just anyone. Sofia was her best friend. She was the sister Kyra never had. And right now, she needed someone to talk some common sense into her.

"Let me order the pizza and then we'll talk."

"You bet we will." Sofia grabbed the magazine and sank down on the couch. "By the way, do you think they have pizza here?"

Kyra shrugged. "Isn't pizza international cuisine?"

"If it isn't, it should be."

In no time, the concierge had them connected with a nearby pizzeria. As the phone rang, Kyra realized it was very likely that the employees only spoke Greek. This would be a problem as Kyra only knew basic Greek at this point. *Gia sou*—hi. *Nai*—yes. *O'hi*—no. *Efcharistó*—thank you. She knew nothing about how to order a large pepperoni pizza in Greek.

Luckily the person on the other end of the phone spoke English although with a heavy Greek accent. And in turn, Kyra learned that when requesting extra pizza sauce they referred to it as gravy. She tucked that bit of trivia away for future use as she loved pizza.

With food on the way, Kyra had some explaining to do. She inhaled a steadying breath. After starting at the beginning of the story, she ended with, "And now I'm planning a lavish wedding."

"To go with that amazing ring. Let me see it again."

Kyra held out her hand. "Do you think I'm making a big mistake?"

After Sofia got done ogling the rock for the third time, she leaned back. "From what you say, he's been the perfect gentleman." When Kyra confirmed that with a nod, Sofia continued, "And you're doing it to help your mother?"

Kyra nodded again. "I've never heard her so worried. She wanted me to drop everything and go home. I tried repeatedly to explain that I could help her better from here, but I don't think it registered."

"Well, since you're doing it for a good cause, I'd say enjoy your no-strings-attached engagement."

"Will you be my fake maid of honor?"

"Hmm…I've never been asked to be a fake before. I don't know whether to be flattered or insulted."

"Be flattered. After all, I'm only a fake bride and this is a fake wedding."

"True." They both laughed.

"But the planning part is going to be all real."

"You mean he's really going to shell out cash for a wedding that's never going to take place?"

Kyra nodded. "He obviously has more money than anyone should be allowed."

"In that case, I'd be more than willing to take some of it off his hands."

Kyra grabbed one of the magazines and leaned back on the couch. "I don't think that'll happen, but you could help me pick out obscenely expensive dresses, flowers and whatever else goes into a society wedding. I asked Cristo to help me, but he bailed on me for some business dinner tonight."

Sofia shook her head. "What is it with guys and work?" And then lines of concern creased her face. "Are you sure he's actually at a business meeting?"

"Yes." Cristo might be a lot of things, but she had no reason to doubt his word. She knew Sofia's trust in men was skewed by the lies her ex had fed her while romancing another woman. "Cristo is a good guy even if his sole focus is his work."

"Too bad. He might have made a great catch."

Just then the pizza arrived. The aroma was divine. They also delivered two espressos and some complimentary limoncello. The wood-fired pizza was fresh and the toppings were plentiful and outrageously good. The evening was shaping up to be a great one…despite the fact she'd been stood up by Cristo.

Why exactly was his business so incredibly important to him?

Did he know what he was missing?

CHAPTER SIX

WHERE HAD THE evening gone?

Cristo loosened his tie and unbuttoned his collar. He stepped into the waiting elevator and pressed the button for the top floor of the Blue Tide Resort. All he wanted to do now was see Kyra's smiling face. He checked his watch. It was almost eleven. Something told him that if she had waited up for him, she wouldn't be smiling.

He'd never meant to be out this late, but after the bank he'd had a meeting with one of the suppliers for the Glamour Hotel chain. Their contract was about to expire and both sides were haggling for better terms. In an effort to soothe rising tensions, one of Cristo's business advisers had suggested they all go out for the evening. It was not what Cristo had in mind, but in the end, an evening away from the boardroom had eased tensions all around. Details were settled in a casual atmosphere to everyone's satisfaction and tomorrow the papers would be signed.

He really hoped Kyra would be waiting up for him. He didn't know why. Perhaps it was just the thought of having someone to unwind with—someone to share the news of his successful evening. Or maybe it was the way Kyra put him at ease as though he could tell her anything.

He slid his keycard through the reader and opened the door. The first thing that greeted him was the peal of female giggles. Giggles? Really?

He stepped into the room and found Kyra sitting on the floor with her back to him. She and another young woman he'd never met were pointing at pictures in a magazine and laughing. Well, it seemed Kyra was quite self-sufficient and capable of making her own entertainment. For a moment, he regretted missing it.

He cleared his throat. “Good evening.”

Both women jumped to their feet and turned to him. Their faces still held smiles. The last thing he felt like doing right now was smiling. Yet there was something contagious about the happiness on Kyra’s face. It warmed his chest and eased his tired muscles.

“Oops. Is it really that late?” Kyra glanced down at the mess of papers on the floor. “I guess we got caught up with wedding plans.”

Cristo’s gaze moved to the young woman at her side. “I see you enlisted help.”

Kyra smiled and nodded. “I needed someone to help me.” The unspoken accusation that he’d bailed on her was quite evident even in his exhausted state. Thankfully, Kyra didn’t appear angry. “So I asked my friend to join me. Cristo, this is Sofia. Sofia, this is Cristo.”

“It’s nice to meet you, Sofia.”

“Nice to meet you, too.” Sofia leaned toward Kyra. “Wow. You weren’t kidding.”

What exactly did that mean? He sent Kyra a puzzled look. Then again, he wasn’t sure he wanted to know.

“Don’t mind her.” Kyra waved off her friend, who was trying to smother a laugh and failing miserably.

Obviously they were very good friends. He didn’t know why that should surprise him. Kyra was easy to get along with. That was one of the reasons he’d asked her to work with him to secure this deal with Stravos. He hoped she’d be able to charm Stravos. So far, nothing else had worked. But what Cristo hadn’t anticipated was that he would be the one charmed.

He cleared his throat. “I’m sorry. I was held up and couldn’t get back sooner.” It was the truth, though by the look on Kyra’s face, she didn’t exactly believe him. “It looks like you two had a good evening.”

"We did. Sofia has agreed to be my fake maid of honor for our fake wedding—"

"You told her?" His jaw tensed. What part of don't tell anyone about their arrangement hadn't she understood?

"Um…I did—"

"I think I should go." Sofia grabbed her purse from the couch and moved toward the door. When she got near him, she paused. "Don't worry. Your secret is safe with me."

"Thank you. There's a lot riding on it." He glanced at Sofia, who didn't look as though she trusted him alone with her friend.

The smile faded from Sofia's face. "Kyra and I go way back. There's nothing I wouldn't do for her. Perhaps I should stay."

Did Sofia think he was going to retaliate in an ungentlemanly way? That was not his style. Not now. Not ever. "You don't have to worry. Kyra will be perfectly safe here. I promise."

Sofia gave him one last assessing glance. Then she turned back to Kyra. "Call me if you need anything, anything at all."

"I will. Thanks."

Once Sofia was out the door, Cristo turned back to Kyra. "It seems your friend doesn't trust me."

"Should she?"

"I suppose that's up to you to answer." Okay. So maybe he hadn't taken it well that Kyra had broken her word to him about keeping this deal on the down-low, but he really didn't think he'd done or said anything out of line. Maybe it was the stress of having his whole career on the line combined with the lateness of the hour that had him a bit sensitive. "Don't worry. I hope to have this deal with Stravos concluded soon."

"Does this mean Stravos agreed to a meeting?"

Cristo shook his head. "Not yet. But I hope to hear from him in the near future."

"Will our arrangement be over as soon as you have your meeting?"

Was there a hopeful note in her voice? Was she that anxious to get away from him? He hoped not. He kind of liked having her around. She certainly made his life a lot more interesting. "We'll need to keep up the pretense of being a happy couple until I have a signed agreement."

CHAPTER SEVEN

KYRA YAWNED AND stretched the next morning.

The weekend had finally arrived. After all of the changes and upheaval that week, it was good to have a chance to regroup. After a quick run, she planned to sit down with Cristo and find out exactly what he had in mind for this wedding. She had a few of her own ideas now that she'd looked over the magazines, but she didn't know if they were what he wanted.

With her hair pulled back in a ponytail and dressed in her running clothes, she headed for the living room. When she didn't find Cristo drinking his morning coffee or looking over one of the many newspapers he had delivered to the suite daily, she took a glance in his office. It was empty. In fact, there was no sign of him. Was it possible he'd actually slept in? She couldn't fathom it.

She contemplated knocking on his bedroom door just to check on him when he came strolling in the front door. She spun around, surprised to find him wearing a suit and tie. "Don't you ever take a day off?"

"Why would I do that?" He wore a serious expression.

"All work and no play makes Cristo a dull boy."

He arched a brow. "You think I'm dull?"

"I don't know. Perhaps." She sent him a smile that said she was teasing him. But her comment wasn't all in jest. She found it frustrating the way he worked night and day. And from all appearances, every day of the week. "You do know that it's okay to take some downtime once in a while, don't you?"

His dark brows drew together as though what she said did not compute. "The world doesn't stop just because it's

Saturday. You'd be surprised to know of all the business deals that are agreed to on weekends."

She sighed. "Well, what about the work we have to do here?"

His phone buzzed and he held up a finger to indicate he would be with her in a moment. She was seriously tempted to take his phone from him and give him a time-out. She crossed her arms and tapped her foot.

He quickly typed something into his phone before slipping it in his pocket. "Now, what did you need?"

"You."

A broad smile lifted his kissable lips. "Why didn't you say so? If I had known you wanted me, I would have been at your beck and call."

She rolled her eyes. "Does that line really work on the ladies?"

He shrugged. "I don't know. I never tried it."

"Lucky for them. No wonder you were so desperate for a fake bride if that's the best you've got."

"What can I say? I'm not used to picking up women."

She wasn't for a second going to believe he didn't have a social life. No way. Not with his dark, tanned good looks. "So you're saying they pick you up?"

"In a manner of speaking. Would you like to pick me up?"

She shook her head and waved him off. "Not a chance. You've already given me enough headaches with this wedding that you refuse to help me plan."

"I never refused."

"I know. You're just too busy." Her voice grew weary. Cristo needed to realize she wasn't one of his employees to slough tasks off on. They were in this together. Perhaps he just needed to be reminded of what was at stake. "Maybe we should call the whole thing off."

"What? But we can't."

She pressed her hands to her hips. "You're too busy to

help me, and from what I can tell, your plan isn't panning out."

"It's working. Remember, our picture was in the paper?"

"From what you're telling me, this Mr. Stravos is very thorough. You don't think he's going to want to see us together—see if we're really a happy couple?"

Cristo shrugged. "How hard can that be? We fooled everyone in the restaurant."

"That was from a distance. What happens when we have to put on a show for someone—someone who is suspicious of us like Mr. Stravos?"

"So what do you have in mind?"

"Stay here today. We can get to know each other better." When his eyes dipped to her lips, her pulse raced. She swallowed hard. "Not like that. I meant talking. If we're going to portray a happy, loving couple, we should know more about each other."

"But my meeting—"

"Can be rescheduled. This was your idea, not mine. I'm just finding ways to make it work. Unless you just want to forget it all—"

"Okay. I get the point." He sighed. "Let me make a phone call."

"And change into some running clothes." Then, realizing that just because he looked like a Greek god didn't mean he exercised, she added, "You do run, don't you?"

He nodded and moved toward the bedroom. The fresh air and sun would do him good. And if she was lucky, it'd erase the frown from his face.

In no time at all, Cristo had changed into a royal blue tank top that showed off his broad shoulders and muscular biceps. Mmm… This man definitely knew his way around a gym. A pair of navy shorts did nothing to hide his well-defined legs.

Cristo didn't say much on their way to the beach. In fact,

he was so quiet she wondered if he was truly upset with her about ruining his plans for the day.

She came to a stop on the running/walking path and turned to him. "If you don't want to do this, I'll understand."

Cristo started to stretch, lifting both arms over his head. "Are you starting to worry that you can't keep up?"

"Are you serious?"

He didn't say anything, but his stare poked and prodded her.

Her pride refused to let her back down. He might look amazing, but since she'd known him, he hadn't run. She, on the other hand, had been running every morning. "I'm not worried at all. We'll see who keeps up with whom."

He smiled confidently.

Once they warmed up, they took off at a healthy pace. Little by little they kept trying to outdo each other. Kyra was used to running solo, so she'd never been challenged this way.

When she started to get winded, she glanced his way. Cristo hadn't even broken a sweat. What was up with that? Shouldn't a man who spends all of his time going from meeting to meeting be tired by now?

As though he sensed her staring at him, he glanced over at her. "I take it I've surprised you."

What did it hurt to be honest? "Well, kinda. It's just that with you working all of the time, um…"

"You thought I'd be out of shape?"

Her face was already warm from the sun and exertion, so she hoped it'd hide her embarrassment. "I know how busy you are—"

He slowed down to a walk. "Between you and me, I do take time out to exercise."

"But when? You're always going from meeting to meeting."

He sent her a smile. "When something is important enough, you make the time. Sometimes I make it to the gym before heading to the office. Other times I do it at lunch. And on the really stressful days, I go in the evening."

Funny how he found exercise important enough to squeeze in, but he didn't seem to have that same philosophy about his social life. "You must really be health conscious."

"I don't know about that. I still enjoy a nice juicy steak. The exercise is more of a stress reliever for me. I played football all through school and always felt better after a strenuous workout. I guess it stuck."

"Football? Here in Greece?"

"No. I grew up in New York City."

"Small world. So did I." Something told her they may have lived in close proximity but they had led very different lives. "Let me guess. You were the quarterback."

He shook his head. "Sorry to disappoint you. I was a wide receiver, much to my father's disappointment."

"Your father wasn't happy that you played football?"

"He was fine with football, but he thought that a Kiriakas should always be the best. In this case, the quarterback and team captain."

"Surely he was…um, is proud of you."

"We should be getting back. I'll race you." When she didn't respond, he added, "I'll give you a head start."

She wasn't too proud to accept his offer because they both knew with his powerful legs that he could easily beat her. "And winner buys lunch."

She took off, all the while thinking about the relationship between Cristo and his father. Her heart swelled with sympathy for the son who failed to live up to his father's expectations. Was that why Cristo seemed to keep to himself?

Minutes later, Kyra and Cristo relaxed at an umbrella-covered table after their race. She'd ended up winning the race. And though she'd teased him about it, she knew he'd let her win. She hated to admit it, but he could easily outrun her. Maybe there was more to Cristo than profit reports and balance sheets after all.

"Looks like you're buying lunch." Cristo's eyes twinkled with mischief.

"So that's why you let me win?"

"Let you?" He shook his head. "I don't throw races. Are you trying to get out of our little wager?" He sent her a teasing smile.

She wished he wouldn't make her pull everything out of him. It'd be so much nicer if they could chat like friends—like her and Sofia. Open, easy and honest. Kyra squeezed the wedge of lemon over her iced tea. "Do you have siblings?"

He nodded. "Three…erm, two older brothers. And you?"

That was a really strange mistake to make. Who forgot the number of brothers they had? His pointed stare reminded her that she still owed him an answer. "I'm an only child. But Sofia is the sister I always wanted."

"Have you known her long?"

"Since junior high. We've been inseparable ever since. She's the yin to my yang. Although lately she's been a bit more yang." When he sent her a puzzled look, she added, "More sunny rather than shady."

He nodded in understanding. "So does that cover everything?"

She arched a brow. "You're kidding me. This isn't an interview. And we've barely scratched the surface of what I'd want to know about my fiancé, but it's at least a start."

"Honestly, there's not that much to know about me."

She eyed him up, surprised to find he was perfectly serious. Well, the guy may be a workaholic but he certainly couldn't be accused of being conceited.

"There's lots to know about you. Like what's your favorite meal?"

He thought for a moment. "I guess surf and turf."

"Who's your favorite musical group?" She'd bet he was a classical fan.

"U2."

Color her surprised. "Coffee or tea?"

"Coffee."

"Sunrise or sunset?

"Sunrise."

"Left or right?"

His brows drew together. "Left or right what?"

"Oops. Preferred side of the bed."

"Left."

Oh, good. She preferred the right. Not that it mattered, since this relationship was an illusion.

"Now it's my turn." Cristo leaned forward, resting his elbows on the table. He launched into his own rapid-fire questions. She played along, enjoying getting to know him better.

"Top or bottom?" His eyes twinkled with devilment.

Oh, no. She wasn't going there with him. "That's nothing you need to know."

"I disagree." His lips lifted into an ornery grin. "Every fiancé should know these things."

Boy, was it getting warm. Kyra resisted the urge to fan herself. The only thing she could think to do now was change the subject. "So why is this deal with Stravos so important to you?"

Cristo sighed as he leaned back in his chair. He took a sip of his iced coffee. "I plan to expand the Glamour Hotel and Casino chain, which is currently only a North American venture, into a global business. Stravos has an upscale hotel chain that spans the globe. I've heard rumors his grandson is interested in condensing the family's holdings in order to concentrate their funds on expanding their shipping business. This is the prime time to make my interest in the hotel chain known before they publicly announce it's for sale."

He hadn't really answered her question. She still didn't know his driving desire to make his business bigger and better than before. And from what she sensed, it was more than just a strategic business move. But she didn't want to push him too hard now that he was finally opening up to her.

"Now that we've gotten that out of the way, I really should get some work done today." He downed the rest of his drink.

"What about the wedding? Exactly how far do you want me to go with these wedding preparations?"

"The whole way." His chair scraped against the colorful tiles as he prepared to stand.

He wasn't going to get away, not until they got a few things straight. "You know, I didn't sign on to guess my way through this whole wedding. Engaged couples, well, at least the ones I know, make some of the decisions together."

His jaw tensed as a muscle twitched in his cheek. "But I don't know anything about weddings."

"And you think that I do?"

He shrugged. "But you're a woman. Don't all women dream about their weddings?"

"Not this woman. It was never a priority. I figured someday if I met a guy who could make me his top priority, that we'd settle down together. But I'm not getting married just because it's what my mother expects."

"So what you're saying is you wouldn't marry someone like me—at least not willingly."

She paused, not sure if she should speak the truth or not. But then she figured that a man as rich and powerful as Cristo Kiriakas probably didn't have many people in his life who spoke openly and honestly with him. After all, what could it hurt?

She took a deep breath. "No. I wouldn't marry you. You're too wrapped up in your own world. You say the right things, but when it comes time to the follow-through, you fail—"

"That's not fair. You're just judging me on this one occasion, when I have everything riding on this pivotal deal with Stravos. You have no idea what's at stake here."

"I'm sure I don't. But I'm guessing in your world there's always some huge deal to be made or some catastrophe to resolve. Face it, your business is your mistress. You don't have room in your life for another woman."

His mouth opened, then snapped shut. She had him and he knew it. What could he say to the contrary? Absolutely nothing.

His phone buzzed.

She sighed. "Let me guess. You're going to get that when we're at last having an open and honest conversation?"

He pulled the phone from his pocket. "It could be important."

"Do you ever get a phone call that isn't important?"

He didn't answer her as he took the call and moved toward the rail overlooking the beach, most likely to gain some privacy. And yet again, he'd proven to her why staying single was her best option. She didn't like being shoved aside and forgotten.

The truth of the matter was she wasn't suited for this job. She was getting too emotionally invested in a man and a relationship that would soon disappear from her life. But how did she turn off her emotions?

As Cristo's conversation grew lengthy, her patience shrank. She finished her tea and was about to return to the suite for a shower when she noticed Cristo's voice rising. She glanced around finding that most of the nearby tables were vacant.

"You're just worried, because when this deal goes through—and it will—my hotel chain will rival yours."

Kyra couldn't help but be curious as to what had made Cristo lose his cool. He might be a busy man, but he was very good at the art of deflection. He'd even taken her harsh assessment of him as husband material without raising his voice. Who was on the other end of the phone?

"I'm not disloyal to the family. This is business, pure and simple. Something you taught me as a kid."

She shouldn't be sitting here listening. Yet she couldn't move. She was entranced by this new side of Cristo—this vulnerable aspect.

"I'm sorry you feel that way, Father." His whole body noticeably tensed. "Do what you need to do, and I'll do what I need to do."

Sympathy welled up in Kyra. She knew what it was like to disagree with a parent. She did it more than she liked with her mother.

"You know what? You've always been disappointed in me." Cristo jabbed his fingers through his hair as he started to pace. "Why should this be any different?" And with that, Cristo ended the call.

The breath caught in Kyra's throat. There was a line being drawn in the proverbial sand between the two men. And that wasn't good. Not good at all.

Okay, so maybe she'd had a few heated arguments about her mother's meddling, but it had never gotten that harsh. She knew no matter what she did in life that her mother would love her. She didn't have anything to prove to her mother.

So what in the world had happened between Cristo and his father? Was there always such discord between them? Her heart went out to Cristo as he leaned forward on the rail, keeping his back to her. She could only imagine the turmoil churning inside him.

If she'd had any thoughts about backing out of this arrangement, they were gone now. It was bad enough that his father thought he was going to fail, but for her to pull the rug out from under Cristo when he'd been working night and day to make this deal a success would just be too much.

Suddenly, grabbing a shower didn't seem quite so urgent. "Cristo, I was thinking about ordering brunch. That run really worked up an appetite. Want to join me?"

When he turned to her, his face was pale. Lines by his eyes and mouth were more pronounced. It was as though he'd aged five years during that one phone call. She was tempted to go up to him and wrap her arms around him while murmuring that it would all be better soon. But she knew that his wounded ego would rebuff her sympathies.

Cristo returned to the table and sat down. "That was my father." She'd guessed that much by what she'd overheard, but she didn't say anything as she waited and wondered if Cristo would open up to her. He cleared his throat. "He saw the press release of our engagement."

"But I thought you said it wouldn't be in the New York papers."

"It wasn't. My father has his sources. I just didn't know he had me under such tight scrutiny." Cristo rubbed the back of his neck. "He also found out about my plan to buy the Stravos hotels."

"I take it he's not happy about either of your plans." When Cristo shook his head, she added, "I'm so sorry."

Cristo's dark gaze met hers. "What do you have to be sorry about? You had nothing to do with my father."

"I'm just sorry that you had to argue."

Cristo's brows drew together. "I don't need your pity. My father is a hard, cold man. But once this deal is concluded, I'll have an international hotel chain. It'll even top my two brothers' accomplishments. My father will have no choice but to acknowledge my success. He'll have to admit I'm no longer that irresponsible boy who stood by helplessly while…while, oh, never mind. It doesn't matter now."

On the contrary, it mattered a great deal. But she wouldn't push him. As it was, she understood so much more about him and his driving motivation to make this deal a success. She couldn't even imagine how much it must hurt to need to prove your self-worth to a parent. She would do her utmost to help him.

CHAPTER EIGHT

WHAT DID HE know about planning a wedding?

Nothing. Nada. Zip. Zero.

Cristo sat on the floor of the suite with his back propped against the couch. His legs were stretched out in front of him with his ankles crossed. He couldn't remember the last time he'd had such a leisurely Sunday.

He frowned as he gazed at the glossy magazine cover that Kyra had just dropped in his lap. His gaze moved over the cover. *Finding the Perfect Dress.* He kept reading. *Wedding Night Confessions.* He groaned.

"Did you say something?" Kyra rushed over to him with an armload of magazines.

"No." He willed his phone to ring with an emergency or anything he could construe as an emergency, but the darn thing for the first time ever remained silent. He was stuck. He stifled another groan.

She settled next to him. "It helps if you open it. I've marked some pages."

He grudgingly started flipping through the pages. What he wouldn't do now for a quarterly profit report to review or the *Wall Street Journal* to peruse. Instead, he was looking at articles on which shade of nail polish go best with your gown. He turned the page to find *Flowers on a Budget.*

"Isn't it amazing all of the subjects they cover?" Kyra sounded impressed. "I've learned quite a bit from reading these magazines."

"I certainly wouldn't have thought of these things." And that was no lie. His gaze paused on the headline *Making Your Wedding Night Unforgettable.* The title evoked all sorts of tempting images of Kyra in skimpy—no, scratch that. She'd be wearing a classy white nightie that tempted and teased. He closed the magazine.

"Are you sure something isn't bothering you?" She sent him a worried look and shifted uncomfortably.

Yes. Lots. He struggled for a different subject to discuss, something that wouldn't have him imagining her on their wedding night. And then it came to him. "Actually, there's something I've been meaning to mention."

She laid her pen down on a pad of paper as though giving him her full attention. "I'm listening."

He set aside the bridal magazine with its taunting headlines and got to his feet. He retrieved his briefcase from next to the bar and removed a manila folder.

"Between meetings, I was able to pull up some preliminary information on your surname." He handed it over to her. Their fingers brushed and a wave of need washed over him. His gaze dipped to her lips. He wondered what she'd do if he were to kiss her again, because that one time just wasn't enough. Not even close.

"You did?" Her face beamed with a hopeful smile.

"Don't go getting too excited. As you probably know, it's a popular name. We're going to need more information to narrow it down. Can you remember any details your father told you? Was he born here?"

"He was born in the States. My grandmother was pregnant with him when they crossed the Atlantic."

"Hmm… That eliminates finding a birth record for your father. Did he ever hear any family names?"

She shook her head. "He said his mother didn't talk much about her family. His father told him it was because she was homesick."

"And your grandfather's family?"

"Died in a flu epidemic. He ended up being raised by friends of the family." Kyra worried her bottom lip. "I do have something that might be helpful in my bedroom."

When she went to stand, he put a hand on her shoulder.

"Let's not get sidetracked from this wedding stuff. We can go over the stuff about your family tomorrow."

"Oh." Disappointment rang out in her voice.

She held out the folder. "Thanks for these names. I know it'll be like finding a needle in a haystack, but it's a start." Her eyes grew shiny. "Who knows, I might be holding the name of a relative in my hand."

In that moment, he realized just how much this search for her family meant to her. With him being so distant from his own, Kyra's need to reconnect with hers intrigued him.

He cleared his throat. "How about we make a trip into Athens?"

"To do what?"

"I thought we'd visit the library. Hopefully they'll have lots of old documents."

She clasped her hands together and smiled. "You'd do that for me?"

He nodded. "I'd like to see you find your family."

"Really?" The smile slipped from her face. "I mean, up until now you haven't seemed very interested in helping."

He raked his fingers through his hair. How did he explain this to her when he hadn't really delved into his motives? Why exactly had this become so important to him?

Cristo cleared his throat. "I guess I know what it's like to feel alone and isolated." Wait. Was that honestly how he felt? He didn't like digging into emotions, but the captivated look on her face urged him on. "And I know that it's different because my family is alive. I chose to walk away. You never got a choice."

"Thank you for understanding." Her eyes filled with warmth. "You know, it's not too late to change your mind about reconciling with your family. In fact, this wedding is the perfect excuse to ask them to visit."

He shook his head. It wasn't going to happen. "Speaking of the wedding, didn't you have more stuff we need to go over?"

* * *

If anyone could help her track down her family, it was Cristo.

The next morning, Kyra awoke before the alarm. As she showered and dressed, thoughts of Cristo circled around in her mind. She had a good feeling about finding her family now that he was on her side. He spoke Greek fluently and could read it. He knew a great many people, including those with the Pappas name. If Cristo could point her in the right direction, she just might meet her distant relatives.

When she rushed into the living room, she found it empty. She made her way to his study. It was empty, too. Was it possible Cristo had slept in? On a Monday—a workday?

Maybe she should check on him. She started toward his room when she noticed a note on the bar. In a very distinctive scrawl with determined strokes, the blocked capital letters were surprisingly legible.

KYRA,
UNEXPECTED PROBLEM AT THE OFFICE NEEDED MY IMMEDIATE ATTENTION. I'LL MAKE IT UP TO YOU. IN THE MEANTIME, BELOW ARE SOME WEBSITES YOU MIGHT WANT TO CHECK. HOPE THEY ARE HELPFUL.
CRISTO

Frustration bubbled in Kyra's veins. Why had she believed him when he said he'd help her this morning? She clenched her hand, crinkling the paper. She should have known he'd be too busy.

She had to get out of the suite. Otherwise, she just might invest in a gallon of ice cream. That would not help slim her hips. Besides, a run in the fresh air and sunshine would hopefully soothe away her disappointment in finding out that Cristo was just like the other men she'd dated. Why in the world did she let herself imagine he would be any different?

She pushed herself long and hard. An hour or so later, she returned to the suite feeling a bit better. She was determined to find her family, with or without Cristo's help. She'd gotten this far on her own. She could make it the rest of the way.

After showering again, Kyra settled on the couch with her laptop. She smoothed out the note Cristo had left her and input the first web address, which took her to a Greek social site. Thank goodness her computer had the option to translate everything to English.

She didn't know how much time had passed when she heard the door open. With effort, she continued to stare at the monitor. Try as she might, she couldn't think about anything but the sexy man now standing behind her.

"Hello, Kyra." His deep voice washed over her.

"Hi." She stubbornly refused to make this easy for him. He was the one who'd broken their date as though she should totally understand that business trumps all else, all of the time.

He moved to stand at the end of the couch. "Aren't you even going to look at me?"

Was that some sort of challenge? She glanced at him and then turned back to her computer, already forgetting the site she wanted to visit next. "Did you need something?"

"So this is how it's going to be?"

She closed her laptop and turned to him. "What is that supposed to mean?"

"That you're mad because I had work to do."

She hated how he made it seem as if her search to find her family was so unimportant. If only he knew how much her mother needed it—how much she needed it. "It doesn't matter. I did fine on my own."

"You did?" There was genuine enthusiasm in Cristo's

voice as he slid off his suit jacket and draped it over the back of a black leather armchair.

She nodded. "I was able to connect with some people online who pointed me toward some helpful information."

"That's great. Were the sites I left you of any help?"

"Yes. Thank you."

Cristo sat down on the couch and rolled up his sleeves. "I know I let you down today, and I'm truly sorry about that." His gaze met hers, making her heart thump. "But I'm here now and I'd like to do what I can to help. And tomorrow we're off to Athens to do research."

She sent him a hesitant look. "You don't have to. I know you have a lot of work to do—"

"And it can wait. I really do want to help. I promise no emergency will hold us up. So is it a plan?"

He'd apologized and it was a soothing balm to her bruised pride. She smiled. "It's a plan."

"Good. Now, why don't I look over what you have so far while you order room service."

That sounded reasonable to her. "I'll be right back." She rushed out of the room, hoping he wouldn't grow frustrated with her lack of documentation. Seconds later, she returned. "Here's everything."

He accepted the black-and-white snapshot of a young couple obviously very much in love. He turned it over to glance at the back before looking at her. His eyes reflected his confusion. "Where are the birth records, marriage certificates or family bible?"

"I…I don't have them. When my mother realized I was going to continue my father's mission, she gave me this photo. Everything else was destroyed in a fire when my father was a kid. That's a picture of my grandparents here in Greece before they moved to the States."

Cristo glanced back at the black-and-white image. "This isn't a lot to go on."

"But it's a start, isn't it?"

He sighed. "I supposed it is. Do you mind if I borrow this?" He hurried to add, "It won't be long. I just want to make a high-quality copy of it."

Her chest tightened. She couldn't stand the thought of losing the only solid link to her past, but as of right now, it was of no help to her. "Go ahead. Do what you need to." Then for her own peace of mind, she asked, "Do you think there are any clues in it?"

He held up the photo. "I'm interested in the background. If we have it enlarged, we might be able to locate where the photo was taken."

"I used a magnifying glass, but I couldn't make out any signs."

"I'm thinking more about the architecture. If it's unique enough, it could point us in the right direction. Now, show me what you came up with online."

Kyra readily opened her laptop, eager to share the tidbits of information. It was a lot like a jigsaw puzzle. She welcomed the help in figuring out how the information fit together and discerning which information didn't belong.

And at last she had Cristo's full attention. Best of all, the more they talked, the more excited he became with the project. He filled her with hope that at last she might find any lingering relatives.

They sat in the living room all evening, scouring the internet and eating room service. Kyra saw a different side of Cristo, a down-to-earth quality. And she liked it. A lot.

Now, how could she get him to let down his guard again? She really enjoyed seeing him smile.

CHAPTER NINE

IT HADN'T WORKED out quite as he'd planned.

Cristo glanced over at Kyra as their limo inched its way through the congested streets of Athens. "I'm sorry our visit to the library wasn't more productive."

"It's not your fault. After all, you helped me search through countless newspapers, journals and books. We may not have uncovered anything, but it wasn't for lack of trying."

He breathed a little easier. "Don't give up. We still have the picture of your grandparents. It's got to have some clues."

She lowered her head and shrugged. "Perhaps."

Even though they weren't able to track down any documents with her grandparents' names, he refused to give up and she couldn't, either. "You know that library is huge. They have thousands of documents. I'm sure we've barely even scratched the surface. We'll just keep at it until we head in the right direction."

"You're right. It's just so frustrating."

"Then think about something else for a while."

"Actually, I do have some questions for you." She withdrew a notebook and pen from her purse. "How many people are you considering inviting to the wedding?"

"You want to do this here? Now?"

"What else do we have to do?"

Some tempting thoughts sprang to mind. "I can think of something a lot more fun."

His gaze moved to the partition that was currently down. If he was to put it up, they'd have all the privacy needed and then he could claim her lips.

A smile tugged at her lips. "That's not what I meant."

"But I promise you'll enjoy it." He playfully reached out for her, but she scooted away. He frowned at her. "Fine. You win. What was it you wanted to know?"

"How big should the wedding be?"

"I'm thinking something small and intimate. Maybe five hundred people."

"Five hundred?" Kyra's mouth gaped. "Are you serious?"

He shrugged. "What were you thinking?"

"Twenty would work for me. But I know you're a very popular person, so how about one hundred people?"

That wasn't many people. There was family, business associates and employees to consider. Still, there was a certain appeal to an intimate gathering. "Considering we'll be having the ceremony here in Athens rather than in New York, I'm guessing you won't be having many guests."

She shook her head.

Surely he could cut back on the invites. He gave it a bit of thought. "I should be able to get out of inviting a number of people because of the location. It'll take some effort, but I think we can make one hundred people work."

She noted something in her day planner. "I've done some online research and there are invitation addressing and mailing services. I think at this late date it'd be our best option. For a fee, I can put a rush on the order."

"Yes. Yes. The price doesn't matter."

She reached in her purse for an electronic tablet. "What's your favorite color?"

"Why?"

"I need it for the invitations." Her fingers moved rapidly over the screen.

"I guess it's blue." He honestly didn't think anyone had ever asked him that question. "And what's yours?"

"My what?" she asked as though she had been lost in thought.

"Your favorite color?"

"It's aqua." She focused on the tablet and then said, "I've got some invitations picked out. It's just a matter of narrowing them down. Ah, here's one that uses both of our colors. How about a beach-theme invitation with the background being the sand and water with a blue sky?" She turned the screen around for him to see a picture of the proposed invitation. "And for a fee they can add a gold ribbon and starfish. They'll be sent in little blue boxes."

If she liked it, that was good enough for him. "Go ahead and place the order. And you're sure it'll get to everyone in time?"

She nodded. "As long as you give me those names and addresses today."

He was afraid she'd say that. "I'll list the names and my assistant can give you the addresses."

"You do know that once we send out the invitations your family and friends will know about this thing between us. How are you going to explain the fact they've never met me or even heard of me?"

He hadn't thought of that. "I'll tell them the truth. That we met here at the resort…and it was love at first sight."

"And you think they'll believe it?"

"Most definitely. You're so gorgeous, how could I not be captivated by you?"

"You're making that up."

"I could never make up something like that. Between your beauty and your warm personality, I'm not sure which won me over first."

He wished he was better with words. If he was, he'd tell her how her big brown eyes glittered with specks of gold. They were utterly mesmerizing. Her cheeks held a rosy hue. And her lips…well, they were so sweet and tempting. He knew that for a fact because the kiss they'd shared was forever imprinted upon his mind.

And when he was alone, it wasn't facts and figures that filled his mind these days, it was figuring out how to steal another kiss. Perhaps he could suggest they practice some more, so that it seemed natural when they had to do it in front of people.

He may not be able to articulate how she made him feel, but he could show her. Going with the moment and refusing to consider the implications, he reached his hand out to her. His thumb traced her jaw. "You're the most amazing woman I've ever known."

She continued to stare into his eyes. His heart pounded against his ribs. Did she have any idea what she could do to him with just a look? He should back away.

But he needed to taste her once more. His gaze dipped to her shimmery lips. Instead of the calm, sophisticated businessman that he liked to portray to the world, right now he felt like a nervous teenage boy.

The tug-of-war between right and wrong raged within him. All the while his fingers continued to stroke her smooth skin. His pulse quickened and the pounding of his heart drowned out the voices.

He leaned forward. His lips claimed hers. Gently and hesitantly. He had no idea if she felt the same way.

But then her hands moved over his shoulders and wrapped around his neck. Her mouth moved beneath his. No kiss had ever rocked his world like hers. He didn't know what was so different about her. He just knew he never seemed to get enough.

His phone buzzed and Kyra pulled away.

Of all the lousy times. Cristo swore under his breath. With the moment ruined, he reached for his phone. "Kiriakas here."

"Mr. Cristo Kiriakas?"

"Speaking." He really should have checked the caller ID, because he didn't recognize the female voice.

"I'm calling on behalf of Nikolaos Stravos. He would like to know if you are available for dinner."

She named a date in the coming week. The acceptance

teetered on the tip of Cristo's tongue, but he held it back for just a moment—just long enough so this employee of Stravos's didn't know just how anxious he was for this meeting. After a slow, deep breath in and out, Cristo said, "As it happens, I could rearrange my calendar."

"He also requested you bring your fiancée. Would that be possible?"

Cristo's gaze moved to Kyra's beautiful face. "Yes, we will both be able to attend."

"Good." The woman filled him in on the details.

When Cristo disconnected the call, he was a bit stunned. His plan was really working. Okay, so he had had a few doubts along the way. And when his father had insisted he was doomed to fail, his confidence had wavered just a bit. But thanks to Kyra sticking by his side, he'd kept moving forward and it had paid off.

Curiosity glittered in Kyra's eyes. "Well?"

"That was one of Stravos's employees. He wants to have dinner."

"Really?" Kyra clapped her hands tightly together. "This is good, isn't it?"

He nodded.

"Yay! Congratulations." A big grin lit up her entire face.

For a moment, he didn't move. He'd been so stunned by her rush of emotions. He wasn't used to people getting outwardly excited. His family and coworkers were quite reserved. But maybe just this once, it wouldn't hurt to follow her lead. He smiled.

"And it's all thanks to you."

"Me?" She pressed a hand to her chest. "I didn't do anything."

He wasn't going to argue with her, but he couldn't have done any of this without her. And it wasn't just the dinner—she'd gotten him to remember that there was more to life than work. And she'd reminded him how good it felt to smile—really smile, the kind that started on the inside and radiated outward.

Cristo cleared his throat. “Dinner is next weekend.”

Her smile turned upside down. “But I have absolutely nothing to wear. I’m presuming this will be a formal affair.”

“Yes, it will be. Mr. Stravos is very old-fashioned and quite proper.”

“What will you be wearing?”

“A black suit.” Then witnessing the mounting stress on her face, he added, “You’ll want something stunning. Something that will turn heads.”

“Really?”

“Most definitely. I want Stravos to see just how amazing you are. Don’t worry. When we get back to the resort, I’ll ring downstairs and arrange to have the boutique send up their best dresses for you to choose from.”

The worry lines faded from her face. “You’d do that for me?”

There was a whole lot he’d do for her, but he kept it to himself. “Of course. After all, you are doing me the favor.”

And with that he made a point of answering emails on his phone. He needed some time to straighten out his jumbled thoughts. Kyra had an effect on him unlike any other. And that wasn’t good. He needed to be sharp and focused for his meeting with Stravos.

CHAPTER TEN

THE WEEK HAD flown by what with wedding plans and studying.

At last Friday had arrived as well as Kyra's generous paycheck.

She frowned. *That just can't be right.* She disconnected the phone call with a bank in New York after attempting to make a payment on her mother's mortgage. The problem was the bank didn't want to take her money. They said the mortgage had been paid in full. *How could that be?*

She immediately dialed her mother's number. Maybe her mother had moved the mortgage to another bank. That had to be it, because her mother wouldn't have called the other week panicked if the mortgage had been mysteriously paid off.

"Hi, Kyra." Her mother's pleasant voice sounded so clear that it was as if she was next door, not an ocean away. "I can't talk long. I'm at work. At least I still have one job—"

"Mom, we need to talk."

"Okay. About what?"

"The mortgage."

"Have you changed your mind about coming home? I'm sure between the two of us, we can make the payment."

"Where's the mortgage?"

"What do you mean? It's at the bank, of course."

Something wasn't adding up. "The same bank Dad used?"

"Yes. But you don't need to contact them. I'm taking care of everything. I…I explained that the next payment might be late. They were very understanding."

An understanding bank? The words sounded off-key. In fact, her mother wasn't quite acting like herself.

"Kyra, I need to go. We can talk later."

At last Kyra could no longer deny the truth. Her mother was lying to her. The knowledge sliced into her heart. The one person she was supposed to be able to blindly trust was capable of deceit. But why?

"Mom! Stop! I know the truth."

"What truth? I don't know what you're talking about." Her mother's voice was unusually high-pitched.

"I just called the bank. They told me the mortgage has been paid in full for the past year since…since Dad died. How could you do it?" A rush of emotions had Kyra blinking repeatedly. "How could you let me believe Dad had let us down—that he left us in debt?"

"Kyra, you have to understand. I did it all for you—"

"Me? No. You did it for yourself. You lied and connived so you could control me."

"You're wrong! You don't understand. I couldn't lose you, too. We need each other."

"Not anymore." Kyra pressed the end button on her phone.

In a matter of minutes, everything she thought she knew about her life and her family had come undone. She swiped away a tear as it streaked down her face. How could her mother let her think the worst of her father—that he was irresponsible and careless? None of it was true. Her father wasn't perfect, but he had taken care of them.

The walls were closing in.

Kyra paced back and forth in the suite. Her thoughts raced until her head started to pound. What she needed was a distraction—something to calm her down. First she phoned Cristo, then she called Sofia. She struck out twice.

Everyone but her had plans on a Friday night. Cristo was away on business. And even Sofia had plans with some friends from the housekeeping department. That left Kyra on her own. And there was no way she was going to thumb through any more bridal magazines, conduct any further internet searches for a clue to her family or study for her online classes.

She opened the French doors leading out to the private balcony. The moon shone overheard and reflected off the serene cove. She leaned against the rail, enjoying the warmth of the evening air.

How was she ever supposed to trust anyone after this? Her mother had lied to her. And not just a little fib, but an ongoing whopper of a tale. If it hadn't been for her mother, she wouldn't be standing in this extravagant suite pretending to be Cristo's bride. Did her mother have any idea what her lies had done to Kyra's life?

The lapping sound of the cove beckoned to her. It would be just perfect for a nighttime dip. After all, she'd been in Greece for several weeks, and she had yet to stick her toes in the clear, inviting water. Tonight she would remedy that.

Determined to wear off some of her frustration after speaking to her mother, Kyra rushed to her room and slipped on her brand-new turquoise bikini. She scribbled a note for Cristo, just in case he returned sometime that evening and actually noticed her absence. With a white crocheted cover-up and flip-flops, she rushed to the beach.

She discarded her cover-up and towel on the sand. The water was warm and she waded farther in. This would be the perfect way to clear her mind. But even then, thoughts of betrayal ate at her.

Ever since her father died, she had worked so hard to be the perfect daughter, to put her mother's needs first, to play by the rules. But no more. Now she was going to do what she wanted—what made her happy.

Kyra moved farther into the water until it was up to her shoulders. Was it wrong that she sometimes wondered what it would have been like if she and Cristo had met under different circumstances? Would he have asked her out just because he found her attractive or intriguing? She sighed with regret over never knowing the answer.

She fell back in the water and began to float. So far, Cristo had been nothing but a gentleman…when he wasn't working. Which wasn't often. She really wondered if anyone would believe he was madly in love with her. She started to do the backstroke. A few strong strokes and then she coasted.

Thoughts of Cristo crowded her mind. Though he could be sweet and was devastatingly handsome, he didn't have room in his life for a woman because he already had a mistress—his work. And his mistress was demanding—too demanding. Or was he using his work as an excuse to avoid a serious relationship? If so, why?

There was a splash of water behind her. The little hairs on the back of her neck lifted. She wasn't alone. Her gaze sought out the shore. She wasn't far from it, but could she get there before whoever it was caught her?

She started for the shore when a hand reached out and caught her foot. A scream tore from her lungs. She started to struggle, splashing water in her eyes.

"Kyra! It's me. Cristo."

She stopped struggling. "What in the world are you doing? Trying to scare me to death?"

"Sorry. You looked so peaceful floating on the water that I didn't want to ruin the moment."

"Well, you certainly did that. I didn't hear you." And then she caught sight of his muscular chest. Okay, so maybe she wasn't so upset about him joining her. The moon reflected off the droplets of water on his bare flesh, making it quite tempting to reach out and slide her fingertips over his skin. Her fingers tingled at the thought.

"It wasn't my intention to startle you. It's just when I got back to the suite and saw your note, a night swim sounded like a good idea. I thought I'd join you, but if you want me to go, I'll understand."

"No. Stay." She tried to catch a glimpse of what he was wearing, but the water was too dark to make out anything.

So she was left to wonder what sort of swimwear he preferred. Perhaps he was skinny-dipping. Nah, not Cristo. He was too proper. Maybe it was a pair of those itty-bitty bikini bottoms. She immediately rejected the image. Perhaps he wore some shorty-shorts—better yet low-slung board shorts.

Cristo's gaze met hers. "You're sure you want me to stay?"

She nodded, still working up the courage to reach out and run her hands over his chest. "I'm actually happy to see you. I thought you'd be working until late."

"I had something better to do." A mischievous smile lit up his face, making him even more handsome.

Was he flirting with her? It sure sounded like it to her. A smile pulled at her lips. "And what would that be?"

His voice lowered. "Spend time with my fiancée. Didn't you say it was important we learn more about each other?"

"I did. Do you swim much?"

"Wait a sec. This was my idea. I get to ask the first question."

"And what would that be?"

His gaze narrowed. "Have you ever gone skinny-dipping?"

Thankfully the moonlight wasn't that bright, because Kyra was certain her cheeks were bright red. "No."

"Oh, come on," he coaxed. "You can tell me."

"I am. I haven't. But I take it you have."

He nonchalantly shrugged. "I was at boarding school. It was a dare. There was no way I could back out."

She shook her head. "You must have been a handful as a kid."

"And you were a straight-A student and a Goody Two-shoes who did no wrong."

Was she really that predictable? She stuck her tongue

out at him. He let out a deep laugh that made her stomach flip-flop.

Still chuckling, he turned and swam away from the beach. The gentle lap of the water filled the quietness of the evening. No way was he getting away that easily. She followed him.

They paddled around the cove, laughing, playing and enjoying the intimacy of having the water to themselves. Okay, so maybe Cristo wasn't a complete workaholic. Kyra's cheeks began to ache as she continued to smile, but she couldn't help herself. Tonight Cristo was engaging and entertaining. Just what she needed to take her mind off her troubles.

She moved up next to him. "I'm surprised you'd take the evening off to splash around the cove with me."

"What, you thought I'd forgotten how to have a good time?"

She shrugged. "Something like that."

"Well, I'm glad to prove you wrong." He cupped his hands together and sent water splashing in her direction.

She sputtered, caught off guard. She swiped the water from her eyes to find Cristo grinning. No way was she letting him get away with that. She held her arm out at her side and swiped it along the surface of the water, sending a much larger spray in his direction. The next thing she knew they were engaged in a heated water battle until Kyra's arms grew tired and she gave up the victory to him.

"Is my water nymph worn-out?" Cristo moved closer.

"Yes." She leaned her head back, dipping her long hair in the water before smoothing it into place. "Aren't you tired, too?"

"Not too tired to do this." His hands slipped around her waist, pulling her close.

His lips claimed hers. What was up with him? He'd kept his distance from her after the kiss in the limo. Perhaps it had confused him as much as it had her. Whatever it was, she approved.

His mouth moved lightly, tentatively as though testing the waters. Her hands moved to his bare shoulders, enjoying the feel of his muscles beneath her fingertips.

As the kiss deepened, her legs wrapped around his waist. The kiss went on and on. They definitely had this part of their relationship down pat. Then again, maybe a little more practice would be good.

Cristo carried her out of the water. All the while their kiss continued, and Kyra's heart pounded. Could this really be happening? Was she really falling head over heels for this man?

She couldn't think clearly. It was as though the full moon had cast a spell over them—anything seemed possible. And she didn't want this moment to end—not now—not ever.

However, when a breeze rushed over her wet skin, a chill set in. She pulled back. In the moonlight, she stared into Cristo's puzzled gaze.

She attempted to steady her rushed breathing in order to speak. "We can't keep this up. What if someone sees?"

"They'll probably get some ideas of their own." His brows lifted. "You do remember we're supposed to act like we're on a romantic getaway, right? Consider this a dress rehearsal."

His words were like a cold shower. Was that really what he thought they were doing here? Putting on a show? The realization stabbed at her heart. Here she was getting caught up in the moment and he was figuring out how to get the most mileage out of their public display of affection.

She untangled her limbs from him. Goose bumps raced over her flesh, but the heat of her indignation offset the chill of the night air. "It's getting late. We should go inside."

"And continue this?" There was genuine hope in his voice.

"Um...no. I think we have this kissing stuff down pat."

"Are you sure? I'm thinking I might need a little more practice."

"You do remember this is all make-believe, right?" With each passing day, she found it harder and harder to draw the line between their fake engagement and real life. The lines kept blurring and they were starting to fade away.

Cristo sighed. "I remember. And tomorrow night will be our big test. Do you think we can pull it off?"

"I think we have a good chance. But when we're alone, we can't keep forgetting about the boundaries in this pretend relationship."

Cristo stepped back. "Is that what you really want? Because while we were out in the water, I got the distinct impression you wanted more."

For a while there, she thought she could play the part of girl gone wild. The truth was, while her mother's actions had hurt her deeply, she was still the same person inside, just a bit more scarred.

"I…I didn't mean to lead you on." She glanced away.

He placed a finger beneath her chin and lifted until their gazes met. "Talk to me. You're not acting like yourself. What's going on?"

"It's nothing."

"It's definitely something." His voice was low and soothing. "I'm your friend. I'd like to be there for you. If you'd let me."

She moved to where she'd left her towel and cover-up. Maybe it would help to talk about it. Cristo would know that he wasn't alone with his problems coping with his parents.

As she dried off, she chanced a quick glance over her shoulder in order to satisfy her curiosity. He indeed was wearing a pair of dark board shorts with a white stripe around each leg. In the moonlight, his shorts hung low enough to show off his trim abs. His head lifted and their gazes met. He ran a towel over his chest, but he didn't say a word. It was as though he was waiting for her to start the conversation.

She slipped on her crocheted cover-up. She spread out her towel on the sand and sat down. "Join me."

He did. His shoulder brushed against hers. She ignored the nervous quiver his touch set off in her stomach.

"The reason I agreed to play the part of your fiancée was because it allowed me to help my mother. But today, I learned that everything I believed is…is a lie." She went on to reveal her mother's duplicity. The whole sordid story.

When it was all out there, Cristo draped an arm over her shoulders and pulled her close. She let her head rest against his shoulder, taking comfort in his touch. He didn't have to say a word. There was comfort and understanding in his touch.

She didn't know how much time had passed before they started for their suite. This gentle side of Cristo was even harder for her to resist. But she knew that if she let Cristo get too close, he'd wedge his way into her heart. From that point forward, she would forever be comparing every man she met to Cristo. And she already knew they wouldn't live up to Cristo's larger-than-life personality.

She couldn't let that happen. She had to stay strong for a little longer.

CHAPTER ELEVEN

So this is what it's like to ride in a helicopter.

Kyra gazed out the window as the lights of the Blue Tide faded into the distance. She was never going to forget this experience.

Thankfully she'd had the forethought to document it. She stared down at the new photo on her phone. It was of her and Cristo standing next to the helicopter in their evening clothes. If she didn't know better, they really did look like a genuine couple. Cristo was so sexy in his black suit, black dress shirt and steel-gray tie. Any woman would be out of her mind not to want to be on his arm. She cast Cristo a glance, surprised to see he was staring back at her. Her stomach dipped.

She would have liked to talk to him, but the *whoop-whoop* of the helicopter blades made that difficult. Even the headset Cristo had given her hadn't done much to offset the rumbling sound. She turned to stare out the window. The brilliant rays of pink, orange and purple of the setting sun took her breath away.

She adjusted the beaded, pearl-colored bodice of her strapless dress. Cristo had told her to go with something stunning. She truly hoped this dress was what he'd had in mind. With him being tense over the upcoming dinner, he hadn't seemed to notice her, much less her dress.

Thankfully the saleswoman assured Kyra the dress was made for her. The crystal-beaded bodice led to a beaded waist followed by a hi-low handkerchief skirt of sky blue. She wiggled her freshly pedicured toes in the new silver heels with a rhinestone strap. She couldn't remember the last time she'd been this dolled up.

Kyra glanced over at her dashing escort. She was really hoping he would notice all of her hard work. As though he'd sensed her staring, he glanced her way. Their gazes met. He reached out, taking her hand in his and giving it a reassuring squeeze. His warm touch calmed the fluttering sensation in her stomach. She wanted so desperately to help him today, but she worried whether she'd be able to pull it off.

The helicopter touched down on a fully lit helipad not far from an impressive coastal mansion. The grounds surrounding the white mansion with a red tile roof were illuminated by strategically placed spotlights. Kyra was awed by the enormity of the home.

After Cristo helped her exit the helicopter, she turned to him. "One man lives here? All by himself?"

Cristo's gaze moved to the mansion and then back to her. "His grandson lives with him. And I'm sure there's a household staff."

"I'd get lonely." She turned all around, not finding any signs of neighbors. "This place really is isolated out here on this island."

"Don't worry." Cristo wrapped his arm around her waist and pulled her to his side. He placed a kiss upon the top of her head. His voice lowered. "You're safe with me."

She lifted her chin and gazed into his eyes. She couldn't read his thoughts. But when he ran a finger along her cheek, her heart went *tip-tap-tap* in her chest. Was he being sincere? Or was this just another performance?

"Welcome." A male voice interrupted the moment. "I'm Mr. Stravos's butler."

With great regret, she turned to find an older gentleman standing off to the side of the helipad. Immediately, her heart settled back to its normal pace. So Cristo had seen the man approaching and it had all been a show.

Right now, all she wanted to do was pull away from Cristo. She felt foolish and gullible. But considering their agreement, she was stuck acting as his loving and devoted fiancée. She choked down her disappointment.

Cristo took her hand and placed it in the crook of his arm. They followed the butler to the grand house. The sand and sea were only a few yards away. The lull of the water pounding the rocky cliff filled in the silence. The walkway led them to a portico that stretched the length of the house. Impressive columns were placed every ten feet or so.

At the center of the structure was a courtyard. A wrought-iron gate stood open, welcoming them into the tiled area. A working water fountain stood prominently in the middle highlighted with different colored lights.

Surrounding the fountain sat various groupings of patio furniture, from a wrought-iron picnic table for four to a couple of cushioned loungers. At the far end stood a fireplace. It glowed as a log burned in it. Kyra was awed by the entire courtyard.

A tug on her arm had her realizing they were being led inside. Kyra grudgingly followed along. She had a job to do this evening and she intended to do her best. The sooner Cristo had a signed agreement, the sooner this arrangement between them would end. Cristo would have his precious contract and she'd have her life back.

Though her stomach quivered with nerves, Kyra knew how to do this. At last there was some benefit from the years of witnessing her mother putting on airs for her friends. Kyra knew how to embellish and imply things without outright lying. It was an art of inflection and knowing what to leave out. Her mother was an expert, and it'd only gotten worse since the death of Kyra's father. Kyra shoved the troubling thought to the back of her mind. Right now, she had a job to do.

The living room was quite formal with two full-length white couches facing each other. There were four wing-backed chairs in burgundy upholstery. At the far end of the room was a prominent stone fireplace. On the perimeter were various types of artwork from a bust of some Greek hero to paintings of historical figures and the Greek ruins.

When Kyra went to free her hand from Cristo's in order to further explore her surroundings, he tightened his grip. What in the world? Was he worried that she'd slip away and leave him on his own?

"Welcome." Another man entered the room. He approached them and smiled. But she noticed immediately that his smile didn't quite reach his eyes. "I'm Nikolaos Stravos III, but please call me Niko."

The man was approximately Cristo's age. Niko was handsome in a tall and dark kind of way. But in Kyra's mind, he didn't hold a candle to Cristo. And it was then she realized she was starting to measure other men according to Cristo's yardstick. Not good. Not good at all.

She tried to see Niko clearly without the comparison to the larger-than-life man at her side. Niko had dark wavy hair, which was finger-combed back off his face. It was a very relaxed look for a man whose grandfather seemed so old-fashioned. Or maybe that was why Niko had a casual appearance—it was opposite of what his grandfather would want. The fact he would stand up to the senior Stravos instead of catering to the older man scored him a few points in Kyra's book.

Cristo shook his hand and introduced himself before turning to her. "And this is my fiancée, Kyra Pappas."

She presented what she hoped was a bright and friendly smile. "I'm pleased to meet you."

Cristo cleared his throat. "Will your grandfather be able to join us this evening?"

Niko's face creased with lines. "I hope you won't be too upset to learn that I'm the one who invited you here."

"You? But why?" It wasn't Cristo who spoke those words but rather Kyra. And it wasn't until the words were out there, followed by an awkward silence, that she realized she shouldn't have spoken so freely. The heat of embarrassment rose up her neck as both men cast her raised brows.

Niko lifted his chiseled chin as he faced Cristo again. "As I was saying, my grandfather is quite set in his ways and I've been trying to talk him into making some changes."

Cristo sent her a warning look not to say anything else. He turned back to their host. "And you are the one considering selling off the hotel chain?"

"How about we dine first? Everything is ready now."

"And your grandfather? Will he be joining us later?"

"He has a lot of work to deal with. But I mentioned the dinner to him earlier today." Niko waved the way to the dining room.

At least food would give her something to do, since talking hadn't gone so well for her. Not a great way to start the evening. The problem was her nervousness. Cristo's tension had rubbed off on her and now she had to relax if she wanted to help her fiancé.

Why had Stravos's grandson requested this meeting?

Cristo attempted to keep up the light conversation about football. All the while, he kept wondering if there'd been a shift in power in the Stravos organization. But how would his investigators have missed such huge news? The answer was they wouldn't have.

Though the dinner itself was quite a delicious affair, Cristo had a hard time enjoying it. He hadn't come here for good food and company. He'd wanted to negotiate a deal or, at a bare minimum, find out what it'd take to strike a deal with Stravos. So far, he knew no more than when he'd arrived at the estate.

"Thank you for the delicious dinner." Kyra folded her linen napkin and set it aside.

"It was my pleasure." Niko pushed back his chair. "I thought we would have dessert out in the courtyard."

"That would be wonderful. I just love what you've done

with it." Kyra continued to chatter on about nothing specific, just making idle conversation to fill in the empty spots in the conversation—empty spots left by Cristo's prolonged silence.

He knew he should be friendlier. But he also knew the grandson didn't possess the control needed to make this venture a reality. Right now, he was left hoping for a miracle.

They made their way to the courtyard. Niko turned back to him. "Would you care for some more coffee?"

When Cristo declined, Niko moved to the wrought-iron table with a glass top that held a tray with a coffee carafe as well as cream and sugar. Once his cup was filled, he took a seat in the chair opposite Cristo.

Now that dinner was over and they'd made idle chitchat, it was time to get to the point of this get-together. "I hate to ruin this lovely evening with talk of business, but I was wondering what your thoughts are regarding the sale of the Stravos Star Hotels."

"I've given the subject of selling off the chain considerable thought. My question for you is, why are you so interested in the purchase when you already have a hotel chain of your own?"

"The Glamour Hotel and Casino chain is a North American venture. What I'd like to see happen is to merge the two chains and give the discriminating traveler the global availability of staying with a chain they are comfortable with—that keeps track of their preferences in our universal concierge system. That way, no matter which location they stay in, they'll feel like they're at home."

Niko's eyes lit up. "I take it you have already implemented this feature in your existing hotels?"

"We have, and it has created a large increase in return clientele. You don't have to worry about the Stravos Star Hotels. Though the name will change, the quality will remain exemplary."

They continued into a more detailed discussion of what each of them would like to see take place with the sale. For the most part, there was mutual agreement. There were other areas that were a bit sticky, but Cristo didn't see them as insurmountable hurdles. No deal was ever achieved without its share of negotiating.

Niko set aside his now-empty coffee cup. "I know that if the time comes, our assistants and attorneys can hash through all of this, presenting us with long, dry memos, but I suppose I'm more like my grandfather than I care to admit. I like to be personally involved when it comes to the decisions that will change the course of Stravos Holdings."

"I can appreciate the personal touch. My father is the opposite. He would rather sit in his ivory tower and read reports."

"What a shame to spend so much time locked away in an office." Kyra's eyes pleaded with him to follow her conversation. "I'd love to hear what it's like to live out here on this private island."

"It's quiet." Niko smiled as he settled back in his chair.

There was more business he wanted to discuss, but perhaps Kyra was right. And Niko seemed like a decent man. "I bet there's good fishing."

"I must admit that I'm not much of a fisherman." Niko refilled his coffee before turning to Kyra. "I'm sure you'd grow bored out here."

"Unless I found something to amuse me."

Was she flirting with Niko? Cristo sat up a bit straighter. Her gaze immediately swung around to him.

"I could definitely imagine some leisurely mornings." Did she just smile and wink at him?

As the playful conversation continued, Cristo forgot about his business agenda and enjoyed the moment. Kyra was captivating and could take most mundane subjects, turn them on their heads and find an interesting angle he hadn't thought of before.

There was a natural warmth and friendliness about her that he hadn't experienced with the other women he'd dated. He started to wonder if this was what life would be like with an amazing lady by his side, one who supported and loved him. And then realizing the dangerous direction of his thoughts, he drew them up short.

Much too soon the conversation wound down and everyone got to their feet. Cristo didn't want the evening to end. He hadn't been this relaxed and happy in a long time.

"Thank you so much for having us." Kyra smiled at Niko.

Cristo held out his arm to escort her back to the helipad. When her hand looped through the crook of his arm, all felt right again. With her by his side, he didn't have to pretend. It felt as though this was how things were meant to be.

They'd just turned for the gate when there was the sound of footsteps behind them. Assuming it was one of the household staff, Cristo kept moving toward the portico.

"Grandfather, come meet our company."

"Very well." There was a gruff tone to the man's voice.

Cristo turned, having absolutely no idea how this initial meeting would go. The one thing he did know through his abundant research was that the senior Nikolaos Stravos was not a social man. The man preferred his privacy, but he loved his grandson above all else. Hopefully Niko would have some sway with the older man.

Cristo's eyes met a slightly hunched man who in his prime would have towered over Cristo. The man's wavy hair was snow-white and his matching beard and mustache were clipped short. On his nose were perched a pair of black-rimmed reading glasses. It appeared he had been hard at work just as his grandson had claimed.

"Grandfather, please meet Cristo Kiriakas."

Cristo stepped forward and held out his hand. "It's good to meet you, sir. I've heard a lot about you."

The man studied him as though trying to decide if he

wanted to shake it or not. At last the man accepted the gesture. His grip was firm and the handshake was brief.

The senior Stravos pulled back but kept his gaze on Cristo. With his arms crossed, he frowned. Cristo did not have a good feeling about this meeting—not good at all. Was the man always this hostile?

"Grandfather, wouldn't you like to meet Kyra—"

"What I'd like is to know why this man has been digging around in my business and my life." The man's voice was deep and rumbled with anger.

"Excuse me?" Cristo feigned innocence while he figured out how best to handle this situation.

"There is no excuse for the level of digging your men have been doing. Did you really think you'd find whatever you were searching for?"

Perhaps Cristo had been a bit zealous with his quest to make this deal a reality.

Before he could find an appropriate response, Kyra stepped forward. "I'm sure Cristo meant no harm. He's from the States and, well, I think we do things differently from how you do them over here."

Senior Stravos cast her a quick glance. "I should say so. We know when not to cross a line. We have respect—manners."

"Cristo does get excited about business. Sometimes he gets wrapped up in a project to the exclusion of everything and everyone."

Why was she making excuses for him? Didn't she think he could handle this situation on his own? Not that he'd done a good job so far.

"What my fiancée is trying to say is that I like to do my research before I start negotiations. I like to know everything about who I'm about to do business with. I'm sorry if that offended you or if my team overstepped. That was not my intention."

The man's bushy brows drew together. "And what exactly do you think you have to offer me?"

"Money. And lots of it for your hotel chain."

The man's eyes widened. He turned to his grandson. "Did you know about this?"

"I did."

"And I suppose you think it's a good idea."

Niko straightened his shoulders and met the older man's gaze straight on. "You know I do. We've talked about it numerous times."

"But I didn't know you'd gone behind my back to bring in an outsider to try to sway my opinion."

"It's not like that. You knew I was still exploring the idea of selling off the chain and you knew I invited Cristo here for dinner. I asked you repeatedly to join us."

Nikolaos sighed in exasperation. "I told you I was busy. Besides, a dinner won't change my mind about selling."

This was worse than Cristo had been imagining. This man could give his own father lessons in being obstinate. How in the world was Cristo going to sway the older man to reconsider his position?

Obviously money for a billionaire wouldn't be a deciding factor. It had to be something else—something more personal. But what?

CHAPTER TWELVE

KYRA KNEW CRISTO was in trouble.

Everything he'd been working toward was about to go up in flames—if it hadn't already. She wanted to help, but she didn't know how. And she didn't want to make matters worse.

"You have a very beautiful home here." Kyra smiled at the older man, hoping the neutral subject would ease tensions. "Thanks so much for having us. I can't get over how charming your courtyard is. I especially love the flowers."

The man gazed at her for a moment before turning away. But then his gaze came back to her. There was a strange look in his eyes—like one would give to a person they loosely recognized but couldn't quite place. "Are you American?"

"Yes, I am. My family's from New York."

Mr. Stravos moved to stand next to her, blocking Cristo from the conversation. "And you're in Greece on a holiday?"

There was a slight pause as she debated how honest to be with him. When Cristo went to step forward and intervene, Niko shook his head. This was all up to Kyra. She swallowed hard. Honesty was always the best policy. "I actually came to Greece to work."

"Work? You work for Cristo?"

Kyra might not be a high-powered businessman like everyone else in the room, but she wasn't stupid. She knew Mr. Stravos was on a fishing expedition. He wanted to know if she and Cristo were truly an item or if this was just a scam to secure a business deal. "It started that way, but when we met it was love at first sight."

"Hmpf." Mr. Stravos didn't sound impressed. "So you two don't know each other?"

"That's not true." She'd been learning lots about Cristo, but what she didn't know was where things stood between them. Those kisses they'd shared weren't just for show—no matter what Cristo said. There had been red-hot passion in them. And the way Cristo had looked at her the other night beneath the moonlight in the cove had gone beyond putting on a show for others. There had been hunger and need in his eyes. And there was the way he made her heart race, unlike any man she'd ever met. "How much do you have to know about someone to know they are very special?"

The man's bushy brows rose. "I knew my late wife from childhood. It was expected we would marry."

"Ours was a whirlwind courtship. Cristo swept me off my feet. I don't think it matters how long a couple is together. They just know when it's right." None of which was a lie. She truly believed this. She just hadn't met Mr. Right yet. Her gaze moved to Cristo. He certainly made a really good Mr. Right Now.

"Why come to Athens to work? Don't they have work where you come from?"

She decided to turn the question around on him. "Why not come here? Athens is beautiful. It's an adventure."

"And that's it?"

There was one more thing. Why not tell him? It wasn't a secret. And there was the slight chance that Mr. Stravos might know something about her family. "I came here in search of my extended family."

Mr. Stravos's eyes widened. "You have family here?"

"I hope so. My father's side of the family came from Greece."

"What are their names?"

"Pappas. Otis and Althea Pappas. Cristo has been kind enough to offer to help me search for the records."

A frown pulled at the man's face. Without a word, he

turned and headed back into the mansion. Oh, no! What had she done wrong? She cast Cristo a questioning glance, but he was staring at the man's retreating back. This wasn't good. Not good at all.

Kyra turned to Niko. "Was it something I said?"

Niko shook his head. "You were fine."

"Then what just happened?"

"I have no idea." Niko shrugged before turning back to Cristo. "What can I say? My grandfather is always full of surprises. But don't give up. I'll talk to him."

Cristo stuck out his hand. "I'd really appreciate anything you can do."

Kyra cast Cristo a sympathetic look, but he turned away. She understood that he was deeply disappointed, but there had to be another way. Something he hadn't thought of yet.

They started for the gate when Kyra paused. She turned back to catch Niko just before he entered the living room. "Niko, would it be all right if I sent over a wedding invitation for you and your grandfather?"

"That would be quite thoughtful. But I can't promise we'll be able to make it."

"I'll send one anyway," she said and smiled.

She didn't want to push any further. At least it was something. Maybe nothing would come of it. Then again, who knew what the future might hold. She looped her hand through the crook of Cristo's arm, as was becoming natural to her.

So where did they go from here?

She glanced over at Cristo. His handsome face was marred with stress lines. Now wasn't the time to ask him.

Once back at the Blue Tide Resort, they walked along the paved path that led back to the main building. She kept waiting for him to say something—anything so she knew where things stood. Unable to stand the prolonged silence, she asked, "How do you think the meeting went?"

He sent her an I-don't-believe-you-have-to-ask look. "Obviously not well."

Was she just being overly sensitive or was his grouchiness directed toward her? Surely he didn't think she intentionally messed things up, did he? She would never do that to him.

"I'm sorry I didn't do a better job convincing Mr. Stravos that we're a happy couple. Perhaps it would be best if we just ended this whole arrangement right now."

Cristo stopped walking and sent her a hard stare. "You're quitting?"

"Don't you think it would be best? I was absolutely no help to you at dinner. And there's no need for us to be in each other's way."

"No." His voice held strength and finality to it.

No? What did he mean no? "You aren't even going to consider letting me out of this arrangement?"

He shook his head. "When I make a deal with someone, I expect them to keep up their end of the bargain."

"But I don't understand. Mr. Stravos looked at me as though he didn't believe a word I said—it was as though he could see straight through our story. I think this whole engagement is a huge mistake. I'm sorry I failed you."

"It wasn't you." Cristo reached out, took her hand in his and squeezed it. "You have nothing to apologize for. You did everything right, and I appreciate it."

She stared straight into his eyes, trying to determine the depth of his sincerity. "You really mean that? You're not just saying it to make me feel better?"

"Trust me. I mean every word." He shifted his weight from one foot to the other. "If anything, this is all my fault for thinking up such a far-fetched scheme."

"There has to be another way to convince the elder Stravos that the sale is good for everyone. After all, his grandson is all for the deal."

"The problem is I'm running out of ideas." There was a worrisome tone in his voice—one she'd never heard before.

She realized that she'd come to care for Cristo far more than she ever imagined possible, and she just couldn't let him throw in the towel now. If Cristo really thought expanding his business was a way to somehow reconnect with his father, he had to keep trying. Somehow, someway this would all work out. "Promise me you won't give up hope."

He glanced up at her. Skepticism shone in his eyes. "You think it's still possible to strike a deal with Mr. Stravos?"

"I do."

His eyes warmed. "What would I do without you?"

"Lucky for you, you don't have to find out." She squeezed his hand. He squeezed her hand in return. When she went to pull away, he tightened his hold on her. Their fingers intertwined and they started along the beach. "I wonder why Mr. Stravos got quiet when I started talking about my family. Do you think it's possible he might know some of them?"

"I wouldn't get your hopes up. If he had known any of them, I don't see why he wouldn't have mentioned it. I'd just write off his peculiar behavior to a man who is very eccentric."

When Cristo led her straight past the walkway leading back to the lobby of the resort, she got the distinct impression his mind was too preoccupied for sleep. To be honest, she wasn't tired, either. When they reached the sand, they both slipped off their shoes. The evening air was calm and the moon was full. It was as though it had a magical pull over them.

With each step they took, her curiosity mounted about Cristo's motivation to close this deal. Maybe if she understood exactly what was at stake, she'd be better able to help him. "Why is this business deal so important to you?"

"I already explained it to you."

Kyra shook her head, knowing that his passionate need to complete this deal came from a deep personal need. "But there's something more to it. After all, the Stravos chain isn't the only hotel chain in the world. So why does it have to be this one—and why now?"

"It's not worth talking about."

"It is or I wouldn't have asked. Talk to me. I know this has something to do with your father. Do you really think your whole relationship hinges on your success?"

He stopped and turned to her. "Does that always work?"

"Does what work?"

"Wearing a man down with that sultry voice and then asking him to confide his tightly held secrets." He smiled at her letting her know that he was just teasing her.

"I guess that means it's working."

"Perhaps." He leaned forward and pressed a quick kiss to her lips.

And then as though it hadn't happened, he started walking again. Kyra didn't say anything else as she waited to learn more about the man who was holding her hand and making her heart race. She was overcome with the desire to know everything about him—at least everything that he was willing to share with her.

Just when she'd given up on him answering her, he spoke. "I was only fifteen at the time…it was Christmas break from school. We were on holiday at the family cabin in Aspen. My parents, grandparents and my three brothers were there."

So far it sounded like a lovely memory. She tried picturing Cristo as a teenager. Something told her that he'd had a whole host of girls with crushes on him.

Cristo cleared his throat. "I didn't want to sit around the cabin and I didn't want to go into town and see the latest action movie with my older brothers. So I talked my younger brother, Max, into going skiing with me." Cristo's thumb rubbed repeatedly over the back of her hand. "It is one of those moments in life where I really wish I could go back in time and redo it. If only…"

Kyra had a sinking feeling in her stomach. She wanted to tell him to stop the story—as though that would keep the tragedy from happening. But something told her he'd kept this bottled up far too long. If he was strong enough to let out the ghosts of the past, she was strong enough to be there for him.

"Max was a really good kid and, being the youngest, he was usually left out of a lot of things my older brothers liked to do. So when I suggested we go skiing, just the two of us, he was excited. Perhaps too excited." There was a catch in Cristo's voice. He stopped walking and turned to stare out at the water. "I should have kept a better eye on him. Maybe then..."

"You were only a kid yourself. I'm sure you did your best."

"But that's just it. My best wasn't good enough." His body tensed and his grip on her hand tightened to the point of it being uncomfortable. And then, as though realizing he was causing her pain, he loosened his hold, but he didn't let go—they were still connected. "Max was showing off. He always felt a need to prove himself. Our father has always been a tough man to impress. Max must have gotten it into his head that he had to impress me, too. He went zipping by me. I tried to catch up to him but he was too far ahead and..."

Tears stung the backs of Kyra's eyes because she knew what was coming next. It was going to be horrible and unimaginable.

"And the next thing I knew...he hit a tree." Cristo's voice was raw with pain. "I watched helplessly as his body went down into the snow. And he didn't move. I tried to help him. I'd have done anything to save him."

Kyra wrapped her arms around Cristo and held him close as the waves of pain washed over him. She had no idea that his scars ran so deep, not only his brother's death, but also his estrangement from his father.

When Cristo pulled back, he started to walk again. For a few minutes they moved quietly beneath the starry sky. She didn't know what to say—what to do. Was it possible to get past Cristo's guilt?

When Cristo spoke there was a hollow tone to his voice. "After the accident, Max lived for a little bit, but the brain damage was too severe. My…my father blamed me. He said it was my fault—that I should have been looking out for Max because I was older. And he was right. I failed."

She squeezed Cristo's hand, letting him know he wasn't alone.

"My father never forgave me. I've done everything I could to make peace with him. But nothing will ever bring back Max."

"And this deal with Stravos—is this a way to prove yourself to your father?"

"It…it's a sound business decision." His gaze didn't meet hers.

Cristo couldn't admit it, but he wanted his father's approval. Kyra was at last figuring this all out. "You're intent on proving yourself…just like Max was trying to do when he had his accident."

Cristo shrugged. "My two older brothers succeeded at everything they tried. Life always came easy to them. One runs a string of golf courses and the other has a restaurant chain."

And then another thought came to her. "Are you driving yourself this hard to prove something to your father or is it something else that has you up before the sun and working until long after sundown?"

"What are you getting at?" He rubbed the back of his neck.

"That you don't believe you're worthy of happiness—of building a life for yourself—"

"I have a life."

"Going from business meeting to business meeting

isn't a life. It's an existence. But you could have so much more—"

"No!" He shook his head and blinked repeatedly. "Not anymore."

Kyra wrapped her arms around Cristo and hugged him close, hoping to absorb some of his pain. "You deserve love, too."

Kyra's heart ached for the boy who'd lost his brother and the son longing for his father's love and respect. Contrary to her original impression, this deal wasn't about power or money. It was about so much more. It was about family, and she wanted desperately to reunite Cristo with his, even if she never found her own.

After a bit, Cristo pulled away. "Don't pity me. I don't deserve it. I only told you because, after all you've done for me, you deserve to know the truth—the whole truth."

"I understand and I will continue to help you any way I can. We're in this together and that's how we're going to stay."

Then without analyzing her actions, she leaned up on her tiptoes and pressed her lips to his. He didn't move at first, as though she'd caught him totally off guard. Was it really that much of a surprise after the intimate talk they'd just shared?

As her lips moved over his, she felt as though this evening they'd taken a giant leap in their relationship—less fake and more real. She knew there was no turning back now. Cristo had snuck past her neatly laid defenses and made his way into her heart.

Her hips leaned into his. Her chest pressed to his. His hands moved around to her back—to the sensitive spot where her dress dipped low. His fingers stroked her bare skin, sending the most amazing sensations zinging through her now-heated body.

She didn't want this night to end. It just kept getting better and better. If only she could be content with taking second place to his work, maybe they'd have a chance at something lasting instead of something temporary. And just like quicksand, she kept getting in deeper and deeper.

Suddenly Cristo pulled back. His gaze didn't quite meet hers. "We can't do this. It's a mistake."

A mistake?

"I'm sorry." He turned and followed the lit path back up to the lobby of the resort.

What in the world just happened?

Had he rejected her? The thought stung her heart. How could he go from opening himself up to her one minute to pushing her away the next?

The questions plagued her, one after another. And she had no answers for any of them. And the one question that bothered her most was where did they go from here?

CHAPTER THIRTEEN

WHAT IN THE world had gotten into him?

More than a week had passed since Cristo had bared his troubled soul to Kyra. And it hadn't made things better. It'd made them worse. It'd dredged up all of the horrific memories he kept locked away in the back of his mind. And when he faced Kyra, she was quiet and reserved. It wasn't just his father. Now that Kyra knew the truth, she'd withdrawn from him, too. Not that he could blame her.

Cristo moved to the bar in the suite and refilled his mug with freshly brewed coffee. His second pot that morning. And he still didn't feel like himself.

He hadn't slept well in days. He spent his nights tossing and turning. There had been no getting comfortable. All he could think about was Kyra.

They'd gotten so much closer than he'd ever intended. Even to the point where she had him opening up about his past—something he never shared with anyone. And something he would never do again.

In the daylight hours, he continued his search for her family. He was more invested in the quest now than ever before. He needed to know that when this arrangement was over that Kyra would be all right. Because try as he might, he still hadn't convinced her to speak to her mother.

Though it was still early, Cristo had placed a call to the private investigator. He normally received weekly reports on Monday afternoons, but he had no patience to wait until after lunch. This search for Kyra's family had hit too many dead ends. They were due for a bit of good luck—at least Kyra was due it.

The conversation was short but fruitful. Cristo clenched

his hand and pumped his arm as the PI gave him their first valid lead. Cristo assured the man he would personally follow up on the findings.

Determined to see this plan enacted immediately, he grabbed his phone and called his PA. He canceled all of his meetings that day. He had something more important to do. And though his PA sputtered on about the number of important meetings he would be missing, he didn't care. For once, he was putting something—rather someone—else ahead of his own business agenda. Something his father would never do.

Kyra strolled out of her bedroom, yawning as she headed for the coffeepot.

She eyed up his khaki shorts and polo shirt. "Is it casual dress day at the office?"

"No. I'm not working today."

"Really?" Her fine brows rose. "Has there been a global disaster? Is it the end of the world?"

"Kyra, stop." He didn't realize he'd turned out more like his father than he'd ever intended. A frown tugged at his lips. "Why does there have to be something wrong for me to take the day off?

"It's just that in all the time I've known you, you've never voluntarily taken a day off. So I figure something big must have happened."

Perhaps he'd been a bit too driven whcrc his work was concerned. "It just so happens that I have other plans today."

"Well, I hope you have a good day. I have to study for a test. I've been catching up on my studies. I need to get my certification." She walked over to the coffee table and picked up her laptop. "It's time I really concentrated on my career. After all, our deal will be over soon, and I want a plan in place so that I can move on to the next stage in my life."

"Do you mean move on from me? Or the Blue Tide?"

"Both."

The wedding was in just a few weeks—the time they'd call everything off. This domestic bliss would be over. The thought of her leaving for good, of never seeing her again, was like a forceful blow to his chest. He swallowed hard. "I noticed you've been studying a lot lately. Does it have anything to do with your fight with your mother?"

"No, it doesn't. Is there something wrong with me getting serious about my future?"

"Not at all." Though he still thought she was using it as a distraction from her family problems, today wasn't the time to dwell on such things—not when at last they had a viable lead. "Could you take today off from your studies?"

She shook her head. "I have my finals soon. I almost have my hotel management certification—my ticket to see the world."

"What if I told you I heard from the investigator and he has a lead on your family?"

Her face lit up with excitement. "Really?"

Cristo nodded. "He used the picture you provided and it led him to the small village of Orchidos."

"Orchidos? I've never heard of it. Where is it?"

"You'll see. Come on." Cristo started for the door.

"Wait. Are you serious?"

"Of course I'm serious."

She ran a hand through her hair. "But I'm not ready to go anywhere. I haven't even had my first cup of coffee yet, and I'm not dressed to go out."

"You can have it in the car." He glanced at his watch. "You've got ten minutes and then we're out of here."

Kyra disappeared to her bedroom, leaving him to pace back and forth in the living room. He checked his phone every couple of minutes for texts or voice mails until he remembered that he'd had his phone calls forwarded to his PA. Today was all about Kyra.

When she emerged from her bedroom, she stole his breath away. He smothered an appreciative whistle. He didn't want to scare her off if she knew how attractive he found her. Still, he couldn't take his eyes off her.

Kyra's long hair was piled on her head with a few loose curls softening the look. A dark teal sleeveless dress with a scalloped neckline and tiny maroon flowers made her look as if she was ready for a picnic on the beach. A brown leather belt emphasized her tiny waist. The skirt ended just above her knees, showing off her legs. On her feet were jeweled flip-flops.

"Is something wrong with what I'm wearing?"

He knew he was staring but he couldn't help himself. At last her words registered in his distracted mind. "No. You look great."

"Are you sure?" She smoothed a hand down over the skirt, straightening a nonexistent wrinkle. "I could change into something else."

"No. Don't. You're perfect." In that moment, Cristo realized his words held meaning that went well beyond her clothes. There was a special quality to her—a warmth and genuineness—that appealed to him on a level he'd never felt before.

This recognition left him feeling off-kilter, not quite sure how to act around her. It was as though something significant had changed between them and yet everything was exactly the same. How was that possible?

At long last, she was about to find out a bit of her family's past. And hopefully about the present, too. She crossed her fingers for luck.

Kyra gave Cristo a sideways glance as they walked side by side through the hotel lobby. And it was all thanks to Cristo. The glass doors automatically slid open and there sat a luxury sports car—the kind of car that cost more than most people's houses.

She went to skirt around it when Cristo asked, "Where are you going? This is your ride."

"It is?" Her gaze moved from the electric-blue super car with a gold lightning bolt etched on the back fender to Cristo's smiling face. "This is yours?"

He nodded. "Why does that surprise you?"

She knew he was wealthy enough, but she didn't think he had a fun side. She thought the only entertainment he found was in closing the next big deal. Perhaps there was hope for Cristo after all. "I just didn't imagine you were the type to enjoy a sports car."

"And what type do I seem?"

"Oh, I don't know. The suit-and-tie kind. The type who reads the *Wall Street Journal* in the back of a limo. The on-the-phone-the-whole-trip type."

"Well, I'm glad to know I can surprise you from time to time." He opened the door for her and she climbed inside, enjoying the buttery soft leather upholstery and the new car smell.

Cristo moved to the driver's seat and started the engine, which roared to life. There was no doubt in her mind that this car had power and lots of it—quite like its owner. They set off, and her body tensed as they headed down the long drive. Any minute she expected him to punch the accelerator.

"Relax." Cristo's voice was calm and reassuring. "I promise I know what I'm doing."

"That's what I'm afraid of. That you might go flying down the road like we're on a racetrack."

"You don't have to worry. You'll always be safe with me." He glanced at her briefly before focusing back on the road.

She wanted to believe him, honestly she did, but she had the distinct feeling that just being around him put her heart in jeopardy. There was something about him—something far deeper than the size of his bank account or his impressive toys—that got to her. And she would have to be careful because she wasn't about to end up playing second fiddle to a man's work—not even when the man was Cristo Kiriakas.

When her phone chimed, she retrieved it from her purse. Her mother's name appeared on the caller ID. It wasn't the first time she'd called since Kyra had uncovered her mother's deceit and it wouldn't be the last. Didn't she understand that Kyra needed to process what she'd done?

The one person Kyra thought she could always depend on had betrayed her trust. It wasn't something that could be righted—at least not straightaway.

Cristo turned down the music. "If you need to take that, go ahead. I don't mind."

Kyra sent the call to voice mail. No way was she speaking to her mother with Cristo listening. "It's not important."

"Are you sure?"

"Yes. I'll deal with it later." Much later.

Kyra turned the music back up and amused herself with the passing scenery. It kept her from staring at Cristo. Besides, she'd promised herself when she finally made it to Greece that she'd get out and see the sights, and so far she hadn't had a chance. There was so much of this beautiful country that she wanted to explore.

The car glided over the coastal roadway. The clear blue sky let the sunshine rain down over the greenery dotted with wildflowers from purples and pinks to reds and oranges. On the driver's side was a rocky cliff that led down to the beach.

Almost an hour later, they arrived in the small Greek village of Orchidos. She soon found out that the village was aptly named. Wild orchids were scattered about the perimeter of the village. Huge blooms ranged in color from apricot to maroon with splashes of white upon the delicate petals. It was truly a spectacular sight.

Cristo pulled off to the side of the road. "Are you ready?"

She eagerly nodded. "Do you really think I have any relatives living here?"

He got out and opened her door for her. "I don't know, but we have an appointment later today with the town elder. Maybe he'll have some answers for you. But first, I thought you might want to explore the village."

"I definitely do."

They passed by the modest white houses with red tile roofs. In the center of Orchidos stood a town square with a charming café, Aphrodite's. White columns surrounded the portico. And a stone carving of what she assumed was Aphrodite stood proudly in the center surrounded by little white tables.

They took a seat and were impressed with the delicious menu. When the food was delivered to their table, it did not disappoint. Kyra found herself eating far too much after Cristo ordered almost everything on the menu, from grilled fish to skewers to a salad and a number of delightful treats in between. She was beginning to think she'd never comfortably fit in her clothes again.

Next up on the agenda was walking up and down the roads and steps that connected this almost vertical village. The buildings were all different shapes and sizes. Each was steeped in history. The people of Orchidos were warm and welcoming as they offered smiles and greetings. Kyra felt right at home.

Cristo held her hand the whole time. It was as though the awkwardness they'd experienced had at last slipped away. He told her what he knew of the history of the village. Most of which he confessed to learning on the internet. They climbed wooden steps that wrapped around the hillside. The effort was well worth it as they ended up in the most stunning lookout spot, overlooking a green valley and patches of more orchids. Kyra took a bunch of photos. She thought of sending them to her mother but quickly dismissed the idea. She wasn't ready to deal with her mother. Not yet.

At one point, Cristo checked his cell phone. She waited for him to say that something had come up and he had to cut their outing short. It wouldn't surprise her in the least. Something always came between them when they were having a good time. But this time, Cristo slipped the phone back in his pocket without saying a word. She didn't mention it, either—afraid of ruining the moment.

Minutes turned into hours and before she knew it, Cristo was leading them back to the town square for coffee. It was only then she realized that her cheeks were growing sore from smiling so much. Then again, her feet ached, too. Sandals weren't the best for long walks, but she wouldn't have missed it for the world. To think her ancestors once walked these streets, too, meant a lot to her.

"Thank you for this." She smiled at Cristo. "I've really enjoyed seeing where my grandparents might have once lived. But in all of the excitement, I forgot to ask how you found this place."

"Remember that photo of your grandparents?" When she nodded, he continued. "It was taken in this village. The building in the background once stood in the town square, but a fire destroyed it many years ago. That's why it took the investigator so long to track it down."

"So this is where my family came from?" Kyra glanced around, taking in the village with a whole new perspective.

"We had better get going. We have an appointment that I'm sure you don't want to miss."

Cristo led her a short distance to a nondescript, white stone house with the standard red tile roof, although it had a few tiles missing. He turned to her. "I hope you find your family."

She did, too. Although she already felt as though she'd found something very special with him, she wasn't ready to name those feelings. It was still so new. And she felt so vulnerable.

CHAPTER FOURTEEN

KYRA'S HEART THUMPED with anticipation.

Please let us find the answers to my past.

The red door of the house opened and an older gentleman stepped out. His tanned, wrinkled face lit up with a smile. *"Yasas."*

Kyra turned an inquiring look to Cristo, who greeted the man in fluent Greek. When Cristo turned back to her, he gave her hand a squeeze. "Our host, Tomas Marinos, welcomes you. I'm afraid he only speaks Greek. But I can ask him any questions you might have."

"Can you ask him if he knew Otis or Althea Pappas?"

Cristo translated for her and the man immediately shook his head. Disappointment sliced through her. But she wasn't giving up. They were so close.

When Cristo guided her inside the very plain house, she whispered, "Why are we staying when he doesn't know my grandparents?"

"You asked to research your family and that's what we're doing."

"Here? Shouldn't we go to the local library and search through old birth records and deeds."

He shook his head. "Not in Orchidos. There's no library. Mr. Marinos is the village elder. He has the best records of anyone, such as they are."

"Oh. I didn't know." Heat warmed her cheeks. She hadn't meant to sound unappreciative.

"I warned you in the beginning that tracking down your family based on one old photo wasn't going to be easy." Cristo's steady gaze met hers. "But I know how determined you are to find out about your past, so I used every resource at my disposal to track Mr. Marinos down and make sure he has photos and papers that stretch back to the nineteenth century. If your grandparents ever lived in Orchidos, their names will be in here."

This was it. Her stomach quivered. She was about to find out what happened to her father's family. In her excitement, she whirled around and gave Cristo a hug. "You're amazing."

"You might not say that when you see all of the papers that need sorted. I've been warned there are a lot."

She sent him a worried glance. "I don't know much Greek and—"

"No worries. I'll be right here by your side."

She nodded. In her heart, she believed her father had a hand in guiding her here. *We made it, Dad. At last we'll find out about your family.* She blinked repeatedly, still feeling the loss of her father.

The kitchen table was lined with boxes, as well as the floor. She had no doubt there was a lot of history in those boxes. She moved to the first box and yanked off the dusty lid. Finding the records were in chronological order, they were able to narrow down their search.

Cristo cocked a dark brow at her as she worked at a fervent pace. "You weren't exaggerating when you said you wanted to find your past, were you?"

She shrugged, lifting out a handful of papers. "You probably don't understand what it's like not to know where you came from. My father and I had started tracing the family tree a couple of years before he died. We started with my mother's family. Her side was pretty easy to trace. My father's side was the opposite. We planned to fly here and do research, but he…he didn't live long enough."

"And what if this information isn't what you're expecting? What if it doesn't lead you to the family you've always dreamed of?"

"I guess I'll have to let go of that dream."

"You know that sometimes the best families aren't the ones we're born into, but the ones we make for ourselves."

Kyra paused. She never would have guessed Cristo ever stopped shuffling papers and signing contracts long enough to contemplate something so deep. "Is that what you plan to do? Make a family for yourself?"

"At first, I thought my work would be enough, but lately I've been reconsidering—"

Their gazes met and her heart picked up its pace. The more this day progressed, the harder it was becoming to remember he was her business associate and not just a really sexy guy with an amazing smile. She couldn't resist his charms or ignore how he was letting his guard down around her.

She placed the aged and sun-stained papers on the table. "If you're worried you'll turn out like your father, you don't have to. I could never imagine you being cold and hostile to your child."

Cristo shook his head. "I don't know if I could split my time between my work and my family. As you've seen, I tend to get absorbed in my work. How about you? Will you choose work or family? Or will you try to balance them both?"

"I don't know what my future holds once I get my certification. I'm going to take it one day at a time."

"You know you don't have to leave the Glamour Hotel and Casino. I could find you a position—"

"No. This is something I have to do on my own."

"If you change your mind—"

"I won't."

Heat warmed her cheeks. She couldn't believe he thought that highly of her. "Thank you. But we better get started on these papers before our host kicks us out."

She glanced around, but Mr. Marinos seemed to have disappeared.

"Don't worry. He's out on the porch. But he said he'd be

more than happy to answer any questions." Cristo glanced down at the papers. "Now that we've found the boxes for the right time period, how about you look through the photos and scan the papers for any mention of Pappas. If you find something of interest, you can pass it to me and I can translate it for you."

She glanced down at the papers and realized they were all in Greek. This search was going from hard to downright difficult. But she wouldn't give up. There was a part of her that needed to know where she'd come from and to connect with any relatives that still might be lurking about. And maybe then she wouldn't feel as if there was a gaping hole in her life where her father used to be.

Hours passed as they sifted over paper after paper. Frustration churned in her stomach as a whole section of papers seemed to be missing. But how could that be?

Cristo returned from speaking to Mr. Marinos. "He doesn't know what happened to the papers."

Kyra blinked away tears of frustration as she placed the lid on the box. "So that's it. We've hit a dead end. Whatever there was of my past is gone. It died with my father."

Cristo stepped around the table. He held out his hand to her and helped her to her feet. He gazed deep into her eyes. "This isn't the end. I promise. We will find out about your past. Maybe not today. And maybe not tomorrow. But we will uncover whatever there is to find. Do you trust me?"

She wanted to—she really did. "How am I supposed to trust you when I can't even trust my own mother?"

He reached out, running a finger along her cheek. "I'm sorry she hurt you, but I am not her. I won't let you down."

Standing here so close to him with her heart pounding in her chest, she couldn't imagine him ever hurting her. "I want to trust you."

He smiled. "I'll take that as a positive sign."

All she could think about at the moment was pressing

her lips to his. He really shouldn't stand this close to her. It did the craziest things to her thought processes.

And then as though he could read her thoughts, he dipped his head and placed a kiss upon her lips. He pulled away far too quickly. "Don't give up hope. Sometimes things work out when you least expect them to."

Was he referring to learning about her family?

Or was he talking about this thing that was growing between them?

She hoped it was both.

He'd been so certain this trip would give Kyra the answers she craved.

Cristo felt horrible seeing the disappointment reflected in her eyes. It was his fault. He'd put it there. He should have followed up better before mentioning the lead to her.

The sports car glided smoothly over the motorway on the drive back to the Blue Tide. Usually sitting behind the wheel of a high-performance vehicle relaxed him—gave him a new perspective on things—but not today. The disappointment in the car was palpable even though Kyra tried her best to cover it up.

His investigator had been certain Kyra would find answers in Orchidos. It didn't make sense. Who removed those papers? And why?

It was almost as if any trace of Kyra's family had been purposely removed—erased—as though they never existed. Who would do such a thing? What were they missing?

Cristo rubbed his neck. He was making too much of this. Why would anyone want to hide the history of Kyra's family? It didn't make sense.

He chanced a glance at Kyra. Her head was tilted back against the seat's headrest, and she was staring out the window. She looked as though she was all alone in this world, but that wasn't true. She had her mother and Sofia. People who cared about her, even if it wasn't the way she wanted them to care.

And she had Cristo. He cared. Perhaps he cared more than was good for either one of them. Because he didn't know how to be there for anyone. He'd never learned that as a child.

He'd been a pawn passed between his mother and a string of nannies and then shipped off to a string of boarding schools—when he got in trouble at one, he'd get shuffled off to another. There had been no consistency—or rather he should say that his life had been one long line of inconsistencies. He could never be what Kyra had traveled the globe in search of—family. The thought saddened him. But he wasn't sure whom he was sadder for, her or himself.

Still, he hated seeing Kyra in such turmoil. He couldn't just sit by and let her feel so dejected—so alone.

He moved his hand from the gearshift and reached out to her. But with her arms crossed, he couldn't reach her hand, so he settled for her thigh. Big miscalculation on his part. A sense of awareness took hold of his very eager body. His fingertips tingled where the heat of her body permeated the cottony material of her summer dress.

Kyra's head turned and their gazes met. He glanced back at the road, relieved to have an excuse to keep her from reading the conflicting emotions in his eyes. He knew he should pull his hand away, but he couldn't—not yet. He hadn't made his point yet.

"Kyra, you're not alone." He tightened his hold on her thigh and his pulse quickened. "You've got people who care about you."

"Does that include you?"

The breath caught in his throat. What was she asking him? Did she mean as a friend? Or did she want something more? Right then the urge was overwhelming to pull back—to keep a safe distance. But a glance at the emotional turmoil in her eyes had him keeping their physical link for just a bit longer.

"I'm here as your friend anytime that you need me." *There. That sounded good. Didn't it?*

His cell phone buzzed. He knew he'd promised not to do any work today, but sometimes promises had to be broken. And this was one of those times when he desperately needed a diversion.

He glanced at the phone as it rested in the console. "It's Niko Stravos. I think I should get it, don't you?"

"You're asking me?" The surprise in her voice reflected his own. He'd never asked anyone if he should take a call. When the phone buzzed again, Kyra added, "Answer it. Maybe he has good news. I could use some about now."

Cristo pressed a button on the steering wheel and, utilizing the car's speaker system, said, "Hello."

"Cristo, it's Niko." They continued to make pleasantries and Cristo let him know that he was on the speakerphone and Kyra was with him. "Sounds like I have perfect timing, then. I'd like to invite you both back for dinner later this week."

Cristo, surprised by the invitation, cast Kyra a glance, finding she looked equally shocked. "Thank you. But perhaps we should get together at my resort. Your grandfather wasn't happy about our prior visit—"

"I wouldn't worry about that. My grandfather can be temperamental at times. Don't take it personally." There was a bit of static on the phone line, but soon it quieted and Niko's voice came through clearly. "In fact, this dinner invitation was my grandfather's idea. He sends his apologies for being abrupt the last time you were here and asks that you join us for a more casual dinner Friday night."

Really? What could this possibly mean? Cristo sure wanted to find out. But he knew Kyra had been disappointed by her lack of discovery today, and he didn't know if she'd be up for putting on a happy front for the senior Stravos.

They were almost back at the Blue Tide Resort now. Cristo slowed the car and turned into the long drive. Cristo hated that he might have to back out of this amazing opportunity, but Kyra's needs had to come first. "Can you hold for just a moment?"

"Sure."

"Thanks." Cristo muted the phone in order to speak with Kyra in private. "What do you think?"

She picked at a nonexistent piece of lint on her sundress. "I think it's an amazing opportunity for you. You should go and see what Nikolaos Stravos has to say."

"And what about you? Will you come with me, too?"

CHAPTER FIFTEEN

PLEASE LET HER AGREE.

After all, they were a team.

Cristo prompted her, anxious for an answer. "Kyra?"

She worried her bottom lip. "I don't know. I really wasn't much help to you on the last visit. You might be better off on your own."

He wanted to argue with her and tell her they made a great team, but he held back the words. After she'd just put him on the spot about being in her life, he didn't want to confuse things further. He was already confused enough.

"I understand." He tightened his fingers on the steering wheel. "After today's adventure, you need some time to regroup. I'll let Niko know."

"Thank you for understanding."

Cristo pressed the button for the phone. "Niko?"

"Yes. By the way, I forgot to mention that my grandfather requested Kyra bring any photos she might have of her family. He said he might have some information for her."

Kyra's face lit up with anticipation—it was such a welcome sight. Cristo didn't have to ask if she'd had a change of heart. He just hoped Nikolaos Stravos's information was better than what they'd uncovered today, which was nothing. "We'll be there."

Niko gave them the details, including the request for casual dress. Cristo knew that the Stravoses' version of casual dress was far from jeans and T-shirts. It was more like a suit minus the tie. Which satisfied Cristo just fine. He always felt more in his element when he was dressed up.

He pulled the car into his reserved spot. One of the attendants would clean it before putting it in his private garage. Right now, the care of his prized car slid to the back of his mind. He turned in his seat. "You did it. Thank you."

Her fine brows drew together. "I did what?"

"Got us a second chance to impress Nikolaos Stravos—"

"I just wish it was under different circumstances. I don't like the tales we're fabricating." Anxiety reflected in her eyes. "What if I say the wrong thing? What if he figures out the truth?"

Cristo didn't like this situation any better than her. This wasn't the way he normally did business, but how else were you supposed to negotiate with someone who was so stubborn and set in their ways?

But this relationship wasn't all a lie. No matter how much he fought it, there was definitely something growing between him and Kyra. He couldn't put a name on it. He just knew that she deserved better than him.

"You'll do fine. You'll charm him just like you do everyone." Anxious to erase the worry from her big, beautiful eyes, Cristo leaned over in his seat and pressed his lips to hers.

She didn't move at first. Had he caught her off guard? His muscles tensed, preparing to be rejected.

And then her mouth started to move beneath his. He started to relax—to enjoy the touch. She tasted sweet like vine-ripened grapes. He doubted he'd ever have another sip of wine without thinking of her.

Cristo had only meant to give her a reassuring kiss, but now that his lips were touching hers, he had no interest in pulling away. What he wanted was more of this—more of Kyra. And she didn't seem to be complaining as her fingers lifted to caress his jaw. No other woman could turn him on the way Kyra could. It wasn't even as if she tried. It was just natural—chemistry.

As her fingertips trailed down his neck to the inside of his shirt collar, he knew he had to stop her before things got totally out of hand. This was not the place to take things to the next level. His fingers moved to cover hers, halting their exploration.

With every bit of willpower, he pulled back and stared her in the eyes. "Now, was that a lie?"

She shook her head. "But—"

His lips pressed to hers again, silencing her protest. He didn't want to know what followed her *but*, not at all. They'd tackled enough problems for now.

He rested his forehead against hers. "No buts. There's something between us. Don't ask me to define it because I can't. And don't expect too much from me because I don't want to let you down. The only thing I can offer you is this—right here, right now."

She pulled away from him. "All the more reason for me not to go to this dinner with you."

"And miss out on a chance to find out what Nikolaos might know about your family?" He knew he had her there. Finding out about her past was too important to her to back out now. "Don't worry, I'll be right there next to you the whole time." He'd just reached for the door handle when Kyra spoke up.

"Do you really think keeping up this charade is the right way to go about things with Stravos? Maybe if we explain everything to him, he'll understand the importance of the deal."

There was nothing about Nikolaos Stravos in his past or present that in the slightest way hinted he was an understanding man who could be swayed by sentimentality. He had a cutthroat reputation in the business world—he wasn't used to sitting back and letting people have their way.

But Kyra had a point. Cristo wasn't comfortable with weaving such an elaborate ruse. "Why don't we play it by ear?"

She stared at him for a moment before nodding her head. "If you think it's best."

As they exited the car and headed back to their suite,

Cristo couldn't dismiss her words. He didn't want Kyra thinking less of him. He wasn't conducting this elaborate ruse because it was fun, although it was with Kyra, or because it was his normal business practice, which it certainly wasn't, but rather because it was what this particular situation necessitated.

His father had taught him to do anything necessary to secure an important business deal. After all, business came first, ahead of all else including family. Cristo supposed he'd learned that lesson quite well. Maybe too well. That was why he'd chosen not to have a family. He didn't want to end up like his father.

And in that moment, he recalled something he'd promised himself as a teenager. After observing his father at the office and witnessing the unhappiness he unleashed on a regular basis, Cristo swore he'd do things differently. Less skirting the truth and with more compassion.

So far he was failing.

Perhaps it was time he considered doing things Kyra's way.

Sleep was elusive.

Kyra tiptoed through the darkened suite late Thursday night. Cristo needed his rest. He had a big day tomorrow. And hopefully Nikolaos Stravos had changed his mind and had decided to go ahead with the sale.

But more than that, she wondered what the older man wanted with her. She recalled their prior meeting and the way the man had stared at her before storming off. He didn't like her, so why was he suddenly willing to help her? Something wasn't adding up, but she couldn't put her finger on exactly what it was.

She sighed and leaned against the wall surrounding the balcony that overlooked the private cove. She was letting her imagination get the best of her. It was Cristo's fault. Ever since their outing, she hadn't been able to get him off her mind. She'd finally found out what it was like to have all of his attention and now she craved more.

"Would you mind some company?"

The sound of Cristo's voice caused her to jump. She turned and had to struggle to keep from gaping at his bare chest and the low-slung dark boxers. Had she fallen asleep somewhere along the way and this was a dream—a very vivid, very tempting dream?

She swallowed hard. "Did I wake you?"

He raked his fingers through his already mussed-up hair. "That would imply I was actually sleeping."

"You couldn't sleep, either?"

"No." He moved to stand next to her. "It's a beautiful night. The moon is so full that it's almost like daylight. But I have a feeling that's not why you're out here. What's bothering you?"

She didn't want to get into another conversation about Nikolaos Stravos. Instead, she said, "I couldn't sleep, and I was bored of staring into the dark."

He reached out and put a finger beneath her chin, pulling her around to face him. "Are you still worried about the dinner?"

"It's nothing."

"I don't believe you. Your eyes tell a different story."

"They do?" She glanced away. Did they say how sexy she found him right now? Did he know how hard it was for her to carry on this conversation when he was barely dressed?

"Obviously you have something on your mind, and until you deal with it, you'll be left lurking in the shadows of the night." His voice lowered, making it warm and quite inviting. "Talk to me."

What would he say if she told him what was weighing on her mind at this particular moment? Her gaze once again dipped to his bare chest. His presence was distracting her—teasing her—tempting her.

How did someone look that good? Cristo certainly knew

his way around a weight room. How did a busy man like him have time for exercise? Somehow he fit it in between boardroom meetings and jet-setting around the globe.

"Kyra? What is it?"

She struggled to center her thoughts on something besides how her heart was thump-thumping in her chest. She licked her dry lips. "I… I was just wondering if this is all going to end tomorrow. You know, after the meeting with Stravos. Will you and I go our separate ways?"

"Is that what you want?"

Her gaze met his. She really didn't want this thing between them to end. She was getting totally caught up in this world of make-believe. And what would it hurt for it to go on just a little longer?

Cristo reached out to her, running the back of his fingers down her cheek. "Tell me what you want."

The pounding of her heart echoed in her ears. Her mouth opened but nothing came out. Her mind went blank. Sometimes words just weren't enough. Without giving thought to the consequences, she lifted up on her tiptoes and leaned forward. Her lips pressed to his.

This was most definitely what she wanted.

His hands gripped her hips, pulling her closer. Her breasts pressed against his muscled chest. Her palms landed on the smooth skin of his shoulders. It was as though an electrical pulse zinged through her fingertips and raced through her body. Every part of her body was alert and needy.

Their kiss moved from tentative to heated in less time than it took his fancy sports car to reach cruising speed. And her engine was revved up and ready to go. Tonight she wasn't going to think about the future or the implications of where this most enticing night would leave them. This moment was all about letting down their guards and savoring the time they had together.

Cristo pulled back. His breath was deep and fast. His heated gaze met hers. "Kyra, are you sure about this?"

She nodded. She'd never been so sure about anything in her life. That not-so-long-ago night when he'd proposed to her, he'd utterly charmed her. But today when they'd toured Orchidos, he'd finally cracked the wall around her heart.

If she walked away now, she would regret it for the rest of her life. Her time with Cristo was the stuff that amazing memories were made of. And she wanted a piece of him to take with her—a tender, special moment.

"I'm sure." Her voice came out as a whisper in the breeze. "I've never been more certain."

His lips claimed hers again. His kiss was hungry and rushed, like a drowning man seeking oxygen. Her hands wrapped around his neck. The curves of her body pressed to the solid muscles of his toned body.

In that moment, she could no longer hide from the truth. She loved Cristo. He hadn't snuck around, no, he'd marched right past her defenses and staked a claim to her heart. She'd tried ignoring it and then denying it, but the truth was she loved him.

As though he sensed her surrender, he stopped kissing her long enough to sweep her off her feet. Her pulse raced. If she was dreaming, she never wanted to wake up.

This night would be unforgettable.

CHAPTER SIXTEEN

THE GLARE OF sunshine had a way of making things look different than they had in the shadows of the night.

Kyra had absolutely no idea what to say to Cristo. So she'd avoided him all day, hoping the words would eventually come to her. But by evening, she was even more confused by her emotions.

Where exactly had their night of lovemaking left them? After all, it wouldn't have happened if not for their make-believe relationship. This whole web of role-playing and innuendos was confusing everything. And now they'd just succeeded in compounding matters even further.

As she recalled the magical night of whispered sweet nothings and the flurry of kisses, her heart fluttered. But was this rush of emotions real? Or was it a side effect of their fake romance? How was she to know?

The only abundantly clear fact was that she would have to be extremely careful going forward. Otherwise, her heart would end up smashed to smithereens when this elaborate ruse was over. And she had no doubt this relationship would most definitely end, sooner rather than later. Cristo had made that crystal clear.

Kyra stepped up to the floor-length mirror in her bedroom and examined her little black dress. It certainly wasn't anything fancy by any stretch, but she wasn't sure what casual dress entailed. So in her mind, a little black dress seemed to work for all occasions—she hoped.

There was a tap on her bedroom door followed by Cristo's voice. "Kyra, are you ready?"

"Um, yes. I'll be right there." There was no time for second-guessing or trying on yet another dress. She was going with black. She snatched up a small black purse with delicate beading on the front and headed for the door, hoping this evening would go much better than their first encounter with Mr. Stravos.

On not-so-steady legs, she made her way to the living room, where Cristo was waiting for her. He looked breathtakingly handsome in a stylish navy suit with a light blue shirt. The top buttons were undone and conjured up memories—heated, needy memories. How in the world was she supposed to get through the evening when she was so utterly distracted?

Cristo gave her outfit a quick once-over. "You look beautiful. Are you ready to go?"

She nodded, still uncertain where things stood between them and not sure how to broach the subject. Apparently she wasn't the only one unsure, because she noticed how Cristo was careful to avoid the subject, too. In fact, he was quieter than normal. It only succeeded in increasing her nervousness.

Once again, they were whisked away in the helicopter. This time she welcomed the *whoop-whoop* of the rotary blades. It was a perfectly legitimate excuse to remain quiet. The only problem was the ride was much too short, and before she was ready, they touched down at the Stravos estate.

This time Niko came out to greet them. "I must apologize for my grandfather. He is delayed by an overseas phone call. But have no worries, he will be joining us."

Cristo gave each sleeve of his suit a tug. "Do you know why he wanted to meet with us?"

Kyra translated that to mean *Is he interested in making a deal?* She had to admit she was quite curious, too. Because she had a distinct feeling her future with Cristo hinged on what happened this evening. And she wasn't ready to let him go, not yet. They'd finally turned a corner in their relationship and she was anxious to see if there was anything real—anything lasting.

Tonight, dinner was served outside in the courtyard. Lanterns were lit and strategically placed around the area, providing a cozy ambience.

"Kyra?" It was Cristo's voice and it held a note of concern.

She glanced over to find both men staring at her. "Um, sorry. I was just trying to memorize the layout of this patio area. I'd love to have something similar someday."

Cristo arched a brow, but he didn't ask any questions. "Niko asked if you'd care for something to drink."

"Yes, please. Would you happen to have any iced tea?"

Niko smiled and nodded. "I'll get that for you."

She was surprised to see her host move to the cart of refreshments and pour her a glass of tea. For some reason, she imagined there would be servants tripping over themselves to do Niko's bidding. Apparently this billionaire was quite self-sufficient. Maybe that was why she liked him so much. And she noticed Cristo had warmed up to him, too.

Kyra struck up a conversation about the architecture of Niko's home and its rich history. Cristo surprised her with his knowledge of Greek history. Little by little, she found herself relaxing.

"Excuse me." A voice came from across the courtyard. Conversation immediately ceased as all heads turned to find Mr. Stravos making his way toward them. "Apologies. Work waits for no man."

Cristo got to his feet. Kyra followed his lead, anxious for this visit to go better than the last one. She lifted her lips into what she hoped was a warm smile even though her insides shivered with anxiety. She noticed that Mr. Stravos didn't smile. Was he angry? Or was that his usual demeanor?

After shaking hands with Cristo, the older man turned to her. He took her hand in his, and instead of shaking it, he lifted it to his lips and pressed a feathery kiss to the back of her hand. She continued to hold her smile in place.

Well, he definitely isn't angry. What a relief.

"Thank you for coming back to visit, my dear. I'm sorry our previous time together was so brief."

"Thank you for the invitation. I was just telling Niko how lovely I find your courtyard. Someday I'd love to have a similar one." She struggled to make polite chatter when all she wanted to do was question the man about her family.

Mr. Stravos glanced around as though he'd forgotten what it looked like. "I must admit that I don't spend much time out here these days. Most of my time is spent in my office."

"You must be quite busy. Too bad it takes you away from this gorgeous courtyard and the amazing flower gardens surrounding your home."

As though on cue, dinner was served at the glass table on the other side of the courtyard. The conversation turned to their adventure to Orchidos. Cristo joined in, explaining that it was also his first visit to the village. Everyone took a turn talking about subjects from the wild orchids growing throughout the village to the architecture.

After dinner, everyone moved to the cushioned chairs grouped together. Cristo took her hand and gave it a squeeze. Her gaze moved to meet his. He smiled at her and her heart tumbled in her chest. No man had ever made her feel so special.

"How long are you going to continue with this charade?" Mr. Stravos asked out of the blue.

Kyra's gaze swiftly moved to the older man. His expression was perfectly serious. They'd been busted. And try as she might, she couldn't keep the heat of embarrassment from rushing to her cheeks.

Cristo's neck muscles flexed as he swallowed. "What charade?"

"This." The man waved his hand between him and Kyra. "You think I'm going to sell you my hotels because you put on a show of marrying her. You two hardly know each other. Am I really supposed to believe that you care for her?"

Kyra hoped Cristo knew what to say because her mind was a blank. If she tried to speak now, it'd be nothing more than stuttering and floundering.

"You're right." Cristo released her hand and sat forward. "I knew how important marriage is to you and I wanted you to take my proposal seriously, so I asked Kyra to act as my fiancée." When the older man's gaze moved her way, Cristo added, "Don't be upset with her. She didn't want to do it, but I convinced her. And a lot has changed since then."

Kyra was not about to let Cristo shoulder all of the blame. The more she got to know Cristo, the more she realized how important this deal was to him. "He has been nothing but kind and generous. I couldn't ask for anyone better in my life." Her gaze moved to the man who'd rocked her world the night before. His gaze met hers. In that moment, she had her answer—their lovemaking hadn't been faked. There was something genuine between them.

Mr. Stravos scoffed at her defense of Cristo. "He is only looking out for himself. He wants this deal so much that he will do anything to get it."

"That's not true. He's been helping me track down my family. It's what led us to Orchidos." She sighed, still disappointed they hadn't unearthed any new information. "But we weren't able to come up with any further information. Which is strange because the investigator traced the photo I have back to that village."

The older man's dark eyes narrowed. "Do you have the photo with you?"

At last she'd gained his attention and hopefully his help. "I do." She reached into her purse and withdrew the black-and-white photo. She held it out to the man. "That's my grandmother and grandfather. They both died before I was born."

The man didn't say a word as he retrieved his reading

glasses from his jacket pocket. He moved the photo closer to the lantern to get a better look. Did he recognize someone? The longer he stared at the photo, the more hope swelled in her chest. What did he know about her family? Would he be able to point her in the right direction?

She sat up straight and laced her fingers together to keep from fidgeting. As though sensing her mounting anxiousness, Cristo reached out to her. His fingers wrapped gently around her forearm and gave her a squeeze before sliding down to her hand. She unclenched her fingers in order to hold his hand.

Her gaze met his, where she found comfort and reassurance. It helped calm her racing heart. No matter what Mr. Stravos said, she knew instinctively that Cristo would be there to help her deal with the news.

Mr. Stravos tapped the photo with his finger. "You're sure this is your family?"

Kyra nodded. The breath hitched in her throat. She had the feeling her life was about to take a drastic turn. She just hoped it was for the best.

There was a long pause before Mr. Stravos spoke again. "I… I knew your grandmother."

Really? There was sincerity written all over his aging face. She expelled the pent-up breath, but she was still cautious. "Why didn't you say so when I told you her name?"

"Because I had to be sure it was her. You don't understand."

"You're right. I don't understand at all. Why would you keep it a secret that you knew her?"

"Because she's my sister. And you aren't the first person to come here claiming to be my long-lost relative—"

"I never claimed to be anything of the sort." She could feel Cristo's grip on her tightening just a bit—cautioning her to move carefully.

"I am sorry." The man's voice was barely more than a whisper. "I've grown too cautious over the years."

She had the feeling the apology was rare for him. His words touched her and immediately soothed her lingering ire. "Trust me. I didn't come here expecting or wanting anything from you. We…we should go."

"No. Stay. Please. We have much to talk about."

She cast Cristo a hesitant look. He nodded his consent. She settled back in her seat and coffee was poured. She tried to relax but she was too wound up, waiting and wondering what information Mr. Stravos would have about her grandparents.

"I haven't seen my sister since I was a kid. She was older than me. Many years ago, our family lived in Orchidos."

"I don't understand. Cristo and I just spent a day there, talking with people and searching through old papers. There was no hint of your family or my grandmother."

Her uncle nodded in understanding. "That's because I had some problems in the past with blackmail. I had as much of my family's history that could be located gathered and brought to me. And the people of Orchidos who knew my family promised to keep what they knew to themselves. Having money comes with challenges that some might not expect. Privacy comes at a premium."

"And how do you know I'm not lying to you?" She didn't like being even remotely lumped in with blackmailers and scam artists.

"That's easy, my dear. You look like my sister when she was younger. When I first saw you, I thought I'd seen a ghost."

Which explained why he'd made such a hasty exit after their first meeting. "But I don't understand. Why don't you know what happened to my grandmother? Did you two have a falling-out?"

"No. We didn't. But she had one with our father. She'd fallen in love with a boy my father didn't approve of. My father did everything possible to break them up but nothing worked. When they eloped, my father disowned her and told her she was never welcome in his home again."

A deep sadness came over Kyra. She couldn't imagine what it would be like for her grandmother to have to choose between the man she loved and her family. "That must have been horrible for all of you."

"There was no reasoning with my father. He was a big man who ruled the household with an iron fist. And he never backed down from a decision."

"So my grandmother married my grandfather and moved to the States?"

Her uncle nodded. "That night was the last time I saw her. My mother and I were banned from keeping in contact with her. When I got older, I thought about checking on her, but back in those days there was no such thing as the internet—no easy way to find someone who didn't want to be found."

They continued to talk and fit together the puzzle pieces of her grandmother's life. And then the conversation turned to Kyra and her life. Uncle Nikolaos seemed genuinely interested in her. He at last let down his guarded exterior, showing her a warm and approachable side.

When she glanced around, she found Cristo and Niko deep in conversation. This evening had turned out quite differently than she'd imagined. And it was all thanks to Cristo. If it wasn't for him, she never would have met her uncle and cousin.

As though Cristo could sense she was thinking about him, he glanced over at her and smiled. Just that small gesture sent a warm, fuzzy feeling zinging through her chest. She loved him more than she'd ever loved anyone. And she knew it was dangerous, because in the end, she would get hurt. But for this evening, she was going to bask in the warmth she found being in the company of the man she loved and her newfound family.

* * *

Cristo had a hard time taking his eyes off Kyra.

There was something different about her that night. Was it that dress? Or was she glowing with happiness from finding her long-lost family? Whatever it was, she was even more captivating than before, if that was possible.

"My cousin seems to be charming my grandfather. That's not an easy feat. Trust me. I've tried in the past. That man is quite set in his ways."

"They do seem to be hitting it off." Cristo finished his coffee. He was tired of dancing around the subject. "What do you think my chances are of putting together a deal to buy the hotel chain?"

"Honestly, I've talked with my grandfather at some length and so far he hasn't shown any interest in parting with it. Between you and me, I think it goes far deeper than a business deal. But for the life of me, I can't figure out why he holds so tightly to it, and he won't explain it to me."

Cristo could feel his chance to seal this deal slipping away. And he'd run out of ideas of how to get through to Nikolaos Stravos, who took stubborn to a whole new level.

Niko set his empty coffee cup on a small table before turning back to Cristo. "I think your best hope lies with your fiancée." His brows drew together. "She's still your fiancée, isn't she?"

Without hesitation, Cristo nodded. "She is. If she'll still have me." A thought came to Cristo of a way to make Kyra happy. "Since you're now family, how would you feel about standing up for me at the wedding?"

Niko's eyes opened wide. "I'd be honored."

"Great." The men shook hands. "Kyra will be so happy."

Cristo turned to gaze over at his adorable fiancée. He didn't know how it had happened, but somewhere along the way, he'd begun to picture her in his future. In fact, he couldn't imagine life without her in it. Marriage would undoubtedly change things as he knew them, but he instinctively knew it would be better with her in it.

When it was time to call it a night, hugs were exchanged between Kyra and her newfound family. Cristo couldn't be happier for her and it had nothing to do with his business… or his hopes to iron out a deal with Stravos.

Nikolaos gave him a stern look. "No more charades. Honesty is the only sound basis for a relationship. And my great-niece deserves only the best."

"I'll do my best, sir."

Nikolaos arched a brow. "You should also know that your involvement with my niece will have no bearing on my decision about selling the hotel chain. Do not have her doing your bidding."

Cristo's body stiffened. "The thought never crossed my mind."

The man's cold, hard gaze left no doubt about his sincerity. "Good. Because if you do, mark my words, I will use every resource at my disposal to destroy you."

Cristo bristled at the threat, but he willed himself not to react for Kyra's sake. At long last, she'd found the family she had been longing for—a connection to the father she lost—and Cristo refused to be the reason for discord between them.

Noting the obvious affection in the older man's eyes when they strayed to Kyra, Cristo understood the man's protectiveness. Cristo cleared his throat. "I would expect nothing less of a caring uncle. I am glad you have found each other."

Nikolaos's eyes momentarily widened as though surprised by Cristo's response. "So long as we understand each other."

"We do, sir. We both want Kyra to be happy." And he truly meant it.

Approval reflected in Nikolaos's eyes. "If you two decide to go through with the wedding, I'd very much like to be there."

"You would?" Kyra interjected. A smile lit up her face.

"Most definitely."

Cristo held out his hand to the man. "We'll definitely keep in touch."

Nikolaos cleared his throat. "As for your offer to buy the hotel chain, I will take it under advisement. My grandson seems to think it would be a good idea to divest ourselves of it and focus on our shipping sector, but I like to remain diversified." He glanced down at Cristo's extended hand, then accepted it with a firm grip and solid shake. "I will take your offer to our advisers and see what they have to say."

"Thank you. I appreciate your consideration."

Cristo didn't know what would happen with his business deal, but he was starting to figure out that the most important thing right now was his future with Kyra.

CHAPTER SEVENTEEN

"I CAN'T BELIEVE IT," Kyra spoke into the phone the next morning.

The sound of footsteps on the tiled floor had her glancing over her shoulder. The sight of Cristo made her heart go *tip-tap-tap*. She smiled at him and he returned the gesture. There was just something about his presence that made her stomach quiver with excitement. He headed straight for the coffeemaker.

"Sofia, I've got to go. I'll talk to you later."

Kyra rushed off the phone. She couldn't stop smiling. She told herself it was because she'd connected with her father's family. And though it wasn't exactly the family she'd been expecting, it was a connection to her father nonetheless. That connection was priceless, especially in light of the discord between her and her mother.

"You can't believe what?"

"I'm just so surprised we found my family. Honestly, after we ran into nothing but dead ends in Orchidos, I'd pretty much given up hope of finding anyone or learning anything about my father's family. I can't believe I've found them."

"I'm really happy for you."

Maybe this was the opening she needed to help Cristo find his way back to his family, which was so much more important than the business deal—if only he could see that.

"Do you really mean that?"

"Of course I do. I know how important family is to you."

"It's just as important to you." When he shook his head, she persisted. "It is, or you wouldn't be so tormented by the memory of your brother or doing everything in your power to gain your father's respect."

He continued to shake his head. "You don't know what you're saying."

"This wedding, it could be a bridge back to them." She had no idea if he was listening to anything she was saying, but she couldn't give up. Someone had to make him see reason.

His dark brows drew together as his disbelieving gaze met hers. "And how is that going to work? Invite them here for a doomed wedding? I'm sure that'll really impress them."

"You're missing the point. This isn't about impressing anyone—it's about reconnecting, talking, spending time together. They'll understand when the wedding is canceled for legitimate reasons."

He raked his fingers through his hair. "Why is this so important to you?"

"Because it's important to you. Just promise me that you'll think about it."

He hesitated. "I'll think about it. By the way, you're welcome to visit with your uncle and cousin as much as you want. Just let me know ahead of time and I'll have the helicopter available. I know you're really missing your mother—"

A frown pulled at Kyra's face. "I don't want to talk about her."

"Wait a second. You're allowed to lecture me on making amends with my family and yet you're unwilling to deal with your own mother?"

"It's different."

"Uh-huh." His tone held a distinct note of disbelief. "And how would that be?"

Kyra huffed. "Because she lied and manipulated me."

"One of these days you're going to have to take her call."

"Not today." Kyra glanced at the clock, finding it was already after eight o'clock. She turned back to Cristo. "Speaking of family, I've received RSVPs from your brothers. They send their regrets."

"I told you they'd be too busy to travel halfway around the world for a wedding." His tone was matter-of-fact. "That's why I asked Niko to stand up for me."

"You did?" This was news to her.

Cristo nodded. "And he agreed. So no worries about my absentee brothers."

The fact he hadn't expected more from his brothers was disheartening. She didn't like the distance between Cristo and his family. Maybe it was because the only family she had now was her mother, but Kyra didn't think there was anything more important than staying in contact with those you cared about.

"I just can't believe they'd miss their brother's wedding."

"Believe it. The apple doesn't fall far from the tree."

"What does that mean?"

"It means they are a lot like my father. Business first. Family a distant second."

How sad.

"Were you ever close?"

"My brothers are a lot older than me. Eight and ten years. It wasn't like we had much in common. I was much closer to Max."

And when Max died, Cristo was left alone with his guilt. *How awful.* She wanted to help him find a way back to his family.

"Maybe if you were to call your brothers—maybe if they knew how important this is to you—"

"No." His voice held a note of finality. "I'm fine on my own."

"Are you? Or are you punishing yourself for Max's accident—something that wasn't your fault?"

"You don't know what you're talking about."

"Don't I?"

She wasn't going to back down and let him waste the rest of his life in a mire of guilt for something that wasn't his fault. "You keep thinking that if you'd said something different or done something different that the accident could have been averted, don't you? It's easier to blame yourself than to accept it was totally out of your hands." Her voice wobbled. "Nothing would have changed what happened."

Cristo's brows scrunched together. "You sound like you're talking from experience."

"I am." She'd never told anyone this. "For a long time, I blamed myself for my father's death."

"But why? I thought he died of a heart attack."

"He did. At home. Alone. My mother had driven me to the movies to meet one of my friends. My mother went shopping until it was time to pick me up. There wasn't anyone there to help him. To call 911."

Cristo moved to her side and wrapped an arm around her shoulders, pulling her close. She let her weight lean into him. Together they could prop each other up. "It wasn't your fault."

"Just like it wasn't your fault."

Cristo didn't say anything, which she took as a good sign. Hopefully he'd let go of the guilt that was only succeeding in distancing him from his family.

Kyra blinked repeatedly, trying to stuff her emotions down deep inside. "Shouldn't you be at a meeting or something?"

His brows lifted. "Are you trying to get rid of me?"

"Not at all. It's just that you're always so busy."

He took a sip of coffee before returning the cup to the bar. "You're right. I am a busy man. Maybe too busy."

"Too busy? Where did that come from?"

"I've been thinking about what you said about slowing down."

Really? He'd listened to something she'd said to him. He certainly had her attention now. "And what did you decide?"

"That there's more to life than work."

It was a good thing she had her hip against the couch or she might have fallen over. Since when did this workaholic have time for fun? "What have you done with the real Cristo?"

"I'm serious."

So it appeared. But she did have to wonder how far he was willing to take this makeover. "And what do you have in mind?"

"I saw there's a beach volleyball game this morning. I signed us up."

Her mouth gaped. She had to admit that she never expected those words to come out of his mouth. Not in a million years.

"You do play volleyball, don't you? I thought I overheard you mention it to Sofia."

She nodded. "I played all through high school. It wasn't beach volleyball, but it'll do."

"Good. How soon can you be ready?" There was a knock at the door. "That will be breakfast. I thought you'd want something to eat first."

"Are there any other surprises I should be aware of?"

He sent her a lopsided grin. "I don't know. Would you like some more?"

This playful side of Cristo was new to her, but she fully approved. A smile pulled at her lips as her gaze met his. She wanted the day to slow down so they could enjoy this time together a bit longer. Okay, a lot longer.

He held up a finger for her to wait as he went to answer the door. After the wide array of food had been delivered and arranged on the table, he turned back to her. "Now, what were we discussing? Oh, yes, surprises. Do you want more of them?"

She didn't have to contemplate the answer. "Yes, more surprises as long as they are this good." She lifted one of the silver lids from a plate, finding scrambled eggs, sausage, bacon and orange wedges. She grabbed a slice of orange and savored its citrusy taste. Once she'd finished it and set aside the rind, she turned back to him. "Definitely."

He moved to stand in front of her, and before she knew what he was up to, his head dipped. His lips claimed hers. His mouth moved tentatively over hers. Was he testing the waters? The thought that he wasn't as sure of himself as he liked the world to think turned her on all the more.

She met him kiss for kiss, letting him know that his advance was quite welcome. Her arms wound their way around his neck as his hands spanned her waist, pulling her snug against him. She definitely liked his surprises.

Much too soon, he pulled back. "Don't pout."

It showed? Or was he just getting to know her that well? "But I liked that surprise. A lot."

He smiled broadly. She loved how his eyes twinkled with merriment. It filled her with a happiness she'd never known before. She forced her lips into a playful frown, hoping to get more of his steamy kisses.

He shook his head. "It isn't going to work. You'll have to wait until later."

"You promise?"

"I do. But right now, we have some beach volleyball to get to."

"You're really serious about this, aren't you?" For some reason, she never pictured Cristo as the volleyball type. But then again, with his shirt off and some board shorts hung low on his trim waist...she could envision it clearly now.

"Yes, I'm serious. And if you don't go change quickly, we won't have time to eat."

Kyra groaned as he pushed her in the direction of her bedroom to put on her bikini. This day was definitely going to be interesting. Very interesting indeed.

How could more than two weeks have flown by?

Cristo had never had so much fun.

He'd really enjoyed this time with Kyra. There had been the volleyball tournament followed by leisurely strolls along the beach. There were late mornings wrapped in each other's arms followed by early evenings for more of the same. If only he'd known what he'd been missing all of this time, he might have taken the chance on love sooner.

Somewhere between the moonlit walks on the beach, the stories of her childhood and the stroll through a nearby village, he'd fallen for his own pretend bride. Now he wanted her for his very genuine wife. But how could he prove his honest intentions to her without her thinking he had an ulterior motive?

His feelings for her were not fleeting. This was not a summer romance to reflect upon in his twilight years. No, this was a deep down, can't-live-without-her love. But he knew Kyra was still holding back—clinging to that wall around her heart.

And he knew why—the fake engagement they'd struck at the beginning followed by her mother's betrayal. Combine them both and it was no wonder Kyra was having problems trusting him. But there had to be a way to convince her of his sincerity. But how?

While Kyra was off checking on flowers for the wedding, he found himself pacing back and forth in the suite. She had left him with one task to complete for the wedding—one task that left his gut knotted up. He had to make a phone call to his parents.

He withdrew his phone from his pocket. His finger hovered over the screen. He'd been very selective on which calls to take this week and which to let pass to his voice mail. Did that make him irresponsible? His father would say it did, but Cristo was beginning to see things quite differently. Every person deserved some downtime now and then. Everyone deserved time to find happiness and love.

And he wouldn't have realized any of this if it wasn't for Kyra. He owed her big-time for the happiness that she'd brought to his life. The least he could do was see if either of his parents were coming to the wedding.

With great trepidation, he dialed his mother's number. She immediately answered.

"Hello, Mother."

"Cristo, don't you ever answer your phone these days?"

She'd called him? This was news to him. He was certain there weren't any voice mails from her. He wouldn't forget something like that. "What's the matter? Is it Father?"

"Your father is fine."

"That's good." Why had he gone and jumped to conclusions? Maybe because his mother didn't call often and certainly not repeatedly. "What did you need?"

"It isn't what I need, but rather, what do you need? After all, you're the one getting married."

"I…I don't need anything." Well, that wasn't exactly true. He needed answers, but he wasn't sure his mother was the person to give them to him.

He needed to know if he was putting too much stock into building a lasting relationship with Kyra. When it was all over, would they end up cold and distant like his parents? The thought chilled him to the bone. He didn't think he could bear it if they did. And he certainly wouldn't want his children growing up in such an icy atmosphere.

He tried to think back to a time when his parents had been warm and affectionate with each other. Surely they must have been at one point. For the life of him, he couldn't recall his father sweeping his mother into his arms and planting a kiss on her lips just because he loved her and wanted to show her. How could they coexist all of these years with such distance between them?

"Mother, can I ask you a question?"

"You can ask, but I don't know if I'll have an answer for you."

His mother was a very reserved woman. She didn't sit down with a cup of coffee and spill her guts. Whatever she felt, she held it in. Maybe she was more like his father than Cristo bothered to notice before now.

"When you and Father married, were things different in the beginning?"

"Different? How so?"

"You know, was he always a workaholic?" Cristo just couldn't bring himself to say *icy* and *cold*.

"Your father made it perfectly clear from the start that his work would always come first."

"And you were all right with that?"

There was a slight pause. "I understood how important his work was to him."

"What about Max's accident? Did that change him?" What Cristo really wanted to know was if he was responsible in some way for his father's chilly distance from his own family.

This time there was a distinct pause. "The accident changed everyone. You included. But you can't blame yourself. It was an accident."

"That's not what Father thinks."

There was a poignant pause. "What your father thinks is that the accident was his fault. But he doesn't know what to do with all of that guilt and grief so he projects it on those closest to him. It creates a barrier around him, keeping us all out. He no longer thinks he deserves our love."

"Really?" Cristo had never gotten that impression. Had he been reading his father wrong all of this time?

"I think your father is afraid of losing someone else he loves, including you. I can't promise he'll ever be the father you want—the father you deserve—but sometimes you have to accept people flaws and all. Cristo, I'd love nothing more than our family to heal."

To heal there had to be forgiveness—a letting go of the past. Would his father be able to do that? More important, would Cristo be able to do it? Could he let go of his guilt over Max's death?

Cristo surprised himself when he realized that Kyra had opened his eyes and shown him the importance of family. Kyra had also pointed out a fact that both he and his father had been overlooking—Max wouldn't have wanted this big rift in the family. He was forever the peacemaker.

Maybe the best way to honor Max's memory was to swallow his pride and make peace with his father. But there was something he needed to know first. "Mother, is that what Father wants, too? For the family to be together again?"

There was a poignant pause. "I think he does, even if he can't bring himself to say the words."

His mother was only guessing. Of course his father wouldn't admit that he needed his family. That would make him look weak. "I don't know how you do it."

"Do what?"

"Make excuses for him and give him the benefit of the doubt. Do you really love him that much?"

There was suddenly a distinct chilliness in her voice. "Cristo, what are all of these questions about? Are you having second thoughts about your wedding?"

He was definitely having doubts, but not as she was thinking. He had to make a choice—his work or his bride. He couldn't have them both in equal portions. One had to outweigh the other. But could he let go of his work—his meetings and his endless phone calls—in order to put Kyra first in his life?

"Cristo, you're worrying me. What are you thinking?"

"That I don't want to end up like my father." It wasn't until the words were out of his mouth that he realized he'd voiced his worst fear. And he didn't have any idea how his mother would take such a statement.

"You have a good heart. Follow it. It won't let you down."

His mother rarely handed out advice, so for her to say this, she had to really believe it. His mother thought he had a good heart. A spot in his chest warmed. Maybe what he needed now was to have more faith in his love for Kyra.

"Thank you. This talk helped. I know exactly what to do. I've got to go."

After getting off the phone, he knew the only way to prove his love for Kyra was real would be to turn his back on the deal with Stravos. His heart beat faster. But how could he do that when he had worked so hard to make this deal a reality? He clenched his hands. How could he give up his chance to finally prove himself to his father—to earn his father's respect?

But then Kyra's smile came to mind and his fisted hands relaxed. He remembered the way her eyes lit up when she was happy. He conjured up the memory of her melodious laughter and the way it relaxed him. She knew what was important in life—family and love.

He had to trust in his love for her.

The rest would work itself out.

CHAPTER EIGHTEEN

WASN'T THIS EVERY little girl's dream?

Kyra turned in a circle in front of the large mirrors that had been specially delivered to her suite. The slim-fitting snow-white lace-and-organza bridal gown was divine. This was her final fitting and she didn't think the dress needed another stitch. It was absolutely perfect. The neckline dipped, giving just a hint of her cleavage. The bodice hugged her waist. She smiled at her reflection, imagining what it'd be like to walk down the aisle and have Cristo waiting for her.

She'd tried on countless wedding dresses from frilly ball gowns to hip-hugging mermaid-style dresses. They were either too flouncy, too clingy or too revealing. She had started to think she'd never find the right dress.

It wasn't until her frustration had reached the breaking point that she stopped and wondered why she was working so hard to find the perfect dress for a fake wedding. Why was it so important to her? As of yet, she didn't have an answer—at least none she was willing to accept.

The wedding was only two days away and Cristo had yet to call it off. She didn't understand why, especially now that her uncle had stated their marriage would have no bearing on his decision to sell the hotel chain. Or was Cristo hoping to really go through with the wedding? Did he think by marrying her that her uncle would feel obligated to follow through with the sale?

A frown pulled at her lips. Was she merely a means to an end? The thought made her stomach lurch. Or was she making too much of things—letting her imagination run amok?

She inhaled a deep, calming breath. That must be it, because Cristo had been nothing but charming and thoughtful. He wouldn't hurt her. It was bride's nerves—even if she wasn't truly a bride. And besides, with Cristo holding off on canceling the wedding there was still a chance his parents would make an appearance. Kyra had even sent them a note pleading with them to come for their son's sake. She never heard back.

A knock at the door curtailed her thoughts. The suite had been a hub of activity all morning in preparation for the big day. She'd never had so many people fuss over her. It was a bit intoxicating. If only it was real…

She spun around one more time, enjoying the breezy feel of the luxurious material. She wondered what Cristo would think of it. Would he want something more traditional? Or perhaps he'd rather she wear something more daring—more revealing? Kyra sighed. The truth was she didn't know what he'd think and she never would.

"Hello, Kyra."

Oh, no! It can't be.

Kyra spun around, finding her mother standing in the doorway of the suite. Her arms were crossed. That was never, ever a good sign.

"Mom, what are you doing here? I didn't know you were flying in."

"You would have known if you'd ever check your messages. But I guess we're even now because I didn't know my own daughter was getting married."

Kyra glanced down at her wedding dress. "I can explain."

Her mother's gaze narrowed. "I can't wait to hear this."

Kyra inwardly groaned. Could this day possibly get any worse?

"Explain what?" Cristo came to a stop next to her mother.

This time Kyra groaned aloud. It was her fault. She shouldn't have tempted fate. Now look at what she'd brought upon herself, her mother and her fake groom all in the same room. Wasn't this cozy?

Her mother turned to Cristo. "And you would be?"

"Cristo Kiriakas. The groom. And you would be?"

"The mother of the bride." Her painted red lips pressed together in a firm line of disapproval. Her gaze flickered between Cristo and Kyra. "And now you've ruined everything."

A look of bewilderment filled Cristo's wide eyes. "Excuse me. I don't understand. What did I ruin?"

"Surely someone must have told you the groom can't see the bride in her wedding gown. Now go. Get. You can't be here."

Cristo's brows drew together and his voice deepened. "This is my suite and no one orders me around."

"Must you be so stubborn? Don't you know being here is bad luck? Come back later. My girl and I have some catching up to do."

He sent Kyra a questioning look. She shrugged. Right about now, her face felt as if it was on fire. This just couldn't be happening. This had to be some sort of nightmare and soon she'd wake up.

Cristo sent her a reassuring smile, letting her know he had everything in hand. "I think she looks absolutely beautiful in her gown." He glanced up at the ceiling. "See, no lightning strikes. I think we're safe."

"Really? Are you really going to stand there and mock me?" Her mother sent him an I-dare-you-to-argue-with-me glare.

Kyra inwardly groaned. She knew that look all too well. Cristo would lose and it wouldn't be pretty. Kyra rushed over to the counter and grabbed her phone. Reinforcements were needed and fast.

Mop&Glow007 (Kyra): 911...suite

MaidintheShade347 (Sofia): What's wrong?

Mop&Glow007 (Kyra): Everything. Hurry.

Tension filled the room.

"Mom, what are you doing here?" Kyra tried to redirect the conversation.

For a moment, her mother didn't move. Eventually, she turned to Kyra. "You surely didn't think I was going to let my only child walk down the aisle without me."

"But I'm not—" Cristo sent her an icy stare that froze the words in the back of her mouth.

Her mother's perfectly plucked brows drew together. "You're not what?"

"I'm not," she said as she glanced at Cristo, who shook his head, "getting married right now."

Her mother sighed. "And you expect me to believe that while you're standing here in your wedding dress? I know you're mad at me, but were you really going to get married without telling me?"

Kyra shrugged. She honestly didn't have an answer because she'd never thought about it, since this wedding was never going to take place. But with Cristo signaling for her to keep quiet about the fake engagement, she couldn't tell her mother the truth right now. And if her mother learned the truth, word would spread quickly. The scandal they desperately wanted to avoid would become a reality. So Kyra said nothing. *What a mess.*

"Mom, how did you know about the wedding?"

"I read it in the paper just like everyone else. Honestly, Kyra, do you know how it made me feel to learn about your engagement that way?"

Kyra sent Cristo a puzzled look. He'd promised that news of their engagement wouldn't be in the United States papers. He shrugged innocently.

"Kyra, what's really going on? Are you pregnant?"

"What? No! Mother!" The heat in her face amplified.

Her mother's suspicious stare moved from her to Cristo

and back again. "I'm only saying what others will think with such a rushed wedding."

"That's it. I've heard enough." Cristo stepped up to her mother. "You can't come in here and upset Kyra. I think you've already caused her enough pain."

"Her pain? What about mine? She abandoned me and now she's trying to get married behind my back—"

"That's enough!" Cristo's voice held a steely edge. "Kyra has done nothing but love you and do everything she could to help you. It's you who owes her an apology."

Her mother gaped at him, but no words passed her lips.

"Kyra, I'm here. What's the emergency?" Sofia came to an abrupt halt in the open doorway. Her gaze moved rapidly between Cristo and Kyra's mother. "Oh. Hi, Mrs. Pappas."

For an awkward moment, no one spoke. The tension was thick in the room as Cristo and her mother continued to stare at each other as though in some power struggle.

Sofia sent Kyra a what-do-I-do-now look.

Kyra snapped out of her shocked stupor. "Sofia, why don't you give my mother a tour of the resort while I get out of this dress."

"I don't want a tour," her mother announced emphatically. "I want to know why you're standing there in your wedding gown in front of the groom. There's still time to fix this. We can find another dress—"

"Mom, no. This dress is perfect."

Her mother gave the dress due consideration and then nodded. "It was perfect, but now it's jinxed."

"It is not. I love it. Now, please go with Sofia." Before her mother could argue, Kyra added, "Really, Mom, go ahead. I have a few things to discuss with the seamstress and then I'll be free."

"But what about him?" Her mother nodded toward Cristo.

"He's not superstitious and neither am I. We'll make our own luck."

"Well, I never..." With a loud huff, her mother turned and stormed out of the room.

Sofia sent her one last distressed look.

Kyra mouthed, *Sorry*.

Once they were gone, Cristo shut the door. "Would you mind explaining what just happened here?"

"Tornado Margene blew into town, huffing and puffing." Kyra stepped down from the pedestal, anxious to get out of the dress.

"So I've seen. But what is she doing here?"

"Why are you asking me? You're the one who promised not to put our wedding announcement in the New York papers. If you want someone to blame for this fiasco, look in the mirror."

"I didn't do it." When she continued to look skeptical, he continued. "Why would I? It just complicates things further." He paused as though a thought had just come to him.

"What is it? Don't hold back now." She approached him.

"Considering the timing of your mother's visit, I'm going to guess my mother received her wedding invitation and arranged for the press to be informed. It would be something she'd do. She's always taking care of details like that. She doesn't know we're not—well, um...that the marriage—"

"Isn't real," Kyra whispered, finishing the sentence though it left an uneasy feeling in her stomach.

He raked his fingers through his hair. "This certainly complicates things."

"You think? And I've got my finals tonight." She should be studying this afternoon, not trying to appease her mother.

Cristo's face took on a concerned look. "Can you get an extension?"

She shook her head while catching the anxious look on the seamstress's face. "I've got to change clothes. I'll be back. Don't go anywhere. We aren't done talking."

This arrangement couldn't go on. She shouldn't have

agreed to it in the first place. In the end, it hadn't worked out for Cristo after all. She felt awful for him.

Would Cristo understand when she called everything off? Would they still be on friendly terms? Or would they go their separate ways and never see each other again? The thought of never seeing Cristo again tore at her heart.

But she realized that's the way it needed to be. He had his work. She had her family. That had to be enough.

Kyra wasn't just beautiful.

She was stunning in her wedding dress. Like a princess.

Cristo paced the length of the living room. Over and over. Her mother making a surprise appearance certainly wasn't how he'd planned for their talk to start.

For days now he'd been trying to decide how to propose for real. At last he had everything sorted out. That was until her mother showed up. Why did her mother pick today of all days to fly in?

He stopped and stared down the hallway. There was no sign of Kyra. What was taking her so long? He paced some more.

He envisioned telling Kyra his decision to make this marriage authentic. Her face would light up with joy as she rushed into his arms and kissed him. Excitement swelled in his chest at the mere idea of it. He'd promise her that they could face anything as long as they were together and she'd agree. Life would be perfect. Okay, maybe that was stretching things with her mother being at the resort, but it would all work out. It had to.

At last Kyra emerged from her room in a pair of peach capris with a white lace tank top. Her hair was in a twist and piled atop her head with a clip. She looked absolutely adorable. Thankfully the seamstress had made a hasty departure.

Cristo drew in a deep steadying breath and then slowly blew it out. "Kyra, we need to talk—"

"If this is about my mother, I'm sorry for accusing you of letting the cat out of the bag."

"It's okay—"

"No, it isn't. I jumped to conclusions and I shouldn't have." Her gaze didn't meet his. "There's something I have to tell you. I know we made a deal, but I… I can't go through with this. I have to be honest with my mother—with everyone."

"I understand."

Her head jerked upward and her wide-eyed gaze met his. "You do? You understand?"

His gaze moved to the windows. Suddenly he felt the walls closing in on him. Or maybe it was a case of anxiety. He'd never considered it before now, but what if Kyra turned him down? What would he do then?

"Cristo? Did you hear me?"

"I have an idea. How about some sunshine and fresh air?"

Her brows arched. "What about our talk?"

"We'll talk. I promise." He moved toward the door. "Come on."

"Cristo, I can't. If you hadn't noticed, my mother is here."

"She can wait. This can't."

He led her to the elevator, out the back entrance and down a windy path to the beach area. Maybe he should have rehearsed what he was going to say to her. Where did he even begin? His jaw tensed. What if he made a mess of things?

Kyra touched his arm. "Hey, what's wrong?"

He glanced over at her. Concern reflected in her eyes. The words wouldn't come. They caught in the back of his throat.

"Just relax." She slipped her hand in his. "Whatever it is, we'll deal with it."

His frantic thoughts centered. All he could think about was how her smooth fingertips moved slowly over his palm, sending a heady sensation shooting up to his chest and farther. His anxious, rushed thoughts smoothed out. He could do this. Anything was possible with Kyra by his side. They were a team.

Hand in hand they walked along the path away from the crowded beachfront. This time around, he didn't want an audience for what he was about to say. He just needed Kyra.

Alone at last, he turned to her. "I have something I need to tell you."

Worry lines creased her beautiful face. "It's okay. I know what you want to talk about."

"You do?" Was he that obvious? He didn't think so but, then again, Kyra knew him better than anyone. He'd opened up to her far more than he'd ever done with anyone.

"It's my mother. Don't worry. I'll send her packing—"

"No, it's not her. And you don't have to ask her to leave on my account. In fact, it might be better if she stayed—"

"Why? Are your parents coming for the wedding, too?"

He shook his head. "My mother called. Neither she nor my father will be attending. She blamed it on my father's hectic work schedule."

"I take it you don't believe her?"

He shrugged. "It doesn't matter. I don't need them here. But it might be nice if your mother stayed—"

"Stayed? Why do you keep saying that?"

He took both of Kyra's hands in his. "It's okay. You don't have to worry. I have a plan."

"A plan? Isn't that what just blew up in our faces? First with my uncle and now with my mother—"

"I guess you wouldn't exactly call it a plan."

Frustration reflected in Kyra's eyes. "Would you please explain what you're talking about?"

He was beating around the subject and making this conversation far more complicated than it needed to be. "The truth is, I called Nikolaos today. And I withdrew my offer to buy the hotels."

“What? But why? That deal means everything to you.”

“Because somewhere along the way, you taught me there are other things more important than business and beating my father at his own game.”

“I did that?”

Cristo nodded. “You taught me that and a lot more.”

He dropped down on one knee. “I know I am supposed to have a ring when I do this, but seeing as you’re already wearing it—”

“Cristo, get up!” Her eyes widened with surprise. “What are you doing?”

“You know what I’m doing. I’m proposing, if you’ll let me get the words out.”

“You can’t. This isn’t right.” She pulled her hands from his.

Wait. What? She was supposed to be jumping into his arms. Lathering his face with kisses. Not standing there looking as though she was about to burst into tears at any second.

He was so confused. He thought at last he’d gotten things right—choosing love over business. But it still wasn’t working out with a happily-ever-after.

Where had he gone wrong?

CHAPTER NINETEEN

THIS COULDN'T BE HAPPENING.

Cristo was saying all of the right things at exactly the wrong time.

Kyra took a step back. She couldn't—she wouldn't—be the woman he sacrificed everything for. The fact he'd withdrawn his offer for the Stravos hotels was too much. Though she loved him dearly, she couldn't let him turn his life upside down to be with her. She wouldn't be able to bear it when later he ended up resenting her.

"I can't do this." Her hands trembled as she slipped the diamond ring from her finger and pressed it into his palm.

"Kyra—"

"I'm so sorry." She turned on shaky legs, hoping they'd carry her back to the hotel.

"Don't walk away. Kyra, I know you care. Why are you doing this to us?"

She paused. If she was honest with him, he would just explain away her worries. He'd be more concerned about the here and now. He wouldn't give the future due consideration. But she could. She had to be the strong one—for his sake.

With every bit of willpower, she turned back and met the pained look on his face. "You have to understand that we've let ourselves get caught up in this fairy tale. Neither of us has been thinking straight."

"That's not true." His eyes pleaded with her.

"Everyone can see we don't belong together. Your parents can't even be bothered to meet me. Why can't you see that this is a mistake?"

"My parents know nothing of love. If they ever loved

each other, it was over years ago. But I do love you. I guess the real question is, do you love me?"

Kyra's gaze lowered to the ground. "You need and deserve more than I can give you. You're an amazing guy. Someday you'll find the right lady and she'll make you happy. You'll see—"

"What I see is you refusing to admit that you love me, too." He reached out to her.

Kyra sidestepped his touch. She knew that if he touched her—held her close—she'd lose her strength. She'd never be able to let him go—to let him find happiness. "I don't want to hurt you. I never wanted to do that. But you have to realize that this dream world we created isn't real. You and I as a couple, it isn't real."

His eyes grew dark and a wall came down in them, blocking her out. Even though they were standing beneath the warm Greek sun, a shiver ran across her skin.

"And that's it? You're done with us?" His voice vibrated with frustration.

"I think it's best we call the wedding off immediately and go our separate ways before we hurt each other any more."

He stared at her long and hard, but she couldn't tell what he was thinking. And then he cursed under his breath and started back toward the hotel—alone.

Kyra pressed a hand to her mouth, stifling a sob. She couldn't let her emotions bubble over now. She had to keep it together a little longer—until Cristo was out of sight.

He would never know how hard it was to turn him away. But she couldn't make the divide between him and his parents even wider—because they'd made it clear with their silence that they didn't approve of her. She was a nobody by their social standards. Her chest ached at the thought they wouldn't even give her a chance.

And now Cristo had sacrificed his chance to merge the Glamour Hotel chain and the Stravos Star Hotels. The enormity of the gesture finally struck her and a tear dropped onto her cheek. No one had ever sacrificed something so important for her. How was she ever going to move on without him?

Kyra dashed away the tears. Somehow she had to make things right once again for Cristo.

But how?

Her phone chimed. She pulled it from her pocket.

MaidintheShade347 (Sofia): Do you want to hang out?

Mop&Glow007 (Kyra): Can't.

MaidintheShade347 (Sofia): Busy with Cristo?

Mop&Glow007 (Kyra): No.

MaidintheShade347 (Sofia): No? What's up?

Mop&Glow007 (Kyra): It's over.

MaidintheShade347 (Sofia): What's over?

Mop&Glow007 (Kyra): Everything.

MaidintheShade347 (Sofia): Where are you?

Mop&Glow007 (Kyra): The beach.

MaidintheShade347 (Sofia): I'll be right there.

Kyra moved to the sand and sank down on it. It didn't matter if Sofia showed up or not. No one could fix this. No one at all. She'd done what was needed. Somehow she had to learn to live with the consequences, as painful as they were.

CHAPTER TWENTY

THE WEDDING WAS TOMORROW.

Correction. The wedding was supposed to be tomorrow.

Still in yesterday's clothes, Cristo paced back and forth in the empty suite. Kyra hadn't returned to their suite since they'd spoken yesterday—when he'd made a complete and utter fool of himself. He'd never begged a woman not to leave him. And yet, baring his soul to her hadn't seemed to faze her. He didn't understand her. He didn't understand any of this.

Kyra was different from any other woman he'd ever known. And he was different when he was with her. She brought out the best in him. And now that she was gone, he had all of the time in the world to catch up with business, but he didn't have the heart to do it. For the first time ever, he'd lost his zealousness for making boardroom deals.

What was wrong with him?

So what if a woman had dumped him? He knew better than to invest too heavily in a relationship. He knew they were likely to turn sour at a moment's notice just like his parents' unhappy union.

He should be happy he'd gotten out of the engagement unscathed. He could have ended up married to a woman who didn't love him. That would definitely be a road map to unhappiness.

How could he have let himself think any of it was real?

They'd been having fun. They'd been laughing and talking. That was all. He'd let himself get caught in those smiles of hers that lit up her whole face. He'd fooled not only those around them, but himself. He'd let himself believe in a fantasy of them creating a lasting relationship. And absolutely none of it had been real.

No matter how hard he tried, he couldn't make himself believe that last part. It had been real, at least for him. And that was what made this so difficult.

Thank goodness his father didn't know what a mess he'd made of things. It would have just reinforced his father's opinion that he was incapable of making important decisions—decisions for a multimillion-dollar business.

Cristo's hands balled as every muscle in his body stiffened. He was losing his edge. And that couldn't happen. He had to get a grip on his life and get it back on track. But how? It was as if by losing Kyra, he'd lost his rudder.

A knock at the door jarred him from his thoughts.

Kyra!

His heart raced. His palms grew clammy. He had to handle this the right way. He would be calm, cool and collected. He inhaled a deep breath and then blew it out.

His footsteps were swift and direct. He yanked the door open. "You came back."

Niko's brow knit together. "I wasn't here before."

"Oh. Never mind. I thought you were someone else." Cristo inwardly groaned as he turned and walked farther into the room.

Niko closed the door behind him. "So, are you ready for tonight?"

"Ready for what?"

"How could you forget? Tonight's your bachelor party. Your last night of freedom."

In truth, Cristo had forgotten, but he wasn't about to admit it. He wasn't about to let Niko read too much into his forgetfulness. "Sorry. I've been busy."

Niko glanced around the suite. "You don't look busy now. Want to grab some dinner before the party?"

Cristo rubbed his stiff neck. "I'm not hungry."

Niko sat down. "So tell me what's wrong."

"Why do you think something's wrong?"

"I didn't want to say anything, but you look like hell. So do you want to tell me what is going on?"

Cristo spun around and faced his friend, who had agreed to be his best man. Cristo hadn't asked him to fulfill the role because of the potential business deal, but rather because they'd struck up an easy friendship. Plus, Niko was going to be family and what better way to draw Kyra into her newfound family than to invite her cousin to be part of the wedding?

But so much had changed since that decision had been made. Cristo might as well let Niko know it was over. What was the point in holding back? Soon everyone would know the truth.

Cristo balled up his hands. "The…the wedding…it's off."

"What? But why? You and Kyra looked so happy together at dinner the other week."

Cristo choked down his bruised ego and pushed past his scarred heart to tell Niko the whole horrible story. He started with Kyra's mother making a surprise appearance and how her mother had lied to her. Then he mentioned the disastrous proposal. Cristo had hoped that by getting it off his chest he'd start to feel better about everything. But in the end, he didn't feel any better. In fact, he felt worse—much worse.

Niko looked him directly in the eyes. "Do you love her?"

Cristo sank down on the couch. "I thought I did but… but I was wrong."

"You don't believe that any more than I do. I know your ego is wounded. Any man's would be. But is it worth walking away from the love of your life?"

"You're just saying that because she's your cousin."

"No, I'm not. I'm saying this because I've never seen

a man look so miserable. Look at you. You're an absolute mess."

Cristo glanced down at his wrinkled clothes. He ran a hand over his hair, finding it scattered. And he didn't even have to check his jaw to know he had heavy stubble. His face was already getting itchy.

"Have you eaten anything recently?"

"I'm not hungry." Though his empty stomach growled its disagreement, he just didn't have any interest in food.

"There has to be a way to fix this." Niko sighed as he leaned back. "Did you ever consider she might have had a case of bridal nerves?"

Cristo shook his head. "It's not that."

"What do you think went wrong?"

"I don't know. That's what I spent all night and today trying to figure out. In the beginning, I never intended to care about her, but somewhere along the way this pretend relationship became the genuine thing."

"Did you tell Kyra this?"

"I started to, but she cut me off and told me I was making a mistake. She thinks everything I'm feeling is just an illusion."

"And is it?"

He shook his head. "It's real. I even called your grandfather and withdrew my offer to buy the hotel chain, hoping to prove my sincerity to her. But it didn't seem to faze her. In fact, it had the opposite effect."

"Trust me. I'm no expert on women and love, but if she means that much to you, you should go after her. Make her understand this isn't some illusion—that your feelings for her are real."

Cristo rubbed his neck again. "I don't know. Why would she believe me this time?"

"Maybe because this time you aren't going to blindside her with a proposal right after an emotional run-in with her mother. Maybe by now she realizes she made a monumental mistake, but she's too embarrassed to come back and face you."

Niko's words struck a chord in him, but Cristo's ego still stood in the way. One rejection was bad enough. Being rejected twice was just too much. "Why should I go after her when she was the one to back out of the wedding in the first place?"

Niko arched a brow. "Would you give up this easily on a business deal?"

Cristo inwardly groaned. His friend knew how driven he was, but that was business and this was…was different.

When Cristo didn't answer, Niko continued. "Wouldn't you try to do everything in your power to secure the deal—even if it meant risking a second rejection?"

Cristo knew all along that Niko was right. At this point, he didn't have anything more to lose. But he did have a chance to gain everything that was truly important. It was a chance to hold Kyra in his arms once more. A chance to gaze into her eyes and tell her how much he loved her. His love for her trumped his wounded pride.

Cristo jumped to his feet. "Don't call off the bachelor party." He started for the door. "I'll catch up with you later."

"Cristo, wait." When he turned around, Niko added, "Don't you think you should shower first?"

"I don't have time for that now. I have something far more important to do."

Now that he had a plan, he couldn't wait around. He had to go to Kyra. He had to apologize for throwing everything at her at once.

At last he realized he'd been so caught up in his own feelings and plans that Kyra's feelings hadn't registered. It hadn't struck him until now how her mother's appearance would make Kyra feel vulnerable. Instead of being there for her, he'd been pushing his own agenda as if their marriage was some sort of business deal.

Now he needed to apologize and be there to support Kyra as she dealt with her mother.

Whatever she needed, he'd do it.

He loved her.

He would wait for her…as long as she needed.

CHAPTER TWENTY-ONE

"STOP! I DON'T need to hear this. It's over. Done."

Kyra glared at Sofia, willing her to drop the subject of her now-defunct wedding. She couldn't take any more of being badgered by her best friend and her mother. They were getting on her case for calling off the wedding. They just didn't understand. She'd lost the only man she'd ever loved and to compound matters she'd just completed her finals even though she'd hardly been able to concentrate on them. Thankfully her test results wouldn't be in for another week.

She sat on Sofia's couch and stabbed a spoon in the now-soft ice cream. She could only deal with one tragedy at a time. And missing Cristo was as much as she could take at the moment.

"Obviously you need to listen to somebody as you're not making any sense." Her mother crossed her arms and frowned at her.

"And you're lucky I'm even speaking to you after the way you lied and manipulated me. How could you do it?"

The color drained from her mother's face. "I told you I'm sorry."

Kyra swirled the spoon in the ice cream. "And that's supposed to fix everything?"

"No." Her mother sounded defeated. "I was wrong. After your father died, I wasn't thinking clearly. I couldn't bear to be alone."

"Why couldn't you have just said that instead of creating elaborate lies and scheming to get me to move back in with you?"

Her mother lowered her arms and then laced her fingers

together. When she spoke, her voice was soft. "You had your own life. Your own friends. I thought you'd say no. And I would be all alone for the first time in my life." Tears splashed onto her mother's cheeks. "I was so lost without your father. He was my best friend."

The anger Kyra had been nursing the past few weeks melted away. As her mother softly cried, Kyra set aside her ice cream in order to put her arms around her. No matter what, she still loved her. "It's okay, Mom. You aren't going to lose me. Ever."

Her mother straightened and Sofia, looking a bit awkward, handed her some tissues. Her mother's watery gaze moved from Sofia back to Kyra. "Really? You forgive me?"

"I'm working on it." It was the best she could offer for now. Her mother's lies had cut deeply. It would take time for the wounds to completely heal. "But you have to promise to always be honest with me…even if you're scared."

Her mother nodded as the tears welled up again. "I promise." She dabbed the tissues to her damp cheeks and then turned her bloodshot eyes to Kyra. "But you can't let what I've done ruin your future with Cristo. I've seen the way he looks at you. He loves you—"

"Mom, don't! That isn't going to help. What's done is done. I don't want to talk about it."

Her mother got to her feet. "You're making a mistake."

Once her mother retreated to the tiny balcony of Sofia's efficiency apartment, Kyra flounced back against the couch. No one understood she'd done what was necessary. Cristo was better off without her.

Sofia moved to stand in front of her. She planted her hands on her hips. "You aren't going to scare me off. So don't try."

Kyra retrieved the carton of rocky road from the end table and took another bite. "Why doesn't anyone believe this is for the best?"

"Because you don't believe it yourself or you wouldn't

be shoveling that ice cream in your mouth with a serving spoon."

"That's not true. It's a soup spoon." She glanced down, realizing she'd single-handedly wiped out half of the large container. This wasn't good. She set aside the melting ice cream and stood. "I need some air."

"Want some company?"

She shook her head. "I have some thinking to do."

"Think about the fact you might have been wrong about Cristo. He really loves you."

"You're just saying that because you want to believe in happily-ever-after." Kyra headed for the door.

"I never stopped believing in them. It's just that they are for other people, like you, not me. I have a habit of picking out the wrong guys."

Kyra opened the door and stepped into the quiet hallway before turning back. "You'll surprise yourself one of these days and find yourself a keeper."

"Oh, yeah, listen to who's talking. You've got yourself a keeper and you're tossing him back."

As Kyra walked away, she realized Sofia was right. Cristo was a keeper for someone—just not her.

The sun was setting as she walked along the path that snaked its way along the beach. The lingering golden rays bounced off the water, making it sparkle like an array of glittering diamonds—like the one that used to be on her finger. She glanced down at her bare hand. Tears stung the backs of her eyes. She blinked them away. Her emotions felt as though they'd been shoved through a cheese grater. Why did doing the right thing have to be so difficult?

As she walked, she kept replaying snippets of her time with Cristo. She loved how he'd started to let down his guard with her—how he'd started to enjoy life instead of going from one meeting to the next. She hoped now he wouldn't revert to his old ways. There was so much more to life than business—even if his future wasn't with her.

"Kyra."

She knew the sound of his voice as well as she knew her own. It was Cristo. How had he found her? Silly question. Sofia and her mother would have tripped over themselves to tell him where to find her.

She turned to him, too exhausted and miserable to put on a smile. But when her gaze landed on him, she found she wasn't the only one who wasn't doing well. Cristo's hair was a mess. His suit looked as though it had been in a hamper for a week. Wait. Weren't those the same clothes from yesterday? And then there were the dark shadows beneath his bloodshot eyes.

She stepped up to him. "Cristo, what's the matter?"

He didn't say anything. He just stared at her. All the while, her concern mounted. Maybe he was ill. Maybe something had happened to his family.

"Cristo, please say something. You're scaring me. Is everything all right?"

"No. Everything is not all right."

"Tell me what it is. I'll do what I can to help."

"Do you truly mean that?"

"Of course." She had already sacrificed her heart and her happiness for him, what was a little more?

CHAPTER TWENTY-TWO

CRISTO WANTED TO believe her.

He wanted to believe Kyra had at last come to her senses.

He wanted to believe she'd been caught off guard yesterday when he'd proposed. But the only way to find out was to put his scarred heart back on the line. His pulse raced and his palms grew moist.

With the lingering rays of the setting sun highlighting her beautiful face, he also noticed the sadness reflected in her eyes. Maybe Niko was right. Maybe too many surprises had been thrown at her yesterday. Maybe it had been bridal nerves. He sure hoped that's all it was.

Cristo stared deep into her eyes, knowing this would be the most important pitch of his life. "Kyra, I'm sorry about yesterday. I shouldn't have sprung that proposal on you after you had the shock of seeing your mother again. I was anxious." His head lowered. "I wasn't thinking clearly."

"It's okay. I'm not mad at you."

He lifted his head to see if she was telling him the truth. In her eyes, he found utter sincerity. "So if you aren't upset, why did you push me away?"

"We don't belong together. These past weeks have been an amazing fantasy and you've been wonderful, but it can't last forever. Things end."

"Are you thinking about your mother and father?"

She shrugged but her gaze didn't quite meet his.

"Well, I'm not your father. And no, I can't promise you that we'll have fifty years together. But you can't predict we won't. The future is a big question mark. But there is one thing that I do know."

"What?"

"That I love you." When she went to protest, he pressed a finger to her lips. "And it isn't part of my imagination. It's a fact. I love the way you laugh. I love the way you can see the important things in life. And I love that you are forever putting other people's happiness ahead of your own."

She removed his finger from her mouth but not before pressing a kiss to it. "It's more than that. I know how much you want your father's approval. They will never approve of a nobody like me."

"First of all, you're not a nobody."

"You mean because I'm Nikolaos Stravos's long-lost great-niece?"

"No. Because you're a ray of sunshine who makes this world a better place just by being in it."

"But your parents—"

"Will come around."

"Really? They won't even come to our wedding. I… I wrote them a note pleading with them to come to the wedding for you. And still they say nothing. I really thought I could get through to them."

His hands cupped her face. "See, there's another thing you've taught me—to quit working so hard to gain other people's approval. Fulfillment has to come from within—knowing that whatever I choose to do in life, I do it to the best of my ability."

"But they're your family."

"No. You're my family. I love you, Kyra. And I will be here to love you and support you."

There was a moment of silence. Oh, no. He prayed he'd gotten through to her.

"I do. I love you." Her eyes filled with unshed tears.

"I love you, too. And when you're ready, I have a question for you. But I won't pressure you. I'll wait. I'll wait for as long as it takes."

She sniffled and smiled up at him through her happy tears. "I'm ready now."

"You're sure?"

She nodded.

He slipped the ring from his pocket and held it out to her. "Kyra, will you marry me?"

She nodded as a tear splashed onto her cheek. "Yes. Yes, I will."

He'd never been so happy in his life. For so long, he thought seeking out bigger and better business deals would bring him the peace and happiness that he'd desired. How had he been so wrong?

"From this point forward, you and I are family." He leaned forward and pressed his lips to hers.

EPILOGUE

Next day...

"TALK ABOUT A perfect day."

"Do you really mean it?" Kyra looked up into her husband's handsome face as they swayed to a romantic ballad. All around them were wedding guests, smiling and talking.

"Of course I mean it. How could you doubt it?"

"It's just that I know this isn't how you'd been hoping things would turn out—"

He placed a finger to her lips, silencing her words. "We agreed we weren't going to discuss business today."

"I know. I just feel really bad you weren't able to work out the deal for the hotel chain. I think me turning out to be Nikolaos's great-niece hurt you instead of helped you."

Cristo arched a brow at her. "I've learned there are more important things in life than a successful business deal… such as an amazing wife and a monthlong honeymoon to look forward to."

Her heart swelled with love as she gazed into Cristo's mesmerizing eyes, and it was there she saw her future. "Do you know how much I love you?"

"Not as much as I love you." He leaned forward and pressed his lips to hers.

Being held in his strong arms and feeling his lips move over hers was something she'd never tire of. It was like coming home. Because no matter where they were, Cristo was her home, now and forever.

He led her from the dance floor and was about to get her a refreshment when Uncle Nikolaos approached them. She

immediately noticed his face was mark
are you feeling all right?"

He waved off her concern. "I'm fine. Just
I guess I'm not used to getting out and about. B
about me. I wanted to congratulate you again. You
mother would have been so proud of you. You're su a
beautiful bride."

"Thank you." Kyra leaned forward and pressed a kiss to his weathered cheek.

Uncle Nikolaos turned to Cristo and stuck out his hand. "Welcome to the family."

"Thank you, sir. Don't worry. I plan to make your niece very happy."

"I'm going to hold you to that promise. And I hope what I have to say won't distract you from the happiness you've found with Kyra, because nothing is more important than family."

Cristo wrapped his arm around her and pulled her close. "Trust me, sir. I've learned that lesson."

"Good. Then if you are still interested, expect a call soon to make the arrangements to have the Stravos Star Hotels sold to you. Consider it a wedding present."

For a moment no one spoke. At last Cristo found his voice. "Thank you. I am quite honored you trust me with the chain. I won't let you down."

"Thank your wife and Niko. They're both quite persuasive. An old man can only hold out so long."

All eyes turned to Niko, who had quietly stepped up and kissed Kyra's cheek. "Congratulations, cousin. You didn't do so bad in your choice of a groom."

"Thanks. I'm kind of fond of him." She flashed a big smile at Cristo.

Niko shook Cristo's hand. "Looks like we'll have a lot of details to sort through when you get back from your honeymoon."

"I'm hoping we won't have to wait that long—"

"Cristo, you promised." Kyra wasn't about to let him off the hook. This month away was supposed to be all about them, not his work.

He sent her a sheepish look. "I haven't forgotten. You won't even know that I'm working."

She really wanted to put her foot down, but she knew better than most how important this sale was to Cristo—it was his chance to step out from his father's shadow. She couldn't deny him this opportunity. "As long as you keep it to an hour in the morning while I'm enjoying my first cup of coffee and getting ready to tackle the day."

He held out his hand to her and they shook on it. "It's a deal."

She pulled on his hand until his face drew near hers and then she pressed her lips to his for a quick kiss. "Now it's a deal."

Everyone laughed.

"It was a beautiful ceremony," said a female voice.

Heads turned to find the new addition to their gathering.

He'd know that aristocratic voice anywhere.

"Mother." Cristo's voice rose with surprise mingled with happiness. "When did you get here?"

"We arrived a little bit ago."

We? Cristo glanced around. His gaze came to rest on his father. Was it his imagination or had his father aged considerably? There was considerable graying at the temples and the lines on the man's face were deeply etched.

When their gazes connected, Cristo detected the weariness reflected in his father's eyes. Cristo was so stunned by his father's appearance that he was at a loss for words. What did this all mean?

"Congratulations, son." His father held out his hand to him.

His father had taken time out of his busy schedule to be here. He wouldn't have done that voluntarily. Cristo suspected his mother had a lot to do with clearing his calendar. Cristo's gaze swung over to his mother, who had a hopeful gleam in her eyes. And then he noticed Kyra prodding him with her eyes to accept his father's gesture of goodwill.

He slipped his hand in his father's warm, firm grip. A smile eased the lines in his father's face. His father pulled him close and hugged him, clapping him on the back.

The hug didn't last long. Cristo quickly extracted himself from the awkward position. He hadn't been hugged by his father since he was a kid. He glanced at the ground unsure of what to do next.

"Thank you both for coming." Kyra stepped forward and held her hand out to his father, who in turn surprised everyone when he hugged her, too.

Cristo's mother stepped up next and gave Kyra a brief hug. "Welcome to the family."

Kyra stepped back to Cristo's side and took his hand in hers. "Thank you. I'm looking forward to getting to know you both."

"I was hoping you'd say that." His mother beamed. "When you return to the States, you're both invited to stay with us. You and I can house-hunt while the men are off tending to business."

Kyra smiled. "You have a date."

This was a surreal moment. Cristo tried to make sense of what had taken place just now. Sure, he was all hyped up by the rush of emotions from the wedding, but deep down, he had the feeling it was a new beginning for all of them.

His mother bestowed a warm smile on them. "May you both have a lifetime of happiness."

Cristo hoped the same thing. He wanted nothing more than to be able to make Kyra smile every day for the rest of their lives.

Kyra turned to her husband. Her husband. She loved the sound of those words. And she loved Cristo even more.

Tiny crystal bells placed at each table setting started to chime in unison, signaling it was time for the bride and groom to kiss. Kyra smiled as she turned to Cristo. He didn't waste any time sweeping her into his arms and planting a loving kiss upon her obliging lips. Her heart fluttered in her chest as if it was their first kiss.

Far too soon, he pulled away. Just then a romantic ballad started to play. Cristo held his arm out to her. "May I have this dance?"

As they moved around the dance floor, Kyra spotted Sofia at the bridal party table alone. Kyra frowned. She'd told her to bring a date, but Sofia had insisted there was no one she was interested in enough to ask to the wedding.

"What's the matter?" Cristo's voice drew Kyra out of her thoughts.

"Nothing."

"Come on now, I know you well enough to recognize the signs of you worrying about something or someone."

He was quite astute. "It's Sofia. She's all alone tonight and I feel bad. Perhaps I should have had you set her up with one of your friends."

"I'm glad you didn't ask."

Kyra stopped dancing and pulled back just far enough to look into her husband's eyes. "What's that supposed to mean? You don't think Sofia is good enough for your friends—"

"Slow down. That isn't what I meant at all."

"Then what did you mean?"

"That I'm not comfortable playing matchmaker. I think it's better when people find each other on their own. Like we did."

She hated to admit it, but he did have a good point. She moved back into his arms and started swaying to the music. "I suppose you're right."

"What did you say? I didn't quite hear you."

"I said you're right." And then she caught his sly smile. "Oh, you. You just wanted me to say you're right again."

"Hey, look." Cristo gazed off into the distance.

"Don't try to change the subject. You're just trying to get out of trouble."

"Is it working?"

"No." She sent him a teasing smile.

"But I'm serious. You should check out the bridal table again. I don't think you have to worry about Sofia having a boring time. Your cousin seems to have taken an interest in her."

"Really?" Kyra spun around to check it out. Sofia was smiling. And so was Niko. "Do you really think anything will come of it?"

Cristo shrugged. "Hard to tell. Niko seems quite wary of relationships. But aren't you rushing things? They just met."

"True." She sighed. "I guess I just have romance on my mind."

"And so you should, Mrs. Kiriakas. This is just the beginning of our story."

"I can't wait to see what's next."

"Neither can I. I love you."

"I love you, too."

* * * * *

THE GREEK DOCTOR'S SECRET SON

JENNIFER TAYLOR

CHAPTER ONE

IT HAD SEEMED like such a good idea back home in England. Now she wasn't so certain any more. What if something went wrong, something she hadn't foreseen? She could end up creating even more problems if she weren't careful.

Amy Prentice could feel her anxiety mounting as she and her eight-year-old son, Jacob, joined the queue for the ferry that would transport them to the small Greek island of Constantis. It had all appeared so straightforward when they had set off that morning. She would take Jacob to Constantis for a holiday and whilst they were there, she would tell him about his father being Greek. At the moment Jacob knew very little about the man who had fathered him apart from the fact that he was a doctor and that he worked in America, which was why they never saw him. Jacob had accepted it without question, or he had done before the other children in his class had started teasing him. Although a lot of them came from single-parent families too, at least they had some contact with their absent parent. Jacob, however, had never met his father and that was all down to her.

Nicolaus Leonides had made his feelings abundantly clear nine years ago. He hadn't been interested in the child Amy had been carrying and there was no reason to imagine that he had changed his mind. Not after everything she had read about him. Nico had achieved everything he had set out to do, establishing himself as one of the world's foremost cosmetic surgeons. The name Nicolaus Leonides had become a byword for perfection and the fact that only those with a great deal of money could afford to be treated at his clinic in California was immaterial.

No, Nico wouldn't be interested in Jacob's problems even if she was prepared to contact him, which she had no intention of doing. Staying on the island where Nico had spent so much time when he was growing up had been the best way Amy could think of to give Jacob an idea of his paternal heritage. So why did she feel so unsure all of a sudden, so afraid that she might be opening up a whole new can of worms? She hung back, the weight of the suitcase dragging painfully on her arm as she debated the pros and cons of carrying on with her plan. Jacob had already skipped up the gangplank but he stopped when he realised that she wasn't following him.

'Come on, Mum! You're going to miss the ferry if you don't hurry up!'

Amy sighed when she heard the excitement in his voice. Coming on this trip had given Jacob a much-needed boost and it was good to hear him sounding so upbeat for a change. He would be bitterly disappointed if she announced that they were no longer going to the island. She worked such long hours in her job as senior sister on the acute assessment unit at Dalverston General Hospital and saw far too little of him. This trip had been a chance to redress the balance as much as anything else.

Amy took a deep breath then hefted their suitcase up the gangplank. She couldn't give up now that they had come this far. And as for creating problems, well, there was no basis for thinking that. After all, there was no danger of them running into Nico. He was thousands of miles away, adding even more dollars to his bulging coffers!

Nico broke into a run. The last passengers had already boarded the ferry and the crew were preparing to cast off. If he missed this boat there wouldn't be another one until the following day and he couldn't afford to stay on the mainland overnight. There was an open surgery in the morning which was always packed full of people requiring his attention and he couldn't let them down.

He put on a final spurt and just managed to leap aboard as the crew cast off the final rope. He nodded apologetically when one of the older men remonstrated with him. Maybe he shouldn't have taken such a risk but it felt good to know that he was fit enough to push himself like that. When he'd had that heart attack three years ago, he had honestly thought that was it, that all he could expect from then on was a sedentary existence. It had taken him a while to adjust to the idea of his own mortality but once he had done so, he had realised that he could still enjoy life so long as he was sensible about it.

He had set about making changes to the way he had lived, starting with the biggest issue of all, the amount of stress he was under. Setting up the practice in

California and making it a success had been his *raison d'être.* He had worked eighteen-hour days and then spent any free time networking; however his cardiologist had made it clear that he couldn't do that any longer. Not if he wanted to avoid another heart attack.

He had sold the practice and moved back to Greece, taken a year out while he worked out what he wanted to do with the rest of his life. It had been hard to imagine doing anything other than what he had devoted himself to for the best part of twenty years and he had struggled to find a new direction. And then one day he had taken a trip to Constantis, the tiny island where he and his sister had enjoyed so many holidays with their grandparents, and he had realised in amazement that he had wanted to live there.

There had been no medical facilities on the island at the time. If anyone was taken ill, they had to be ferried to the mainland for treatment. Nico had contacted the IKA, the body which ran the Greek health service, and they had been cautiously enthusiastic about his proposal to build a clinic providing primary health care as well as a ten-bed hospital unit. It had taken a lot of negotiation but in the end he had been given the go-ahead, mainly, he suspected, because he had been willing to fund the building costs himself. The Ariana Leonides Clinic had been open for twelve months now and it was thriving.

Nico moved further along the deck, smiling as he passed several people he knew. Although he had a staff of ten working with him at the clinic, he was well known to the islanders and he had to admit that he enjoyed that aspect of the job too. Although he had led a busy social life in California, he had been aware that the invitations had been extended because of his status more than anything else. His name on a guest list had been seen as real kudos by the hostess, something to brag about. He was rich, successful and that was what had mattered most of all.

A sudden commotion made him glance round and he frowned when he saw a crowd starting to gather near the railings. Forcing his way through it, he spotted a girl lying on the deck. She was obviously a tourist from her clothing—tiny denim shorts and an equally skimpy top—and she appeared to be unconscious. There was a young man kneeling beside her and he looked up in panic when Nico approached.

'I don't know what happened. One minute she was taking photos with her phone and the next second she just collapsed!'

'Does she have a history of fainting?' Nico asked, crouching down beside the girl.

'I don't know! We only met a couple of days ago so I have no idea if this is something she does regularly,' the young man explained.

'I see. What's her name?' Nico asked, checking the girl's pulse which was extremely rapid.

'Jane.' The boy gulped. 'She's from Australia although I don't know where exactly. As I said, I only met her a couple of days ago and we've spent most of the time since then partying.'

Nico sighed. *Partying* implied that the young couple had been drinking and maybe even taking drugs. He had dealt with several such cases recently and the most difficult task of all was getting the youngsters to admit what they had taken so they could receive the appropriate treatment. He stood up and drew the boy aside so they could speak in private.

'Has she taken something? I'm a doctor and you need to tell me if she has taken any drugs or I can't help her.'

'No, no! It's nothing like that,' the young man protested but Nico could tell he was lying.

His tone hardened. 'This isn't the time to worry about your own skin. If Jane has taken drugs then I need to know what I'm dealing with. To put it bluntly, she could die if she doesn't receive the appropriate treatment.'

'I don't know anything about any drugs!' the young man claimed. He suddenly spun round, forcing his way through the crowd and disappearing from sight.

Nico cursed under his breath as he knelt down beside the girl again. He couldn't afford to go after him when he needed to stay here. He rolled her onto her side, working on the assumption that she had taken some kind of narcotic and could start vomiting. She was burning hot and her breathing was shallow which all supported his theory that an overdose of drugs was to blame for her collapse. The problem was finding out exactly what she had taken.

'My mummy's a nurse,' piped up a small voice. 'She can help make the lady better—shall I get her?'

Nico glanced up and saw a boy of about eight years of age watching him. He had light brown hair and dark brown eyes and for some reason he looked strangely familiar… He blanked out the thought and smiled at the child. It would be a huge help if he had someone to assist him, especially if Jane's heart stopped beating, as could very well happen.

'Yes, please. I could do with an extra pair of hands.'

The child nodded gravely then hurried away. Nico turned back to the girl, checking her pulse once more as well as her breathing. Neither seemed to have improved but there again they didn't seem to have got any worse either which was something to be grateful for.

'Jacob said you needed help.'

The clear tones cut through the babble of voices and Nico felt his heart come to a dead stop. He looked up, squinting against the glare of the sun. It couldn't be her, he told himself, his gaze resting on the slender figure standing over him, not here, not now, not on this ferry. It was too big a coincidence to imagine that fate had brought them together after all this time.

'You!'

The word exploded from her lips yet she hadn't shouted; it was said so quietly, in fact, that only he could have heard her. Nico rose to his feet, his breath coming in laboured spurts as he tried to make sense of what was happening. He regretted very little that had happened in his life simply because he had worked out what he had wanted and how he would achieve it too. Every decision he had made had been thought through and deliberated upon. Except one. He had never planned for her to get pregnant.

'Amy.'

Her name flowed so easily from his lips that it shocked him all over again. It was years since he had seen her and yet there was no hesitation about recalling who she was. His eyes skimmed over her, taking stock of the light brown hair falling to her shoulders, the brilliant gleam of her green eyes, the slender curves of her body. She didn't look a day older than the last time he had seen her, he realised in amazement. It was hard to believe that all those years had passed…

'Do you know what's wrong with her?'

The abruptness of the question brought him back to earth with a bump. Nico crouched down beside the girl again, doing his best to steer his thoughts in the direction they needed to go. He had a patient who required his help and this wasn't the time to start thinking about how much he regretted what had gone on between him and Amy Prentice.

'I suspect it may be a drug overdose,' he said, relieved that he was still able to function on a professional level. He nodded towards the girl's backpack. 'Can you take a look in there and see if there's anything that may give us a clue as to exactly what she's taken?'

'Of course.'

Amy knelt down and unzipped the bag, trying her best not to let him see that her hands were shaking. Meeting Nico like this had been a massive shock and she could feel the aftermath of it rippling through her like a series of seismic explosions. It was difficult to maintain her control but she had to do so for Jacob's sake. There was no way on this earth that she wanted her son to guess that this man was his father!

A moan slid from her lips and she hurriedly turned it into a cough when she saw Nico glance at her. She turned away, focusing on the contents of the girl's bag. There were all the usual items: T-shirts, underwear, toiletries. And then right at the bottom, tucked into a corner, she found what they were looking for. Holding up the small glass bottle, she showed it to Nico.

'GBL if I'm not mistaken. The bottle's half full though there's no way of knowing how much she's taken today.'

'Right.' Nico's tone was grim. 'At least we know what we're dealing with although that doesn't guarantee that we'll be able to help her.'

Amy nodded. Gammabutyrolactone, GBL for short, had become increasingly popular with the student population. Even a small dose could have a powerful sedative effect and if mixed with alcohol could be extremely dangerous, often leading to unconsciousness or even death. The girl would need immediate treatment if she was to have any chance of pulling through.

'What's that, Mummy? Is it medicine to make the lady better?'

Amy tried not to show her dismay that Jacob was witness to what had happened. He was only eight and she wanted to protect him from things like this for as long as possible. She opened her mouth to explain that it was nothing for him to worry about but Nico beat her to it.

'It's not medicine. Medicine makes people better but this is something very different,' he explained quietly. 'Something she shouldn't have taken.'

'Oh, you mean drugs.' Jacob nodded sagely. 'They told us about them in school. I don't know why anyone wants to take them when they make them ill, do you?'

'No, I don't.'

Nico smiled up at the boy and Amy felt her heart turn over in fear. The resemblance between them at that moment was so marked that she couldn't believe Nico hadn't noticed it. Although Jacob had her colour hair, he had inherited Nico's olive skin and chestnut-brown eyes. Even his nose was a smaller, childish version of Nico's, arrow straight without even the hint of a tilt to it. It was all she could do not to whisk Jacob away and hide him so that Nico would never guess he was his son. After all, he didn't deserve a son like Jacob, did he? Not after what he had said when she had suffered that miscarriage.

It's for the best, he had stated coldly when she had told him that she had lost the baby. They had never planned on having a child and the fact that she had lost it made things simpler.

Even though Amy had known from the outset that Nico hadn't been overjoyed when she had realised that she was pregnant, she had been deeply hurt. They had met at the hospital where Amy was completing her nursing degree. She was in her final year while Nico was on the exchange programme. The hospital was a centre of excellence in the field of plastic surgery and Nico had taken up the offer of a consultant's post there.

They had both attended a fundraising event one evening. It had been very well supported and the room had been crowded. She had, quite literally, bumped into him and managed to spill her drink all down the front of his jacket. She had been absolutely mortified but Nico had taken it remarkably well, brushing aside her apologies and insisting on fetching her another drink. They had got talking and one thing had led to another; he had asked her out for dinner, she had accepted. After a couple of months, she had been more than a little in love with him and had thought—hoped!—that he had felt the same way. However, his reaction first to her pregnancy and then to the miscarriage had soon put paid to that idea. Amy had realised that all she had ever been to him was a pleasant little interlude, someone to spend time with while he was in London, someone to sleep with. He definitely didn't want to tie himself to her with or without a child.

That was why she had ended their relationship. She simply couldn't bear to carry on seeing him, knowing how he really felt about her. It was also the reason why she had decided not to tell him when she had discovered a couple of months later that she was still pregnant, that she must have been carrying twins and had miscarried only one of them. Nico had finished his stint on the exchange programme by then and had left London and moved to Los Angeles to further hone his skills. Although she could have tracked him down if she had wanted to, there hadn't seemed any point. Nico hadn't wanted her or their child, and he had made it clear.

He probably still wouldn't want them now either, Amy thought bitterly. Which meant that she would need to be very careful. Maybe she had coped with having her heart broken but she wouldn't allow the same thing to happen to Jacob. She took a deep breath. She couldn't afford to panic, not when she had to make sure that Nico didn't find out that Jacob was his son!

CHAPTER TWO

NICO USED THE ferry's radio to contact the clinic so an ambulance was waiting when they docked at Constantis's tiny, picturesque harbour. He supervised the transfer himself, wanting to get the girl back to the clinic as quickly as possible. She was still unconscious and the longer she remained so, the greater the risk that she might not recover.

Once the ambulance was on its way he went to fetch his car, pausing when he saw Amy and the child disembarking. He couldn't just drive off without speaking to her, could he? Even if they had been total strangers, at the very least he would have to thank her for helping him, and they were a long way from being strangers. Heat poured through his veins as he found himself recalling the time they had spent together in London. Even though it was years ago, he could remember only too clearly how he had felt when they had made love. Amy had touched him in ways that no woman had ever done.

The thought shocked him, unsettled him, made him feel all sorts of things, and that was another first. He had learned to contain his emotions at an early age and preferred to keep his feelings under wraps. To find himself feeling so churned up wasn't a pleasant experience and he did his best to get a grip. Maybe Amy had aroused feelings he had never experienced before or since but that was all in the past and a lot had happened in the interim. His gaze moved to the boy at her side and his mouth thinned. How old was he? Eight? Nine? Whichever it was, the child was proof that Amy hadn't wasted any time getting over him.

That thought accompanied him as he made his way over to them. He forced himself to smile even though it wasn't as easy as it should have been. The realisation that Amy had found someone to replace him so quickly didn't sit comfortably with him, funnily enough. He found himself recalling her distress when she had suffered that miscarriage and frowned. Had that been a key factor? Had she felt the need to replace not only him but the child she had lost? It made a certain kind of sense and yet he couldn't quite believe it. Amy had never struck him as the kind of woman who moved from one man to another without a great deal of thought.

'Thank you for your help,' he said formally, determined to get back on track. All this soul searching was unsettling and he needed to call a halt. He glanced at the suitcase at her feet. 'I take it that you are staying on the island?'

'That's right. We're staying at the Hotel Marina, right on the beach. We're really looking forward to it, aren't we, Jake?' She smiled at the child although Nico saw a flash of something that looked almost like fear cross her face.

'I'm sure you will enjoy it,' he said politely, wondering what had caused it. He brushed aside the thought, determined that he wasn't going to be sidetracked. 'My sister and I spent many happy holidays here with our grandparents when we were children.'

'Is that why you're here now?' she said quickly. 'For a holiday?'

'No. I opened a clinic on the island twelve months ago and I live here now.'

'Really?'

'Yes.' He shrugged. 'I'm very fortunate to live and work in such a beautiful place.'

'You are, although I don't imagine that was the main reason you set up a clinic here.' She gave a soft little laugh and Nico felt his skin prickle when he heard the contempt it held. 'No doubt it's the ideal place to tap into the lucrative European market. There's a huge demand for cosmetic surgery procedures from across the whole of Europe, I believe, and travelling to Greece must be a lot quicker than travelling to the USA.'

'The Ariana Leonides Clinic doesn't offer cosmetic surgery procedures. Its aim is to provide primary health care for locals and tourists.' He shrugged when he saw from her expression that he had surprised her. For some reason he couldn't explain, he knew that he wanted to set matters straight. 'There's also a ten-bed hospital unit for minor surgery cases.'

'I had no idea…' She broke off and shrugged. 'It all sounds very different from what I would have expected, but there again it's been a long time since I saw you, Nico. There's bound to have been changes in your life.'

'In yours too,' he agreed, looking pointedly at the child standing beside her.

'Indeed.' She gave him a brief smile but once again he saw that flash of fear cross her face and it intrigued him. It was on the tip of his tongue to ask her what was wrong when she picked up her suitcase. 'Anyway, I won't keep you. I'm sure you must be anxious to check how your patient is doing. It was nice to see you again, Nico. Take care.'

With that, she made her way to the taxi rank. There were only three taxis on the island and as luck would have it, there happened to be one free. Nico watched her hand her case to Aristotle, the driver, then usher the boy into the back of the cab. It roared away in a cloud of exhaust fumes, leaving him wishing that he had said something, done something, at least made arrangements for them to meet again. Even though he knew it was crazy, he couldn't help feeling, well, *bereft* as he watched the taxi disappear around the headland…

Nico shook his head to rid himself of that foolish notion. Going over to his car, he got in and started the engine. He had everything he needed *and* wanted. He had made up his mind a long time ago that he would never commit himself to a relationship. He was too much like his father to take that risk. Maybe he had made a lot of changes to his life since his heart attack, but, basically, he was still the same person he had always been. One couldn't escape one's genes, after all. No, getting involved with Amy was out of the question even if she had been willing, which he very much doubted.

As for having a family, well, that was another non-starter. To put it bluntly, he refused to subject any child to the kind of upbringing he'd had. That was why he had been so dismayed when Amy had announced that she was pregnant. He had kept thinking about his own childhood, remembering how he had felt growing up as the son of Christos Leonides. Although his father might be revered by the business community even today, few people knew what he was really like.

Christos Leonides was a cold and ruthless man who had always put his business interests first and had cared nothing for his wife and his children. While neither Nico nor his sister, Electra, had been physically mistreated when they were growing up, they still bore the mental scars of their father's indifference. Their mother had done her best while she'd been alive to compensate for it but it had had a lasting effect on both of them, especially on Nico. Although Electra seemed to have come to terms with the past since she had married and had her own family, Nico had been unable to rid himself of the fear that he would turn out exactly the same as his father.

That was why he had ruled out the idea of having children and why it had been a relief when Amy had miscarried their baby, even though part of him had grieved for their lost child. He had been so shaken when he had realised it too that he had buried his feelings beneath a veneer of disinterest and it didn't make him feel good to know that he had hurt Amy. Badly. She had suffered one of the worst experiences any woman could go through and he had made it so much worse by pretending that he hadn't cared.

Nico's heart was heavy as he set off for the clinic. He didn't regret many things in his life, but he regretted that.

* * *

Amy finished unpacking and stowed the suitcase in the corner out of the way. Glancing around the small, whitewashed bedroom, she felt some of the tension start to seep out of her. Meeting Nico had been a shock but the upside was that she had got through the experience relatively unscathed. She had often wondered how she would react if they met again, but surprisingly she didn't feel much different from normal. Although her heart was beating a shade faster than usual, it certainly wasn't racing, and her breathing was only the tiniest bit laboured. She was functioning perfectly well and if that wasn't proof that she was over him then she had no idea what was.

'Can we go to the beach now, Mum?'

Amy glanced round when Jacob came racing into the room. She had allowed him to explore the small hotel where they were staying while she unpacked, although he had been under strict instructions not to leave the building. Now she smiled at him. 'I can't see why not. Do you want to put your swimming trunks on? We may as well have a swim while we're at it.'

'Yes!' Jacob punched the air in delight as he ran over to the wardrobe and took out his swimming trunks. Stripping off his clothes, he put them on and raced towards the door.

'Hold it right there, young man.' Amy picked up the bottle of sunscreen, ignoring his grimace as she started to apply it to his skin. 'There's no point pulling a face. I told you before we came here that you have to use sunscreen before you go outside. The sun is a lot hotter here than it is at home and you don't want to get burned, do you?'

'I bet *he* doesn't wear sunscreen,' Jacob muttered, screwing up his face as she applied a layer of cream to his nose.

'Who doesn't?' Amy asked, busily rubbing it in.

'The man on the ferry, that doctor—Nico, you called him.' Jacob tilted his head to the side and looked questioningly at her. 'How come you knew his name, Mum? He knew yours too 'cos he called you Amy, so have you met him before?'

'I…erm… Yes. But it was a long time ago.' Amy screwed the top back on the bottle, feeling her hands trembling. She had forgotten how observant Jacob was and she should have realised that he would pick up on something like that.

'Where did you meet him? I thought you said that you hadn't been to this island before,' Jacob continued, making it clear that he didn't intend to let the subject drop.

'I haven't.' Amy picked up her beach bag, making a great production out of checking that she had everything they needed: towels, sunglasses, water…

'So you met him somewhere else?' Jacob persisted. 'Was it at the hospital? Did he used to work in Dalverston?'

'Not Dalverston, no. We met in London while I was studying to be a nurse,' Amy explained, hoping that would satisfy him.

'London? That's where you met my daddy, wasn't it? Does he know him?' Jacob's voice was filled with excitement. 'Maybe he has some photos of my daddy or knows where he lives. Can we ask him, Mum? *Please!*'

'Jacob, stop it! Nico—I mean that man—doesn't

know anything about your daddy.' Amy took a deep breath, struggling to stay calm, but it wasn't easy. Maybe it wasn't a total lie; after all Nico had no idea that he was Jacob's father. Nevertheless, it didn't make her feel good to have to fudge the truth and she hurriedly changed the subject. 'Now come along. No more questions. Let's go and have that swim. Last one in the water is a lazy monkey!'

Jacob responded to the challenge as she had hoped he would, racing out to the terrace that led onto the garden. Amy followed more slowly, needing to get herself together so that he wouldn't suspect anything was amiss. She sighed. Jacob had become increasingly curious about his father since the other children had started teasing him and it was only to be expected when he knew so little about him. Jacob had never seen a photograph of Nico, never been told anything about his father's background, and it was all her doing too.

She had blanked out that period in her life because it had been too painful to think about it. However, she couldn't continue blanking it out, certainly couldn't refuse to answer Jacob's questions for ever. At some point she would have to tell him about the man who had fathered him, which was why she had decided to bring him to Constantis. Giving Jacob a sense of his true identity was the first step, she had reasoned, and the rest would follow later. However, she was very aware that things might happen sooner than she had anticipated now that Nico was on the scene. Should she get it all over and done with? she wondered suddenly. Tell Nico who Jacob was and then tell *Jacob* that Nico was his father?

Amy immediately dismissed the idea. She couldn't tell Jacob that Nico was his father until she was sure of Nico's reaction and even then she might have to keep the truth from him. After all, there was no reason to believe that Nico would welcome the news that he had a son, was there? The one thing she wouldn't risk was Jacob getting hurt if Nico rejected him, as he might very well do.

'We'll keep her here overnight. She may need to be transferred to the mainland tomorrow but it's too risky to move her at the moment. Can you keep an eye on her, please? She may have recovered consciousness but she's not out of the woods yet.'

Nico smiled his thanks when Sophia nodded. As acting sister on the hospital unit, Sophia Papadopolous had proved her capabilities more than once. He was planning on making her position permanent and only hoped that she would agree. Sophia had returned to Constantis after a long stint of working in Italy. Although she hadn't said anything to him, he had heard via the clinic's redoubtable grapevine that she had returned following the break-up of a relationship. Sophia had been disappointed in love and had come home whereas he had come here for the good of his health. Everyone had their reasons for being on the island, it seemed, even Amy. Had she come here simply for a holiday? Or had there been another reason for her visit? From what she had said, she'd had no idea that he was living here so that couldn't have been a factor and yet it seemed strange that she should have chosen this island rather than one of the more popular tourist destinations.

He tried to dismiss the unsettling thought as he went to his office and put through a call to the Australian Embassy in Athens. He had found Jane's passport tucked into the pocket of her haversack and now had her full name and address. He spoke to one of the attachés who promised to contact the girl's parents. According to her passport, Jane Chivers was eighteen years of age and although legally an adult, Nico guessed that her parents would want to know what had happened to her. In their shoes, he would have done.

Nico frowned as he ended the call. It was the kind of thought that would never have occurred to him before and yet it had appeared, fully fledged, in his mind. Why? Had it anything to do with meeting Amy and her son? Had it somehow triggered a reaction to see the boy and wonder what would have happened if she hadn't lost their baby? He sensed it was true and it alarmed him. He didn't want to go down that route. It was pointless. Pointless and strangely upsetting too.

Nico left his office and went to check that there was nothing that needed his attention before he went home. There had been an antenatal clinic that afternoon but Elena Delmartes, one of their most experienced doctors, had dealt with it and there had been no problems. Offering a comprehensive health care package to the islanders had been his aim when he had set up the clinic and he knew that the women appreciated not having to travel to the mainland for their antenatal care. Although most still preferred to have their babies delivered at home by the local midwives, they came to the clinic for their check-ups. It was a system that worked extremely well. According to the latest figures, very few women had missed an appointment at the clinic which certainly hadn't been the case when they had needed to travel to the mainland. It meant that every baby born on the island had an increased chance of being born healthy.

He drove home, taking his time as he travelled along the familiar route. Once his proposal for the clinic had been given the green light, he had set about finding himself a place to live. Although a few luxury villas had sprung up along the coast, he had preferred a more rural location and had opted to search the villages tucked into the foothills of the mountains for somewhere suitable. He had come across the tumbledown old farmhouse at the end of a particularly long day and had fallen instantly in love with it. With views of the mountains to the rear and a sweeping view of the sea from the front, it had been exactly what he had been searching for. He had immediately put in an offer then had to wait months while the various members of the family who owned it were contacted and persuaded to sell him their shares.

He had taken possession twelve months ago and there was still a lot to do, but he had discovered to his surprise how much he enjoyed working on the property. There was something deeply satisfying about crafting and replacing the old worn stone. It was a little like performing cosmetic surgery, he often thought; he was taking something less than perfect and improving its appearance.

Nico parked the car and stood for a moment, drinking in the view. The air was ripe with the heady smell of the vines that grew in the nearby fields and he inhaled appreciatively. There was a good crop of grapes this year so maybe he should think about making his own wine. It would be a treat to sit out here next year, sipping a glass of wine that he had produced himself. He closed his eyes, picturing the scene: the sun turning the sea blood red as it sank below the horizon; the sky darkening before the first stars appeared; the woman seated beside him, raising her glass and smiling at him…

Nico's eyes flew open. Hurrying inside, he set about his nightly routine—shower, change of clothes, make himself a meal—all the things he did every night when he got home. However, no matter how hard he tried, he couldn't erase that final, disturbing picture, the one of Amy seated beside him, smiling at him with such warmth in her eyes. Maybe it *was* a long time since he had seen her but it didn't feel like it, not when he could conjure up her image in the blink of an eye. However, the most worrying thing of all was that now her image was in his head, he knew that he was going to have the devil of a job getting rid of it.

CHAPTER THREE

'*EFHARISTO.* THANK YOU. That was delicious.'

Amy smiled her thanks as she and Jacob got up from the table. Breakfast had been simple but delicious: thick creamy yoghurt with honey and fresh figs followed by a selection of tiny sweet pastries. It proved that she had been right to choose this small, family-run hotel. Jacob would gain a much better idea of the Greek way of life by staying here than he would have done if they had stayed in a hotel that was part of an international chain. Hopefully, it would help him develop a better understanding of his paternal heritage.

She sighed as she followed Jacob out of the dining room. Maybe he would gain an insight into the Greek side of his heritage but unless she was prepared to tell him that Nico was his father what would it achieve? Jacob needed something solid to give him a true sense of his identity—photographs, meetings, *conversations*. At the moment his father was some shadowy figure he had never met and it wasn't enough to arm him against the taunts that had made his life such a misery lately. He needed proof that he *had* a father and the only way to give him that was by introducing him to Nico.

Amy was still worrying about it as they made their

way to the beach. Although it was still early, the sun was strong so she went through the routine of applying sunscreen to Jacob as well as to herself. There was another English family staying at the hotel but the parents didn't seem concerned when their two children ran off to play before they could apply sunscreen to them. The mother shrugged when she noticed Amy watching.

'They hate having to use sun cream. I have the devil of a job putting it on them.' The woman laughed as she dropped the bottle into her beach bag. 'Mind you, I'm a bit like that myself. There doesn't seem much point coming all this way to get a tan and then coating yourself with that stuff, does there?'

Amy smiled, although she disagreed wholeheartedly with what the other woman had said. She had seen too many cases of people being badly burnt after they had failed to take adequate precautions even in England. She checked that Jacob was playing safely in the shallows with the other children then took her book out of her bag. It was the latest mystery by a favourite author but it failed to hold her attention. She kept thinking about Nico and what she should do, whether she should tell him who Jacob was or not. It all depended on how he would react and that was something she couldn't foretell. She sighed. If it was anything like the way he had reacted when she had miscarried Jacob's twin, it would be better to keep Jacob's identity to herself.

The morning flew past. Amy spent some time helping Jacob build a sandcastle then decided it was time they got out of the sun. It was almost noon and the sun was at its peak so she opted to take him for an early lunch. Once they had put on dry T-shirts, they strolled around the headland and discovered a small *taverna* in the next bay. There was a shady terrace overlooking the beach where a couple of local fishing boats were unloading their morning's catch and she elected to sit out there, ordering a Greek salad for herself and a toasted sandwich for Jacob. They had just started to eat when Nico appeared.

Amy felt her heart leap into her throat when she saw him standing at the foot of the steps leading up to the terrace. It was obvious that he had come straight from the clinic because he was wearing a lightweight suit with an open-necked white shirt that made his olive-toned skin look more bronzed than ever. With those deep chestnut-brown eyes, that crisp black hair and those clean-cut features, he was an arresting sight and she noticed several of the women in the restaurant looking at him with interest.

Amy took a quick breath as her gaze ran over him, comparing how he looked now to how he had looked nine years ago. He was definitely thinner, she decided, thinner and even more commanding. Nico had always projected an air of confidence, of authority, of being completely in charge of himself, and it was more apparent than ever these days. He looked exactly what he was, a handsome, successful man in his prime, and the thought scared her. Once Nico found out about Jacob then she wouldn't be in control of the situation any longer. Nico would try to take charge and that was the last thing she wanted. How could she be *sure* that Nico would put Jacob's needs first? How could she *guarantee* that Jacob wouldn't get hurt?

It was that last thought which frightened her most

of all, although she did have other concerns, ones which she refused to dwell on. How it would affect her to have Nico back in her life wasn't the issue.

Nico felt his breath catch when he saw Amy sitting on the terrace. Just for a moment he was tempted to turn around and leave only that would have been far too revealing. Did he really want her to think that he had a problem about seeing her? he thought as he made himself walk up the steps. Of course not! He stopped by her table, dredging up a smile that he hoped appeared more natural than it felt.

'Hello again. I see you've discovered my favourite lunchtime haunt.'

'I had no idea that you came here,' she snapped.

'Of course not.' Nico had to stop himself taking a step back when he heard the defensive note in her voice. It was obvious that he had touched a nerve, although he wasn't sure which nerve it was. That remained to be seen. 'It's just a happy coincidence.'

He thrust that tantalising thought aside. Digging into the reason for her touchiness would be a mistake. He needed to remain detached, aloof, *distant* if he wasn't to find himself being drawn into a situation he would regret. He and Amy Prentice had had an affair—that was the long and the short of it. He hadn't made her any promises, hadn't wanted anything more than they'd had. If Amy hadn't got pregnant then he probably wouldn't even have remembered her name…

Would he?

The question buzzed around inside his head like a pesky wasp around a jam pot but he swatted it away. He didn't intend to go down that route—it was a waste of time. Maybe he hadn't thought about her for a long time but he was very aware that somewhere in the depths of his mind, she had occupied a small space all of her own. Amy and the miscarriage had been a milestone in his life, even though he hated the idea. It implied that she had a hold over him and that was something he didn't appreciate. He preferred to live his life on his own terms and not have to account to anyone else for his actions.

'So how are you enjoying your holiday so far?' he asked, pulling out a chair. There were several empty tables he could have chosen but he was determined not to make an issue out of this encounter. The more significance he bestowed on it, the more important it would become.

'We've only been here for a day,' she shot back then flushed when she realised how rude that must have sounded. Her tone softened as she glanced at her son. 'It's been great so far, though, hasn't it, Jacob?'

'Uh-huh,' the boy mumbled, his mouth crammed full of sandwich.

Nico laughed with genuine amusement. 'I'll take that as a yes. Obviously, Jacob has worked up an appetite, so what did you get up to this morning?'

'We went to the beach for a swim and then made a sandcastle,' Amy told him, spearing a juicy black olive with her fork.

Nico looked away as she popped it into her mouth, not proof against the feelings it aroused as he watched her lips close around the ripe fruit. He took a deep breath as he picked up the menu and studied it. There was no point thinking about Amy's beautiful mouth and the kisses they had shared. It was never going to happen again purely because he didn't intend to put himself in the position of kissing her. Not if he had any sense! As he had already discovered, Amy had the power to disrupt his life and the last thing he needed was her turning it upside down. He mustn't forget that the main reason he had moved to Constantis was for his health and he didn't need the stress.

'Dr Leonides, how lovely to see you!'

Maria Michaelis, who ran the café with her husband, Stavros, greeted him warmly as she came to take his order. Maria had been one of his first patients when he had opened the clinic. She was diabetic and had had many problems over the years, including the biggest one, her inability to get pregnant. However, after a change of medication, everything had been sorted out, although it was a little embarrassing that she now believed he was some kind of a miracle worker.

'*Kalimera*, Maria.' Nico stood up and kissed her. 'How are you today?'

'Very well, Doctor, thank you.' She patted her swollen tummy. 'This little one is certainly keeping me on my toes.'

'You mustn't do too much,' he admonished her, sitting down. He glanced at Amy, wanting to include her in the conversation as it would appear more normal that way. And keeping everything normal was vitally important, he suddenly decided. 'Maria is seven months pregnant with her first child and I keep telling her that she should rest more.'

'How wonderful! Congratulations.'

Amy smiled at the other woman and Nico felt his heart skip a beat when he realised how lovely she looked. With her light brown hair pulled back into a ponytail and her face free of make-up, she looked far too young to be the mother of the child sitting beside her. His gaze moved to Jacob and he frowned when once again he was struck by a sense of recognition. Had he met Jacob's father? Was he someone Nico had worked with in London perhaps? All of sudden he realised that he wanted to know about the man who had supplanted him in Amy's affections and fathered her child.

'Do you know if it's a boy or a girl yet? Or have you decided to wait and see when it's born?'

Amy was still talking to Maria and Nico forced himself to concentrate on the conversation. Maybe he did want answers but this wasn't the time to start asking questions. He preferred to do it when he and Amy were alone. A shiver danced down his spine at the thought of them spending time alone together but he ruthlessly suppressed it. He wasn't going down that route either!

'I wanted to wait but Stavros couldn't bear to.' Maria laughed as she patted her tummy. 'We've waited such a long time for this baby, you see, and Stavros had to know what it was. It's a boy and we're going to call him Nicolaus after the doctor because without his help we would never have had the chance to become parents. Dr Leonides did far more than we could have hoped.'

Amy smiled politely when Nico made some dismissive remark about only doing his job but she had to admit that she was surprised. Although the Nico she remembered had been an excellent doctor—thorough, committed, focused—he had never really related to his patients on a personal level. However, from what Maria had said, that was no longer the case.

The thought was intriguing. Amy had no idea what had brought about such a change in his attitude but she knew that she wanted to find out. She glanced at him, studying the strong lines of his profile as he gave Maria his order. Had something happened to make him reassess his outlook on life? He had been driven by the need to succeed when she had known him, by a desire to prove himself at the very highest levels, and yet she sensed that it was no longer the case. Nico might look much the same on the outside but inside he was a very different person, it seemed.

It was a disturbing thought when it made her see that she didn't know him as well as she had thought she did. By the time his lunch arrived, Amy had had enough of thinking about it. She and Jacob had finished eating so she asked Maria for their bill. Nico looked up and frowned.

'Please. You must allow me to pay for your lunch.'

'Oh, no, I really can't let you do that,' Amy protested, taking her purse out of her bag. 'If you can just let me know how much I owe you,' she said, glancing at Maria. Maria looked uncertainly from her to Nico, obviously unsure what to do, and Nico sighed as he put down his knife and fork.

'Let's not make an issue of it. If you prefer to pay your own bill then it's fine. I'm not going to argue with you, Amy.'

Amy flushed, realising how churlish it must have sounded to refuse his offer. She gave a little shrug as she put her purse back in her bag. 'Then thank you. It's very kind of you, isn't it, Jacob?'

Jacob nodded, although she could tell that he was growing bored and wanted to leave. Maria said something to Nico and Amy saw him frown as he glanced at Jacob and shook his head. Although Amy had no idea what Maria had said, judging by Nico's expression it was something that bothered him. All of a sudden she was struck by a need to get away. Maybe she was overreacting but there was something about the way Nico was looking at Jacob that had set all her internal alarm bells ringing. Grasping hold of Jacob's hand, she led him to the steps, pausing reluctantly when Nico called her name.

'Yes?'

'I thought you'd like to know that the girl we treated on the ferry has regained consciousness.' He shrugged but his gaze was oddly intent as it travelled from her to Jacob again.

'Oh. Right. That's good, isn't it?' Amy replied, her whole body trembling as fear overwhelmed her. Had Maria noticed the resemblance between Nico and Jacob? she wondered sickly. Noticed it and remarked on it too?

She shot a glance at her son and felt her breath catch. Even though she had been at such pains to protect him from the sun, his skin had started to tan, making the resemblance between him and Nico all the more apparent. It didn't take a genius to see it or to realise that Jacob's chestnut-brown eyes were the mirror image of Nico's and that his nose was an exact, albeit smaller, replica of the man's. Anyone looking at them could tell they were related and all of a sudden she didn't know what to do.

Amy's heart was racing as she muttered a hasty goodbye and hurried Jacob down the steps. She could try to brazen it out, of course, deny it if Nico asked her if he was Jacob's father, but deep down she knew it would be a waste of time. Nico was already suspicious and now all she could do was try to minimise the damage it could cause. No matter what happened, she had to protect Jacob and if that meant them leaving the island then that's what they must do.

Nico returned to the clinic after lunch although he had intended to take the rest of the day off. There were no surgeries scheduled that afternoon and he had been planning to enjoy some much-needed down time. However, meeting Amy had aroused so many questions that he knew he wouldn't rest until he found out the answers to them. He went straight to his office and closed the door, letting the silence wash over him in the hope that it would help to clear his head, but it didn't work. One question kept hammering away in his mind: was it possible that Amy's son was his child?

He sat down at his desk, struggling to make sense of the idea. It wasn't easy when he had thought that Amy had miscarried the baby they had conceived. Admittedly, it had been very early on in her pregnancy—barely six weeks, in fact—and she had refused to go to hospital afterwards, claiming that early miscarriages were extremely common and that there was nothing anyone could do. And yet as soon as Maria had asked him if Jacob was related to him, he had seen the resemblance for himself.

Closing his eyes, he pictured the boy's face, examining in his mind's eye each and every feature from the child's deep brown eyes, which were the exact same colour as his, to the shape of his nose, which was undeniably a Leonides nose. His sister, Electra, had three boys and each of his nephews had inherited the family nose. Why, they had even joked about it—he and Electra often remarking that the children could never deny their heritage with noses like that!

Nico opened his eyes and stared blankly across the room. Everything pointed towards the fact that Jacob was his son but how could he be? How could Amy have given birth to a child she had lost…unless she had lied about the miscarriage? Was that the answer? Had she deliberately misled him? Claimed that she had lost their child so she could bring it up on her own? Used it as an excuse to get *him* out of the picture? Maybe that had been her intention from the outset—she had wanted a baby but had not wanted him. He knew there were women like that, women who wanted to raise a child without any input from the father, yet he couldn't see Amy doing that. She had been too open, too honest, too *transparent* to have devised such a scheme—or so he had thought.

Anger roared through him as he realised that he really didn't know what she was capable of. He had accepted her at face value, accepted her kindness, her sweetness, her apparent lack of guile. But what if it had all been a front, a means to an end, and the end result was the child she had wanted? What if he had been nothing more than a *sperm donor* in her eyes, an unwitting one, granted, but no more than that when it came down to it? He couldn't bear to think that he had been used that way, used and then discarded, but what other conclusion could he reach when all the evidence pointed towards it being true?

Nico shot to his feet, his anger soaring as he strode to the door. Amy had a lot of explaining to do!

* * *

Amy had just finished her shower when there was a knock on the bedroom door. Jacob was lying on his bed, playing on his games console, so once she had wrapped a towel around herself, she went to answer it. It was Helena, who ran the hotel with her husband, Philo. She smiled apologetically when she saw Amy.

'*Kalispera.* I am sorry to disturb you but there is someone asking to see you.'

Amy felt a rush of fear swamp her. There was only one person who would seek her out and she wasn't sure if she was ready to face Nico yet. Not until she had worked out what she was going to say to him.

'Oh, right. Thank you.' She glanced down and shrugged, playing for time. 'I'm not really fit to see anyone right now, I'm afraid.'

'Do not worry.' Helena smiled reassuringly. 'I have shown the doctor into the sitting room and given him something to drink. There is nobody in there so you will be able to talk in private once you are dressed.'

Amy closed the door as Helena went on her way. She couldn't think of anything she wanted to do less than have a private conversation with Nico but what choice did she have? Knowing him, he wouldn't give up and go away if she failed to appear. No, he would be far more likely to come to her room and that was something she wanted to avoid. The last thing she needed was Jacob overhearing their conversation.

Gathering up her clothes, she hurriedly dressed, opting for a cotton dress in a delicate shade of green which she knew suited her. A slick of coral lipstick and a flick of mascara helped to relieve the pallor that had invaded her skin. Her hair was still wet from the shower but she didn't have time to dry it so she brushed it back from her face and secured it at the nape of her neck with a silver clip. Maybe it was silly to make such an effort with her appearance, but she needed to feel that she was in control of herself, especially as she had a feeling that she was going to need every scrap of control she could muster when she faced Nico.

'I just need to have a word with someone,' she told Jacob, slipping her feet into a pair of tan leather sandals. The heels weren't all that high but they did add an extra inch or two to her height and that would help. Nico was over six feet tall and she hated the thought of him towering over her, although at one time she had loved the way he had made her feel so small and feminine—

'I'll be in the sitting room if you want me.' Amy blanked out that thought, knowing how foolish it was. The last thing she needed at this moment was to start harking back to the past. 'I shan't be long so you're to stay here until I get back. Understand?'

'Uh-huh.' Jacob barely glanced at her, too absorbed in his game to worry about her absence.

Amy wasn't happy about leaving him on his own, however. As she made her way to the sitting room, she decided to make it clear to Nico that she had no intention of getting into a protracted discussion. Whatever he had come to say would need to be said as quickly as possible. Taking a deep breath, she pushed open the door. Nico was standing by the window and he turned when he heard her enter the room. He had his back to the light, making it impossible to discern his expression. She felt at an immediate disadvantage and decided to take the impetus from him in the hope that it might help to ease the situation.

'Helena said that you wanted to speak to me.' She gave a little shrug, as though the request didn't worry her although it did. 'I don't mean to be rude but I've left Jacob on his own, so can we keep it brief?'

'Of course.' He inclined his head although his eyes never left her face, she noticed. 'It's quite simple. I just have one question I would like you to answer: Is Jacob my son?'

CHAPTER FOUR

A DOZEN ANSWERS flew through her head but Amy knew in her heart that only one would satisfy him. What was the point of dragging this out by lying when Nico already suspected the truth?

'Yes.'

His eyes closed for the briefest of moments before he started walking towards her. Amy stepped aside, unsure what was about to happen, but he merely opened the door and left without uttering another word. Amy sank down onto a chair as all the strength drained from her limbs. Was that it? Now that Nico had his answer, was he not going to pursue the matter any further? Didn't he care that he had a son, or at least not enough to ask her any more questions?

Tears filled her eyes, tears of disappointment for Jacob, tears of disillusionment for herself. Quite frankly, she couldn't remember feeling so let down, not even when Nico had reacted with such a sad lack of emotion when she had miscarried Jacob's twin. It made her see that any hopes she may have harboured about Nico wanting to get to know Jacob had been a waste of time. Nico wasn't interested in Jacob any more now than he had been interested in him nine years ago.

* * *

Nico sat in his car and stared across the shimmering blue expanse of the sea. He couldn't actually see it. All he could see was this greyness that seemed to have enveloped him. It felt as though it had leaked out from his very soul and consumed him.

He had a son. It should have been a time to take stock, to reassess his life and make plans for the future, but he couldn't see through the greyness. He had a son who he had known nothing about, a child who had grown up knowing nothing about him either. He didn't doubt for a moment that Amy had kept him a secret from Jacob just as she had kept Jacob a secret from him, but why? It was a question he should have asked her, one of many that needed answering, but he couldn't face it. Not now, not when everything felt so grey and hopeless.

His hands shook as he started the engine and drove away from the hotel. It was late afternoon and the roads were busy with locals and tourists heading back to begin their preparations for the evening. Nico took his time, aware that his concentration wasn't what it should have been. It took him almost an hour to get home but it didn't matter. Nothing mattered apart from that answer Amy had given him, that tiny life-changing word: Yes.

The first stab of feeling pierced his heart and he winced. He got out of the car and watched as the sun sank below the horizon. He could see the colours now, see the gold turn to orange, see it begin to fade to a rusty red. He had no idea how long he must have stood there but there was the barest glow shimmering along the horizon when he finally roused himself. He went inside and took a bottle of water out of the fridge, gulping it down as though he had just returned from the desert. In a way, he had. He had escaped from that grey wasteland and now he needed those answers, all of them, no matter how unpalatable they might turn out to be.

Tossing the empty bottle into the bin, he went back to his car. This wasn't over, not by any means. Amy had a lot of explaining to do.

Jacob's eyelids were drooping by the time they had finished dinner. Although he put up a token resistance when Amy took him back to their room, she could tell that he was merely going through the motions. He fell asleep before she got to the end of the chapter in the book they were reading. Switching off the bedside lamp, she let herself out onto the terrace. They had a ground floor room overlooking the garden and it was peaceful out there with just the sound of the waves rolling up the beach to disturb the silence.

Sitting down on one of the wicker chairs, she let the peace wash over her, hoping it would calm her, but her nerves were too tightly strung. She didn't know when Nico would seek her out again but he would. Even if he didn't want anything to do with Jacob, he would want to make his position clear, make sure she understood exactly what she could expect from him. That was his way. He took control, made decisions, and didn't confer with anyone. However, it wasn't that simple in this instance. What Nico decided wouldn't affect only him but Jacob as well. She had come to Constantis specifically to give Jacob a link to his paternal heritage. Even though she had never expected to run into Nico, it had happened and now she needed to protect Jacob at all costs. She couldn't bear to imagine how hurt he would be if he found out who Nico was and then learned that his father had rejected him.

Quite frankly it was a risk she wasn't prepared to take so they would leave Constantis first thing in the morning. Jacob was bound to want to know why they were leaving, especially when she had made such a big deal of them staying there, but she would think up some sort of an excuse, maybe tell him they were going island hopping like the pirates of old had done. He loved stories about pirates and with a bit of luck it would convince him that there was nothing strange about the sudden change to their plans.

'We need to talk.'

Amy jumped when a figure materialised out of the darkness. She had been so lost in her thoughts that she hadn't heard Nico approaching. She pressed her hand to her throat to still the rapid pounding of her pulse. She needed to stay calm if she hoped to deal with this situation as she had to do.

'Do we?'

'Yes.' Nico stepped onto the terrace, pausing briefly to glance into the bedroom. 'I take it that Jacob is asleep.'

His tone gave nothing away and Amy bit her lip. He didn't sound angry or upset and it was hard to know how to respond. She took a quick breath, trying to match her tone to his, not an easy thing to do when she could feel the fear tumbling around inside her.

'He fell asleep before we'd finished reading his book. He was worn out from playing on the beach, I expect.'

'I expect so.' He sat down beside her. 'That and the heat. It makes a difference when you're not used to it.'

'It does. This is the first time Jacob's been away. Oh, we've had a couple of holidays in the UK but we've not been abroad before, so it's a whole new experience for him.'

'But he's enjoying it?'

'Oh, yes.' She gave a little shrug, struggling to contain her impatience. Why were they discussing the merits of this holiday when they had so many more pressing matters to worry about?

'Good. Constantis is a very beautiful place, although I doubt that was the reason you chose it for your holiday, was it, Amy?' His tone had hardened and Amy realised that the small talk was over. It was time to get down to the nitty-gritty, the real reason why Nico had come to see her.

'No. I came here because of you, Nico,' she told him bluntly.

'Really?' His brows rose. 'I thought you said that you had no idea I was living here?'

'I hadn't. I was as shocked as you were when we met on the ferry.'

'I see. So if you didn't come here to see me, then why did you come?'

'Jacob has been going through a tough time recently. He's been bullied at school because he doesn't have any contact with his father.' She shrugged. 'You never really spoke about your family, Nico, but you did mention the holidays you enjoyed here with your grandparents. I thought it might give Jacob something to relate to if we came here and he got an idea of the lifestyle, but I'm beginning to see that I made a mistake.'

'Is that a fact?'

Once again his tone gave nothing away but Amy refused to worry about it. Now that she had come this far, she intended to finish what she wanted to say.

'Yes. Jacob needs more than just a taste of the Greek way of life. He needs a real sense of his identity, solid facts about his father and his paternal heritage, and it's obvious that you aren't prepared to provide him with any of those things. That's why I've decided that we should leave Constantis. Better that than run the risk of Jacob finding out that his father doesn't give a damn about him!'

She laid it all out for him—Bang! Bang! Bang!—unconcerned as to how it made him feel. She didn't care about the effect it had had on him to discover he was a father, Nico thought bitterly, but then she had never really cared about him, had she? If Amy had felt anything for him then she wouldn't have lied about the miscarriage to get rid of him. Anger licked along his veins as he rounded on her.

'So that's it, is it? You pack your bags and leave without asking me what I want?' He laughed harshly. 'I don't know what to say, to be frank. I'm not sure if I'm more stunned by your arrogance or your stupidity!'

'There's nothing stupid about it.' She turned to him, her eyes blazing with an anger equal to his. 'You made your position perfectly clear nine years ago. You didn't want a child then or, rather, you didn't want *our* child, and it's obvious that you haven't changed your mind. What's the point of dragging this out, Nico? The sooner Jacob and I leave here, the sooner you can forget all about us. Is that really so difficult to understand?'

'Yes! It is!'

Nico could feel the emotions bubbling up inside him. It was as though the stopper had shot out of the bottle where he had kept them confined for all these years and they were suddenly free: anger and excitement, hope and fear all mingled into one huge surge of feeling that threatened to drown him. He struggled back to the surface, trying to clear his head enough so he could think, but all these feelings were getting in the way. Turning, he gripped tight hold of Amy's hands, needing something to hold on to so he wouldn't get swept away.

'Nine years ago you told me that you'd had a miscarriage and now I discover that you lied to me and that you didn't lose the child as you claimed you had. Do you have any idea how that makes me feel? Do you care?' He laughed harshly. 'I doubt it if you were prepared to go to such lengths to get what you wanted!'

'What lengths?' she demanded, trying to pull away, but he held her fast. 'I don't know what you mean.'

'Oh, come on! Of course you do. You wanted a baby, didn't you, Amy, and it just so happened that I was on the scene so you decided that I could be its father.' He shook his head. 'I'm not sure if I admire your single-mindedness or what, but you used me to get pregnant, didn't you? And then, once you'd achieved your objective, you told me that you had lost the baby. It was all very clever, really. You got exactly what you wanted and you *didn't* have to put up with the inconvenience of me cluttering up your life!'

Amy stared at him in horror. Surely he didn't believe that she was capable of such deceit? She opened her mouth to disabuse him of the idea but nothing came out, not a single word in her defence, and Nico obviously took it as proof that he was right.

'I've heard about women like you, although I've always found it hard to believe that anyone could be so cold and calculating. However, it appears that it can and does happen. Some women are prepared to go to any lengths to get what they want.

She had to say something, had to make him understand that he was wrong. She hadn't planned any of it, neither her pregnancy nor the miscarriage, or the fact that Jacob had been a twin. 'No, you're wrong, Nico. Completely and utterly wrong. I didn't…'

'Save it.' Standing up, he glared down at her and she trembled when she saw the contempt in his eyes. 'We shall leave it to our lawyers to sort this out.'

'Lawyers,' she echoed numbly.

'*Ne.* This is far too complex an issue to resolve ourselves, especially when I can't trust you to do what's right. I shall contact my lawyer in the morning. I expect he will be in touch with you very shortly.'

With that, he spun round, making it clear that he had said all he intended to say. Amy shot to her feet, knowing that she couldn't let him leave like this. She had to make him understand what had really happened before the situation deteriorated any further. She ran after him, catching hold of his jacket sleeve as he was about to step down from the terrace.

'Wait! You can't just leave like this, Nico. We can sort this out without getting anyone else involved. Once I've explained what really happened then I'm sure you'll feel very differently.'

'Really?' He turned to look at her, his eyes filled with a derision that cut her to the quick. 'You're going to make up some sort of a sob story to explain why you used me, are you?' He gave a soft little laugh that made the hair on the back of her neck stand on end when she heard the threat it held. 'Come along then, Amy, let's hear it. It should be entertaining if nothing else.'

'There's no point me telling you the truth if you refuse to believe me.' She let go of his sleeve and stepped back. 'Contact your lawyer if it's what you want to do, Nico. Maybe *he* will be prepared to listen to what I have to say, listen and believe it too!'

She went to walk away but this time it was Nico who stopped her. His hand fastened around her bare arm, his strong fingers holding her fast.

'I doubt it. I doubt if anyone will believe a word you say after I've explained how you lied and deceived me.' He hauled her to him, holding her so close that she could feel the heat from his body seeping into hers and shuddered. 'Oh, you're a highly accomplished liar—I'll give you that. I thought you were so sweet and caring but I was wrong, wasn't I? You were playing a part, that's all. You pretended to care about me and you put on a good show, good enough to fool me, and I'm not easily taken in, believe me. However, the truth is that you couldn't have given a damn about me.'

He skimmed his knuckles down her cheek in a gesture that was an insult rather than a caress. 'You were willing to trade sex for what you really wanted—a baby. And you achieved your objective, didn't you?' He laughed softly and the disgust in his voice made her cringe even though she knew it wasn't justified. 'You certainly fooled me. I actually thought it meant something when we made love but it was just a means to an end. It makes me wonder what else you're prepared to do to get what you want. It could be interesting to find out.'

Amy wasn't prepared when he bent and claimed her mouth in a searing kiss. His lips were hard, unyielding, seeking to punish more than anything else. Tears sprang to her eyes because this wasn't what she wanted. She didn't want Nico to hate her, to blame her, to feel this bitterness towards her. Maybe she should have contacted him after she had discovered that she was still pregnant but she had honestly thought she was doing the right thing. Nico hadn't wanted a child. He hadn't wanted *her*. And punishing her this way wasn't fair.

She turned her face so that his mouth slid from hers and came to rest on her cheek. She could feel the anger in his lips, feel their harshness against her skin, and her heart ached. It was obvious that he was deeply hurt as well as furiously angry and it was her fault for not making him understand what had really happened.

'I never tried to trick you, Nico.' Her voice held a desperation that made him go still. Amy knew that she had just seconds before he pushed her away and hurried on, the words spilling from her in a frantic rush. 'I never planned on getting pregnant—it just happened. And I truly thought I had lost the baby when I had that miscarriage only it turned out that I'd been expecting twins.'

Her voice broke as she tipped back her head and

looked into his eyes. Even after all this time it was painful to think about the child she had lost. 'I lost one of the babies, Jacob's brother or sister, but I didn't lose him.'

CHAPTER FIVE

THE SOFT SWISH of the waves rolling up the beach was the only sound to disturb the silence. Nico could hear them rushing ashore but it felt as though he was a million miles away. It was as though he had been cut adrift, deprived of everything that was familiar. Amy hadn't lied or tried to deceive him. She had carried his child, the twin to the one she had lost, and had given birth to him. On a scale of earth-shattering events that had occurred in his life recently this had to register as a big fat ten.

Nico took a deep breath, feeling himself tremble as reaction set in. He knew that he needed to work out what he intended to do, but it was too soon. His brain simply couldn't cope with anything else at the moment. In the space of a few hours he had discovered that he was a father and that the woman who had borne his son hadn't used him as he had believed. That was more than enough to be going on with.

'Nico?'

Her voice was low, anxious, and he tensed. Amy needed his reassurance. She wanted him to tell her that everything would be all right, but he couldn't do that. Not yet. Maybe not ever. Having a child was going to make a massive difference to his life. Although he didn't know exactly how it would change, he knew that it would. He had never wanted children but it was too late now. It was a fait accompli and now he needed to readjust his whole outlook on life. Fear rushed through him at the thought and he cleared his throat, not wanting Amy to suspect how terrified he felt.

'Obviously, we have a lot to talk about but not tonight, Amy. We both need time to think about what has happened. *Ne?*'

'You do believe me, though, Nico? Believe that I never tried to trick you?' Her voice held an urgency that made him sigh.

'Yes, I believe you. I only wish that you had told me about Jacob before now.'

'There didn't seem any point. You made it clear after the miscarriage that you didn't want a child, Nico. When I found out that I was still pregnant it seemed wrong to force you into a situation you wouldn't welcome.'

Nico grimaced because it was no more than the truth. He wouldn't have welcomed the news, although he would have accepted responsibility, of course. He would have done what was right for Amy and their baby, but would it have been enough? he wondered suddenly. Would it have been enough for Jacob to grow up knowing that his father had maintained contact with him purely out of a sense of duty?

Nico understood only too well how that felt. His own father had never made any secret of the fact that he hadn't wanted children. Christos Leonides had only agreed because it was what Nico's mother had wanted. Ariana Leonides had come from a very wealthy family and it had been her money which had allowed his father to set up in business. Nico had always suspected that Ariana had insisted on them having children before she would agree to marry Christos. Although Christos may have acceded to her demands so he could achieve his business ambitions, he had never cared about Nico or his sister, as he had made it clear.

What if he turned out the same as his father? Nico thought sickly. What if he found it impossible to care about Jacob? At the moment Jacob seemed to be a happy and well-adjusted child. Although Amy had told him that Jacob had been bullied at school, Nico could tell that the boy knew he was loved and that made a world of difference. He could cause untold harm if he took on the role of Jacob's father only to discover that he couldn't relate to him as a father should do. It made it even harder to know what to do. Should he get involved when he wasn't sure if it would be in the child's best interests?

Amy had no idea what Nico was thinking but it was obviously something troubling if his expression was anything to go by. She bit her lip, wishing she could think of something to say to make it easier for him. Obviously, his views on fatherhood hadn't changed but if they were to deal with this situation then they had to find some sort of a compromise. The one thing she refused to do was to upset Jacob.

'Look, Nico, I realise this must have been a shock for you,' she began then stopped when a woman stepped out onto the adjoining terrace. It was Donna Roberts, the woman Amy had spoken to at the beach that morning, and she came hurrying over when she saw them.

'Have you got any aftersun?' She glanced back at her room and grimaced. 'Only Darcey's caught the sun and she's carrying on something dreadful. She's not stopped crying all evening, not even when we were trying to have our dinner. She just keeps complaining that her shoulders hurt and she feels sick.'

'I've a bottle in the bathroom,' Amy said at once. She hurried inside and fetched it, handing it to the woman with a frown. 'How bad is she?'

'Oh, not that bad. There's just a few blisters on her shoulders but they'll soon heal.' Donna sighed. 'She's driving us all mad with her moaning. Tim couldn't stand it any longer so he's taken himself off for a drink. I just wish I could have gone with him!'

'Would you like me to take a look at her?'

Amy glanced round when Nico spoke. He came over to them and she forced herself not to flinch when his arm brushed hers. All of a sudden all she could think about was that kiss. Maybe Nico had kissed her in anger, his lips seeking to punish rather than to arouse pleasure, yet the memory seemed to have lodged itself in her mind. She couldn't help comparing it to all the other times he had kissed her. Nico's kisses had aroused her like no other man's kisses had done before or since.

'I'm Dr Leonides. I run the Ariana Leonides Clinic in the town centre,' he explained and the very calmness of his tone acted like a douse of cold water.

Amy shivered as she realised how foolishly she was behaving. It didn't matter how she had felt nine years ago. The only thing that mattered was the effect it was going to have on Jacob if he found out that Nico was his father. Could she trust Nico to put Jacob's interests first? Could she trust him to care? She needed to be sure before she decided what she should do.

'Oh. Well, I don't know.'

Amy forced her thoughts back to the present when she heard the wariness in Donna's voice. 'I can vouch for Nico. He really is a doctor.'

'It's not that.' Donna gave a little shrug. 'We didn't bother buying any travel insurance, you see. Tim said it was a waste of money and it would be better spent on something else. He'll be furious if we end up with a huge medical bill.'

'There is no need to worry,' Nico said smoothly. 'I wouldn't dream of billing you for a consultation after hours.'

'Oh, I see. Well, in that case then thank you very much. It might stop Darcey moaning if a proper doctor looks at her.'

The woman smiled in relief as she led the way into her room. Amy followed her and Nico inside, pausing in the doorway as she didn't want to add to the general clutter. The room was extremely cramped thanks to the addition of two camp beds. Nico had to pick his way over to the far side where the little girl was lying huddled up, sobbing. Amy frowned. Even from this distance, she could see how red the child's skin looked.

'Hello, Darcey,' Nico said softly, crouching down beside her. 'I'm Dr Nico and I'm going to take a look at your shoulders. Your mummy said that they are very sore.'

Darcey nodded, her blue eyes awash with tears. She was about six years old and was obviously in a great deal of discomfort. 'They hurt a lot,' she whispered miserably.

'I'm sure they do.' Nico replied gently. He carefully examined the red-raw skin, his brows drawing together when he came to a patch on the child's left shoulder which was covered with a number of large fluid filled blisters. He didn't touch them, just examined them from several different angles before he stood up. His tone was flat when he addressed the child's mother but Amy could hear the anger it held.

'Your daughter has second-degree burns to her left shoulder. I suspect she is suffering from heat stroke as well. She needs immediate treatment so I shall arrange for her to be admitted to the clinic's hospital bay.'

'Hospital!' Donna exclaimed. 'Oh, no, surely that's not necessary. I mean, it's only a bit of sunburn—nothing serious.'

'Burns like this are serious whether they are caused by the sun or anything else,' Nico said sternly. 'Your daughter will need to be closely monitored for the next few days.'

He turned to Amy and she felt a rush of warmth envelop her when his expression softened. Did it mean that he had forgiven her for keeping Jacob's existence a secret from him? She hoped so. Maybe it was foolish but all of a sudden she realised that she didn't want to be at odds with him.

'Can you get Darcey ready? She'll need something placed over those blisters to protect them. There will be less chance of scarring if they are allowed to heal in their own time.'

'Of course,' Amy replied, rapidly running through the contents of her first aid box. She had brought it with her out of habit, not wanting to be unprepared if Jacob tripped over and cut his knee or something similar. She nodded when she remembered that she had added a pack of lint-free dressings to its contents. 'I've some dressings in my room which should be ideal.'

'Good.' Nico nodded his approval then turned to the child's mother again. 'I shall drive you to the clinic. I suggest you contact your husband and let him know what's happened.'

'I…erm… Yes. Of course.' Donna didn't look happy as she picked up her mobile phone and went outside to call her husband.

Amy returned to her room, found the first aid box and took it back with her. Nico was speaking on his phone, making arrangements to have Darcey admitted to the hospital. Amy left him to deal with it and concentrated on making the little girl comfortable. Darcey's brother, Harvey, watched her, obviously enjoying the drama, especially as he wasn't the one who was suffering. He grinned when Amy finished.

'Darcey won't be able to go swimming now, will she?' he said gleefully.

'No.' Amy patted the little girl's hand when she started to cry. 'There'll be lots of other times when you can go swimming, sweetheart.'

'But not on this holiday,' her brother persisted. His smile widened when Darcey let out another wail. 'Cry baby! Cry baby!'

'That is enough. It's unkind to make your sister cry like that, young man. Stop it right now.'

Nico came over to them, looking very stern as he stared at the boy in distaste. Amy hid her smile when she saw Harvey flush. She had a feeling that he didn't get reprimanded very often and couldn't help thinking that it would do him the world of good. It was her firm belief that children needed to be told when their behaviour was unacceptable and obviously Nico felt the same.

For some reason the thought filled her with a fresh sense of hope. Maybe it was wrong to see it as a sign that she and Nico could reach an agreement when they had so much to discuss, but it seemed like a good omen. She carried on getting Darcey ready, wrapping her in a sheet when the child started to shiver as the effects of her sunstroke set in. There was still no sign of her mother and she could tell that Nico was growing impatient at the delay.

'I'll go and see where Donna is,' she offered, moving to the French doors.

'Efharisto.' Nico glanced at the child and his mouth tightened. 'I would like to get her to the clinic as soon as possible.'

Amy nodded. The sooner Darcey started receiving treatment, the better. She went outside and found Donna standing at the end of the terrace. It was obvious that she had been crying and Amy sighed. She could do without another drama tonight, thank you very much.

'Tim's blazing,' Donna announced when Amy went over to her. 'He seems to think it's all my fault, but why should it be down to me all the time? They're his kids too and it's about time he started taking an interest in them. Most weeks he hardly sees them and when he does, he does nothing but shout at them. I tell you, it'd be easier if I was a single parent. At least I'd get some sympathy then for what I have to put up with!'

'I'm sure it's the shock that's made him so angry,' Amy replied, although she doubted it. However, it wasn't the time to have a discussion about the man's parenting abilities. Her heart gave a little jolt as she was immediately reminded of her own concerns about Nico's abilities as a father. Could he adapt to the role? Did he even want to? She forced the questions from her mind. They were too disturbing and she would deal with them later.

'Dr Leonides is keen to leave. Have you arranged to meet your husband at the clinic or is he coming back here to look after your son?'

'He's going to meet us there.' Donna shrugged. 'After he's finished his drink, naturally.'

Amy didn't say anything. It wasn't her place to comment on the father's behaviour. She checked on Jacob, who was fast asleep, then went next door. Nico had picked Darcey up and was ready to carry her out to his car and for some reason the sight of him standing there with the child in his arms brought a lump to her throat.

She had missed all of this, missed the interaction between him and Jacob, missed seeing him holding their son in his arms when Jacob had been a baby. There was no guarantee that it would have happened, of course; who knew how Nico would have reacted when Jacob was born? However, the thought that she *and* Nico had been denied those precious memories because of her refusal to contact him not only hurt but made her feel guilty too. She had a lot of making up to do. If Nico would let her.

'We'll be off then.' Nico paused beside her and his gaze was intent as he stared down at her. Amy hastily tried to put aside those disturbing thoughts, afraid that he would read her mind. She must never forget that it was Jacob's happiness that was the most important issue. Even if she did feel guilty about what she had done, she couldn't afford to let it affect her judgement.

'Darcey's father is going straight to the clinic,' she informed him, praying that her tone of voice gave nothing away. 'He will meet you there.'

'Good. At least we won't have to wait for him to return.' He paused before he continued flatly. 'Promise me that you won't do anything hasty, Amy. We need to talk about what's happened and I don't want you leaving Constantis, if that's what you were planning to do.'

'If you're sure it's what you want, Nico,' she said softly, searching his face.

'It is.'

There was a moment when she thought he was going to say something else but in the end he swung round and left. Amy watched him carry the little girl to his car then turned away, her heart thumping heavily inside her as she went back to her own room. Jacob was fast asleep, mercifully oblivious to what had happened that night. Amy smoothed back his hair, feeling love well up inside her. She loved him so much and wanted only what was best for him but how could she be sure that involving Nico in his life would be in his best interests? She had promised Nico that they would stay on the island but there was an awful lot that needed sorting out before she reached any decisions.

She bit her lip as a wave of fear washed over her. She would never forgive herself if she did something that, ultimately, might hurt Jacob.

Nico arrived at the clinic earlier than usual the following morning. He went straight to the hospital unit, wanting to check on Darcey Roberts before he did anything else. Although the child's injuries weren't life-threatening, he felt a strange kind of connection to the little girl. He *cared* what happened to her, cared that her parents appeared to take such little interest in her welfare. No child should be treated so indifferently. Every child should be loved and cherished, just as he wanted to love and cherish Jacob.

The thought brought him up short. Nico stood stock still as he tried to make sense of it. How could he care about the boy when twenty-four hours ago he hadn't even known Jacob had existed? The logical part of his brain rejected the idea but another part insisted it was true. He cared about Jacob. And he cared about Amy too.

Nico's heart was hammering as he entered the hospital. He had no idea what was going on but all these unfamiliar feelings scared the life out of him. It was an effort to dredge up a smile when Sophia came to greet him.

'*Kalimera*, Sophia.'

'*Kalimera*, Dr Leonides. I expect you have come to check on our new little patient.'

'*Ne*. How is she this morning?' Nico's voice sounded strained and he cleared his throat. He needed to get himself back on track rather than carry on behaving so out of character. 'Have her parents arrived yet?' he continued more firmly, glancing around the sunlit room.

He had thought long and hard when he had been planning the hospital unit, wanting to make it a pleasant place to stay as well as to provide his patients with the privacy they needed. If there were both male and female patients in the unit then a partition could be slid into place to divide the room into two separate sections. Although it wasn't possible to provide individual rooms—there simply wasn't enough space—each bed was set in its own bay. It allowed a degree of privacy that people appreciated.

'No.' Sophia's mouth thinned as she led the way to the end bay. 'They left shortly after you did last night and they haven't returned yet.'

'I see.' Nico was hard-pressed to hide his anger but there was no way that he wanted to upset Darcey. He smiled at her. 'So how do you feel this morning, little one? A bit better than you did last night, I hope.'

'My shoulders are still sore but my head doesn't hurt,' she told him solemnly. She peered hopefully past him. 'Have you brought my mummy to see me?'

'No. But I'm sure she will be here very soon,' Nico told her, gently smoothing back her hair. Darcey didn't say anything, leaving him with the distinct impression that she didn't believe him. Maybe her mother made a habit of not turning up, he thought grimly as he examined her. If that were the case then he would make it clear to her parents that it was unacceptable while the child was in his care.

He told Sophia to carry on with the treatment. Darcey's temperature would be monitored and the area that had been burned would be kept scrupulously clean but he didn't plan to do anything else. Second degree burns—where the skin was damaged enough to cause blisters to form—usually healed on their own. Although the epidermis had been burnt, the dermis—the deeper layer of the skin—should heal without scarring. Darcey had been very lucky in many respects because the area of damage was relatively small. If it had been more extensive, it could have required plastic surgery to repair it.

'I shall come back later,' he told Sophia. 'Let me know when the parents arrive, would you? I would like a word with them.'

'Of course, Dr Leonides.' Sophia took a quick breath then hurried on. 'I'm afraid I have some news that may upset you. I shall be leaving at the end of this month. I am getting married, you see.'

'Ah. Congratulations. I am delighted for you, Sophia, although I am very sorry that you are leaving us. I had hoped to make your position here a permanent one.'

'I would have loved that, but my fiancé has been offered a job in Boston.' She sighed. 'That is the reason why we parted. I wasn't sure if I wanted to move to America to live.'

'It must have been a big decision for you but I'm sure it's the right one,' Nico said quietly.

He repeated his congratulations then went to his office, wanting to make a start on the ever-present paperwork. Although he had staff who dealt with the complexities of the Greek health service, there was always something that needed his attention. He made a note on Darcey Roberts's file to the effect that no bills should be raised. He had promised her mother that there would be no charge for her treatment and he always kept his word…

If he promised Amy that he would play a role in Jacob's life then he would have to keep his word about that too.

CHAPTER SIX

THE THOUGHT SENT alarm scudding through him. Nico got up, unable to sit calmly at his desk while his mind was in such turmoil. Walking to the window, he stared across the bay. It was too early yet for the ferries to be running but there were several fishing boats bobbing up and down on the water. Usually, he found the sight of them soothing but not that day. His head was too full of what had happened in the past twenty-four hours.

It had been the same last night—he had found it impossible to sleep when his head had been filled with so many thoughts, so many unfamiliar emotions. Discovering that he had a child had affected him in ways he was only just beginning to grasp. However, it wasn't just the thought of Jacob that had kept him awake; it was Amy as well. How did he feel about her? Because if he agreed to play a role in Jacob's life then Amy would be part of the deal too.

Nico closed his eyes, hoping that he would get a clearer idea of how he felt if he blocked out everything else. Seeing Amy again had been a shock and there was no denying it. Although he hadn't thought about her in a long time, he had quickly realised that he hadn't forgotten her. She had been tucked away in his mind and seeing her again had unleashed a lot of memories. His head began to spin as he found himself suddenly beset by some of them: long walks in the park, holding hands; pizzas eaten in front of the television while watching one of her favourite soap operas; passion-filled nights which they had spent making love…

His eyes flew open because he didn't dare go any further down that route. Not when he felt so confused. Making love with Amy had always been an emotional experience even though he had done his best to hold back. He had never had that problem with other women; in fact someone had accused him once of being so emotionally disconnected that it had felt like making love with a stranger. However, it had been very different with Amy. Right from the beginning she had made him feel things he had never felt before, engaged him both mentally as well as physically. Amy had touched him in ways he would never have believed possible and the thought alarmed him.

Nico gazed at the fishing boats without actually seeing them. If he agreed to be Jacob's father then how could he be sure that he wouldn't fall under Amy's spell once more? Oh, he could tell himself that he was strong enough to resist, but was he? Really? Recalling that kiss they had shared last night, he couldn't put his hand on his heart and swear that he was immune to her. Maybe he had kissed her in anger but there had been a moment just before she had turned away when anger had been replaced by another emotion equally strong, and it was that which worried him.

How could he get involved with her and Jacob when

the future was so uncertain? Although he had made a full recovery following his heart attack, his doctor had warned him that it could happen again. Although he hoped to live a long and full life, he couldn't guarantee it, which meant he had to consider the impact it could have on other people. That hadn't been an issue before; however, the situation had changed. To put it bluntly, what good would it do Jacob and Amy if he fostered a relationship with them only to have it cut short?

Amy was surprised to see the Roberts family in the dining room when she and Jacob went in for breakfast. Donna Roberts waved as they sat down and Amy waved back, although she couldn't help wondering what they were doing there. If Jacob had been rushed off to hospital then nothing would have induced her to leave his side. Donna came over as Amy was pouring herself a cup of coffee.

'I just wanted to say thanks for last night. At least we didn't have to put up with Darcey's moaning all night long!'

'Oh, right.' Amy summoned a smile although it was hard to believe that anyone could be so heartless. 'You decided not to stay at the hospital with her then?'

''Course not! She's perfectly safe there and to tell you the truth I was glad to get a break from her.' Donna laughed. 'There's nothing gets you down more than a kid who won't stop whining, is there?'

Amy didn't say anything as Donna returned to her table. The family had finished their breakfast and, from the look of it, they were ready to head off to the beach. It was hard to believe that they were going to spend the day enjoying themselves instead of rushing off to be with their daughter.

She and Jacob finished their breakfast and went to the beach as well but Amy found it difficult to settle. The memory of what had happened the previous night preyed heavily on her mind. Should she have promised Nico that they wouldn't leave the island? At the time, she had felt that she'd had no choice, not when he had been so anxious to get Darcey to the clinic, but had it been the right thing to do? She had no idea how he truly felt about Jacob and that was the most worrying thought of all. There was no way on earth that she would she risk Jacob getting hurt. She intended to protect him at all costs, as any parent should protect their child.

The thought naturally reminded Amy about poor little Darcey, all on her own in the clinic. She couldn't bear to imagine the little girl's distress when her parents failed to turn up and decided that she had to say something. She got up and went over to where Donna and her husband were sunbathing.

'I was just wondering when you were going to visit Darcey,' she explained when Donna looked up.

'Oh, sometime this evening, I expect.' Donna yawned. 'There's no point wasting the day sitting around in the hospital, is there?'

'Won't she miss you, though?' Amy persisted.

'Maybe.' Donna shrugged. 'But you can't spend your whole life running round after your kids. You need a bit of time to yourself.'

Donna closed her eyes, making it clear that the subject was closed. Amy went back to her towel and lay down but she still couldn't relax. It was as though her thoughts were on a merry-go-round—she kept thinking about that promise she had made to Nico and the possible repercussions from it. In the end she couldn't stand it any longer so when Jacob came back to get a drink she told him that they were going into town, using the excuse that they would pop into the clinic to see Darcey. Hopefully, she might get a chance to speak to Nico while they were there too. Quite frankly, anything had to be better than sitting here, wondering what was going to happen!

Jacob grumbled a bit about having to leave the beach but he soon cheered up when he discovered they were going to use the local bus. It meandered its way to the town centre, stopping at several villages en route to pick up more passengers so that it was packed when it finally arrived. Amy helped Jacob alight then looked around, wishing she had asked Helena for directions to the clinic. There were a number of roads leading off from the main square and she had no idea which way to go. They could be wandering around for ages, trying to find the place.

'Look, Mum. Over there. It's a fort!'

The excitement in Jacob's voice brought her mind back to the fact that this holiday was supposed to be for his benefit. Maybe she did need to speak to Nico, but not at the expense of ruining Jacob's day. She smiled at him.

'Want to go and take a look?' she suggested, laughing when he bounced up and down with excitement.

'Yes!'

He went haring off, leaving Amy to follow at a more sedate pace. It was market day and there were a number of stalls set up around the square. She decided to take a look at what they were selling after they had visited the fort and treat them to a few souvenirs to remind them of Jacob's first holiday abroad. She grimaced. Bearing in mind what had happened since they had bumped into Nico on that ferry, she was unlikely to forget it!

Nico saw his final patient out then checked with Theodora, their receptionist, that there were no last-minute appointments. Morning surgery had been unusually quiet which meant he had finished early for once. He decided to make the most of the time and go into town. With all that had happened recently, he hadn't given any thought to the contents of his fridge and he was fast running out of fresh food. Maybe he should think about inviting Amy and Jacob for dinner one night, he mused as he set off and then just as hurriedly dismissed the idea. Until he and Amy talked everything through and decided what they intended to do, he shouldn't get too involved.

The thought weighed heavily on him as he walked into the town centre. He knew what he wanted to do but he wasn't convinced it was right. Leaving aside the matter of his health, what if his initial enthusiasm waned? He had never had very much to do with children other than during the course of his work. Although he was fond of his sister's boys, he certainly hadn't yearned for a child of his own, never felt that he was missing out by not having a family. It wasn't difficult to imagine the damage it could cause if he formed a relationship with Jacob only to discover that it wasn't what he wanted and disappeared from the child's life at a later stage. The last thing he wanted was for Jacob to grow up thinking that his father hadn't wanted him. He knew from bitter experience how that felt.

Nico made his way to the main square where the weekly market was being held and bought a selection of fruit and vegetables as well as some *horiatiko psomi*—a type of bread that was baked outdoors in wood-burning stoves. He knew most of the stallholders and exchanged pleasantries with them, thinking as he did so how different his life was these days. When he had lived in California he'd had a housekeeper to make sure his every need was catered for. Although he had taken it for granted at the time, it struck him now what an unreal existence it had been. He much preferred this hands-on approach. It kept him grounded, made him see what really mattered, which wasn't success and making money as he had believed once. How surprised Amy would be if he told her that.

As though thinking about her had conjured her up, she suddenly appeared. She had Jacob with her and they were standing beside a stall that sold baklava—the delicious, honey-soaked pastries that were so popular all over Greece. Nico felt his heart start to pound as he came to a sudden halt. They were too interested in selecting their pastries to have noticed him so all he needed to do was make his way through the stalls and he would be able to avoid them. It was the sensible thing to do bearing in mind that he still had no real idea what he should do about Jacob, so why did he feel this knot of excitement building inside him? Why did he suddenly want to be with them more than he had wanted anything before?

Nico couldn't explain it. All he knew was that his heart was telling him to go over to them even though he knew it could be a mistake. And for a man like him, who had always known his own mind, it came as a shock to find himself so ambivalent. What hope did he have of reaching any major decisions about the future when he couldn't even make up his mind about this?

'Try some of those. The ones with the pistachio nuts on them. They're my favourite.'

Amy swung round, a silent *Oh!* forming on her lips when she saw Nico standing behind her. Maybe she had been planning to go to the clinic but she hadn't expected to see him here in the market and it threw her completely off balance. Heat rushed up her face as she hurriedly turned back to the pastries.

'They all look so delicious, it's hard to choose,' she murmured, not wanting to think about the reasons why her heart was racing. It was only natural that she should feel keyed up when she still needed to find out what he planned to do about Jacob, she told herself, but deep down she knew it was only partly true. Being near Nico affected her and there was no point trying to pretend that she was indifferent to him. She took a deep breath and used it to shore up her emotions. At the end of the day, this was all about Jacob; it wasn't about her and Nico.

The stallholder popped the pastries into a box. She obviously knew Nico and chatted away to him as she fastened the box with a length of pale pink ribbon. She handed it to Amy, shaking her head when Amy tried to pay her.

'They are a gift,' Nico said quietly beside her. 'Kara and her husband are patients of mine and it's her way of thanking me.'

'Oh, but I couldn't possibly accept them without paying for them,' Amy protested, taking out her purse.

'Kara will consider it an insult if you refuse.' Nico caught hold of her hand. 'Just thank her and she will be more than happy, believe me.'

'I…ehem…*efharisto*,' Amy murmured, holding herself rigid when she felt the tremor that was working its way up her arm. She quickly withdrew her hand, determined that she wasn't going to let Nico think that his touch still had the power to affect her. The days when Nico could turn her insides to jelly with the lightest of touches were long gone. 'Thank you very much. I'm sure we shall enjoy them.'

The woman nodded graciously then said something to Nico and even though Amy couldn't understand a word, she knew it was about Jacob. Had Kara spotted the resemblance between him and Jacob? she wondered, glancing at him. She sighed because it was obvious from his expression that she was right. People only had to see him and Jacob together to know they were related. Now all she could do was pray that nobody would say anything to Jacob.

The thought made her feel sick with worry. As they moved away from the stall, Amy realised that she needed to avoid it happening again until she knew exactly what Nico intended to do. Taking hold of Jacob's hand, she led him towards the bus stop. Although she felt bad about not visiting Darcey, she couldn't take the risk of going to the clinic and having other people remark on the resemblance between them. Jacob would be devastated if he found out that Nico was his father only to learn that Nico didn't want anything to do with him.

'We'd better make our way back to the hotel,' she said, adopting her most upbeat tone. The thought of Jacob's hurt and bewilderment if he suffered such a rejection was more than she could bear. She smiled as she held up the box of pastries, not wanting Jacob to suspect that anything was wrong. 'Thank you for these, although by rights they belong to you. Are you sure you don't want them, Nico?'

'Certainly not.' He laughed, his handsome face lighting up with sudden amusement. 'I shall be as fat as pig if I eat them all myself.'

Amy grimaced. 'Hmm, maybe I should give them a miss too. I'm not sure if my waistline can cope with all those zillions of calories.'

'Oh, I don't think you need worry about that. Your figure is perfect, if you want my opinion.'

Amy felt heat invade every cell in her body as his eyes swept over her. That he liked what he saw wasn't in doubt. Although she'd had her share of admirers over the past few years, she had avoided getting involved in another relationship. It hadn't been difficult. Jacob came first and there was no way that she would risk upsetting him by bringing a stranger into their lives, plus she had never met anyone who she had wanted to spend her life with…

Except Nico.

Pain pierced her heart and she turned away. She had loved him so much but she had learned the hard way that love wasn't always reciprocated. Nico hadn't loved her. He couldn't have done if he had been so relieved when she had seemingly lost their child. The thought was almost too painful to bear but she had to see the situation for what it was. Even if Nico did agree to play a role in Jacob's life, he wouldn't be interested in playing a role in hers.

'Would you like to come to my house for dinner one evening?'

'I beg your pardon?' Amy stopped when Nico spoke, wondering if she had misheard him.

'You and Jacob. Would you like to come to my house for dinner one evening?' Nico's expression softened as he glanced at Jacob who had wandered off to look at a stall selling hand-carved wooden toys. 'It would be an ideal opportunity for us to get to know one another better.'

'Does that mean you've decided what you intend to do?' Amy asked, holding her breath.

'I suppose it does.' He shrugged and she could tell by the bemused expression on his face that it was as big a shock to him as it was to her.

'You need to be sure, Nico. Once we tell Jacob who you are, you can't change your mind. You do understand that?'

'Yes. Which is why I am not proposing that we tell him just yet.' He took a deep breath and his expression was sombre all of a sudden. 'There are things I need to tell you first, Amy, and they could influence how you feel about my involvement in Jacob's life.'

'What things?' she demanded. 'What are you talking about, Nico?'

'We can't discuss it here. We need to speak in private.' He glanced round when the rumble of an engine announced that their bus had arrived. 'How would tomorrow evening suit you? Do you have plans or can you come then? I can pick you up after clinic closes. Around five p.m. if that's convenient.'

'That's fine,' she murmured, her head spinning. What on earth did Nico have to tell her that was so important it could affect how she felt about them telling Jacob that he was his father? As they boarded the bus, Amy tried to make sense of it but it was impossible. She would have to wait until the following evening to find out what Nico meant and the thought of having to wait all that time wasn't easy. She had a horrible feeling that she wasn't going to like what Nico told her.

CHAPTER SEVEN

BY THE TIME surgery ended the following day, Nico was having serious doubts about what he had done. Inviting Amy and Jacob to dinner had seemed like a good idea at the time. After all, he needed her to know exactly what it could mean if he became involved in Jacob's life and subsequently suffered another heart attack. However, he had to admit that he wasn't looking forward to telling her. Admitting that he was vulnerable in any way didn't come easily to him, and it was especially hard when it was Amy who would be hearing his confession. Although he knew it was stupid, he hated to think that she might view him as less than the man he had been afterwards.

He tried to shrug off the thought as he drove to her hotel. It was a little after five when he arrived and Amy and Jacob were sitting on the terrace, waiting for him. Nico took a deep breath before he opened the car door. Maybe his ego was about to suffer a major blow but there was no way that he could avoid telling Amy the truth.

'All ready?' he asked, walking over to them.

His gaze skimmed over her, taking stock of the coral-pink dress she had chosen to wear. Although it wasn't an expensive designer number like the women he had known in California would have worn, it suited her, he decided, the colour setting off her soft brown hair and adding a glow to her lightly tanned skin. She looked so young and so lovely as she stood there holding Jacob's hand that he was overwhelmed by a sudden need to touch her. Bending, he kissed her on the cheek, his lips lingering on her warm, sweet-smelling skin as a host of emotions flowed through him. He cared about her and there was no point pretending that he didn't. He cared about her and, what's more, he always had.

Nico drew back, trying to hide his shock as he turned to Jacob. It was hard to maintain a calm front but he didn't have a choice. He couldn't let Amy know how he felt, especially when she had no idea about his heart attack. It was bound to affect how she viewed him when she found out that he was damaged goods.

'I thought we could go down to the cove and try our hand at fishing before dinner,' he told Jacob, doing his best to ignore the pain that thought aroused. 'Have you ever been sea fishing before?'

'No.' Jacob's face lit up with excitement. 'If we catch any fish then can we cook them for dinner?'

'I don't see why not.'

Nico ruffled the boy's hair, feeling his heart swell as he was overwhelmed by an unfamiliar rush of emotion. It was an effort to stop himself scooping the child into his arms and hugging him. It was what he should have done from the day Jacob was born, he thought. He should have been there for him right from the beginning and the fact that he hadn't been was something he would always regret. If he hadn't reacted so crassly when Amy had miscarried Jacob's twin then she would have told him that she was still pregnant and he wouldn't have missed out on all that precious time.

Nico's heart was heavy as he led the way to the car. He helped Jacob into the back and fastened his seat belt then opened the passenger door for Amy. She looked up as she slid into the seat and he could tell that she had guessed how emotional he was feeling. He closed the door and went round to the driver's side without saying anything. Until she knew about his heart attack, he couldn't reveal his feelings, shouldn't by rights even have any.

He took a deep breath to batten down the pain as he started the engine. If it turned out that Amy considered he wasn't a good enough prospect to take on the role of Jacob's father then her decision had to be final.

Amy could feel her anxiety building as they drove to Nico's home. On any other occasion she would have enjoyed the journey too. The scenery was stunning, the vivid blue of the sea contrasting dramatically with the deep greens and greys of the mountains. However, she couldn't rid herself of the memory of how Nico had looked when he had ruffled Jacob's hair. It had been the sort of casual gesture anyone might have made and yet she knew that it had been a defining moment for him. She had seen it in his eyes and understood the effect it had had on him. What she didn't understand was why he had looked so sad afterwards. Whatever secret he was harbouring, it was obviously important.

The thought triggered another bout of anxiety so that she didn't realise they had arrived until she heard

Jacob scramble out of the car. She got out as well and looked around in astonishment. If she had been asked to guess where Nico lived, she would have opted for somewhere far more palatial than this rustic old farmhouse. True the views were stunning but it was a world away from what she had expected.

'So, what do you think?' Nico came and stood beside her, pushing his hands into his pockets, and Amy realised in surprise that he was nervous.

'The view is stunning,' she told him truthfully, trying not to read any significance into the fact that he seemed to set any store by her opinion. She gave a little shrug. 'I suppose, if anything, I'm surprised that you chose a place like this. It's not what I expected.'

'You thought I'd opt for something flashier, a huge, luxurious, modern villa with all the bells and whistles.' He laughed wryly. 'Been there, done that, and I am not planning to do it again!'

'Really. It sounds as though you have had a massive change of heart, Nico. A luxury lifestyle was always high on your agenda before.'

'True.' He shrugged but his expression was guarded all of a sudden. 'I did have a major rethink about my life and how I intended to live it, but then a lot of people do. Things happen that make you redefine what you really want, as you must have discovered for yourself. Having a child and deciding to raise it on your own can't have been easy, Amy.'

'If that was meant as a rebuke—' she began, but he shook his head.

'It wasn't. I didn't invite you here to start an argument. I just wondered how you coped with looking after a baby. You must have had to go back to work, I imagine, so how did you manage then?'

'My parents helped. They were wonderful and looked after Jacob until he was old enough to go to nursery,' she explained quietly.

'It still can't have been easy for you,' he said flatly.

'No, it wasn't but it was worth it.' She gave a little shrug because it seemed pointless getting hung up on past events. 'That's all over and done with now and we need to decide what happens from here on. You said that you had something to tell me?'

'That's right. I do. But let's leave it until after dinner. I promised Jacob that we would go fishing and if I'm not mistaken he intends to hold me to it too!' he added wryly as Jacob came rushing over to them.

He took Jacob inside so they could sort out their fishing tackle but Amy stayed where she was. She couldn't insist that Nico explain what the problem was right this very minute. He would tell her in his own good time and until then she would have to try not to worry too much. She grimaced. Bearing in mind that it was obviously going to have a major impact on any decisions she made, it wasn't the easiest thing to do.

They caught three fish and Jacob was ecstatic because he had caught the biggest one of all. Nico helped him to reel it in then showed him how to scrape off its scales.

'Well done!' he declared after Jacob had finished. He asked Jacob to descale the other fish while he performed the messier job of gutting them, realising to his surprise how much he enjoyed teaching the child to perform such tasks. His grandfather had taught him when he'd been roughly the same age as Jacob was and it felt remarkably good to discover a link to those happy times. Somewhere along the way he had forgotten how much he had enjoyed spending time with his grandfather; however, being with Jacob like this had reawoken a lot of wonderful memories.

Once the fish were ready, they popped them into a plastic bag and carried them back to the house. Amy had opted to sit on the terrace rather than accompany them to the beach and he had been relieved. Not only had it given him a chance to spend time alone with Jacob but it had afforded him some welcome breathing space as well.

He sighed as he and Jacob made their way back up the path. He knew that Amy was longing to hear what he had to say but he was nowhere near as eager to tell her. He kept wondering how it would affect the way she saw him even though he knew how foolish it was. However, foolish or not, he couldn't bear to think that he would be somehow diminished in her eyes. He grimaced. Even if his ego did suffer a massive dent, he still had to tell her the truth. It wouldn't be right to withhold information like that when it would influence any decisions she made about his involvement in Jacob's life.

'We caught three fish, Mum, and I caught the biggest one!' Jacob was bubbling over with excitement as he showed Amy the fish.

'Brilliant! Well done,' she declared, smiling at him. She looked up when Nico came to join them and he had to steel himself when he saw the warmth disappear from her eyes. 'He's a natural fisherman, wouldn't you say?'

'Indeed I would.'

Nico cleared his throat. There was no point wishing that Amy had looked at him with the same degree of warmth. After all, he had let her down, hadn't he? Oh, maybe he hadn't known that she was still pregnant but he hadn't made any attempt to contact her after he had left London. At the time he had honestly believed it was for the best; their relationship was over and they needed to make a clean break. However, now he couldn't help thinking that he had should have kept in touch. She had been so upset after the miscarriage and he had been less than supportive…

He drove the thought from his mind because he simply couldn't deal with it when there was so much else to think about. Taking the bag into the kitchen, he set about filleting the fish. Jacob had followed him so Nico showed him how to remove the bones from the fish, another task the boy obviously enjoyed doing.

'Excellent,' he told him. 'You've made a first rate job of that.'

Jacob looked as pleased as punch on hearing that and Nico couldn't help recalling his own childhood and how he had longed to receive a word of praise from his father. It had never happened but he made a note never to forget to praise Jacob when he had done something well. He bit back a sigh because who knew if he would get the opportunity again. It all depended on what Amy decided once she learned about his health.

That thought kept him company as he fired up the barbeque. He showed Jacob how to rub the fish with olive oil and seasoning then placed the fillets in a metal cage and laid them on the grill. He held up his hand when Jacob eagerly stepped forward to help. 'This is really hot so you mustn't get too close. Perhaps you could help your mum make a salad? Everything's in the fridge plus there's some bread in that big stone jar on the dresser—we'll have that as well.'

Jacob happily led Amy inside, chattering away about how much fun it had been to catch his own supper. Nico turned the fish over, not wanting them to burn and ruin the whole experience for his son. His heart caught because Jacob *was* his son and he always would be no matter what Amy decided to do.

It was a moment of such profundity that he had to force himself to concentrate on what he was doing. However, he could feel the tension that had been gathering momentum all day reach a crescendo. So much depended on Amy's decision. It wasn't overstating the case to say that his whole future was in her hands.

Jacob decided to watch some cartoons on one of the television channels after they had finished dinner. The fact that the characters were speaking Greek didn't seem to faze him one bit. Amy gave him a bowl of ice cream and left him to enjoy the programme. Nico had already cleared away the dishes when she went back outside and had a pot of coffee ready as well. Her brows rose.

'My, my, you are domesticated. What happened to the guy who didn't know how to boil water let alone turn it into coffee?'

'He had a rude awakening when he moved here.' Nico grinned but she could see the wariness in his eyes. Her heart caught because there was no doubt that whatever he wanted to tell her was going to have a major impact. 'Hiring a housekeeper to tend to my every need wouldn't have gone down well with the islanders, believe me.'

'So you do it all—the cooking, the cleaning, the shopping?' Amy knew that she was talking for the sake of it. While they were discussing such mundane matters, she could put off the moment when he would tell her his secret.

'Mmm. I also do most of the work on the house as well.' He waved a hand around the terrace. 'This is all my own handiwork. The terrace had collapsed when I bought this place and I rebuilt it.' He gave a self-mocking laugh. 'Maybe I haven't wasted all that training I underwent to become a plastic surgeon!'

'Do you miss it?' she asked quietly, sitting down. 'Surgery, I mean.'

'Sometimes.' He shrugged. 'But I don't miss the lifestyle I had. I prefer it here. It's far more real.'

'So what happened to your desire for fame and fortune?'

'I discovered that it wasn't what I really wanted at the end of the day.' He paused and she held her breath, sensing that he was about to reveal whatever was troubling him. She steeled herself, but nothing could have prepared her for what he said.

'I had a heart attack, you see. Quite a serious one, serious enough to put me in ICU for a couple of weeks.' He looked at her and she could tell that he was trying to gauge her reaction.

Could he tell how shocked she was? she wondered sickly. How terrified she felt at the thought of him having been seriously ill, possibly dying? The pain that thought aroused was so intense that she gasped and she saw his expression darken.

'Are you all right?' He took hold of her hand and held it tightly. 'I'm sorry. I shouldn't have dropped it on you like that without any warning...'

'You're all right now, though, aren't you, Nico?' Her voice echoed with a fear she couldn't disguise and she felt him go tense.

'Yes. I've made a lot of changes to the way I live and I'm fine.' He released her hand and stood up, walking to the end of the terrace to stare out across the bay. His voice sounded strained when he continued, as though he was struggling to contain his emotions, and her heart ached for him. Dealing with such a life-changing event couldn't have been easy.

'My doctors put it down to the fact that I had been under far too much pressure so that's why I decided I needed to reassess my life. However, it would be wrong to assume that it will never happen again, Amy. That's why you need to decide what we should do about Jacob. What happens if we tell him I'm his father and in a few years' time I have another heart attack and die?'

Amy couldn't bear it. She simply couldn't bear to hear him say such a thing. Jumping to her feet, she went and put her arms around him. His body was rigid, unyielding. Nico was holding on to his control because it wasn't his way to give in to his emotions. But if ever there was a time when he needed to drop his guard, it was now.

'Don't say that, Nico. You mustn't even think it!' She drew him closer, feeling the rigid muscles relax the tiniest bit, and it was all the encouragement she needed. Nico was hurting and she wanted to comfort him any way she could.

Reaching up, she slid her hands around his neck and drew his head down so she could kiss him. His lips were cold at first, cold and stiff, and her heart ached at the thought of the rejection she was about to suffer. Then all of a sudden she felt a rush of warmth flow from his mouth into hers, flow right through her in a hot and hungry tide that made her head spin. Now it was Nico who was kissing her and kissing her with a desire she remembered only too well. As his lips claimed hers, teasing, tasting, arousing her passion, she gasped. She had never felt this desire with anyone else, never longed for any other man's kisses the way she had longed for Nico's. She wasn't sure what it meant but it must mean something.

She was trembling when he let her go. It took every scrap of strength she could muster to walk back to her chair and sit down. Nico was still standing at the end of the terrace and the expression on his face was impossible to read. Had the kiss affected him as much as it had affected her? She couldn't tell but she knew that she mustn't make the mistake of reading too much into it. At the end of the day, she didn't want to be left with a broken heart again. And she most definitely didn't want Jacob to suffer.

The thought made her go cold. All of a sudden she could imagine the harm it could cause if Jacob grew to love Nico—as he would—and something happened to him. Would it be fair to place the child in that position? To allow Jacob to grow attached to his father when there was a chance that he might lose him? Questions whirled around inside her head, making her feel so giddy that she couldn't separate one from another let alone find any answers to them. It was a moment before she realised that Nico was speaking to her.

'I'm sorry,' she murmured, desperately trying to pull herself together, but it was impossible when she found herself suddenly beset by a whole new set of questions. How would *she* feel if something happened to Nico? Lost? Devastated? Bereft? She knew that she would feel all of those things and yet she couldn't understand why. Nico hadn't been part of her life for so long that it shouldn't matter this much if anything happened to him.

'I think it's time I took you and Jacob back to the hotel,' he repeated in a tone that revealed very little about how he was really feeling.

Amy nodded, realising that it would be for the best. She needed time to think about what she had learned, base her decision on logic rather than emotion. She shuddered because she knew just how hard it was going to be. Nico aroused far too many emotions inside her to separate them from rational thought. All she could do was hope that she could find a solution that would work for all of them: her, Nico and, most important of all, Jacob.

Amy went inside and told Jacob they were leaving. He was reluctant to abandon his cartoons but cheered up when she told him he could play on his games console when they got back to the hotel. Nico ushered them both into the car and drove them back, pulling up outside the front door. Dinner had just finished and she could hear the clatter of china coming from the dining room as Helena and Philo cleared up. Their teenaged son, Yanni, was helping them, loading glasses onto a tray to carry them down to the basement kitchen. It all appeared so normal that Amy had difficulty believing what had happened in the past hour. Nico had told her that he could die: could it be true?

'Nico,' she began then stopped when there was a loud crash followed by a blood-curdling scream from inside the hotel.

Nico leapt out of the car before she could unfasten her seat belt and raced inside. Amy went to follow him, pausing when she realised that Jacob was hard on her heels. Until she had a better idea of what had happened, it seemed wiser to keep him out of the way.

'You go and wait in here,' she told him, opening the sitting room door. 'I'll be back in a moment once I've seen what's happened.'

Jacob didn't argue, thankfully enough. He went and sat down on the sofa, looking scared. Amy bent down and gave him a hug. 'It's OK, sweetheart. Nico's a doctor so if anyone's hurt then I'm sure he can help them.'

Jacob brightened up at that. Picking up an abandoned comic left there by some previous holidaymakers, he settled down to read. Amy hurriedly made her way to the dining room, her heart sinking as she took in the scene that met her. Yanni was lying in a sea of broken glass at the bottom of the steps leading down to the kitchen. There was a huge gash down his right arm and another down the right side of his chest. Both were bleeding copiously so she grabbed some clean napkins off the shelf and hurried down the steps.

'Here. Use these.' She handed Nico several napkins then used another couple to stem the blood flowing from the teenager's arm. The cut was deep, a huge slice of flesh having been partially severed and hanging by a thread. Yanni was moaning in agony and Nico shook his head.

'He needs something for the pain. Can you stay with him while I fetch my bag from the car?'

'Of course.'

Amy carried on with what she was doing, using both hands to stem the flow of blood. Yanni was shivering violently now and she guessed that he was going into shock. He urgently needed fluids to compensate for the blood he was losing so it was a relief when Nico returned and handed her a bag of saline and everything she needed to set up a drip. Helena was standing in the corner, sobbing, while Philo was staring blankly at them. Amy beckoned him over, knowing it would help if she gave him something to do.

'Can you find something to hang this drip on?' she asked, deftly inserting the cannula into Yanni's arm. 'We need to get some fluids into him as quickly as possible.'

Philo hurried away, coming back a few minutes later with an old-fashioned coat stand. Amy had the line set up by then and she nodded her approval as she hung the bag of saline on one of the coat hooks. 'That's perfect, thank you.'

Nico had administered an injection of morphine along with an anti-emetic so Yanni wasn't in quite so much pain. However, it was obvious that he urgently needed treatment. She wasn't surprised when Nico quietly informed her that he had called an ambulance. It arrived a short time later by which time she and Nico had managed to stop the bleeding.

'I'll take him straight to Theatre,' he told her as they helped the paramedics load the boy onto a stretcher.

'I need to check that there's no muscle damage to the arm or that will cause problems for him in the future.'

'His chest is badly cut too,' Amy said, sotto voce, although it was doubtful if Yanni could hear her now that the morphine had taken effect.

'It is. It's going to need plastic surgery if he isn't to be left with an ugly scar.'

'Well, he couldn't be in better hands,' she said, smiling at him.

'Thank you.'

Nico returned her smile. He appeared to be about to say something else but in the end he turned away. Amy frowned as she watched him help Helena into his car. What had he been going to say? Had it been something to do with his patient or had it been of a more personal nature?

A shiver danced down her spine and she hugged her arms around herself as she went back inside the hotel. She knew that she was allowing her emotions to get the better of her and it was scary to realise just how vulnerable she was. What Nico had told her tonight had been a massive shock and there was no point denying it. Maybe she hadn't seen him for a very long time, but somewhere at the back of her mind, the thought that he was living his life as he had chosen to do had lingered. In a strange way it had been a comfort. Now everything had changed and she needed to weigh up the effect it could have on Jacob if Nico died.

She took a deep breath, trying to batten down the searing pain that pierced her heart at the thought. It was Jacob's feelings which mattered. Not hers.

CHAPTER EIGHT

IT HAD BEEN a while since Nico had performed such delicate and intricate surgery but he soon found his confidence surging back as he set about the familiar routine. As he had feared there was damage to one of the major muscles in the boy's arm and he attended to that first, painstakingly piecing everything back together. Although Yanni would probably suffer some after-effects—possible weakness in the arm or a lack of co-ordination—Nico knew that his swift intervention would save the boy years of heartache and was pleased. Maybe he should think about utilising his skills to help other people in Yanni's position?

It was the first time that he had reconsidered his decision to forsake surgery and it was unsettling. He had been so sure of what he was doing but all of a sudden everything seemed to be up in the air. He forced the disturbing thoughts from his head as he concentrated on the job at hand, tidying up the flap of skin before stitching it back into place with the most exquisitely tiny stitches. Sofia, who was acting as lead theatre nurse, shook her head.

'I did not know it was possible to produce work like this, Doctor. It's amazing!'

'I'd be rather good at embroidery, don't you think?' Nico replied, smiling at her over his mask.

'Very good. I know who to ask if I need my wedding dress embroidered!'

Everyone laughed and it helped to lighten the rather tense mood. Although they were all skilled professionals, Nico knew that none of them had dealt with this type of situation before. Leonardo, the young doctor he had hired a couple of weeks earlier, seemed particularly fascinated so Nico made sure that he could see what he was doing. Maybe he should also think about passing on his skills to some of the younger doctors? he mused. After all, it seemed a shame to possess all this knowledge and not make use of it.

By the time everything was sorted it was five a.m. and he could tell that everyone was as exhausted as he was. 'Thank you all,' he said, looking around the small group who had worked so hard to support him. 'You've done a wonderful job and it's thanks to you that Yanni should regain full use of his arm eventually.'

He was deeply touched when a spontaneous round of applause broke out and had to leave Theatre in rather a rush in case he broke down. He felt incredibly emotional and put it down to being back in Theatre after such a long absence, although deep down he suspected that there was more to it than that.

He went to find Helena and Philo, who had spent the night in Reception. They leapt to their feet when he appeared and he saw the fear on their faces and understood. Now that he had a child of his own, he knew how it must feel to fear the worst.

'Yanni is fine,' he said, swallowing the lump in his throat that thought evoked. 'The operation went extremely well and although there are bound to be a few problems, I'm confident that in time your son will regain full mobility in his arm.'

Helena burst into tears and sank back down onto a chair. Philo shook his head, seemingly unable to take it all in. Nico patted him on the shoulder, an unprecedented move for him. 'Yanni will be fine, Philo. Believe me.'

Philo still couldn't get any words out and settled for vigorously pumping Nico's hand instead. Nico gave the couple a moment to collect themselves then explained that a nurse would be along shortly to take them to see Yanni. Although the boy needed peace and quiet to recover from the operation, he knew that the parents desperately needed to see him. If it were Jacob lying in that bed, he would definitely want to see him.

The thought gave rise to another upsurge of emotion and he hurriedly excused himself. He checked with Sofia that all was well then went to his office. The couch pulled out into a bed but he couldn't be bothered setting it up and simply lay down. He ached with tiredness but it was a good kind of tiredness, one that stemmed from a job well done. Once again the thought that he was wasting his talents struck him and he knew that he needed to rethink his plans for the future.

He sighed. There were an awful lot of things he needed to think about as well as the direction his career should take. When would Amy decide what she intended to do about Jacob? They had been interrupted by last night's emergency but he needed to know if she was willing to allow him to play a role in Jacob's life now that she knew about his heart attack. He also needed to know if she felt any differently about *him* even though he wasn't sure why it should matter. His main concern had to be Jacob, surely?

Philo's elderly parents were in the dining room when Amy took Jacob for breakfast the following morning. They had been drafted in to cover for their son and daughter-in-law who were still at the hospital. Although they spoke very little English, through a series of mimes Amy was able to deduce that Yanni had come through the operation extremely well. She expressed her relief then went to pour her and Jacob a glass of orange juice each. Donna Roberts was at the buffet and she pulled a face when she saw Amy.

'I don't think much of the choice this morning, do you? There's only one type of bread and no jam, just this honey.' She poked at the pot of local honey as though it was something revolting rather the delicious confection it actually was.

'I don't suppose Philo's parents have had time to sort things out,' Amy said soothingly, helping herself to some of the bread. 'It must have been hectic, what with Yanni's accident and everything. You do know about that, don't you?' she added as an afterthought.

'Oh, yes.' Donna picked up a fig and poked her fingernail into it. She put it back in the dish and sighed. 'Tim and I saw the ambulance when we were coming back from the *taverna* and then Harvey told us that Yanni had cut himself. He was here, you see, and had a ringside seat.'

'Harvey was here on his own!' Amy exclaimed.

'*Yes*. He's almost ten and well able to amuse himself for a couple of hours while we go out,' Donna retorted.

She went back to her table, obviously not appreciating the fact that Amy had seen fit to question her childcare arrangements, or rather, the lack of them.

Amy returned to her own table, trying to tell herself that it was none of her business how the other family behaved, but it was hard to ignore what had happened. Leaving the boy on his own was a definite no-no in her opinion, although she wasn't sure what she should do about it. Jacob wanted to spend the morning on the beach again so once breakfast was finished, they made their way there. Donna and her husband and son were already there so it appeared they were going to do the same as the previous day—spend the day sunbathing and visit Darcey in the evening.

Amy determinedly turned her thoughts away from the other family as she helped Jacob build a sandcastle. They had almost finished when Harvey came racing over and leapt on top of it. Jacob's face crumpled in dismay and Amy immediately sprang to his defence.

'You are a naughty boy,' she told Harvey but her words had no effect whatsoever. Sticking out his tongue, he jumped up and down on the sandcastle, trampling it underfoot.

Taking hold of Jacob's hand, Amy led him away. There was no point remonstrating with the boy when it obviously wouldn't have any effect. She gathered up their belongings and went back to the hotel, wondering what she could do to take Jacob's mind off what had happened. There was a ferry trip to some caves that she had planned to take him on as a treat and it would be the perfect day for it.

They hurriedly changed and went to catch the bus. The ferry left from the harbour and they were just in time. Jacob loved being on the boat and especially loved it when they saw some dolphins swimming alongside. The caves were spectacular too, enormous great chambers which the sea had carved out of the cliffs and filled with an eerie green light given off by the plankton that lived in the water. Jacob was entranced and took lots of photographs to show his friends when they got home. Amy's heart lightened when he told her that. Jacob seemed to have forgotten about the bullying that had made his life such a misery. Maybe she didn't need to tell him about Nico being his father, after all?

The thought stayed with her as they sailed back to the harbour. It was tempting to leave things the way they were, but she knew deep down that she was taking the coward's way out. It was easier not to say anything but what if the bullying started again and she was forced to tell Jacob the truth? He would be both upset and bewildered because she hadn't told him who Nico was when she had had the chance and it would make the situation even more difficult.

She sighed. There was only a week of their holiday left and she would have to make up her mind soon.

Nico got through his morning list with very few problems. There were a couple of tourists suffering from sunburn although their injuries weren't serious. He advised them to drink plenty of water and stay in the shade. Aloe vera cream, available from the local pharmacy, would help to soothe the burns but they would be well advised to keep covered up for the remainder of their holiday. They thanked him politely but they looked very glum when they left. Keeping out of the sun obviously wasn't high on their list of priorities when they had come away on holiday.

Once surgery ended, he went straight to the hospital. Yanni's bed had been partitioned off from the main part of the ward to afford him some peace and quiet. He was wide awake, however, when Nico arrived.

'*Kalimera*, Yanni. You look a lot better this morning, I must say.'

'I feel better,' Yanni replied, smiling shyly. He was a rather reserved young man who was studying archaeology at Athens University. He had come home for the holidays to help out at the family's hotel.

'Good.' Nico pulled up a chair. 'I'm not sure what your parents have told you but I think it's best if you know exactly what I needed to do last night.' He briefly outlined the procedure he had used to repair Yanni's arm. 'You will find that your arm is very stiff and unresponsive at first. However, I'm confident that it will improve with time and the appropriate physiotherapy.'

'So I will still be able to use it?' Yanni asked anxiously. 'Obviously, I'll need two good arms if I hope to become an archaeologist. I won't be able to go on a dig if I'm…well, handicapped in some way.'

'It will take time,' Nico told him truthfully because Yanni needed to know exactly what he was up against. 'And you'll need to follow an extremely gruelling physiotherapy programme if you hope to regain full mobility in your arm—I shall contact the head of physiotherapy at the hospital on the mainland today and make arrangements for them to see you. However, I'm confident that it can be done as long as you are determined enough.'

'There's no question about that,' Yanni told him quietly. 'I'll do whatever it takes, Dr Leonides.'

'In that case, then I'm sure you won't have a problem.'

Nico smiled his approval then left Yanni to mull over what he had said. However, he was convinced the boy would succeed and it was good to know that he had played a major part in his recovery. All of a sudden he realised that the tentative plans he had made to help other people in a similar position needed to be firmed up. It was a waste of his training and experience to give up surgery, although it would mean making some changes to his life. If he was working on the mainland several days a week, he would need to find someone to take charge of the day-to-day running of the clinic.

He sighed, aware that he had been coasting for the past couple of years. His confidence had been badly shaken when he had suffered that heart attack and he had taken the easy way out by turning his back on surgery. Now it was time to get back into the fray, although he had no intention of putting himself under the kind of pressure he had been under before. Nevertheless, it would be good to pick up the threads again. He would feel more like himself, more like the man Amy had known nine years ago.

Nico frowned. How much of his desire to return to surgery could be attributed to his need to convince Amy that he was no less of a man than he had been? He had no idea but he knew that it had played a major part in his decision and it worried him. At the end of the day, returning to surgery might make no difference whatsoever to the way Amy viewed him. And it might make no difference either to what she decided to do about Jacob. He would be well advised to bear both those points in mind. It could save him a great deal of heartache.

Jacob chattered non-stop about what they had seen on the journey back to their hotel. As soon as they got into their room, he begged Amy to let him see the photographs he had taken so she loaded them onto her iPad and left him to look at them while she took a shower. Once she was dressed, she went back into the room expecting to find him still poring over the pictures, but he was nowhere to be seen. Hurrying outside, she came to a dead stop when she found him sitting on the terrace with Nico. They had their heads bent over the iPad and her heart ached when she saw them. Jacob looked so like Nico that it was uncanny.

Nico looked round and smiled when he heard her footsteps but Amy could see the wariness in his eyes. Was he worried about the reception he would receive by turning up unannounced? Or was he more concerned about what she had decided to tell Jacob? After all, it couldn't be easy for him to acknowledge Jacob as his son when he had made it clear in the past that he hadn't wanted children. It was hard to hide how much that thought hurt as she sat down beside them.

'Nico said that he's been *swimming* in these caves!' Jacob looked up, his face alight with excitement as he held up the iPad for her to see. 'How cool is that, Mum?'

'Very cool,' Amy replied, trying and failing to maintain a neutral tone. She saw Nico look at her and hurried on, wanting to deflect his attention away from her. She knew how he felt about having children and it was silly to feel hurt. 'Maybe you can do the same one day.'

'Can I? Really?' Jacob shot to his feet. 'When?'

'I…erm…I'm not sure,' she replied, wishing she hadn't said that. 'You're not allowed to swim from the boat—they told us that. And I have no idea how you can get to the caves any other way.'

'I bet Nico knows, don't you, Nico?'

Amy swallowed her groan of dismay as Jacob turned imploringly to Nico. She knew where this was leading but before she could say anything to defuse the situation, Nico replied.

'Yes. In fact, I can drive you there, if you like. There's a very strong undercurrent where the boats anchor which is why they don't allow visitors to swim there. However, you can swim closer in to the land. It's quite safe there.'

'Brill! So when can we go? Tomorrow?'

Amy sighed. Now that Jacob had heard that he wouldn't give up, and the thought of him *coercing* Nico into driving them to the caves didn't sit easily with her. 'I expect Nico is busy tomorrow, sweetheart. After all, he isn't on holiday like us. He can't just go swanning off when he has patients to see.'

'Actually, I'm free tomorrow afternoon as it happens. I usually try to catch up with any paperwork that needs my attention but it can wait.' He looked calmly back at her, giving no indication as to his true feelings. 'I'd be happy to drive you and Jacob to the caves.'

'Oh, I couldn't let you do that,' she protested, desperately trying to come up with a bona fide reason to refuse the offer. After all, it wasn't as though he had made it willingly when he had been more or less *forced* into it.

'Why not? I could do with some R & R and I can't think of anything I'd enjoy more than swimming in the caves. It's very soothing, believe me. I'm sure you'd enjoy it too, Amy.'

His tone was so bland that Amy couldn't understand why a wave of heat flashed through her body. Nico wasn't inviting them along because he wanted to spend time with *her*, she told herself sternly, but it was hard to accept that. There was just something about the way he was looking at her, his deep brown eyes holding a light that she hadn't seen in them for a very long time…

She blanked out that foolish thought as Jacob started to perform a happy dance across the terrace. It was obvious how thrilled he was at the thought of the forthcoming trip and all of sudden she didn't have the heart to disappoint him. 'In that case then thank you. We would love to go, wouldn't we, Jacob?'

'Yes!' Jacob roared at full throttle.

Amy grimaced as he went racing inside. 'You've made one little boy very happy from the sound of it.'

Nico laughed. 'We aim to please.' He sobered abruptly. 'I hope I didn't push you into it, though, Amy. That was the last thing I intended to do.'

'Of course not.' She fixed a smile to her mouth, not wanting him to guess that she had reservations. She was very aware that the more time Jacob spent with Nico, the more he would grow to like him. It was what was happening to her, after all. Whenever she spent time with Nico, she found herself liking him more than ever.

It was a disturbing thought so it was a relief when Nico got up to leave. At the end of the day it didn't matter how she felt, she reminded herself. This was all about Jacob and how it would affect him if he found out that Nico was his father. Should she tell him or should she keep it a secret for a while longer?

It should have been easy to know what to do, but meeting Nico again had changed everything, especially in light of what he had told her about his heart attack. Would it be wise to allow Jacob to grow to love him when there was a chance that Nico might not be around to watch him growing up? The thought was so painful that it was hard to hide how devastated it made her feel when Nico turned to her. Maybe her feelings didn't count, but she couldn't bear to imagine a world where he no longer existed.

'I'll be off then. I only called in to have a word with Darcey's parents. She was discharged this afternoon and I wanted to make sure that her parents understand how important it is that she stays out of the sun for the rest their holiday. However, it appears that they've gone out for the evening.'

'Oh, I see.' Amy frowned. 'Let's hope they've got the sense to follow instructions.'

'Let's hope so,' he agreed, glancing round as though he was eager to leave.

'Well, thanks again,' she said hastily, not wanting to delay him. Maybe he had plans for the evening, she mused, plans that included dinner with an attractive female companion. After all, Nico was a very handsome and personable man and there must be lots of women eager to spend time with him. The thought was depressing and she hurried on. 'It's really kind of you to offer to drive us to those caves tomorrow. I do appreciate it.'

'It's my pleasure.' He smiled at her and once again she felt heat roar through her when she saw the warmth in his eyes. It seemed like the most natural thing in the world when he bent and kissed her lightly on the lips. '*Kalispera*, Amy. Until tomorrow.'

'Kalispera,' she murmured, her heart racing as she watched him walk away. He disappeared from sight and a moment later she heard a car engine roar to life. Only then did she start to breathe again.

Amy touched a fingertip to her mouth, feeling the heat that Nico's lips had left behind. The kiss may have been meant as no more than a token gesture but it didn't feel like that, not when her mouth was burning this way. Panic suddenly engulfed her as she realised just how precarious the situation was. She couldn't afford to let her judgement be clouded by emotion, couldn't allow herself to be swayed by desire. She had to do what was right for Jacob and not what *she* wanted.

She groaned. What she wanted more than anything at that moment was Nico holding her, kissing her, *making love* to her, and it was foolish to wish for such things. Nico had done all of that nine years ago—kissed her, held her, made passionate love to her—but it hadn't meant anything, had it? Why should she imagine that it would mean anything now? Why should she even care? The answers to those questions hovered at the back of her mind but she was too afraid to search them out. It was safer—much safer—to leave them where they were.

CHAPTER NINE

NICO TOOK A deep breath as he drew up outside the hotel the following afternoon. He had found it impossible to rid himself of the memory of that kiss. Maybe it had started out as a mere token gesture yet it had filled his mind to the point where it had required a huge amount of effort to focus on his patients' needs all morning long.

That was something which had never happened to him before. Work had *always* taken priority in the past. However, every time he had relaxed his guard, he had found himself recalling how sweet Amy's lips had tasted, how seductive; how much he wanted to kiss her again! Now he could only pray that he wouldn't do something foolish. Maybe Amy hadn't pushed him away last night but there was no reason to think that she wanted him to kiss her again.

He dismissed that depressing thought as he went into the hotel. Helena was behind the reception desk and he saw the colour drain from her face when she saw him coming in and silently cursed himself. 'Yanni is fine,' he said hastily. 'I saw him shortly before I left the clinic and he was sitting up and chatting to one of the other patients.'

'Oh, thank heavens!' Helena pressed a hand to her heart. 'We have guests arriving today so I stayed behind to get everything ready while Philo went to visit him. I thought it must be bad news when I saw you.'

'On the contrary, Yanni is making excellent progress. In fact, if he carries on like this he should be able to come home next week.'

'Really? Oh, that is good news!' Helena exclaimed. She looked past him and smiled broadly. 'Dr Leonides has just told me that Yanni might be able to come home next week. Isn't that wonderful news?'

'It is indeed.'

Nico felt the skin on the back of his neck prickle when he recognised Amy's voice. He turned slowly around, doing his best not to react when he saw her standing behind him, but it was impossible. She was wearing another sundress in the palest shade of pink. It had narrow straps which tied at the shoulders and a scooped neckline that immediately drew his eyes to the curve of her breasts. She looked so lovely and so desirable that he wanted nothing more than to sweep her into his arms and kiss her until they were both senseless, but how could he do that when he had no idea if it was what she wanted too? The thought was deflating so it was a relief when Jacob came racing across the hall and almost bowled him over.

'Hey, steady on, young man,' Nico said, putting out a restraining hand. 'We don't want any more accidents, do we?'

'He's been so excited,' Amy said softly. 'I can't count the number of times he's asked me when you would be coming to collect us.'

'Well, I'm here now so we may as well get off.'

Nico smoothed his face into a suitably noncommittal expression. Maybe he *was* behaving irrationally but he had no intention of letting her know that. The last thing he wanted was Amy thinking that he was vulnerable in any way. 'Have you everything you need? Towels, swimsuits, et cetera?'

'I think so.' She showed him the extra-large holdall she was carrying. 'Jacob's also brought along his snorkel and mask, plus his flippers. He obviously intends to make the most of this trip,' she added dryly.

'Good for him!'

Nico laughed as he ruffled the boy's hair. It felt remarkably good to know that Jacob was looking forward to the outing so much. Children obviously didn't need expensive presents or lots of money spent on them: they just needed attention. Nico logged the thought for future reference as he turned to Helena. 'Sorry again about giving you such a fright. As I said, Yanni is making excellent progress and there really is no need for you to worry.'

'Thank you, Doctor,' Helena replied, glancing from him to Jacob.

Nico swallowed his sigh when he saw her expression change. It was obvious that Helena had noticed the resemblance between him and Jacob and it made him wonder how much longer Amy could keep their relationship a secret. Surely it wouldn't be long before Jacob himself became aware of it?

That thought accompanied him as he led the way to his car. Although he didn't want to force the issue, he was more convinced than ever that Amy needed to make up her mind about what she intended to do. If she planned to tell Jacob that he was his father then it would be better to get it over with as soon as possible. Quite frankly, he couldn't understand what was taking her so long…unless she was still unsure about him. After all, he had made no bones about the fact that he hadn't wanted children nine years ago, but surely she could see that he had changed?

Nico's heart started to pound as he slid into the driver's seat. Maybe he hadn't wanted a family in the past but he definitely wanted one now. He wanted to be a proper father to Jacob and he wanted it more than he had wanted anything in his entire life. It was a huge shock to realise just how important it was to him too. Now all he needed to do was to convince Amy that she could trust him.

He squared his shoulders as he started the engine. Bearing in mind everything that had happened in the past, it wasn't going to be easy to convince her, but somehow, some *way*, he intended to play a role in Jacob's life from now on!

It took them just half an hour to reach the caves. Amy had expected it to take much longer than that and wasn't prepared when Nico announced that they were there. She fixed a smile to her mouth as she got out of the car but she could feel her stomach churning with nerves.

It had been easier while they had been driving. Nico had needed to concentrate on the narrow, winding roads so she had been spared having to make conversation with him. However, now that they had arrived, she would have to play her part for Jacob's sake. Jacob would think it very strange if she didn't talk to Nico, yet the thought made her feel on edge. Maybe it was silly to keep thinking about that kiss but she couldn't help it. The memory seemed to fill every tiny corner of her mind even though she knew she mustn't allow it to influence her. She had to focus on doing what was right for Jacob and not what she wanted.

'The entrance to the caves is down there.' Nico pointed to a path leading down the side of the cliff and she hurriedly gathered her thoughts.

'It looks very steep to me. Are you sure it's safe?'

'Yes. Steps have been cut into the rock and there's a handrail to hold on to so there shouldn't be a problem getting down.' He smiled reassuringly. 'I'll carry everything down while you keep an eye on Jacob.'

Amy nodded as she opened the back door and let Jacob out of the car. He immediately went racing towards the path but she called him back. 'Stay here until we've got everything out of the car,' she told him firmly. He pulled a face but he did as he was told, waiting impatiently while she retrieved her bag from the footwell.

'I'll take that.' Nico took it off her, grimacing as he swung it over his shoulder. 'I don't know what you've got in here but it weighs a ton!'

'Just the usual things,' she told him defensively. She held out her hand. 'I'll take it. It don't expect you to carry my bag as well as your own.'

'I don't have a bag. Only this,' Nico replied, taking a towel out of the boot of the car. He tossed it over his shoulder and grinned at her. 'I was only teasing about the bag, Amy. It's fine, really.'

'Oh.'

Amy felt the colour rush to her cheeks as she realised that she had overreacted. She hurried over to where Jacob was waiting, wishing that she wasn't so aware of Nico that even the smallest comment seemed to take on a huge significance. She wasn't normally so sensitive but it was different with Nico; *she* behaved differently when she was with him. It had been exactly the same nine years ago too and it worried her that so little had changed. Surely she shouldn't react this way after all that time?

The thought lingered as they made their way down to the beach. Amy looked around, sighing with pleasure at the sight of the turquoise-blue water lapping at the glittering white sand. They were the only people there and it was like stepping into a tiny piece of heaven.

'It's beautiful, isn't it?' Nico came and stood beside her. 'It's one of my favourite places on the island, mainly because very few people ever come here.'

'It is beautiful,' Amy murmured, shading her eyes as she stared across the glittering blue water. 'I'm sure it would be one of my favourite places too if I lived here.'

She turned towards him and felt her breath catch when she saw the way he was looking at her. There was such hunger in his eyes that she felt herself start to tremble. When he held out his hand, she took a step towards him, drawn by the longing she could see in his eyes…

'Where's the caves, Mum? I can't see them.'

Jacob's voice brought her back down to earth with a bump. Amy took a shuddering breath, fighting to control the waves of desire that were rippling through her. She knew what would have happened if she and Nico had been alone, knew that they would have made love right here on the shimmering white sand. It was what Nico wanted. And it was what she wanted too.

Nico could feel himself shaking as he fought to control the hunger that filled every cell in his body. How had that happened? he wondered dazedly as he watched Amy walk over to Jacob. One moment he had been admiring the view and the next he had been overwhelmed by the need to make love to her. What shocked him most, however, was the fact that he knew it was what Amy had wanted too.

A shudder ran through him as he stripped off his clothes. He was wearing swimming trunks beneath as it had seemed easier to come prepared rather than have to change when they got here. Amy must have had the same idea as she was in the process of taking off her dress. Nico groaned under his breath as he took stock of the modest one-piece swimsuit she was wearing under it. Although there was nothing the least revealing about the swimsuit, it certainly pushed all his buttons! His body responded in time-honoured fashion and he hurriedly grabbed hold of his towel, using it to hide his discomfort when she turned to him.

'Should I put sunscreen on Jacob or will he be safe enough without it in the caves?' she asked in a tight little voice that immediately set all his internal alarm bells ringing.

'He'll be fine without it,' Nico replied, calling himself every kind of a fool. Maybe he *did* want to make love to her, and maybe it *was* what she had wanted too, but they both knew it would be a mistake. They needed to concentrate on Jacob, on doing what was right for him. At the end of the day, Amy wouldn't want him disrupting her life when she had managed perfectly well without him for the past nine years.

It was a sobering thought and Nico knew that he must bear it in mind as he continued. 'It's best not to pollute the water with any kind of oils as it can affect the plankton that live in the caves. Anyone swimming there is advised not to use sunscreen for that reason.'

'Oh, I see.' She picked up a towel and draped it across Jacob's shoulders to protect him from the sun until they reached the caves then looked at Nico. 'We're ready whenever you are.'

'Fine. You'll need to leave your sandals on as we have to climb over those rocks,' he told her, relieved to have something practical to focus on rather than all the conflicting thoughts and feelings that plagued him. 'Once we reach the caves, though, you can take them off as we'll be walking over sand.'

He led the way, pausing at intervals to make sure they were keeping up. They reached the entrance to the caves and he helped Jacob jump down off the rocks then turned to help Amy, feeling his breath catch when she placed her hand in his. He quickly released her once she was safely down on the sand.

'The entrance to the caves is rather low and quite narrow,' he explained, trying not to think about how small and fragile her fingers had felt when they had gripped his. 'However, it widens out after a couple of metres so it shouldn't be a problem. You're not worried about confined spaces, are you?'

'Not that I know,' she replied.

Nico's skin prickled when he heard the tension in her voice. It was obvious that she had felt something too when she had held his hand and it was all he could do not to say anything only he knew it would be a mistake. Maybe they were both incredibly aware of one another but it wasn't going to lead anywhere. They'd had their chance and it would be foolish to think they could take a step back in time. They were very different people these days and they could never recapture the feelings they'd had for one another all those years ago.

His heart was heavy as he ducked into the entrance to the caves. Even though he knew how pointless it was, he couldn't help wishing that he had behaved very differently nine years ago. If he could have the time all over again, he would never let Amy go.

CHAPTER TEN

THEY SWAM FOR almost an hour before Amy decided that she had spent enough time in the water. She got out and wrapped herself in her towel, watching as Jacob scooped up a handful of water and splashed Nico with it. He shrieked with delight when Nico picked him up and tossed him into the water, and she sighed. Although she did her best, she couldn't play with him the way Nico did. It made her see how much Jacob had missed by not having his father around.

'Right, that's it. You've worn me out, young man.' Nico waded out of the water, shaking his head when Jacob pleaded with him to go back in. 'Once I've had a rest then maybe I'll come in again. OK?'

Amazingly, Jacob accepted his decision without arguing. Amy's brows rose as Nico sat down beside her. 'I'm impressed. Jacob doesn't usually give in so easily when he wants something.'

'No?' He shrugged as he picked up his towel and started to dry himself. 'Maybe he decided I needed a break.'

Or, more likely, Jacob had realised that Nico wasn't a push-over and had reacted accordingly, she thought wryly. It was yet another point in Nico's favour, another reason why Jacob would benefit from having him around. Jacob needed a male presence in his life, a role model he could look up to. It was on the tip of her tongue to tell Nico that but she held back. Although there were many plus points to having Nico play a part in Jacob's life there were minuses too, the biggest one being the matter of his health. Although he appeared to be as fit as ever, she couldn't ignore what he had told her about the increased risk of him having another heart attack. She couldn't bear to imagine Jacob's anguish if anything happened to him. She couldn't bear to imagine her own anguish either.

Amy lay back on her towel, closing her eyes while she tried to deal with the thought. She knew without the shadow of a doubt that she would be devastated if anything happened to him yet she didn't understand why. After all, he hadn't been part of her life for a very long time. She hadn't seen or spoken to him for nine long years, in fact. Admittedly, she had thought about him frequently during that time but that was only to be expected when Jacob was a constant reminder of Nico's existence. In truth it shouldn't make a scrap of difference what happened to Nico, but she knew in her heart that her world would fall apart if he died.

It was a shock to have to face up to that fact, so it was a relief when Nico announced a short time later that it was time they left. Amy helped Jacob dry himself after he reluctantly waded out of the water then she quickly gathered up their belongings. She desperately needed a breathing space, time on her own to get her thoughts into some sort of order. Being around Nico only seemed to confuse her and that was the last thing she needed when she still had to decide what to do about Jacob. She still wasn't sure that telling him Nico was his father would be a good idea.

Nico glanced around, checking that they hadn't left anything behind. There was a rusty drinks can wedged into a crevice in the rocks and he picked it up. 'Somebody must have tossed it over the side of a boat. They don't realise the damage they can cause by not taking their litter home with them. Things like this—cans and plastic bottles—are a real hazard for the local sea life.'

'There's always someone who can't be bothered to clear up after themselves,' Amy agreed then stopped when she heard shouting. 'Did you hear that? It seemed to be coming from one of the other caves.'

'It did.' Nico's expression was grim as he turned and made his way along the narrow strip of sand that bordered the water.

Amy followed him, keeping tight hold of Jacob's hand in case he slipped into the water. There were several more caves leading off from the one they had swum in but Nico had told her that it wasn't safe to swim in them. Apparently, there were strong currents flowing through them which could catch an unwary bather off guard. They came to the entrance to the largest of the caves and stopped. Nico shook his head when they heard people shouting.

'It sounds as though someone is in difficulty. I'd better see what's happened.'

With that he ducked into the cave and disappeared. Amy hesitated but there was no way that she was letting him go on his own. She turned to Jacob, wanting to impress on him just how serious this was. 'We're going to go with Nico but you are *not* to go into the water. Do you understand?'

Jacob nodded. He looked decidedly scared as they followed Nico into the cave. Amy gave his hand a reassuring squeeze, hoping that she was doing the right thing. She didn't want to frighten him but, equally, she didn't want to leave Nico to deal with this on his own. She sighed. Talk about being trapped between a rock and a hard place!

The cave was much bigger than the one they had swum in. It was also a lot brighter as it led directly out to sea. Amy had to wait while her eyes adjusted to the light then gasped as she took in the scene. There was someone in the water, a teenaged boy from what she could tell, and he was obviously in difficulty. She could see a boat anchored close to the mouth of the cave and recognised it as the same boat she and Jacob had sailed on the previous day. She could only assume that the teenager had either jumped or fallen off the boat. The crew were in the process of lowering a dinghy into the water but it was doubtful if they would reach him in time. The current kept dragging him under and her heart plummeted as he disappeared from sight once more.

'I'm going to swim out there and keep him afloat until the dinghy gets to him.'

Nico waded into the water before Amy could say anything. She pressed a hand to her mouth as she watched him start to swim out to the teenager because it was obvious that he was having problems with the current too. He finally reached the boy just as he was dragged under again and she cried out in alarm when she saw Nico dive beneath the waves. It seemed to take for ever before he surfaced, holding the boy with one arm as he struggled to keep them both afloat. The dinghy was in the water now and she held her breath, praying that Nico's strength would hold out long enough for it to reach them.

The boy was finally hauled into the dinghy and then the crew helped Nico in as well and brought him back to where she and Jacob were waiting. He jumped out, pausing briefly to instruct the crew to take the teenager straight to the clinic once they arrived back at the harbour. Amy handed him her towel, unable to put into words how she felt. She had been so scared when she had seen him disappear beneath the waves... Tears filled her eyes and she turned away but not quickly enough to stop him seeing them.

'Amy? What is it? What's wrong?' He bent to look at her, but she shook her head.

'Nothing. I'm fine.' She glanced at Jacob. 'That boy was very silly to try to swim in this cave, wasn't he?'

'Yes.' Jacob turned to Nico and there was an expression of hero worship on his face. 'It was really cool the way you dived under the water and saved him.'

'If I hadn't done so then I'm sure someone else would have done it,' Nico said lightly. He ruffled Jacob's hair. 'Anyway, that's quite enough excitement for one day, young man. It's time I took you and your mum back to your hotel.'

'Oh, do we have to go back to the hotel? Can't we go to your house?' Jacob pleaded. 'We could go fishing again!'

'Not today,' Amy said firmly. 'Nico has spent enough time entertaining us. Anyway, I'm sure he would appreciate some peace and quiet after what's just happened.'

'On the contrary, I would love some company.' Nico's voice was soft and deep. It stroked along her raw nerves like a velvet-gloved hand and she shivered. 'There was a moment back there when I did wonder if I had been overly confident about my prowess as a swimmer. The current in that cave is extremely strong.'

Amy knew that he was telling her the truth and it placed her in a very difficult position. If she refused to go back to his house, both Jacob and Nico would be disappointed, but was it really wise to go there when her emotions were in such turmoil? Seeing Nico disappear beneath the waves had crystallised her earlier thoughts and added to them as well: she couldn't bear it if anything happened to him. She couldn't bear it because she still had feelings for him.

She bit her lip as panic assailed her. Admitting how she felt had been the easy bit—keeping it from him would be the hard part. However, no matter how she felt about Nico, she must never forget that Jacob came first. If she didn't think it was in Jacob's best interests to tell him that Nico was his father then once they left the island, they would never see him again.

Nico could feel the tension building as he drove them to his home. He had called into the clinic on the way to check on the teenager but, thankfully, the boy had seemed none the worse for his adventures. He had given him a stern talking to before he had sent him on his way and could only hope it would stop him doing anything so foolish again. All it took was one rash decision and the consequences could prove catastrophic.

He groaned under his breath when it struck him that he was a fine one to be handing out advice. If he had thought about the consequences, he would never have invited Amy to his house again tonight. Having her in his home was going to test his self-control to its absolute limit and he could only pray that he would manage to hold out. He certainly couldn't afford to think about how much he longed to take her to his bed!

Nico breathed in deeply as he drew up in front of the house, trying to contain the rush of desire that flowed through him. He got out of the car and waited while Amy helped Jacob out of the back. She turned and he could tell at once how nervous she was and was overwhelmed by sudden tenderness. No matter how hard it was, he would always protect her, he vowed. He had hurt her once before and he would make sure that he never hurt her again, no matter what the cost was to him personally. And if that meant him stepping out of her and Jacob's lives then that was what he would do.

Amy finished preparing the salad and placed the bowl in the fridge to keep cool. She glanced at her watch, wondering how much longer Nico and Jacob were going to be. The sooner they came back, the sooner she and Jacob could eat their supper and leave. Even though Nico had done nothing whatsoever to alarm her, she was feeling very much on edge. If she carried on this way then Jacob could start to wonder what was wrong with her. The last thing she wanted was him thinking that she was keeping something from him, even if it were true.

'We only caught *one* fish, Mum, and Nico caught it, not me!' Jacob couldn't contain his disappointment as he burst into the house. Amy quickly set aside her qualms and adopted an upbeat expression.

'Never mind, sweetheart. You can always try again another day,' she said encouragingly, then winced. She certainly didn't want Nico thinking that she was angling for another invitation, did she?

'That's what I said.'

Nico smiled as he followed Jacob into the house, but she could sense a definite tension about him and frowned. Was he having second thoughts about them being here, wishing that he hadn't invited them? She sighed softly. Quite frankly, she wouldn't blame him if he was. After all, the situation must be no less stressful for him than it was for her. The thought made her come to a swift decision.

'Well, seeing as you haven't caught enough fish for our supper, I think we should go back to the hotel.' She shook her head when Jacob started to protest. 'No. It isn't fair to expect Nico to provide a meal for us, darling.'

'It isn't a problem,' Nico said quietly. 'There's plenty of food in the fridge so we certainly won't go hungry.'

'Please say we can stay, Mum!' Jacob pleaded. *'Please!'*

He sounded so desperate that Amy found herself wavering, even though she knew that she should insist they leave. It was the sensible thing to do, to put some space between her and Nico while she thought everything through. She couldn't afford to rush into a decision that was founded on emotion rather than solid common sense.

'It just doesn't seem right that Nico should have to cook for us again,' she began but Nico interrupted her.

'I'm not. We shall share the work and all make dinner.' He turned to Jacob before she could say anything else. 'Right, you're in charge of the pudding, young man.' He opened the refrigerator door and stepped aside. 'There's fruit, yogurt, cheese—whatever you fancy. I shall leave it up to you to decide what we have.'

'Yes!' Jacob was grinning from ear to ear as he began to plunder the contents of the fridge.

Amy groaned. 'You do realise that we'll probably end up with all his favourite food piled into one dish?'

'It can't be any worse than some of the meals I made when I first started cooking for myself,' Nico said wryly as he took cutlery out of a drawer.

'Oh, dear!' Amy laughed. 'That bad, was it?'

'Worse.' He glanced round and she could see a hint of embarrassment on his face. 'I hadn't a clue, basically. There had always been someone to cook for me in the past and I am ashamed to admit that even doing something as simple as boiling an egg was a major feat.'

'But at least you had a go. And you've obviously come on in leaps and bounds if that meal you cooked for us the last time we were here was anything to go by. It was delicious.'

'Thank you. I knew I had to make some major changes to my life after my heart attack and learning how to cook was one of them.' His tone was grave all of a sudden. Amy felt her heart start to flutter when he continued because she sensed that whatever he was about to say was important to him.

'I suppose what I'm trying to say is that I'm not the same person I was when we knew each other before, Amy. I…well, I'll understand if you view me differently these days.'

CHAPTER ELEVEN

NICO HELD HIS breath as he waited for Amy to reply. Maybe it was asking too much to expect her to declare her feelings but he couldn't help himself. He needed to know if she viewed him as less than the man he had been: the man who had been her first lover.

Heat flashed along his veins as the words awoke all sorts of memories. He had been both surprised and oddly moved when Amy had admitted that she hadn't slept with anyone before him. He had never set any store by a woman's innocence before; if he had thought about it at all then it would have seemed more of a hindrance than anything else. The sort of women he usually dated were exactly like him—independent, single-minded women who viewed sex merely as a pleasurable experience and not a prelude to a lifetime's commitment. And yet discovering that Amy had been a virgin had triggered the strangest response inside him. Not only had it felt as though she was giving him a very special gift, knowing that he was to be her first lover had been a big responsibility too. He had resolved to make the experience as wonderful for her as it could possibly be, and it had been too.

Nico shuddered as he recalled how sweetly responsive she had been to his kisses and caresses. It may have been Amy's first time but, amazingly, he had felt as though it had been his first time as well. Nothing had prepared him for the sheer depth of feeling she had evoked inside him. Why even now he could recall how he had felt that night, how aroused he had been, how much he had desired her, and it was another shock to realise that the memory of that time was as clear and as vivid as ever.

He had truly thought that he had put it all behind him but he had been wrong. Meeting Amy had been a milestone in his life and if he hadn't been so stubbornly set on proving himself then he would have recognised just how important their time together had been. He wouldn't have left her if he had. He would have stayed with her. Stayed with her and Jacob so that now they wouldn't be facing this dilemma because one thing was certain: Amy wouldn't have abandoned *him* after his heart attack. She would have remained with him, cared for him, *despite* what had happened.

Regret filled him even though Nico knew how pointless it was. He had had his chance and no amount of wishing that he had acted differently would change things. It was a relief when Amy didn't say anything because he couldn't have borne it if she had tried to be kind. He didn't want her pity. It was the last thing he wanted!

Nico took a package of lamb out of the fridge and set it on the counter with a thud. It was hard to contain his emotions but he'd had years of practice and it stood him in good stead now. Nobody would have guessed that it felt as though his heart was bleeding at the thought of what he had lost through his own stupidity.

'How about kebabs?' he suggested, blanking out any trace of emotion from his voice. Inside he might be suffering the torments of the damned but, by heaven, he wouldn't show it. 'It won't take long to prepare them and then we can cook them outside on the barbecue.'

'That would be lovely.'

Amy's voice was flat and all his senses immediately went on alert. Was she trying not to let him know how she felt? he wondered grimly. Trying to hide the fact that in her eyes he was no longer the man he had been, the lover who had aroused her passion to previously undiscovered heights? Now his body had failed him, shown that it was only too fallible, didn't she find him attractive any more?

The thought made him want to rant and rail but it wouldn't help, certainly wouldn't change things, neither her view of him nor the fact that he wasn't a perfect specimen of manhood any longer. Nico concentrated instead on preparing their supper, spearing the lamb onto long wooden skewers and rubbing it lightly with garlic and olive oil ready to cook it on the barbecue. He had already lit the fire and the smell of pine burning greeted him as he carried the skewers outside. He smiled bitterly as he tossed a handful of fresh herbs onto the embers to infuse the meat with extra flavour. If he couldn't prove his prowess as a lover then at least he could prove that he could cook a decent meal.

Amy wished with all her heart that she had said something. As they ate their supper, her mind kept returning to what Nico had said about her viewing him differently. The worst thing was that she knew it was true. She did see him in a different light but that was because he *was* different.

The Nico she had known nine years ago had been harder, more focused, far more self-centred. He had changed a lot and whether it was because of his heart attack or what, there was no denying it. How could she have claimed that her view of him hadn't altered, especially when nine years ago she had been madly, crazily in love with him? It would have been tantamount to admitting that she still felt the same way about him today.

Her heart knocked painfully against her ribs and she bent over her plate, spearing the last tender morsel of lamb with her fork. She popped it into her mouth then turned to check that Jacob was eating his supper. Her eyes slid over Nico, stopping abruptly when she realised that he was watching her, and she felt her heart give another of those painful leaps when she saw the expression on his face, a mixture of pure longing and intense regret…

She turned away, her breath coming in tight little spurts as she helped Jacob to cut up the last few pieces of his kebab. She wasn't sure what had prompted the regret on Nico's face but she understood only too well what had provoked that longing. Nico wanted her. He wanted her as a man wanted a woman he found attractive. It was only too easy to understand how he felt when it was how she felt too.

It was a relief when they all finished their main course and Jacob hurried inside to fetch the pudding as it provided a welcome distraction. He came back and carefully placed the bowls on the table, looking as pleased as punch. Amy stared at the assortment in front of her, unsure what to say. Yogurt, some mangled-looking figs, several great dollops of honey, all topped off with chunks of feta cheese made for an eclectic dessert.

'Mmm, this looks interesting.'

She glanced up when Nico spoke, watching as he picked up his spoon and dipped it into his bowl. Was she still in love with him after all this time and everything that had happened? Oh, admittedly she felt *something* for him but something was a long way from being love, surely? How could love survive without any encouragement? Without any reason to hope that it would be reciprocated? Surely, the way they had parted had killed the love she had had for Nico stone dead?

Amy struggled to reason it out and yet the harder she tried, the less sure she was. If she had felt nothing at all for him then it would have been easier but there was no point lying to herself. She felt something for him and only time would tell exactly what it was.

Nico finished loading the dirty dishes into the dishwasher. Night was drawing in and the lanterns he had placed around the terrace provided a soft glow in the encroaching darkness. He watched as Amy picked up her glass and drank the last of her wine. It was time he drove her and Jacob back to their hotel and yet he hated the thought of them leaving. If it had been up to him they would have stayed the night but he knew it wouldn't be wise. If Amy stayed then they would end up in bed together and that was the last thing he should allow to happen, even though he knew it was what she wanted as much as he did. However, allowing desire to dictate their actions was a recipe for disaster.

A gust of wind suddenly blew in from the sea and Nico saw one of the patio chairs topple over. He hurried outside and quickly righted it, frowning when he felt the first drops of rain start to fall. It rarely rained at this time of the year and when it did, it usually heralded one of the violent storms that occasionally swept over the island. If he was to return Amy and Jacob to their hotel then they needed to set off straight away.

'I'm sorry to cut the evening short but I really need to drive you back before the storm sets in,' he explained. 'These summer storms can be incredibly fierce and I don't want us to get halfway there and end up stranded.'

'Of course.' Amy hurriedly stood up, making a grab for her chair as another gust of wind threatened to blow it over. 'That wind came from nowhere!' she exclaimed, tucking the chair under the marble-topped table.

'It did,' Nico agreed, quickly gathering up the lanterns and carrying them inside. 'That's why it's so dangerous. One minute everything is as calm as can be and the next moment the wind springs up. A lot of fishing boats have been lost because of it.'

'How awful!'

Amy shuddered as she followed him inside and Nico sighed. He had forgotten how tender-hearted she was and hated to think that he might have upset her.

'Most of the fishing boats will be safely moored in the harbour by now,' he assured her. 'Very few boats go night fishing these days, mainly because the sea around the island is so difficult to navigate. There are too many partly submerged rocks to take the risk.'

'That's good to know.' She gave him a quick smile then went through to the sitting room where Jacob was playing on his games console.

Nico made sure the candles in the lanterns were safely snuffed out then found his car keys. The rain was beating down now so he went into the hall and dug out a couple of rarely used waterproof jackets from the cupboard. Amy and Jacob would get soaked if they didn't put something over their clothes.

'Here. Put these on,' he instructed when they appeared. He held up a jacket so that Jacob could slip his arms into it. It was way too large for the child but Nico zipped it up anyway and pulled the hood over Jacob's head.

'Your turn,' he said, turning to Amy. He held the jacket while she slid her arms into the sleeves then automatically started to zip it up just as he had done for Jacob. His fingers brushed against the soft curve of her breast and he felt a rush of heat pour through him at the accidental contact.

'It's all right. I can manage, thank you.'

She stepped away from him, making a great production out of zipping the jacket the rest of the way and pulling up the hood, but he could see that her hands were trembling and knew she had felt it too, felt that rush of desire that had hit him.

Nico dragged on his own jacket and led the way outside. The rain was pouring down now, huge great drops that stung their faces as they ran to the car, but he was barely aware of the storm raging around them. Quite frankly it couldn't compete with the storm that was raging inside him. He wanted Amy so much! Wanted her with a passion that belied all reason. It was as though every atom of his being had been consumed by this need to make love to her again.

Was it simply because it had been a while since he had made love to a woman? he wondered as he helped Jacob scramble into the back of the car. He wanted to believe that was the true explanation, but there was no point lying to himself. It was only Amy he wanted, only Amy who could arouse his desire to this extent. And it was such a devastatingly profound thought that his heart seemed to scrunch up inside him. Even if he could never have her, he would always want her.

Amy sat on the edge of her seat as Nico drove them along the narrow winding road. It took all his skill to keep them on course as the wind roared around them but in truth it wasn't the storm that scared her but what had happened before they had left his house. She had felt it too, felt that surge of desire that had passed between them when he had accidentally touched her breast, and it simply confirmed her worst fears. Making a decision about Nico's involvement in Jacob's life would be all the more difficult when her emotions were in such turmoil.

'What the devil…?'

Amy was roused abruptly from her thoughts when Nico slammed on the brakes. Peering through the windscreen she could see that the road ahead was blocked by boulders which had tumbled down off the mountainside. Nico turned to her and his expression was grave.

'Stay here while I check to see if we can get past,

although I doubt it. It looks like the whole road has been blocked.'

Amy bit her lip as he got out of the car, bending almost double as he fought his way against the wind. He had almost reached the landslide when there was an almighty roar and more rocks started to roll down onto the carriageway. Instinctively she went to get out of the car to make sure he was all right but he was already heading back.

'Get in.' He slammed her door then hurried round to the driver's side. 'We need to get away from here as quickly as possible,' he told her tersely as he started to back up the car. He found a turning place and turned the vehicle around, picking up speed as he drove them away from the danger point. He didn't slow down again until they came to a section where the road widened out.

'I'm afraid you won't be able to go back to your hotel tonight.' He glanced at her, his expression impossible to read in the glow from the dashboard lights. 'You and Jacob will have to stay at my house until they manage to clear the road.'

'How...how long will it take?' Amy asked, her voice barely above a whisper.

'I've no idea.' Nico shrugged but she could see his knuckles gleaming through his skin as he gripped the steering wheel. 'It all depends if that is the only landslide or if there are others further along the way. It could be a few hours or a few days before they manage to clear it all away.'

Amy swallowed, trying to dislodge the knot of panic that seemed to be constricting her throat. A few hours she could cope with, but a few days... Closing her eyes, she did her best to calm herself down but it was a losing battle from the outset. The thought of spending several days in Nico's house was daunting, especially in her present frame of mind. Could she behave sensibly or would temptation prove too much? Too much for both of them?

Opening her eyes, she shot a glance sideways at him and felt her heart give a little jolt compounded of both fear and excitement. Who knew what might happen if she and Nico were forced to spend several days together.

CHAPTER TWELVE

'YOU SHOULD BE comfortable enough in here. I'm afraid there isn't a lot by the way of furniture—I haven't got round to furnishing all the bedrooms yet. However, there is an en suite bathroom if you or Jacob need to use it during the night.'

Nico opened the door to what would eventually become a guest bedroom, stepping aside when Amy came forward to take a look.

'It's lovely. Thank you.'

She dredged up a smile but Nico could tell how on edge she felt and couldn't blame her either. The very air seemed to be thick with tension as it pulsated around them and he knew that if it weren't for the fact that Jacob was standing there beside them, he and Amy would be behaving very differently at this moment. He certainly wouldn't be pretending to be the perfect host—that was certain!

Desire twisted his guts, turned them to red-hot liquid fire, and he groaned under his breath. For a man who had always prided himself on being in control of his emotions it was humbling to find himself at their beck and call. He took a deep breath, forcing himself to get a grip. He couldn't give in to these feelings;

it wouldn't be right. Amy had to be free to decide if she wanted him in Jacob's life without him employing some kind of *emotional* blackmail. The thought steadied him.

'Good. I'll just fetch some sheets and make up the bed for you.'

He half turned to leave but Amy stopped him by placing her hand lightly on his arm. It was the sort of instinctive gesture that anyone might have made but there was no doubting that it had a galvanising effect on both of them. Nico gritted his teeth when he felt desire surge through him once more, felt it flood into every atom of his being. There wasn't a tiny, minuscule bit of him that didn't want to drag her into his arms, hold her, kiss her, let their bodies become one—

'If you'll show me where everything's kept then I'll sort out the bed.' She removed her hand and the moment passed, although Nico could see a matching desire in her eyes before she turned away. 'I don't expect you to wait on us while we're here, Nico. Really I don't.'

'In that case the linen is in here.'

He had no idea how he managed to carry it off, how he could behave as though everything was completely normal when it was so far from being that. He led the way to the huge old-fashioned linen press that had been installed when the farmhouse had been built. It stretched from floor to ceiling, the cedar wood shelves as smooth as glass after so many years of use.

'Help yourself to whatever you need,' he said, gesturing towards the beautifully ironed piles of linen. He had drawn the line at doing his own laundry and one of the women from the village did it for him. He saw

Amy inhale appreciatively as she lifted an armful of sheets off a shelf and breathed in the intoxicating mix of fresh mountain air and lavender that infused them.

'These smell gorgeous!' She looked up and smiled at him and he felt his heart dance with pleasure when he saw the delight in her eyes.

'They do, although I can't claim any credit for that. One of the local women does my laundry and it always comes back smelling wonderful.'

'Ah. So you're not completely domesticated then?' she said with a teasing little laugh that helped to dispel some of the tension.

'Sadly, no. Ironing is one skill I don't intend to master.'

He returned her smile then made himself turn away before it could become something more meaningful. He needed to be wary of that happening, careful not to allow a shared moment of pleasure to take on an even greater significance. Who knew how long Amy would need to stay here? He simply couldn't afford to lower his guard and allow his emotions to dictate his actions.

'I shall leave you to sort everything out. There's blankets in the cupboard as well as towels so take whatever you need. I'll make some more coffee. I'm sure you could do with a cup. I know I could.'

His tone was brisk and far more in keeping with how he needed to behave throughout his guests' unplanned sojourn. Amy followed his lead because she too sounded much more detached and perversely Nico found himself regretting the change of mood. Foolish or not but he missed the feeling of intimacy that had surrounded them just moments earlier.

'Coffee would be very welcome. Thank you.'

Nico inclined his head then went to the kitchen and set about preparing the coffee. It was a simple enough task but he gave it his undivided attention—carefully measuring the coffee into the pot, adding hot, not boiling, water and heating the milk. Although he preferred his coffee black, Amy liked hot milk in hers…

Bam! That was all it took, just the thought of her likes and dislikes, and his mind was off and running again. Nico gripped hold of the worktop as he was assailed by a whole flood of memories: Amy's nose wrinkling as she added milk to her coffee and inhaled its aroma; her mouth pursing as she took a first tentative sip; the taste of coffee on her lips when he leant forward and kissed her…

Nico clung to the worktop as his legs threatened to buckle beneath him. He couldn't believe that the scene was so sharp and so clear. He wasn't just remembering what had happened in some abstract and distant fashion: he was reliving it. He could actually taste the coffee as it had tasted all those years ago, hot and rich, imbued with the natural sweetness of Amy's lips. It was so real that it was difficult not to believe it was actually happening right here, right now, this very second. Would it be the same if he re-enacted the scene? Would his blood quicken as he watched Amy lift the cup to her mouth, watched her lips purse in readiness to taste it? Would he be filled with the same desperate urge to kiss her as he had felt then?

A groan escaped him. Of course he would!

Amy finished tucking in the sheets and stepped back to admire her handiwork. Every corner was precisely folded, each wrinkle carefully smoothed out. It was the perfect example of how a bed *should* be made but, best of all, making it had helped to use up several potentially dangerous minutes.

She sighed softly as she went to the old-fashioned dressing table and peered into the mirror. The glass was foxed with age so that her reflection wasn't as clear as it could have been but that was a blessing. Opening her bag, she took out a comb and ran it through her hair, trying not to think about what Nico might see in her eyes at that moment. Desire? Definitely. A worrying lack of self-control? Almost certainly.

She couldn't remember the last time she had felt so conflicted by her emotions. Her head was telling her to get a grip and she was listening—truly she was! However, her heart was sending out an entirely different message, one that was far too beguiling to ignore: would it really matter if she gave in to her feelings, did what she longed to do and slept with Nico again? If she accepted that it must be a one-off and didn't mean anything, then what harm would there be in indulging herself for once?

After all she was a grown woman, a mother, someone who held down a highly responsible job, not some innocent young girl who didn't understand the facts of life. If she had needs like any other woman then why not do what most women would do in the circumstances, sleep with Nico and satisfy this hunger that was gnawing away inside her? No one would blame her. No one would know. They could spend the night together and enjoy one another's bodies without the world coming to an end, surely?

Amy stared into her own eyes and saw the growing temptation that shimmered in their depths but somehow she had to find the strength to fight it. Maybe another woman could have slept with Nico and walked away afterwards without any regrets but she couldn't. She would be haunted for ever by what she had done and she couldn't bear to think that her life and, more importantly, Jacob's might be affected by her actions. If she slept with Nico then she could never be sure if she had allowed any decision she made to be influenced by desire rather than common sense, could she? At the end of the day it wasn't her needs that were paramount but her son's. She had to do what was right for Jacob. Nobody else.

Turning away from the mirror, Amy made for the door. Jacob was in the kitchen with Nico when she tracked him down. He had an empty glass in his hand and a rim of milk around his mouth. Amy fixed her face into a suitably amused expression as she went to join them. There was no way that she wanted Jacob picking up on her mood and worrying.

'No need to ask what you've been up to, young man. I only hope you haven't drunk all Nico's milk. He's a real milk fiend,' she explained politely for Nico's benefit. 'I can't keep up with him when we're at home. I'm always running out.'

'There's no need to worry about that here,' Nico answered evenly. 'One of the local farmers keeps me well supplied with milk, although it's goats' milk, not cows'. There's no cattle on the island—the terrain isn't suitable for them. Although cows' milk is imported and served in most of the hotels, the locals prefer goats' milk.'

'Really!' Amy exclaimed. 'And you liked it, did you, Jacob?'

'Uh-huh. Nico said I could try it. It tasted a bit funny at first but it was OK,' Jacob replied nonchalantly. When he asked if he could go and watch television, she readily agreed, still surprised by his easy acceptance of the different milk.

'You seem surprised, Amy. Why? Is Jacob a faddy eater normally?'

'Not really.' She gave a little shrug, trying to batten down her heart which seemed to want to perform somersaults all of a sudden. If she was to stay in Nico's house until the road was reopened then she would have to talk to him, she told herself sternly. However, there was no denying that the sound of his deeply mellifluous voice was playing havoc with her willpower.

'Like most children he has his likes and dislikes but he's pretty good about trying new things. It's just that with milk being one of his absolute favourite things to drink, I was a bit surprised that he would enjoy something different.'

'Maybe it's his Greek genes coming to the fore,' Nico suggested. He laughed. 'I've always loved goats' milk so Jacob must take after me.'

'Probably.'

Amy laughed as well although the thought that it was yet another thing the pair had in common was a poignant one. As Nico busied himself pouring their coffee she couldn't help thinking how wrong it would be to keep him and Jacob apart. Maybe she did have concerns but were they really grounds enough to withhold the truth from Jacob? Surely he had a right to know that Nico was his father despite what might happen in the future?

Amy sighed as once again she found herself beset by the same old questions; however, at some point soon she would have to make up her mind what she intended to do. There was less than a week of their holiday left and if she wanted Jacob to know who Nico was then she needed to tell him before they left the island. It would give the child a chance to talk to Nico which was vital if they were to form the basis for their future relationship.

A shiver danced down her spine as she glanced over at Nico who was in the process of adding hot milk to her coffee. If she told Jacob the truth then she and Nico would also need to establish some rules for their own relationship.

Nico couldn't sleep. Whether it was all the coffee he had drunk he didn't know, but after an hour spent tossing and turning in his bed, he finally admitted defeat. Getting up he went to the window and opened the French doors, breathing in the rain-washed purity of the night air. It was just gone midnight and although the storm had started to die down, the sea was still very rough, huge white-topped breakers pounding against the shore. From where he stood, he could just make out the glimmer of the lights around the harbour and sighed.

Once the aftermath of the storm had been cleared away, everything would go back to normal and people would resume their daily routines. He would too although it wouldn't be easy to pretend that tonight had never happened. He had come so close to making love to Amy tonight and even though nothing had happened, the fact that he had wanted her so much couldn't be ignored. Of all the women he had known, Amy was the only one who affected him this way.

A sudden movement caught his eye and he turned, feeling his heart leap when he saw Amy standing on the terrace. She was still wearing the clothes she had worn that evening, making him wonder if she had even attempted to sleep. The wind was still very strong and as he watched, he saw her tip back her head so that her hair streamed out behind her like a silken banner. The effect was mesmerising.

Nico wasn't aware of moving; he wasn't aware of anything as he left his room and made his way through the house. Amy was still standing on the terrace, her eyes closed, her head tilted back, her hair twisting and turning in the wind. She couldn't have heard him approaching above the noise of the wind yet she didn't cry out when he laid his hands gently on her bare shoulders. Maybe she had known he would come and find her. Hoped he would.

'Amy.'

The wind caught her name as soon as it left his lips and carried it away but it didn't matter. They didn't need words. They didn't need anything at that moment except each other. Nico bent and kissed the side of her neck where a pulse was beating out its own insistent rhythm, a tender, gentle kiss that would have soothed her if she had wanted soothing only that wasn't what she wanted. Her eyes opened as she turned to look at him and he could see the same questions in their depths that pounded inside his own head: *Was this right? Should they do it? Would a night of passion satisfy their hunger for one another and bring them peace?*

Stepping back, Nico held out his hand, filled with a strange sense of resignation. Maybe there were no answers to those questions. No firm negatives or positives. Only consequences. His heart trembled at the thought but it wasn't enough to make him withdraw his hand and turn away. When Amy placed her hand in his, he led her back inside, holding her lightly so that she would know that she was free to pull away if it was what she wanted. If she changed her mind.

His bedroom door was open but he paused on the threshold, giving her time, giving her space. This had to be her decision as well and not just his. When she walked past him into the room, leading him in after her, he could barely contain his joy. Even though they both understood the problems it could cause, it made no difference. They still wanted one another.

CHAPTER THIRTEEN

THE FRENCH DOORS were open, letting a flood of cool night air flow into the room. Amy could hear the waves breaking on the shore below, hear them pounding against the rocks in a rhythm that seemed to mimic the beating of her heart. Oddly enough she didn't feel afraid. For the first time in days, she knew that this was what she wanted. What she needed to do. Trying to bottle up her feelings and force them back inside her was as fruitless as trying to rebottle spilled Champagne. She had to deal with these feelings, deal with them and move on from here. If she could.

A thread of panic ran through her at that thought but it wasn't enough to make her change her mind. Nothing was. Not when Nico was standing there, behind her. She turned slowly around, letting her eyes drink in every detail. Unlike her, he had obviously tried to go to sleep because he was wearing his nightclothes—dark grey cotton-jersey pyjama pants and a matching T-shirt that moulded the leanly muscled contours of his body. His black hair was ruffled and there was the shadow of beard darkening his jaw too. Amy felt her stomach lurch, swooping swiftly down then back up again as she realised how sexy he looked stripped of his usual formal attire. With those dark eyes staring down at her and that deeply tanned skin he was an arresting sight and she couldn't help being drawn to him.

Stepping forward, she closed the gap between them until she could feel the heat of his body seeping into hers. She was still holding his hand and she felt his fingers tighten momentarily before he deliberately loosened his grip. Did he still have doubts? she wondered as she looked into his eyes. Was he unsure about the wisdom of what they were about to do? Was he concerned about the effect it could have on Jacob or on him? More questions joined the ones that were already resident in her mind, making her feel giddy. Unsteady. Unsure.

'You don't have to do this, Amy. We don't have to do it. In fact, it would be sheer madness if we went ahead!'

The anguish in his voice was so alien that it drove everything else from her head. Amy stared at him in shock. 'You really believe that?'

'Of course I do!' He let go of her hand, his handsome face mirroring the conflict he was feeling. 'If we sleep together then it will make it that much harder for you when you make your decision about how much input I should have in Jacob's life.'

'And that's your only concern, is it?'

'No. But it has to be my main concern.' His eyes bored into hers. 'How I feel doesn't count. It's Jacob and how it could affect him that we have to focus on. I don't want you to do something you may regret in the future, Amy. That's the last thing I want.'

'Why can't this be simply a one-off?' she suggested. 'A sort of swansong rather than the start of something more.'

'And you honestly think you can treat it as that?' he said sceptically. 'You can sleep with me and then put it out of your mind?'

'Yes. Why not?' She gave a little laugh, hoping that he couldn't hear the underlying pain it held. Was that what Nico would do? Sleep with her and then forget about it afterwards? She hated the idea but could she blame him when it was what she needed to do too? 'We're both adults, Nico. We both understand that people don't need to be madly in love to enjoy having sex.'

'So that's all it would be, a means to satisfy our desire for one another?' he said slowly.

'Yes. It's obvious that we still find each other attractive so why not get it out of the way now rather than have it lurking in the background like the proverbial elephant in the room.'

He gave a deep laugh. 'Hmm, I've never heard it described that way before but maybe you're right. Maybe it would clear the air and help us both to think rationally.' He took hold of her hand and gave her a gentle tug so that she was brought into more intimate contact with him. 'I'm willing to give it a go if you are, Amy.'

Amy didn't have time to respond; she didn't have time to think even as Nico bent and claimed her mouth in a searing kiss. She kissed him back, closing her mind to the tiny voice that was telling her it was wrong, that it shouldn't be like this, that she would regret it if they made love for the wrong reasons. Who knew what was right or wrong any more? She certainly didn't! She could only follow her instincts and let them lead her down whichever path they chose.

When Nico led her to the bed, she went willingly, lying down on the cool cotton sheets that smelled of lavender. There were no lights on in the room so that everywhere was in shadow and it seemed to add to the feeling that they were cocooned in their own space. Nico was a darker shadow as he stripped off his clothes and lay down beside her but even though she couldn't see him clearly, she knew every inch of his body. Her mind had logged it away, made a blueprint of it that had been tucked into a special little corner and kept safe.

Amy ran her hands over the familiar contours, marvelling at the fact that her fingers still recognised the muscles and bones, the skin and hair that covered them after all the time that had passed. Her palm skated over the scar on his upper arm—a memento from a childhood accident when he had fallen out of a tree—and she smiled. It was like rediscovering a much-loved path, one that led to such delicious pleasures.

Her fingers travelled on, delicately skimming over his chest, following the trail until she came to his hard, flat stomach where they paused. His skin was hot to the touch, hot and dry and tense. Amy could tell that he was holding his breath, that he was doing his best to contain his desire for her. Nico had always been a generous and considerate lover, wanting to give her pleasure and not just pleasure himself, and nothing had changed in that respect, it seemed. The thought sent a wave of tenderness washing over her and her fingers moved on, grazing over the crispness of hair until she could gently wrap them around his manhood and she heard him gasp.

'Amy…!'

His voice grated with the effort it cost him to speak and she bent and quickly covered his mouth with hers. She didn't want to hear what he had to say, neither arguments nor encouragement. She was doing this for her sake as well as his. If she could slake this desire she felt for him, reduce it to a more bearable level, then surely it would make the situation so much easier to understand.

Her tongue snaked out, probing his lips, enticing them to open for her as passion flared inside her. There was a moment when she thought he was going to resist, when she thought that he was having second thoughts, and then the next second he was rolling her over onto her back, his powerful body pinning her to the mattress. His mouth was so hungry as it took hers, so demanding and yet at the same time so giving that she felt tears well into her eyes. Maybe they were doing this for the wrong reasons but it didn't feel like it. Not when Nico kissed her this way. Not when it felt as though he truly cared.

Moonlight bathed the room in a silvery haze. The clouds had blown away and the sky beyond the open window was inky black and clear. Nico lay on his back and stared out at the night, knowing that he would remember this night for the rest of his life. He had never thought that he would fall in love but he had been wrong. Tonight he had fallen in love with Amy, if he hadn't been in love with her already.

Sighing, he turned to look at her lying curled up, fast asleep, at his side and felt his heart ache. Had he been in love with her nine years ago? He wasn't sure. He had been so focused on carrying out his plan to prove himself that he had been deaf, dumb and blind to everything else. He had refused to acknowledge his own emotions, refused to accept that he had any feelings at all. He had been set on making a success of his life and everything else had been pushed aside. Even Amy and their children. The one she had lost as well as the one she had given birth to. His son. Jacob. How could he ever make up for what he had done? How could she ever forgive him enough to trust him? Should he even expect her to when he wasn't sure if he could live up to the role of being Jacob's father?

Panic assailed him and he closed his eyes, trying his best to contain it. While he wanted to be a proper father to Jacob, and wanted it desperately too, was he fit to take on the responsibility? Oh, it wasn't only the issue of his health, although that was a major factor, obviously. It was his own upbringing that worried him most of all. He had no role model to refer to, no wonderful childhood memories of him and his father enjoying time together. His father had had no interest in him and he had made it perfectly clear too. He had mentioned family genes tonight and although he had been joking about Jacob's apparent liking for the same things he liked, what if he had inherited *his* father's genes and turned out exactly like him? He couldn't bear to think that he would ruin Jacob's life.

'Regrets already?'

Nico sighed when he realised that Amy was awake and watching him. Whilst he wanted to spare her any more pain, he knew that he couldn't lie. 'Doubts more than regrets.'

'Because we slept together?' she said quietly.

'No. I neither regret what we've done nor have doubts about it.'

He dropped a kiss on her mouth, forcing himself to draw back when he felt the familiar tug of desire flare inside him. This wasn't the time to think about making love to her again even if it was what he wanted more than anything. The thought of burying all his fears while she was in his arms was so very tempting but Nico knew he had to resist. It was too important that he got this right. Too important to Jacob and his son's future happiness.

'Then what's wrong? Obviously something is troubling you, Nico.'

There was the faintest tremor in her voice, a reflection of her uncertainty, and Nico silently cursed himself for causing her more distress. Even though he intended to resist temptation, he couldn't stop himself as he pulled her into his arms and cradled her against him.

'I'm afraid that I won't be able to be a proper father to Jacob,' he told her honestly, although it wasn't easy to bare his soul like this. He had told no one about his unhappy childhood. It had never been a topic for discussion. Why, even he and his sister rarely spoke about their father, both of them preferring not to dwell on the negative aspects of their upbringing. To come out and actually admit how unhappy he had been made him feel incredibly vulnerable but Amy deserved to know the truth and have all the facts laid before her before she made her decision.

'I understand how daunting it must be for you, Nico—' she began but he didn't let her finish.

'It is. Although probably not for the reasons you

imagine.' He took a quick breath but now that he had started, he needed to continue. 'I never told you about my father, mainly because there is very little to say. To put it bluntly, he is a cold and ruthless man who cared nothing for me and my sister when we were children. He never showed us any affection or even interest. The only thing he is interested in is making money and he has dedicated his life to doing that.'

'And you're worried in case you behave the same towards Jacob?' she guessed astutely and shook her head. 'No. That's ridiculous, Nico. Why, I've watched you with him and you're great—kind, caring, *supportive.*'

'But it's early days,' he countered, wanting her to listen to what he was saying. Maybe she didn't want to believe it but she had to face the facts. And the facts pointed towards him turning out the same way as Christos Leonides had done. After all, he had never wanted children, had he? In fact, he had taken great care to avoid having any. Surely that was proof that he was very much his father's son.

The thought sent an ice-cold chill through him but he forced himself to carry on. 'It could turn out to be a sort of...well...knee-jerk reaction to finding out that I'm a father. Once I get accustomed to the idea then who knows what will happen?'

'You're going to turn into the proverbial Jekyll and Hyde character?' she scoffed. 'No. I am not buying that, Nico. It's ridiculous!'

'Why? We were only talking about the effect genes can have on a person earlier tonight, so why is it ridiculous? What if I have inherited my father's genes and find that I can't love Jacob as he deserves to be loved?'

'You honestly think that could happen? Or is it merely an excuse you've come up with?'

'An excuse?' he repeated uncertainly.

'Yes!' She sat up and even though the room was dark he could see the contempt on her face. 'You've got cold feet, haven't you, Nico? You've suddenly realised that if you do take on the role of being Jacob's father it's going to change your whole life and you're not sure if you like the idea.'

'It isn't that,' he said quickly but she refused to listen to him. Tossing back the sheet she climbed out of bed and picked up her clothes, and began dragging them on.

'Don't bother. I understand, Nico. Really I do. I'm only glad that we got this sorted out before Jacob became involved.'

She swept out of the room without another word. Nico leapt out of bed and went to follow her then stopped. What could he say? He couldn't swear that he would be there for Jacob for ever and ever, could he? Even if it did turn out that he wasn't anything like his own father, there was his health to consider. Although he felt perfectly fit and hoped to remain that way, he couldn't make any promises. Having suffered one heart attack, his chances of having another one were increased. Oh, he was religious about taking his medication and leading a healthy lifestyle but there was no guarantee it wouldn't happen. How would it affect Jacob if he was taken ill or possibly died if they had forged a close father-and-son bond?

Nico sank down onto the bed, overwhelmed by a feeling of despair as he was forced to face the truth.

Not only would he have to let Jacob go but he would have to let Amy go as well.

The road was finally reopened shortly before midday. As soon as the phone call came from the clinic to tell Nico that the road was clear, Amy gathered together her and Jacob's belongings and carried them out to the car. She felt strangely removed from what was happening but she knew it wouldn't last. At some point soon the full impact of what had happened that morning would hit her.

'Have you got everything?'

'Yes.'

Nico opened the car door for her and Amy slid into the seat, barely glancing at him as she fastened her seat belt. By tacit consent they had avoided one another since that discussion in his bedroom. Quite frankly, Amy had nothing to say to him, not now that he had made his position so very clear. Nico had rejected the idea of playing any part in Jacob's life and by doing so he had also rejected her. It was a repeat of what had happened nine years ago so she shouldn't have felt surprised or hurt but she did.

Tears stung her eyes as she placed her bag in the footwell but she blinked them away as Jacob scrambled into the back. There was no way that she wanted Jacob to know what had happened, no way at all that she would allow him to be hurt. It would be far better if Jacob never learned the truth about Nico rather than discover that his father didn't want him.

'I wish we could stay. We could go to the caves again this afternoon, couldn't we, Nico?' Jacob exhorted, glancing hopefully up at Nico who was fastening his seat belt.

'I'm afraid not.'

Nico's voice was even but Amy could hear a thread of something beneath the carefully level tones. Was he feeling uncomfortable? she wondered. Feeling guilty perhaps about rejecting his own flesh and blood? She sighed, realising that she was attributing to him emotions he didn't possess. Nico had had no difficulty rejecting her and their child nine years ago so why should she imagine that he had any qualms about doing so again?

'I have to go to the clinic so I shall be busy for the rest of the day. I am sure that your mother will take you to the beach or think of something exciting you can do instead.'

'S'pose so,' Jacob muttered, obviously not enthralled by the idea. He suddenly brightened. 'What about tonight? You won't have to be at the clinic then, will you, Nico?'

'No. Nico is extremely busy and can't spend all his time entertaining us.' Amy held up her hand when Jacob opened his mouth to protest. 'I said no, Jacob, and that's the end of it.'

Jacob sank back in his seat, obviously realising that he wasn't going to win this particular argument. Amy swung round and faced the front as Nico closed the rear door. The sooner they were back at the hotel, the better. There were just a few days of their holiday left and then she and Jacob could leave the island and forget all about what had happened here…

'I'm sorry. I've made a complete mess of everything, haven't I?'

Nico's voice was low so that Jacob couldn't overhear what he was saying but she still flinched. She shot a glance at him then turned and stared through the windscreen again, not wanting anything to pierce the cocoon of numbness that enveloped her. It would be a mistake to imagine that his apology was genuine, that he cared. The only person Nico cared about was himself.

Thankfully, he didn't say anything else as he drove them back to the hotel. Maybe he had realised that it would be a waste of time to dredge up any more meaningless excuses. He drew up outside the front door, not bothering to switch off the engine as he turned to her. 'I hope you don't mind if I don't come in with you. It's bound to be busy at the clinic with appointments having been disrupted and I need to go straight there.'

'Of course.' Amy opened the car door and went to get out, pausing when Nico placed his hand on her arm. Even though he only held her lightly, she could feel the imprint of his fingers burning into her skin and bit her lip when desire surged through her once more. She couldn't afford to feel this way. Nico wasn't going to be part of her life from this point on and she had to forget about him.

'I'm sorry, Amy. Truly I am.'

There was nothing she could say, nothing that would help to alleviate the pain of being rejected a second time. Amy shook off his hand and got out of the car then helped Jacob out of the back. Nico bent forward to look at them and there was such anguish in his eyes that she almost weakened, almost but not quite. If he had felt anything—really felt anything—

then he couldn't have turned his back on their son or on her.

Amy turned away, taking hold of Jacob's hand as they mounted the steps to the front door. She heard the car engine rev to life followed by the crunch of tyres on gravel as Nico drove away but she didn't stop or look back. There was no point. Nico had gone from her life a second time. And this time she would make sure he never came back.

CHAPTER FOURTEEN

TIME PASSED IN a blur. Although Nico did everything that was expected of him, it felt as though he was functioning at one step removed. He was haunted by the memory of how Amy had looked when he had left her at the hotel. Several times he was tempted to go to see her and try to explain why he felt it was better that he didn't get involved in Jacob's life but somehow he managed to resist. Even if she believed him, it wouldn't change anything. The truth was that Jacob would be better off without him. All he would be doing was applying a little salve to his own conscience.

The day when Amy and Jacob were due to leave the island rolled around. Nico knew they would need to take the ferry back to the mainland so they could catch their flight. Jacob had mentioned that they were flying home in the dark so he guessed they would catch the noon ferry from Constantis. He busied himself with the clinic's affairs then emailed a former colleague who now worked in Athens. He intended to go ahead with his plan to utilise his skills by working in reconstructive surgery. Apart from the fact that he wanted to do it, it would give him something to focus on. He couldn't bear to imagine that he would live out the rest of his days feeling the way he did at this moment—empty and desolate. Concentrating on the demands of such a taxing job would help to fill the gap in his life. *Hopefully.*

Amy had packed their cases the night before so there was very little to do on their last day on the island. She took Jacob to breakfast, only half listening as he chattered away. It was three days since she had seen Nico, three days that she had spent missing him every hour and every minute and every second. Even when she finally fell asleep at night, he was there in her head, smiling down at her in the moments before they had made love. It was as though the intervening years had never happened and she was right back where she had been: aching and hurt, her heart broken at being rejected. It was hard to maintain a happy front for Jacob's benefit but she refused to do anything that might upset him.

Donna Roberts and her family were already in the dining room when Amy arrived. She was poking the figs, piercing their skins with her bright orange fingernails. She pulled a face when Amy joined her at the buffet table.

'I'll be glad to get back home to some proper food. I mean, who wants stuff like this for breakfast? My Harvey is dying for a bowl of his favourite choco-pops!'

Amy merely smiled, not wanting to be drawn into a discussion about the merits of Donna's children's usual diet. She selected a couple of ripe figs and filled a bowl with yogurt then reached for the bread basket.

'It's all right for you. Your kid probably enjoys this sort of food 'cos he's used to it.'

'I'm sorry?' Amy glanced uncertainly at the woman, unsure what she meant by the comment.

''Cos he's Greek. Well, part Greek, anyway. He's that Dr Leonides's kid, isn't he?' Donna didn't wait for Amy to answer. 'They're the spitting image of one another, aren't they? There's no way the doc can claim not to be his dad when they're like two peas in a pod!'

Amy had no idea what to say. Picking up her tray, she hurriedly carried it over to their table but her hands were shaking as she unloaded it. The thought of how easily the truth could have come out if Donna had said anything in Jacob's hearing gave her hot and cold chills but she forced herself to sit down and eat her breakfast as though nothing had happened. The last thing she must do was panic. She just needed to get through another couple of hours and then they could leave the island for good.

Amy took Jacob to the beach after breakfast, wanting to fill in the time before they were due to catch the ferry. She had been intending to travel into town on the local bus but decided to order a taxi instead. A couple of times the bus had failed to turn up because of engine trouble and she didn't want anything going wrong and delaying them. Leaving Constantis was her main priority. Once they had left the island then she might be able to put what had happened into some sort of perspective. She sighed, realising that it was wishful thinking. The repercussions from this holiday were going to stay with her for a very long time.

She stopped at the desk on their way to the beach and asked Helena for the number of a local taxi firm. Helena immediately offered to make the call for her and arranged for her and Jacob to be collected at eleven thirty. Helena shook her head when Amy thanked her for her help and also for their stay at the hotel.

'It has been our pleasure to have you here. Philo and I hope that you will come back again to see us very soon.'

Amy managed to smile but she could feel her throat closing up with tears. She wouldn't come back to Constantis, not while Nico was here. Even though he had merely lived up to her expectations of him, she couldn't bear to see him again and suffer another rejection. At some point the time would come when she would have to tell Jacob the truth but not right now. Not while she felt so hurt and so wounded. No, a few years down the line she would be able to explain the situation to Jacob with equanimity. She would lay out her reasons for keeping Nico's identity a secret, and also explain Nico's reasons for wanting her to keep it to herself. When Jacob was older, he would be better able to understand the complexities of the situation. Or she hoped he would.

Amy collected Jacob, who was playing in the garden, and took him to the beach for a final swim before they left. And if her heart was full of dread at the thought of what lay ahead at some point in the future then she tried not to dwell on it. Nico had made it clear that he wanted nothing to do with their son so she had no choice in the matter. She had to focus on the fact that Jacob would be better off without a father rather than have someone in his life who didn't care about him.

Nico had had absolutely no intention of going to see Amy before she and Jacob left. He had said all he had to say and even though he found it almost unbearable, he had to stick to his decision. Jacob would be better off without him and Amy would be too. They could get on with their lives and look towards the future.

Who was to say that Amy wouldn't meet someone and fall in love? Now that he thought about it, he was surprised it hadn't happened already. She was so beautiful and kind, so sweet and generous that he would have expected her to have been snapped up by some lucky guy, but from what he could gather there didn't appear to be anyone on the scene, no boyfriend or lover, although maybe he was mistaken about that. After all, why would she discuss her love life with him? Even if they had slept together? There could be someone back in England waiting to welcome her home.

The thought ate away at him all morning long despite the fact that they were even busier than usual. An outbreak of food poisoning at one of the larger hotels along the coast resulted in numerous calls for assistance. As most of the people involved were in no fit state to travel to the surgery, Nico offered to drive to the hotel and visit them in their rooms. He took Sophia with him and was glad he had done as several more guests had presented with the same symptoms. All in all, there were thirty-three people suffering from sickness and diarrhoea and he wouldn't be surprised if there were many more before the end of the day. A bug like this could quickly run riot.

Nico worked his way through the list of people, offering advice as well as handing out sachets of rehydration medication. Sickness and diarrhoea soon caused dehydration and the very young as well as the very old and infirm were most at risk. Fortunately, they had picked up supplies on the way but even so they barely had enough for everyone. Nico wrote out a prescription and handed it to the hotel's manager then explained that he would need to report the incident to the relevant authorities. Checks would need to be made on the hotel's kitchens to find the source of the outbreak.

It was well after three by the time he and Sophia arrived back at the clinic. Nico parked his car and thanked Sophia for her help then sent her home. She had been due to take the afternoon off and he appreciated the fact that she had offered to go with him. There was an antenatal clinic that day but as Elena was taking it, he was free to leave as well, but he went to his office first and phoned the local health inspector and explained what had happened. It was almost half past the hour by the time that was done and he sighed as he got up to leave. If nothing else, the incident had stopped him going after Amy. The ferry would have docked by now and she and Jacob would be on their way to the airport. One thing was certain: they wouldn't come back again.

The thought hung heavily over him as he made his way to Reception. Theodora was manning the desk and she handed him a couple of messages that had come while he was out. Nico glanced through them as he left but there was nothing urgent that couldn't wait until tomorrow…

'Nico! Is he here?'

Nico looked up, his heart surging when he saw Amy running up the drive towards him. She was out of breath when she reached him and he caught hold of her arm and steadied her.

'What is it? What's happened?' he demanded.

'It's Jacob. I can't find him. He's disappeared.'

She was gasping for air, panic making it even more difficult for her to speak. Nico led her back inside to his office and sat her down then crouched in front of her. 'Tell me what happened, right from the beginning,' he instructed, trying to stay calm, not an easy task when his heart was hammering with fear.

'I booked a taxi to bring us into town so we could catch the ferry,' Amy explained. 'There's been a few occasions recently when the bus hasn't turned up and I didn't want to risk it happening again today.'

Nico nodded, refusing to dwell on her reasons for wanting to ensure their departure went smoothly. He couldn't blame her if she was anxious to leave the island after what he had told her. 'So you took a taxi. Then what happened?'

'The taxi was late collecting us so we had to rush when we reached the harbour. Most of the passengers had already boarded the ferry so I told Jacob to stay close to me and ran up the gangplank with our suitcase.' She had to pause to drag in some more air and Nico took hold of her hand and gently squeezed it.

'Take your time, Amy. I know how hard this is but I need to know exactly what happened.'

'Of course.' She took another shaky breath. 'There were several other latecomers as well as us and it was chaotic as everyone tried to get on board at once. I looked round to make sure that Jacob was all right and spotted him at the bottom of the gangplank. I just assumed he was following me but when I got on deck I couldn't see him.'

Tears began to run down her cheeks. 'I looked everywhere, Nico, asked people if they had seen him, did everything I could think of, but there was no sign of him on board the boat. The crew helped me look but they couldn't find him either. The ferry had set sail by the time we had finished checking every conceivable hiding place and the captain explained that he couldn't turn back.' She gulped. 'I had to travel all the way to Athens then come back here on the same boat. I was hoping that Jacob would be waiting at the harbour but he wasn't there and no one has seen him.'

She clutched his hand, her nails digging into his skin as panic overwhelmed her. 'Where is he, Nico? What's happened to him?'

CHAPTER FIFTEEN

AMY CLOSED HER eyes and tried to calm herself as Nico saw the police officer out. There were just a handful of police officers on the island but they had promised to start searching for Jacob immediately. As the officer had said in a bid to reassure her, he couldn't have gone very far because the island was so small. He would soon turn up, the policeman had stated confidently, and she hoped and prayed he was right. She would never forgive herself if anything had happened to him.

'They will phone me when they find him.'

Nico came back into his office, his handsome face etched with the same concern that must be on hers. That he was worried about their son wasn't in any doubt and it surprised her. Why should Nico care so much when he wanted nothing to do with Jacob?

'*If* they find him,' she murmured, too upset to delve into the reason why.

'We will find him, Amy.' He swung round and she could tell from the tension that gripped him the battle he was having to maintain his control. Nico cared; he really cared. It made his decision not to play any part in Jacob's life all the more difficult to understand… Unless it was the thought of having to be around her that had been the deciding factor? Nico might want to be a father to their son but it didn't mean he wanted to become involved with her.

The thought was just too much on top of everything else that had happened. A sob welled from her lips then another and another. It was as though a dam had burst and all the pain and disillusionment that had built up in the past few days came flooding out. Nico crossed the room in a couple of long strides and knelt in front of her but she resisted when he tried to take her in his arms. She didn't want his pity! She didn't want anything at all from him when it was only being offered out of a sense of duty.

'No!' She pushed him away and leapt to her feet, almost overturning the chair in her haste. 'I don't need you consoling me, Nico. I know how you feel about me so let's not pretend.'

'How I feel?'

'Yes. I'm nothing more than a nuisance as far as you are concerned. Not only did I give birth to a chid you never wanted but I had the audacity to turn up here and disrupt your life all over again.' She gave a bitter laugh. 'Maybe you could have accepted Jacob as your son but not if it meant having to see me as well. That was way too much for you to put up with, wasn't it? No wonder you decided that you wanted nothing more to do with us.'

'You're wrong. So wrong that it would be laughable if it weren't so insulting.'

He rounded on her, his eyes blazing with anger, and Amy took an instinctive step back. He didn't follow her, however, just stood there, glaring at her with undisguised contempt as well as something else, something that made her racing heart beat even faster. To see such anguish in his eyes was a shock, especially when she had no idea what had caused it.

'I didn't decide not to become involved in Jacob's life because of you, Amy. On the contrary, it was one of the biggest inducements of all. I had to constantly remind myself that it was Jacob's well-being that mattered and not what *I* wanted.'

'What you wanted?' she said, feeling dizzy from the rush of blood that was surging through her veins. It took her all her time to concentrate when her thoughts seemed to be swirling around. 'I don't understand. What exactly do you want, Nico?'

'You.'

Nico closed the gap between them, praying that he wasn't about to make matters worse, but the time for pretence was over. He had to tell Amy the truth about how he felt and if it wasn't what she wanted to hear then so be it. His voice grated as he continued but that was only to be expected when it was the first time he had opened his heart and laid himself bare. 'I want you, Amy. I want you so much it hurts but I won't run the risk of hurting Jacob.'

'You want me?'

Her voice was the merest whisper and he sighed, understanding her confusion. Why should she believe him after the way he had behaved? He had rejected her, not once but twice, after all. He caught hold of her hands, willing her to believe what he was saying or at least not pour scorn on his declaration.

'Yes. I love you, Amy. I realised it when we spent that night together, although I think I was probably in love with you way before then only I wasn't ready to admit it.'

'I don't know what to say…' She tailed off, her eyes huge and luminous as they stared into his, searching for the truth.

'You don't have to say anything.' He gave her hands a gentle squeeze then let her go. It would be unfair to press her for a response when their main concern had to be finding Jacob, even more unfair to hope that she might feel something for him too. He didn't deserve her love after the way he had behaved. 'Right now we need to focus on finding Jacob. How did he seem today? Was he his usual self or was he behaving differently in some way?'

'I'm not sure.'

Amy made an obvious effort to collect herself but he heard the tremor in her voice and knew that his declaration had been a shock for her. And the fact that she hadn't suspected how he felt seemed to confirm that she didn't love him. If she had loved him then surely she would have realised how he felt about her?

'Was he excited about going home to see his friends?' he asked, trying to squash that unhappy thought.

'He was first thing this morning but now that I think about it, he seemed unusually quiet when we got back from the beach.'

'And nothing happened while you were there? You didn't tell him off for instance about doing something he shouldn't?'

'No, not at all. We had a swim then he played with the Roberts children for a while.' She shrugged. 'He just seemed a bit subdued when we went back to the hotel to have a shower before we caught the ferry.'

'I see. Why did you think he might be here?'

She sighed. 'Because he's asked umpteen times when were we going to see you again. Even this morning, when we were in the taxi on our way to the ferry, he asked about you and if you were at the clinic today.' She shrugged. 'I told him that you probably were but it was too late to call in and see you.'

'So it's possible that he may have come here looking for me,' Nico said slowly, his heart aching at the thought of Jacob wanting to prolong contact with him. Had he been right to rule himself out of the child's life? He had thought he was doing the right thing but he was no longer certain any more.

'It's possible, I suppose. But you would have seen him if he had come here, wouldn't you?'

'I might not have done.' He quickly explained about the outbreak of food poisoning at the hotel. 'Jacob could have assumed I wasn't here today when he didn't see my car parked outside.'

'So he probably wouldn't have come in,' Amy said slowly. She looked at Nico. 'You don't think he would have tried to find his way to your house, do you? I mean, it's a long way and he doesn't know the roads around here all that well.'

'I think it's a possibility and definitely worth checking out.' Nico snatched up the phone and rang the police station, quickly explaining their suspicions. He hung up after the officer promised to send a car to his house to see if Jacob was there. Picking up his keys, he slipped his arm around Amy and hurried her to the door. 'We'll drive straight there and hope we find him sitting on the doorstep.'

'I hope so.' Her voice was choked with emotion and Nico acted instinctively as he held her close for a moment while he planted a gentle kiss on her forehead.

'We'll find him, Amy. I promise you we will.'

He let her go and hurried her outside, pausing only briefly to ask Theodora to phone him immediately if a young boy came into the clinic and asked for him. It seemed unlikely that Jacob would turn up there again if he had been there earlier in the day but he wanted to cover all bases. He sighed as he started the car. Sometimes it did more harm than good to over-think a problem. If he had gone with his gut instinct then none of this might have happened. He would never have told Amy that he didn't want anything more to do with Jacob and when they found him he intended to rectify matters.

If Amy would let him.

Amy sat on the edge of her seat as Nico drove them to his home. Let Jacob be there, she prayed, clinging tight hold to the hope that somehow he had found his way there. However, as the miles passed she realised what a long shot it was. Jacob was only eight and there was no way that he could have walked all this way even if he had remembered which direction to take.

'I can't see him managing to walk this far.'

Amy's heart turned over when Nico voiced her fears. 'Neither can I but where else could he have gone? I mean, he doesn't know that many places, just the hotel and your house…'

'And the caves!' Nico exclaimed. 'He knows that I

sometimes go there on my day off so do you think he might have gone there to find me when my car wasn't parked outside the clinic?'

'I don't know. Maybe.'

'It's worth checking. The caves are on our way so we may as well try there first.'

Nico swung the car down a side road, bumping over the uneven ground as he drove at some speed towards the bay. He drew up and got out then ran to the edge of the cliff where the path led down to the cove. Amy hurriedly followed him, shading her eyes as she searched the ground below where they were standing. Her breath caught when she spotted a patch of red half-hidden in the undergrowth on a narrow ledge to the left of the path.

'Look! Over there. That patch of red. Jacob was wearing a red T-shirt today.'

'I see it.'

Nico didn't hesitate as he plunged down the steep path. Rocks skittered from under his feet but he ignored the danger as made his way down. Amy's breath caught as she watched him step off the path and start to make his way over to the ledge. The cliff face had sheared away at this point and there was nothing to stop him if he fell. He made it safely to the ledge and she gasped when he parted the bushes and she saw Jacob lying on the ground. She started to make her own way down the path, stopping when Nico shouted up to her.

'He's breathing but he's unconscious. Can you go back to the car and phone the clinic? We need an ambulance here as quickly as possible.'

Amy turned round and ran back to the car. The

number for the clinic was already logged into Nico's phone and she had no difficulty contacting them. She quickly explained what had happened and was relieved when the receptionist told her that an ambulance would set off immediately.

'It's on its way,' she told Nico as she went back to the head of the path.

'Good.' He looked up and she could see the worry in his eyes. 'I think he may have hit his head when he fell. He needs a CT scan to check what damage has been done.'

'Can you do that at the clinic?' she asked anxiously.

'No. We don't have that facility so he will need to go to the mainland.'

'He will be all right, though, Nico, won't he?' Amy pleaded. She glanced round, trying to work out how she could get down to them. Nico must have realised what she was intending to do because he shook his head.

'You stay there. There isn't room for both of us on this ledge—it's far too narrow. It doesn't feel that stable either and I don't want to risk it breaking away.'

Amy shivered as she glanced at the sheer drop below them. Nico and Jacob wouldn't stand a chance if the ledge gave way. It seemed like a lifetime passed before the sound of an ambulance siren cut through the noise of the waves pounding ashore. Amy went to meet the paramedics, quickly explaining the situation as she led them to the path. The police arrived a few minutes later along with several local men who were kitted out with ropes and harnesses. In a remarkably short time the rescue operation was underway.

Jacob was brought up first, securely strapped to a

stretcher that was winched carefully up the cliff face. He looked so small and defenceless that Amy couldn't contain her tears as she bent over and kissed his cheek. His eyelids fluttered as he opened his eyes and looked at her in confusion.

'Mum…'

'It's all right, darling. You're safe now. We're going to take you to the hospital and make sure you're all right.'

'Is Nico here?' He tried to sit up but she stopped him. Until they knew exactly what damage he had done to himself, he mustn't be allowed to move.

'Yes. He'll be here in a second. The men are just helping him up the cliff… Oh, here he is now.'

Amy moved aside as Nico came to join them. His face was grey with a combination of fear and fatigue but he managed to smile as he crouched down beside Jacob.

'So you're awake. How do you feel?'

'My head hurts,' Jacob muttered before his eyes closed again.

Nico didn't waste any more time as he told the ambulance crew to load the stretcher on board. He helped Amy into the back. 'I'll go on ahead and make arrangements to have Jacob moved to the mainland. The sooner we get him there, the happier I'll be.'

'It's still over an hour by boat,' she said anxiously.

'Which is why I propose to have him transferred by helicopter.' He bent and kissed her on the mouth. 'He will be all right, Amy. I shall do everything in my power to make sure he is.'

Amy wanted to believe him; she wanted it more than anything but she knew just how serious the situation was. She sat down as the crew closed the ambulance doors and her last sight of Nico was the anxiety on his face as he ran over to his car. It wasn't just professional concern for a patient either. It was the deep, gut-wrenching fear a parent felt for their child. She knew then that she had been wrong to doubt Nico, that *he* had been wrong to doubt himself. He loved Jacob and loved him as a father should. And it was a love that would last a lifetime too if it had the chance.

The CT scan showed a bleed on the left side of Jacob's brain. Nico tried to maintain the necessary professional detachment as he and the consultant studied the monitor but his heart was pounding. If left untreated the build-up of pressure inside the child's skull could become life-threatening so it needed to be dealt with immediately.

He thanked the other man and went to find Amy who was in the waiting room. She leapt to her feet when he appeared and he saw the fear on her face. The fact that he was about to add to it made him feel doubly wretched but there was nothing he could do. He led her back to a chair and sat her down.

'There's a small bleed on the left side of Jacob's brain,' he told her quietly, knowing that he didn't need to explain how serious the situation was. As an experienced trauma nurse she understood only too well the implications of such an injury.

'Oh!' She pressed her hand to her mouth and Nico sighed.

'I know. But at least we know it's there and they can deal with it. The fact that we got Jacob to hospital so quickly will also go in his favour.'

'Where did you manage to find a helicopter at such short notice?' Amy asked, dabbing away the tears that had welled to her eyes.

'I phoned my father and asked him if we could use his,' he explained shortly. It was the first time he had asked Christos Leonides for anything since he had grown up but it had been essential that they got Jacob to the hospital as quickly as possible. In the event his father had come up trumps: not only had he sent his helicopter but he had arranged for Jacob to be flown straight to the main hospital in Athens where he could be seen by one of Greece's leading neurosurgeons. Nico was aware that he owed Christos a debt of gratitude but decided that he would worry about that later.

'Thank heavens he agreed!' Amy exclaimed, clutching hold of his hand. 'So what happens now? Are they going to operate?'

'Yes. Jacob is being prepared even as we speak so it shouldn't be long before he's in Theatre. I had a word with the surgeon and he is quietly optimistic, although there are no guarantees at this stage.' His voice broke and he couldn't continue as fear for his son overwhelmed him once more.

'He will get through this, Nico. I'm sure about that.'

Amy leant forward and hugged him while Nico tried to get a grip on his emotions. He drew back and sighed, feeling worse than ever about not being able to offer her the reassurance she needed so desperately.

'He will.' He stood up, unable to sit there while Jacob was in such danger. 'I think I shall go and have a word with the theatre sister if you don't mind.'

'You do that.' Amy smiled bravely up at him. 'You concentrate on our son, Nico. I'll be here waiting.'

Nico felt his heart surge as he left the room. Maybe they hadn't worked out the details but he knew that he and Amy would find a way to resolve any issues. It was too important that they did; important to Jacob and important to them as well. If they were to become a family then they had to start behaving as one. If being a family was what Amy wanted.

A tiny doubt flew into his mind but he swatted it away. He made his way to Theatre and spoke to the sister in charge, deriving comfort from her assurance that the surgeon who was carrying out the procedure was highly skilled. He went back to the waiting room, taking hold of Amy's hand and holding it tightly as the minutes ticked past. Now it was a waiting game. All they could do was wait and pray that Jacob responded to the treatment.

Amy was exhausted by the time morning came. She and Nico had spent the night at Jacob's bedside. Nico had tried to persuade her to go to the parents' room and rest but she had refused. She needed to be there when Jacob woke up. She looked up when a nurse came to check Jacob's obs again. Nico had explained that the surgeon planned to keep Jacob sedated to allow his brain time to heal. There was a degree of swelling and it would help his recovery. Amy knew it was standard procedure but she couldn't help wishing that Jacob would open his eyes so that she would know he was all right. Having to wait like this was almost unbearable.

The nurse finished her task, smiling sympathetically at them before she left. All the staff had been wonderful, going out of their way to make sure that they had everything they needed. It was obvious that they knew Jacob was Nico's son and she found herself wondering if Nico had told them or if they had worked it out for themselves, not that it mattered. The only thing that mattered was that Jacob should recover. Tears stung her eyes once more and she blinked them away. Nico put down the chart and reached across the bed to squeeze her hand.

'He's doing well, Amy. His obs are fine and he is more than holding his own.'

'Good.' She managed a watery smile. 'I never realised how stressful it is keeping watch like this. Your mind starts conjuring up all kinds of awful scenarios.'

'It does. But I have a feeling there is going to be a happy ending from this. Hopefully, for all of us.'

'You've changed your mind about wanting to be involved in Jacob's life,' she said simply. It wasn't a question when she already knew the answer.

'It's what I've wanted for a while now. If you will agree, of course, and I wouldn't blame you if you weren't happy with the idea.'

'I am. It's what I want more than anything, Nico, but only if you're sure it's what you want.'

'I can't think of anything I have ever wanted more.' His eyes held hers. 'I want to be a proper father to Jacob and be part of his life. I also want to be part of your life, Amy, if you will allow me to be.'

'It's what I want too. More than anything.'

'Darling!' Nico got up and came around the bed. He drew her to her feet and held her tightly against him so that she could feel the heavy beat of his heart echoing through her body. 'I can hardly believe that you are willing to give me another chance after the way I hurt you. I would do anything to make up for what I did nine years ago, my love. Anything in the whole world!'

'You've already done it.' She smiled up at him, loving him more than ever at that moment. That Nico was telling her the truth wasn't in doubt and her heart overflowed with happiness. 'You've accepted Jacob as your son and I know that you will come to love him as much as I do. That's more than enough.'

'I don't deserve you.' He kissed her hungrily, his lips seeking a response she was only too willing to give. He sighed as he drew back. 'My only concern now is my health and the impact it could have on you and Jacob if I was to have another heart attack. I can't bear to think of you two suffering because of me.'

'Don't.' She placed her fingers against his lips. 'There's no point worrying about something that may never happen. All right, so maybe you are at greater risk than other people but you are fit and healthy at this moment and that's what matters.' She glanced at their son. 'We shall concentrate on Jacob getting better and on making plans for our future together.'

'Thank you.' He captured her hand and pressed his lips to her palm. 'Thank you for giving me such a wonderful gift as Jacob and for being you. I am so very lucky, Amy.'

'No, I'm the lucky one,' she murmured.

Two years later...

'Careful!'

Amy ran across the grass and scooped up her daughter before she toppled into the paddling pool.

Twelve-month-old Luisa had just learned to walk and loved exploring her surroundings. Amy had only taken her eyes off her for a moment and the little girl had managed to stagger over to the paddling pool.

'It's OK, Mum. I'll look after her.'

Jacob abandoned the game of football he was enjoying with his cousins and came racing over to take his sister from her. Carefully holding her hand, he helped her into the pool and climbed in beside her. Amy smiled when the sound of laughter rang around the garden.

'He's so good with her, isn't he?' Nico came and flopped down on the grass beside her. Having followed through with his plans to return to reconstructive surgery by taking a part-time post at the hospital on the mainland, his days were extremely full. However, he refused to allow work to interfere with their family life and spent as much time as possible with Jacob and Luisa.

Nico had proved himself to be a wonderful father and Amy knew that any doubts he may have had in that respect had disappeared and was glad.

'He is. Jacob really adores her.'

Amy smiled down at him, thinking how lucky she was. She and Nico had been married for almost two years now and they had been the most wonderful years she could have imagined. Jacob had quickly recovered from his injuries and thankfully hadn't suffered any after-effects. As soon as he had been well enough they had told him the truth about Nico being his father, although it hadn't been the surprise they had imagined it would be. It turned out that Harvey Roberts had overheard his parents discussing the fact that Jacob was Nico's son and had told Jacob, which was why Jacob had wanted to find Nico on the day they were due to leave the island. He had been delighted when they had confirmed that it was true which had been a huge relief.

Amy had needed to return to England once Jacob was better to sort out her affairs, but she had soon returned to Constantis. She had taken over from Sophia as senior sister at the clinic and had worked there until she had left to have Luisa. Although her parents had been a little wary when she had told them about Nico, they had soon got over their initial reservations once they had met him. As her father had said, it was obvious how much Nico adored her and Jacob and that was good enough for them. They were coming to stay the following week to spend time with their grandchildren and Amy was looking forward to seeing them, although apart from family and friends, she missed very little of her old life in England, mainly because she had everything she needed right here on the island.

As for Nico's relationship with his father there had been a cautious improvement. Although Christos would never be a doting family man, he had made an effort to maintain contact with them and seemed to enjoy spending time with his grandchildren, albeit for very short periods. Amy knew that it had helped Nico to put the past behind him and concentrate on the future, a future that seemed to be filled with so much promise that sometimes she had to pinch herself to know she wasn't dreaming. Now as Nico bent towards her, she felt her heart spill over with love and gratitude for everything he had given her.

'As I adore you.' Cupping her face in his hands,

he kissed her softly and with great tenderness. 'I love you, my darling. Now and for ever.'

'And I love you too. Now and for ever,' she echoed, kissing him back.

* * * * *